As if there was no one else in the room, Richard moved up the table until he stood beside her and held out both his hands. 'Rose, I'm so sorry it's been such a long time. I know what you must have been thinking. I asked my mother to get in touch with you, but it seems she didn't and since I wrote that letter I've been on the run and there was no chance to write. But I'm here now. Eighteen months ago, when I asked you to marry me, you said it was too soon and that you thought my feelings for you wouldn't last. And I asked you, if I came back in a year's time and repeated my offer, would you reconsider – and you said you would. Well, it's been longer than that and my feelings for you haven't changed. So now I'm asking you to keep your promise. Darling Rose, I've never stopped loving you. Will you marry me?'

Also by Hilary Green

We'll Meet Again
Never Say Goodbye

THE FOLLIES SERIES

Now is the Hour
They Also Serve

About the author

Hilary Green is a trained actress and spent many years teaching drama and running a youth theatre company. She has also written scripts for BBC Radio and won the Kythira short story prize. Hilary now lives in the Wirral and is a full-time writer.

HILARY GREEN

THEY ALSO SERVE

HODDER

Copyright © Hilary Green 2007

First published in Great Britain in 2007 by
Hodder & Stoughton
An Hachette Livre UK company

First published in paperback in 2007

This edition published 2008 for Index Books Ltd.

6

A CIP catalogue record for this title
is available from the British Library

ISBN 978 0 340 89899 4

Typeset by Hewer Text UK Ltd, Edinburgh

Printed in Great Britain by
Clays Ltd, St Ives plc

Hodder Headline's policy is to use papers that are natural, renewable
and recyclable products and made from wood grown in sustainable
forests. The logging and manufacturing processes are expected to
conform to the environmental regulations of the country of origin.

Hodder and Stoughton Ltd
A division of Hodder Headline
338 Euston Road
London NW1 3BH

www.hodder.co.uk

This book is dedicated to the memory of all the brave men and women, of various nationalities, who sheltered and helped escaping Allied servicemen in occupied France.

ACKNOWLEDGEMENTS

I am grateful, as always, to my agent, Vivien Green, and my editor, Alex Bonham, for their help and encouragement, to the members of my writers' group for their trenchant but always constructive criticism, and to my husband David for proof-reading.

I

'I don't know who the hell you are, but you're too late. Rose is going to marry me.' Matthew's voice combined surprise and indignation in equal measures.

For a moment Rose Taylor felt as if she had left her body and was observing the scene in the crowded kitchen as if it were a still from a film. There was the long table, covered with the debris of a festive meal, the wineglasses still full, ready for the New Year toast that would now never be proposed. There were her mother and her sister Bet, wide eyed and open mouthed with shock; and Jack and Enid Willis, whose home this was and who had taken them in as refugees from the Blitz, gazing at her in puzzled embarrassment. By the door, Merry and Felix were frozen in the act of shaking hands, the snowflakes still melting on the shoulders of Merry's overcoat, Felix's handsome, ravaged face further distorted by surprise. And on either side of her, Matthew and Richard; Matt with his weather-beaten farmer's face creased with anger and confusion, and Richard, so thin and gaunt, with his dark hair plastered to his head by the snow and a terrible realisation slowly dawning in his brown eyes.

It was that look which undid her. Suddenly she was no longer an observer. She felt something rising and swelling within her, like a balloon that must either burst or suffocate her. For a moment she thought she might vomit or faint, then the balloon burst in an inarticulate howl of despair. She thrust her hand into her mouth to stifle it and ran out of the kitchen.

As the door slammed behind Rose, Merry felt the mood of happy triumph in which he had entered the kitchen turn to one of anguished disappointment. He had brought Richard with him, expecting his arrival to add the crowning surprise to the celebrations, and the result had been disaster. At the same moment, the people in the kitchen seemed to come to life. Both Matthew and Richard started after Rose, both calling her name, but Jack Willis interposed his burly frame between them and the door.

'Now then, gents, hold your horses. Happen she needs a few minutes to collect herself.' He looked at Richard. 'I don't know who you are, son, but you've certainly given some of us a shock.'

Merry stepped forward and laid an arm across Richard's shoulders. 'This is Richard Stevens, Jack. He was with us all in the Follies in the summer before the war. For a long time we thought he'd bought it at Dunkirk, then we found out he was a POW. I still haven't discovered how he came to be thumbing a lift a couple of miles outside the village.'

'Well . . .' Jack extended his hand. 'I'm sure we're all glad to see you back, Richard. I'm sorry things aren't quite what you anticipated but I expect Rose'll be down in a minute to explain.'

'I'll go up and speak to her – get her to come down,' Bet said.

'Good idea, love,' Jack agreed, and went on as Bet left the room, 'Now, why don't we all sit down so Richard can tell us what's been happening to him? Mother, these two chaps are starved, I'm sure. Can we find enough for both of them?'

'Of course we can.' Enid moved to the kitchen range. 'I was keeping a plate hot for Merry, anyway, and there's still some meat on that capon and plenty more veg. Sit down, both of you.'

Merry propelled Richard gently to the table. He could feel that he was shivering, but whether from shock or from the effects of a long wait in the blizzard that had been raging all day he could not be sure. He had not spoken since he blurted out his proposal, except to call Rose's name, but as Mrs Willis set a steaming plate in front of him he stirred as if awakening from a nightmare.

'I'm terribly sorry. I seem to have ruined your evening. I had no idea . . . It was stupid of me to assume that nothing would have changed . . . stupid . . .'

'You weren't to know,' Merry said. 'None of us had any idea, until tonight.'

'Well, what did you expect?' Rose's mother spoke for the first time. 'All these months and never a letter. You gave her nothing to hope for. Was she supposed to wait indefinitely?'

'I couldn't write.' Richard looked at her, his face haggard. 'I've been on the run since August. How could I have written?'

'Tell us about it.' Felix sat opposite them. 'How did you get away? When did you get back to this country?'

Merry watched as Richard picked up a forkful of chicken and crammed it into his mouth. He recognised the impulse. He had learned on the retreat to Dunkirk what it was like to be starving, and how, even after weeks, the sight of food could produce an almost Pavlovian response.

'I was wounded at Dunkirk,' Richard said, through a mouthful. 'Both legs shot up. I couldn't walk so they had to leave me on the beach. For months I was in a prison hospital. I can't fault the Huns. I had several operations and I was well looked after. But I never let them know I could walk properly again. One day, when we were being transferred by ambulance from the hospital to a prison camp, I managed to escape. I hid out in the forest with a wonderful family of woodcutters for a while. Then they passed me on to one of the escape lines that are springing up. It's amazing. There are people in France, men and women, who are risking their lives to get escaped POWs back to England. They got me into the unoccupied zone and down to the south coast, and then to the Pyrenees. Then a guide took us through the mountains to the Spanish border.'

'What a fantastic story,' Felix said. 'So when did you get home?'

'That wasn't the end of it,' Richard said. He laid down his fork and took a gulp of the wine Jack had set in front of him. 'The Spanish police caught us and we were interned in a hellhole called Miranda. I can't tell you . . .' He stumbled into silence, but as Merry was about to speak he seemed to revive and went on. 'The conditions were appalling. We were all covered in lice and nearly starving and the guards were sadistic brutes . . .'

'Oh, you poor man,' Enid Willis murmured.

'In the end,' he said, 'the British consul managed to get me out and smuggle me into Gibraltar. And from there I got a ship back to Liverpool. I got there just before Christmas but the army kept me cooped up in a hotel in London for several days, asking a lot of bloody silly questions.' He raised his eyes and sought out Mrs Taylor. 'As soon as they let me go, I came to look for Rose. I had the address in Lambeth but the place was all boarded up. There was an air raid on and I couldn't find anyone who knew where you'd gone. The army had given me a travel pass for Didsbury, so in the end I just had to get the train north. I got home on Christmas Eve.'

'Your family must have been so delighted to see you – at that time of all times,' Enid said.

'So how did you find out where we were?' Mrs Taylor asked.

He looked at her and the bitterness in his face made Merry

wince inwardly. 'I found out yesterday that my mother had known all along. You told her, didn't you, Merry?'

'It's true,' Merry said unwillingly. 'I happened to run into her when I was giving a concert in Didsbury. She's the president of the local music society. That was when I found out that Richard wasn't dead but a POW. I gave her this address and asked her to get in touch with Rose.'

'A fact that she only let slip by accident,' Richard confirmed. 'So I got the first train this morning and managed to get as far as Winchester. From there I hitched, but if Merry hadn't happened along I'd be out there still.' He sat back, his shoulders drooping. 'Anyway, it doesn't matter. Like you said, I'm too late.' He looked across at Matthew, who had listened in silence. 'I've ruined your big moment. I'm truly sorry. I'll push off now and get out of your way.'

'Good Lord!' Jack Willis exclaimed. 'You can't go anywhere at this time of night, and in this weather. Surely we can find him a bed somewhere, Enid?'

'I don't know,' his wife said doubtfully. 'Of course he can't go out in this, but we're bursting at the seams already. We managed to squeeze Felix in, while he's waiting to go into hospital, by putting Bet's boys up in the loft, but as it is poor Merry has to share a bed with him when he comes to stay . . .'

Merry caught Felix's eye and looked away quickly. As far as he could tell, both the Willises and Mrs Taylor were too innocent to guess how well that arrangement suited both of them.

'I don't understand,' Richard said. 'Why are you all here like this?'

'Oh, that's easily explained,' Mrs Taylor responded. 'We came to get away from the Blitz. Bet and her boys were bombed out, and Rose and I didn't fancy spending another night in a shelter with the bombs coming down all round us, so Rose telephoned Enid and Jack here and they offered to put us up.'

'Well, it was the least we could do, in the circumstances,' Enid Willis put in. 'With Barbara away in the Wrens we had the space. You remember Barbara, Richard? She was one of the dancers with you in the Follies, that last summer season before the war.'

'Oh, Babe?' Richard's confused expression cleared slightly. 'That's what we called her, because she was the youngest.'

'Yes, that's right. Rose was always a good friend to her, so when she telephoned and we heard she's had to give up dancing . . .'

'Give up dancing? Why?' Richard looked from Enid to Rose's mother.

'She had an accident,' Mrs Taylor explained. 'She was in a show in France, entertaining the troops before Dunkirk. The building where they were performing was strafed by an enemy plane in the middle of a performance. All the lights went out and in the confusion Rose fell off the edge of the stage. She broke her ankle and tore the ligaments and the surgeon told her she'd never be able to dance again.'

Merry saw the look of shock deepen on Richard's face. 'Oh, that's terrible! Poor Rose!'

'Well, she's over it now,' her mother said. 'We all moved down here and then she felt she wanted to make herself useful so she joined the Land Army and went to work for Matthew here.'

'But then,' Enid Willis added, 'Merry phoned to say that Felix had got to leave the convalescent home and had nowhere to go. We couldn't let him spend Christmas all on his own, so we moved Bet's boys up into the loft and put him in Barbara's room.'

Richard turned to Felix and Merry saw him swallow hard. He guessed it was the first time he had taken in the scarring on his face.

'Felix, Merry told me in the car about you being shot down and the Spit catching fire. Rotten luck!'

Felix smiled. 'Not to worry. Some chaps have had much worse to put up with. I'm waiting for plastic surgery and everyone tells me that the surgeon is an absolute wizard. I'll be good as new in no time.'

It was Merry's turn to swallow. Both he and Felix knew that that was a vain hope.

Richard's attention switched to Merry. 'So where do you come in? How did you know Rose and her family were here?'

'Because I've been using their flat in Lambeth as a base,' Merry explained. 'When I was seconded to the Central Pool of Artistes, which is what the army calls its entertainments unit, I had to find somewhere to live in London and the Taylors kindly took me in. I still stay there when I'm not touring.'

'I'm beginning to get the picture,' Richard said slowly. 'It's just really odd to find all you old Follies people together in one place, after everything that's happened.'

'Well,' Felix said with a smile, 'you know what Monty Prince used to say. Once you've done a season with the Follies, you're family.'

'This is all very well,' Jack Willis remarked, 'but it doesn't get us any nearer finding Richard a bed for the night.'

'Perhaps I could just stretch out on the floor,' Richard murmured. 'It wouldn't be the first time.'

'To hell with that!' Matthew cut in. 'There's plenty of spare room in my farmhouse. You come up with me.'

Richard began to protest but Jack overrode him. 'Good idea, Matt. Now, it's very late and some of us have to be up early, so I suggest we call it a night. It doesn't look as if Rose is coming down. Let's all get some sleep and sort things out in the morning.'

There was a general scraping of chairs and clatter of dishes as the women began to clear the table. Matthew got up. 'Come on, if you're coming. Like Jack says, some of us have an early start.' He turned to Mrs Willis. 'Thanks for inviting me, Enid. Sorry the evening turned out like this.'

Merry accompanied Richard to the door. As they reached it Felix intercepted them. 'It's good to see you, Richard. I'm sorry the circumstances haven't been happier, but don't give up hope. I'm sure things will sort themselves out.'

Richard held out his hand. 'Thanks, Felix. And good luck with the plastic surgery.'

Felix shook his head. 'Sorry. This hand's u/s at present.' He held up the claw-like fingers of his right hand. 'Another job for McIndoe.'

'You coming, Richard?' Matthew called from the porch, and Richard ducked his head, muttered 'Goodnight' and disappeared into the darkness.

Upstairs in the bedroom she shared with her sister, Rose sat huddled in the eiderdown, her hand still pressed to her lips to stifle her sobs. She was shaking all over and the only thought she could frame was 'What am I going to do? *What am I going to do?*' It went round and round in her brain, like a rat in a wheel.

'Rose? *Rose!*' Bet's voice broke through the tumult in her head, sharp with anxiety. The handle of the door rattled. 'Rose, open this door! You can't hide in there all night.' She began to pound on the door. 'Let me in – or do I have to fetch Matt to break the door down?'

Rose got up and stumbled across the room. As soon as she had turned the key Bet pushed past her.

'Rose, for God's sake pull yourself together! You can't leave everyone dangling like this.'

'What am I supposed to do?' Rose cried. 'What can I say?'

Her sister looked at her. Her face was flushed with an expression that could have been exasperation, or perhaps embarrassment, but the sympathy Rose craved was missing.

'Well, Matt's proposed and you've accepted, haven't you? Just come down and explain to Richard that you'd given up hope of ever hearing from him and now it's too late. Who does he think he is, turning up out of the blue and just taking it for granted that you're still free? He'd hardly got through the door before he was proposing to you.'

'But I can't just turn him down,' Rose wept. 'He's waited for me all this time. I promised him that if a year passed and he still loved me I'd marry him. What can I tell him now?'

'You've promised Matt now,' her sister said mercilessly. 'What are you going to say to him?'

'I don't know. I don't know.'

Bet's face softened. She took hold of Rose's arm and pulled her down to sit on the edge of the bed. 'Look, you always said that that fling with Richard was just a summer romance. You never expected it to last.'

'But it has!' Rose protested. 'I didn't realise until it was too late how much I loved him. But then the months went by and he didn't write and he didn't write . . . I thought he must be dead. Then, when we heard he was a POW and he still didn't write I decided he'd forgotten all about me, just like I thought he would. That's why I said yes to Matt this afternoon.'

'But you love Matt, don't you?'

'I thought I did. Now I don't know any more.'

Bet got up. 'Your trouble is, you never know when you're well off. There's Matt, a good man, solid, reliable, owns his own farm – and he adores you, any fool can see that. Richard's not right for you. I've always said that. Too stuck up, with his fancy ideas about being an opera singer. And it's obvious he's never mentioned you to his family, or they'd have been in touch. If he thinks you're not good enough for his posh folks, what sort of a future is there for you? You come down and tell him it's all off and you're going to marry Matt. That's my advice.'

Rose gazed up at her. She felt chilled to the marrow and utterly alone. 'Go away, Bet. For God's sake, let me be! You don't understand. You've never understood. Please, *please*, just shut up, will you?'

She twisted round and stretched herself out on the bed, burying her face in the pillow. After a moment she heard the door slam and her sister's departing footsteps.

The first hours of 1941 were the worst Rose had ever spent in her life. She cried for a while, silently so as not to wake Bet, feeling the tears well up in her eyes and run down the sides of her face to soak into her hair. After her tears were exhausted she lay staring up into the darkness, going over and over the events of the previous evening, until the alarm clock beside the bed showed 5 a.m. Then she got up quietly and gathered up her clothes in the icy, pre-dawn gloom of the winter morning. She crept out of the room and splashed her face with cold water in the bathroom, then tiptoed downstairs to the kitchen. It was a relief to find the room empty. She had half expected to discover Richard asleep on the wooden settle against the wall. The big iron kettle was sitting on the side of the range. She pulled it on to the hob and began to put on the heavy sweater and the bib-front dungarees that were the working uniform of the Women's Land Army.

She had just finished dressing when a sound at the door made her swing round. Merry and Felix stood in the doorway, tousled and unshaven, woollen dressing gowns over their pyjamas. They were old friends, from the summer of 1939 when she had been a dancer with the Fairbourne Follies concert party, and now both their faces were creased with concern. Her throat tightened on a fresh sob. The last thing she wanted at this moment was to have to talk through her dilemma, even with these two.

'I'm sorry,' she croaked. 'I didn't mean to wake you. I tried to be quiet.'

'We weren't asleep,' Felix said. He came into the kitchen. 'Rose, what are you doing? You're not planning to go up to the farm today, are you?'

'The cows need milking, New Year's Day or not, war or no war,' Rose replied.

'But surely, after last night . . . you can't just carry on as if nothing has happened.'

Rose sank down on to a chair and rested her arms on the table. 'I know,' she mumbled wretchedly. 'But what can I do?'

Merry moved behind her and poured boiling water into the teapot. 'Stay here,' he said. 'You're in no fit state to make decisions right now.'

Felix said, 'Is it true, Rose? Have you promised to marry Matt?'

Rose nodded miserably. 'He asked me at Christmas and I said I needed time to think. Then yesterday he wanted to know if I'd made up my mind and I said yes – yes, I would marry him. It seemed . . . I dunno, right. It seemed the only sensible thing to say.'

'You can't go up to the farm, Rose,' Felix said. 'They're both there, Richard and Matt.'

'Both?' she queried, startled. 'You mean Richard is staying with Matthew? How on earth did that happen?'

'We couldn't let him go off out into the night,' Merry pointed out, 'and there was no bed here for him, so Matt offered.'

'Which was big of him, under the circumstances,' Felix concluded.

'So they went off together?' Rose caught her breath. 'Oh, you don't think . . . ?'

'Fisticuffs in the farmyard? Pitchforks at dawn?' Felix queried. 'Not a chance! They're both far too civilised for that

– and anyway, from the look of him, Richard wouldn't have had the energy.'

Merry sat beside her. 'What are you going to say to them, Rose?'

She shook her head miserably. 'I don't know! I just don't know!'

'But it's Richard you've been waiting for all these months, isn't it?' he prompted.

'Yes . . . no. That is . . . I don't think I ever really believed in it. It was just a sort of dream. I'm not the right wife for him. I've always known that, deep down.'

'What makes you say that?'

'You've heard him sing. You know what a wonderful voice he has. He was wasted on a little end-of-the-pier show like Follies. It was just a way of filling in a summer for him. One day he's going to be a great opera singer. I couldn't fit in to that sort of world. I'd just be a drag on him.'

'That's rubbish!' Merry said. 'You'd be perfect for him. You're a fellow performer. You know all about the stresses and strains of the profession. What better sort of wife could he want?'

'Oh, someone much cleverer, more sophisticated than me.'

'But he's proved that it's you he loves. It's not his fault that he's been out of touch for so long,' Felix said.

'I know. But now I've promised to marry Matt. Poor Matt! He's had enough misery, with his first wife being killed like that. What would people say if I went back on my promise?'

Felix leaned across and put his good hand over hers. 'Rose, listen to me. I want to give you a bit of advice from my own experience. For years I tried to ignore my real feelings, tried to pretend I was someone different from my real self, all because I was afraid of what "society" would do to me if I was honest. It was only when this happened . . .' He raised his claw-like right hand towards his damaged cheek. '. . . that I had to face up to who I really am. And I was lucky.' He glanced towards Merry. 'In my case, it wasn't too late.' He gripped her hand. 'You have to follow your heart, Rose! To hell with what people will say.'

Rose met his blue eyes. It was the first time she had ever heard him allude to his relationship with Merry and she was amazed by the intensity of feeling in his voice. This was Felix, the ladies' man, the conjuror whose most potent magic was his own charisma. Felix who, in the old days when they were all in the concert party, had always had girls queuing at the stage door for his autograph. Mysterious Felix, whose real name was the Hon. Edward Mountjoy, but who always refused to talk about his family. All through their summer seasons with the Follies she had watched Merry suffering in silence while Felix flaunted his latest lady friend. Yet it had been Merry who had telephoned to say that Felix had got to leave the convalescent home where he had been recovering from his injuries and had nowhere to go for Christmas, and to ask whether the Willises could fit him into their already overcrowded home. And now the roles seemed to be reversed, with Felix relying on Merry for comfort and support. She had assumed that it was the result of his disfigurement, but now he was suggesting something much more fundamental.

'Felix is right,' Merry said.

'But I don't know what my heart is telling me!' she said, her voice breaking. 'I thought I loved Richard, but then I met Matt and he's kind and gentle and . . . and solid. I can imagine living with him on the farm. I can't imagine what living with Richard might be like. Oh, I don't know. I don't know what to do.' She put her head down on her arms and wept again.

Merry put his arm round her shoulders. 'What you need is a good sleep. Why don't you go back to bed?'

'But I can't,' she wailed. 'There's the cows to milk.'

He gave a brief chuckle. 'Anybody would think you'd grown up on a farm. How long have you been a Land Girl? Two months? Three? Before that you didn't know one end of a cow from the other.'

'I've still got my job to do,' Rose said doggedly.

'Look,' he said, 'Felix and I will go up to the farm and give Matt a hand. And while we're there we can recce the situation from Matt and Richard's point of view. They may have come to some understanding. At least we should find out. You take a couple of aspirins and go back to bed. Everything will be clearer when you've slept on it.'

Rose lifted her head and looked from him to Felix. 'You're very kind. I'm lucky to have such good friends.'

Felix squeezed her hand. 'Nonsense. We're all old pros, after all, and show-business people look after one another. Remember the saying – "the show must go on".'

'Except there isn't a show,' Rose mumbled.

'Oh yes there is,' Merry said heavily. 'A bloody great, dangerous show. We may only have bit parts but we've still got to do the best we can with them. Come on, Felix. Let's get dressed and see what's going on up at the farm.'

When they let themselves out of the front door Merry saw that the snow must have gone on falling all night. It had stopped now but the ground was covered in a thick, unblemished carpet, and theirs were the first footprints to sully it as they trudged up the lane towards the farm. Felix yawned and pulled his greatcoat closer round him.

'You OK?' Merry asked.

'More or less,' was the gruff reply.

Neither of them had slept much that night. Merry tried to suppress a sense of injustice. He had forty-eight hours' leave, two precious nights to spend with Felix, and one of them had been wasted in uselessly going over and over the events of the evening. Still, he told himself, there were more important things to worry about now.

They found Matthew at work in the cowshed. He looked up from milking, his face bleak. 'Don't tell me. She's not coming to work this morning.'

'She's not feeling too good,' Merry said, 'so we volunteered to take her place. And before you say anything, I can milk a cow. I used to help out on a local farm during the school holidays. Just point me to one that doesn't kick.'

Matthew got up. He moved like an automaton and Merry felt a stab of sympathy for his tightly controlled grief.

'I'll get you an overall and you can start on that old girl in the next stall,' he said.

'And I'll just pop in and see if Richard's awake, if that's OK,' Felix said.

Matthew shrugged. 'Please yourself. Door on the right at the end of the passage.'

Merry had just got into the rhythm of milking again and was almost beginning to enjoy himself when Felix reappeared. He hunkered down beside Merry and said softly, 'Richard's done a bunk.'

'*What?*' Merry exclaimed, and the cow stamped irritably.

'Bed's not been slept in and I found this.' Felix held out a folded piece of paper torn from a notebook and addressed to Rose.

'Christ!' Merry said. 'You don't think he's . . . ?'

'No, surely not. Oh God, I hope not! What should we do?'

Merry considered for a moment. 'I think we'd better read it, just in case.'

'Are you sure? It's not intended for us.'

'I know, but we need to know that he hasn't done anything bloody stupid. Rose will understand.'

'Here goes, then.'

Felix unfolded the paper and held the letter so that they could both read it.

Dear Rose,

I can't begin to tell you how sorry I am about last night. I obviously blundered in and upset everyone. It was stupid of me to imagine that everything had stayed the same while I've been away. I have to report for duty by six o'clock tonight so I'm going to make an early start. Please thank Matthew for his hospitality. I hope you and he will be very happy.

Yours,
Richard

'Sod!' said Merry, in an undertone. 'The silly bugger! Now what do we do?'

'God knows,' sighed Felix. 'Better explain this to Matt for a start, I suppose.'

'He's gone, then?' Matthew said when they told him about the note. 'Left her in the lurch again? Might have had the decency to hang around until we found out what she's decided.'

'I think he probably thought he was doing the right thing, for both of you,' Merry said defensively.

'He won't have got far,' Matthew said. 'I don't suppose there'll be any trains today – or not till later, anyway.'

'He's probably hitching,' Merry said.

Matthew grunted. 'He won't get far that way, either. There won't be many people about, not this early.'

Felix said, 'You don't think he might still be standing down on the main road, waiting for a lift, do you?'

Merry looked at Matthew. 'Matt, can you cope on your own? I'm sorry, but I'm a bit worried about Richard. I think we ought to go and see if we can find him.'

'I've managed on my own for years,' Matthew responded.

'Don't see why today's any different. You get off. Silly bugger'll be half frozen by now, I shouldn't wonder.'

They hurried back to where Merry had parked Felix's Lagonda the night before and drove down the icy lanes. The recent snow had covered any tracks but there were only three routes Richard could have taken. They followed them all, without seeing any sign of him. In Wimborne Minster there were a few people about, heading for work or opening shops, but no Richard.

When they reached the main London road Merry stopped the car.

'He may have walked on,' Felix pointed out. 'He could have covered quite a few miles by now.'

'That's just the point,' Merry replied. 'Look at the petrol gauge. If we go much farther I shan't have enough to get back to town myself and I've no more coupons.'

'I guess that's it, then,' Felix said. 'We'd better go back and break the news to Rose.'

2

Back at the Willises' smallholding Merry and Felix found the family at the breakfast table, with the exception of Rose.

'Where have you two been, this early?' Jack Willis asked.

'Up to the farm,' Merry said. 'Where's Rose?'

'Asleep still,' Bet said.

'Have you seen Matt and Richard?' Mrs Taylor asked.

'We saw Matt. Richard's not there. He's left a note for Rose.'

'You mean to say he's just gone off again? Without even talking to her?'

'I think he probably feels that he was intruding, and that she'll be happier without him.'

'Best thing he could do, if you ask me,' Bet said with a sniff.

Merry went upstairs and pushed Richard's note under Rose's bedroom door. After breakfast he managed to catch Bet on her own, feeding the chickens.

'Bet, did Rose talk to you last night, about Richard?'

Bet straightened up, an uncharacteristically stubborn look on her usually easygoing face. 'I tried to talk to her, but I couldn't get any sense out of her. Told me to mind my own business – good as.'

Merry said, 'She can't go ahead and marry Matt now.'

Bet shrugged. 'Why not? That Richard's buggered off again, without so much as a word. If he really cared for her he'd have hung around to say goodbye, at least.'

'I don't think it's that, Bet,' Merry replied. 'I think he just couldn't cope with the situation. I mean, imagine coming back from what he's been through, hoping to find Rose waiting for him, only to be told she's marrying another man.'

'Well, he wants to make his mind up,' Bet said brusquely. 'He didn't have the guts to pop the question before he went off to the war, then he doesn't write for months . . .'

'Bet! He was a prisoner, and then he was on the run,' Merry protested.

'Hmm.' Bet sounded unimpressed. 'Well, if you ask me, she's better off with Matt. He's a good bloke and he's mad about our Rose. And what's more he's got his own farm. Better than a highfalutin opera singer who'll probably be out of work more than in. He'll give her a decent life, will Matt.'

'Oh, sure!' Merry exclaimed sardonically. 'Up at five to milk the cows every morning. And there's nothing highfalutin about Richard.'

But Bet had turned away and was occupying herself with the chickens.

Merry returned to the house to find Bet's two boys in a state of high excitement because Jack Willis had produced an old toboggan from the back of a shed.

'Uncle Merry! Uncle Merry! Will you take us tobogganing?' pleaded seven-year-old Billy. 'You and Uncle Felix? Come on, it'll be fun.'

'Oh do, Merry, please!' said Mrs Taylor. 'Get them out from under our feet for a while.'

So Merry and Felix took Billy and Sam up on the hill above the farm. In other circumstances it would have been a thoroughly enjoyable morning. They tobogganed and played snowballs, 'just like four kids together', as Mrs Taylor remarked indulgently when they returned, faces glowing and fingers numb from the cold. After lunch Sam, who could hardly keep his eyes open after staying up late the previous evening, was persuaded to go to bed for an hour while Billy settled at one end of the kitchen table to finish a model aeroplane from a kit he had been given for Christmas. Merry and Felix sat at the other end and played chess while Mrs Taylor and Mrs Willis sat by the wireless, knitting and listening to the Light Programme. It was the sort of peaceful, domestic interlude that Merry yearned for during his travels around the country, giving piano recitals in hospitals and works canteens, but today he could take no pleasure in it.

Rose reappeared at teatime, dry eyed and pale. 'I've thought it out,' she announced, 'and I know what I'm going to do.'

They all gazed at her. 'Well?' her mother said. 'Who's it to be?'

'Neither of them,' Rose said. 'It's all quite clear to me now. I can't marry either of them.'

'Rose, are you sure?' Merry asked, and Felix murmured a protest.

'I can't marry Matt because as soon as Richard came in I knew I'd only said yes to Matt because I'd convinced myself I'd never see Richard again. And Matt would know that. He'd know I was only marrying him as a kind of second best, and that's not fair on him. And I can't marry Richard because if I'd really been in love with him I'd never have thought of marrying someone else. Anyway, he's gone away again, so he obviously wasn't that keen. He probably thought he owed it to me, after what he said that summer, but now he thinks I've got someone else he's free to get on with his life. So there it is.'

Merry gazed at her set, miserable face and his heart went out to her. 'Don't make up your mind too quickly. Give yourself time.'

'Merry's right,' Bet said unexpectedly. 'Don't go telling Matt you're throwing him over. You'd be a fool to let him go.'

'That's not what I meant,' Merry protested.

'You keep out of this!' Bet said sharply. 'This is family business.'

'Stop it!' Rose said, her voice cracking. 'I've told you, I've made up my mind.'

'But what will you do now?' her mother asked. 'You can't go on working up at the farm as if nothing had happened.'

'Obviously not,' Rose said, with an uncharacteristic sharpness. 'I'll go up tomorrow morning and explain to Matt. Then I'll go and see Mrs Heatherington-Smythe and tell her I'm resigning from the Land Army.'

Rose arrived at the farm at 5.30 the next morning, as usual. The cows were already in the milking parlour and Matt was milking and hardly looked up when she said good morning. Rose put on her overall and settled into the routine she had become used to over the past three months. When the milking was finished and the dairy had been cleaned, she went into the farmhouse kitchen and prepared breakfast, as she always did, for Matt and herself and old Fred, the ploughman – porridge sweetened with honey and boiled eggs fresh from the hens that scratched in the yard. It was not until Fred had gone about his work and she and Matt were washing up that she opened the conversation she had been rehearsing in her head through two sleepless nights.

'Matt, I need to talk to you.'

He finished drying a plate and put it down carefully. 'You're not going to marry me, are you? I've been expecting this ever since that Richard walked in.'

Rose looked at him with tears in her eyes. The expression of dogged resignation on his face touched her more than any protestations of surprise or disbelief could have done. For a moment she longed to tell him he was wrong, that she had made no such decision, but she knew that it would be cruel to both of them to prevaricate.

'I can't, Matt,' she said softly. 'It wouldn't be fair on you, for one thing. I'm sorry, so sorry. I wouldn't have hurt you for the world, but I can't marry you knowing that we might both regret it later.'

He turned away and picked up another plate. 'Why didn't you tell me there was someone else?'

'I didn't think there was. I met Richard that last summer before the war. We talked about getting married once, but I told him we should wait. I thought he'd probably change his mind when the summer season was over. Then, when he went off to join the army, it was all left sort of in the air.'

'If he came down here meaning to ask you to marry him, why did he clear off so fast the next morning?' Matt asked, with the first hint of belligerence. 'Strikes me he can't be that keen.'

'I don't know,' Rose said, in distress. 'I think he probably went away because he didn't want to cause trouble between you and me. The point is, it made me understand how I feel. I'm very fond of you, Matt, and if I'd never met Richard things might have worked out all right for us. But I can't marry you knowing that he's alive, and he hasn't forgotten me and perhaps . . .' She trailed off into silence, unwilling to articulate the hope that she would not put into words, even in her own mind.

Matthew folded the tea towel and laid it on the back of a chair. 'What will you do now, then?'

'I can't go on working here,' Rose said sadly. 'That would be too difficult for both of us. I think I'll go back to London and open up the shoe shop again. The Blitz seems to have eased up a bit. Maybe I could even start dancing again. My ankle's so much better now, I'm sure I could get back into training if I really made up my mind to it. I'll go and see Mrs Heather-ington-Smythe tomorrow and explain things to her and ask her if she can get someone to take over my job. I don't want to leave you stranded.'

'You'd better get down there now, then,' Matthew said, still with his back to her.

'Oh no,' Rose replied quickly. 'I'll finish up today. I can't just walk out and leave it all to you.'

'I coped before you came,' he said. 'I guess I'll cope now. You get off. Best all round.'

He headed towards the door, pulling his coat off the hook as he went.

Rose said, 'Matt, please! Let me help you clear out the cowshed, at least.'

'You get off,' he repeated. 'I'll manage.'

He went out of the door and she heard him pulling on his wellington boots in the porch, then saw him pass the window, striding towards the cowshed. Slowly, she finished drying and putting away the last dishes, then stood for a moment gazing out across the yard and beyond to where the cows were huddling in the snow-covered meadow. She remembered how they had frightened her when she first came to the farm. Now she knew each of them by name, knew which ones were placid, easy milkers and which were likely to kick or knock over the bucket. She looked round the kitchen, taking in the worn red quarry tiles on the floor, the rag rugs, their colours muted by wear, the dishes on the dresser, the comforting warmth of the old black range. In such a short time it had come to feel like home, and it came over her in a sudden rush that she was throwing all this away. This could have been her kitchen, her farm, to share with Matthew. She visualised the life that might have been – could still be perhaps, if she went now and told him she had changed her mind. They could have ridden out the rest of the war here, not untouched by its hardships but out of danger and protected from its worst privations. And afterwards? She hardly ever let herself think about that mythical time 'after the war', but she had never had any doubt that one day it would end in victory. There would be a time of peace, of returning prosperity, and between them she and Matthew could make sure that the farm flourished. There would still be the routine of early morning and evening milking, of course, but perhaps they would be able to afford some help with that. Even leaving aside that distant prospect, the immediate future could be bright. Soon the days would begin to lengthen. Spring was coming. There would be calves and lambs and mornings full of birdsong – and later, when the war was over, there might be children . . .

Rose turned from the window and forced her mind back to the present. It was no good dreaming! She had made her decision and in her heart she knew it was the right one. She could never live happily with Matthew, wondering all the time whether Richard was really still in love with her. Whatever finally happened between them, even if she never saw him again, she knew now what her true feelings were and no amount of wishing would change that. She pulled on her coat and went out, closing the door carefully behind her. The yard was empty but she could hear the sound of Matthew sweeping out the milking stalls. For a moment she hesitated, wondering whether she should go over and say goodbye. In the end, she took her bicycle from its place by the wall and rode out and down the lane towards Wimborne.

As luck would have it, Mrs Heatherington-Smythe was in the WLA office in the village. She looked up in surprise as Rose entered.

'Good morning, Rose. What are you doing here at this time of day? I hope there isn't a problem.'

Rose pulled off her broad-brimmed uniform hat and sat down in the chair opposite her.

'I'm afraid there is, Mrs Heatherington-Smythe,' she said. 'Matthew Armitage has asked me to marry him.'

Mrs Heatherington-Smythe's face positively glowed. 'But, my dear girl, that's not a problem! I'm delighted for both of you. You've fitted in so well at the farm, and Matthew really needs a wife. It's a wonderful arrangement!'

'You don't understand,' Rose said. 'I've refused him.'

'You've what! Whatever for?'

'Because I'm not in love with him.'

'You mean to say you've been leading him on all this time and now you've turned him down?' The glow had faded from the big woman's cheeks, to be replaced with the frosty hauteur Rose remembered from their first encounter.

'I haven't been leading him on!' Rose exclaimed indignantly.

'Going out to parties with him, letting him take you to the pictures. Oh, you needn't worry, I know all about it. You can't keep much hidden in a small place like this, you know.'

'I haven't tried to hide it,' Rose said, trying to quell the angry tears that welled up in her eyes. 'He asked me to go with him, and it was fun for both of us. I don't call that leading him on.'

'Well, perhaps you don't where you come from,' Mrs Heatherington-Smythe retorted with a snort, 'but round here if a girl lets a man spend his money on her it's taken to mean that she is serious about him. You city girls are all the same – just out for a good time!'

'That's not true!' Rose protested, but she was miserably aware that a lot of people would find some truth in the accusation. 'I was serious, Mrs Heatherington-Smythe. I thought I could marry Matthew, until the other day. Then an . . . an old friend turned up out of the blue. He'd been a prisoner of war. I thought I should never see him again.'

'I see.' The other woman's face conveyed the impression that all her worst suspicions had been confirmed. 'So while one boyfriend was suffering for his country, you thought you'd find someone else to provide for you, and now he's back you want to ditch poor Matthew. You want to make up your mind, my girl, and stop trifling with honest men's feelings.'

'I'm not! I never meant to hurt anyone!' Rose cried. 'I'm just as upset about it as anyone is.'

Mrs Heatherington-Smythe glared at her for a moment in silence and then said abruptly, 'Well, what do you expect me to do about it?'

'I can't stay at the farm,' Rose said, trying to control herself and speak calmly. 'It wouldn't be fair to Matthew. I wondered if you could find someone else to take my place.'

'And what are you proposing to do?'

'I thought I would go back to London and reopen my mother's shop.'

'Oh no you won't, my girl!' The large woman opposite her seemed to swell with rage. 'Let me remind you, you volunteered for the Women's Land Army as your choice of war work. You can't just walk out, as and when you please. What would happen if we all behaved like that?'

'But . . . but what am I supposed to do?' Rose stammered.

'I shall have to try to arrange a transfer for you, though God knows I've got enough to cope with without the extra work that entails.'

'A transfer? Where to?'

'That remains to be seen. I'll make sure it's somewhere well away from here, so poor Matthew won't have the embarrassment of bumping into you.'

'But my family are all here – my mother and my sister. I don't want to leave them.'

'Perhaps you should have thought of that sooner,' Mrs Heatherington-Smythe replied implacably. 'Now, if you don't mind, I've got work to get on with. I'll let you know where you are to go as soon as I hear from headquarters. Good morning!'

Rose cycled back to the Willises' house with tears streaming down her cheeks. Her mother and Bet were in the kitchen, peeling potatoes for lunch. Her mother put down the knife and dried her hands.

'Well, how did it go? Did you tell him?'

Rose nodded, unable to speak.

Bet gave her a narrow look. 'You've actually turned him down? You stupid . . .'

'Oh, for God's sake, Bet!' Rose found her voice in a cry of anguish. 'Leave it be, will you? What's it got to do with you?'

'Rose is right,' their mother said. 'If you can't say something helpful you'd best keep your mouth shut.'

Bet turned away sulkily. 'Oh, pardon me for breathing!'

'I'm sorry,' Rose said, sinking into a chair. 'But it's not just this business with Matt. Things just seem to be going from bad to worse.'

She told them what Mrs Heatherington-Smythe had said and Mrs Taylor was all for going straight down to Wimborne to give 'that stuck-up bitch' a piece of her mind. But Jack Willis, who came into the kitchen in the middle of Rose's story, pointed out as kindly as possible that the WLA organiser was within her rights. All single women were expected to sign up for some form of war work and Rose was now in something closely equivalent to one of the armed services. She could not simply resign.

Merry had already left for London at the end of his leave, but Felix was still waiting for the summons to attend Archibald McIndoe's burns unit at East Grinstead hospital. Rose was in the sitting room, staring gloomily out of the window at the gathering dusk, when he sought her out. He came over to stand beside her and squeezed her arm gently.

'Chin up, old girl. It'll all come out in the wash.'

'I don't see how,' Rose said.

'Look, why don't you write to Richard? Tell him you're not engaged to Matthew. I don't mind betting he'll be back here like a shot.'

'How can I?' Rose asked. 'I still don't have an address for him. All I know is he's in the South Lancashire regiment, but I've no idea where they're stationed and the War Ministry won't give out that information.'

'Why not write to his home address and ask them to forward it?'

'Because I don't know that either.' Rose's voice had an edge of desperation. 'Anyway, his mother would probably burn it. She's never wanted him to have anything to do with me.'

'Hang on a minute,' Felix said. 'Merry ran into her at that concert he gave. If it was organised by his unit there must have been some form of communication – you know, letters backwards and forwards. His HQ must have an address for her. He's still using your flat in Lambeth as a base, isn't he?'

'Yes, when he's in London.'

'Why don't you write a letter to Richard and send it to Merry at your address with a covering letter asking Merry to ferret out Mrs Stevens' address and send it on? He could probably even put it in a War Ministry envelope, so she'd never guess it was from you. She couldn't risk not forwarding it then.'

Rose turned to him and smiled for the first time in two days. 'Felix, you're brilliant! At least then Richard will know what the situation is here. After that, it'll be up to him.'

She went up to her room and got out a writing pad and her pen.

Dear Richard,

I don't know if this letter will reach you, but I think Merry has your home address so I am going to send it to him and ask him to forward it. I wish you had not rushed off so early on New Year's Day, as there are so many things I would like to explain to you.

The most important thing I want you to know is that I have broken off my engagement to Matthew. I know this makes me sound fickle and as if I don't know my own mind. Perhaps that's true, but I was sure that you had decided you didn't want to keep in touch and that I would never see you again. And I really did think I could make Matt happy. I realise now that I was wrong and I am very, very sorry for all the unhappiness I have caused.

You came all the way to Wimborne to ask me to marry you, and it must have been a terrible shock to hear that I was engaged to someone else, so you may have changed your mind now. I can't blame you if you have. But I need to know how you feel. I really can't get my life sorted out until I do. I'm being transferred to another farm because, of course, I can't go on working for Matt. I don't know where it is yet, but it will be a long way from here. Please write to me and let me know how you feel. If you send the letter here my mother will forward it to me.

Don't be afraid to tell me honestly if you think it would be better for us not to see each other again. I don't want you to feel guilty, or responsible for me breaking up with Matt. I've learned one thing in the last day or two, and that is that the most important thing is to be absolutely honest with yourself and everyone else about these things.

I hope you are getting over your awful experiences in France and Spain and that the army will give you a chance to get really well again. We all worry about you. Take care of yourself.

She hesitated for some time over how to finish the letter and in the end wrote simply 'Yours, Rose'.

Then she wrote a covering letter to Merry and addressed it to her own flat in Lambeth. The next day Mrs Willis posted it for her on her way to market.

3

'Private Stevens reporting for duty, sir!' Richard came to attention in front of his commanding officer's desk and saluted, then obeyed the sergeant major's command to stand at ease.

The CO looked up and beamed. 'Good to see you back, Stevens. Stand easy. Thank you, Sergeant Major.'

The SM did a sharp about-turn, stamped and marched himself out of the door. As it closed behind him Richard relaxed and allowed his gaze to drop to the officer's face.

'Good leave?' the CO enquired.

Richard drew a breath before answering. Repetition of the deceit did not make it any easier. 'Not bad, sir, thank you.'

'Not bad, eh?' The officer regarded him shrewdly for a moment, but it was apparent that no further confidences were forthcoming so he went on, 'You certainly look a good deal fitter than you did when you got back from Spain.'

'Yes, I'm fine, sir, thank you.'

'Family all well?'

'Yes, thank you, sir.'

'Relieved to have you back safely, I'm sure.'

'Yes, sir.'

'Hm.' There was a pause. Then the officer resumed, 'Bloody good show, getting yourself out of that prison hospital and back across France like that. Bloody good!'

'Thank you, sir.'

'Showed a lot of initiative, a lot of guts.'

'I was lucky, sir. I had a lot of help. They're the people with the real guts.'

'So I understand.' The CO was looking at a file on his desk. 'I've had very good reports of your conduct on the retreat to Dunkirk, too. Singing to keep up the morale of the men, for one thing. And then there was that child you saved from being strafed.'

For the first time Richard allowed a trace of emotion, mainly of surprise, to cross his face. He was touched by the realisation that the young lieutenant in charge of his platoon, who had himself been so close to exhaustion that he could barely stand by the time they reached the coast, had remembered when he got home to mention that one incident out of so many. He had almost forgotten it himself.

'Instinctive reaction, sir,' he said.

'An instinctive reaction that might have got you killed,' the officer commented. He leaned back in his chair and Richard felt that he was being studied. 'Tell me something, Stevens. Why have you never put in for a commission?'

'Never felt I was officer material, sir.' The response was almost glib in its promptness.

'Why not? You're a well-educated chap, intelligent, well spoken. You've proved you have courage and initiative. You're exactly the sort of man we need as an officer. Tell you what I'd like to do. I'd like to put your name forward for promotion. What do you say?'

Richard hesitated briefly, then he met the CO's eyes and smiled faintly. 'Yes, thank you, sir. I think I'd like that now.'

'Good man! Meanwhile . . .'

'There's something else, sir, if I may?'

'Go on.'

'I'd like to put in for a transfer, sir.'

'Transfer? To what? If you're worried that the men in your

own outfit won't accept you as an officer, I think you can forget it.'

'No, it's not that, sir. I'd like to volunteer for special duties. I'm not quite sure what the outfit is called, but I'm sure there must be one. Those people I mentioned in France, they're going to need help if they are going to go on getting our men back to this country. They need money, and some way to keep in touch with this side – wireless operators perhaps. Already there are a lot of pilots who have been shot down over France and there will be more. They all need help to get out. I speak quite good French now, and I could improve it. I want to go back to France and help out over there.'

He had spoken rapidly, almost breathlessly, wanting to get the words out before his courage failed him and he changed his mind. The officer regarded him in silence for a few moments. Then he said, 'You do realise what danger you would be putting yourself in? I understand the Gestapo have a pretty brutal way with anyone caught helping escaped British servicemen.'

Richard swallowed. 'I know that, sir. But there are women and kids helping out, nuns even. If they can take the risk, so can I. I owe them that much.'

Once again the CO regarded him for a moment in silence. Then he said, 'Very well. I'll make some enquiries in the right quarters. We'll be sorry to lose you, but I can see that there is a need for the kind of operation you've outlined. I'm not making any promises, mind you. I don't know how these things are being organised. But I'll see what I can do.'

'Thank you, sir.'

'All right, dismiss.'

Richard came to attention, turned on his heel and marched out of the door.

On the evening of that same Thursday Merry pushed open the street door of the Taylors' flat in Lambeth and found a small pile of letters on the mat. It was apparent that the next-door neighbour, who had been asked to forward them, had not been doing so. He gathered them up and took them upstairs to the living room.

As soon as he stepped inside a wave of depression hit him. It was not an unfamiliar sensation, but one he had not had to contend with since that magical night the previous November when Felix had finally dropped his disguise and admitted his true feelings. The room was icy cold, with the musty dampness of a place that has not been lived in for months. But it was not the physical chill which bothered him. It was the absence of Rose and her mother. Since he had come to lodge with them, getting on for a year ago now, he had come to feel more at home in the cosy flat than he did in his own empty house down in Seaford. He had been there only intermittently, but there had always been a warm welcome and a good meal, in spite of rationing. More importantly, there had been Mrs Taylor's indefatigable cheerfulness and Rose's gentle affection. Now, after the companionable hubbub of the Willises' crowded home, the flat seemed all the more desolate.

Worst of all was the thought that it might be weeks before he saw Felix again. He cast his mind back to the previous night, when for an hour or two they had forgotten the war, and Felix's forthcoming operation, and Rose's dilemma, and concentrated solely on each other – on the intensity of desire and the drowsy tenderness that followed its satisfaction. It was a memory to cherish in the dark days ahead, but also one that brought with it a poignant sense of loneliness.

Merry lit the fire and made himself a frugal meal of sardines on toast. Then he unpacked and sat down to go through the pile of letters. He readdressed those that seemed important and then fetched a notepad and began a letter of his own, which he had mulled over in his mind on the drive up from Dorset.

Dear Richard,

We were all very distressed by the events of New Year's Eve. I hoped that it would be a wonderful reunion for you and Rose and I had no idea that there was any question of her marrying Matthew. I am quite sure that if she had known that you were still in love with her she would never have considered his proposal. It was a great pity you didn't wait until the next day. If you had had a chance to talk to her I think she would have told you so herself.

Please write to her, or better still go down to Dorset and see her again, if you can possibly get away. At least give her – and yourself – a chance to sort things out.

And please keep in touch. We all missed you and worried about you and it was wonderful to see you safe and well. I look forward to hearing from you.

Yours ever,
Merry

He sealed the letter and put it in his pocket and then left the flat and crossed the road to the Queen's Arms pub, where he knew he would find a welcome.

The next morning Merry reported to his commanding officer, Colonel Basil Brown of the Army Welfare Department. The colonel greeted him with a cheery grin.

'Ah, Merry. Just the man I want to see. How were your New Year celebrations?'

Merry hesitated. 'Rather overshadowed by an unfortunate incident, I'm afraid. Nothing to do with me, personally. Just one of those sad mix-ups that must happen all over the country in wartime, I suppose.'

'I'm sorry to hear that,' Brown commented. He paused, but it was clear that Merry did not intend to elaborate so he went on, 'Well, back to the grindstone. There are developments that concern you – rather exciting ones.'

'Oh?' Merry withdrew his thoughts from Rose and Richard and looked enquiringly at his CO.

'You know I've felt for a long time that there is a great deal of talent being wasted in the army – talent that could be used to better effect in providing entertainment for the troops. Your little expedition to France last spring was by way of a trial run and, as you know, it was generally regarded as being a great success. You and your company were able to take a first-rate show right up to the front line, with definite results in boosting morale. So, now that things have settled down a bit after the debacle at Dunkirk, we're ready to build on that. I've got two very good men to come on board – George Black and Bill Alexander. Have you come across George?'

'Not George Black who owns the Palladium and created the Crazy Gang?' Merry queried.

'His son, who has taken over where his dad left off. Born and brought up in the entertainment world. What George doesn't know about variety isn't worth knowing.'

'I'm sure you're right,' Merry agreed.

'And Bill Alexander's a very well-respected straight actor, of course. So between them we've got a very useful team. Now, you've actually had experience of working on the ground, which will be invaluable. We'll go on using the facilities at Greenford Barracks for the moment. I want you to report to George Black there.'

'No more solo touring, then?'

'Not for the time being. Do you mind?'

Merry shook his head. 'To be honest, I was getting a bit browned off with being on my own. It will be good to work as part of a team again.'

'Good man. Now, are you still living out at Lambeth with the Taylors?'

'Well, I'm still using their flat,' Merry agreed. 'But they aren't there. They went down to Dorset to get away from the bombing.'

'Don't you find it a bit of a trek out to Greenford from there?'

'Well, yes.' Merry nodded. The colonel's comments chimed with his own thoughts.

Brown went on. 'There's no accommodation at the barracks, as you know. Everyone involved will have to live out. But I think they will have a list of possible boarding houses and small hotels near by. Tell you what. Today is Friday. Pop over to Greenford and find yourself somewhere to live. Then you'll be ready to start on Monday.'

On his way out Merry looked into the room occupied by the young corporal who acted as Colonel Brown's secretary. The boy looked up from his desk.

'Oh, Lieutenant Merryweather! Glad you looked in, sir. There's a phone message for you. Can you call a Flight Lieutenant Mountjoy? He said you'd know the number.'

Merry felt a jolt of alarm. Now what? he asked himself. Aloud he said, 'Right, thanks. Look, while I'm doing that, can you check something in the files for me? I did a concert in Didsbury last November, for a local music society. I think it was arranged through the secretary of the society. Can you see if you can find me her address?'

The corporal turned away to rummage in a filing cabinet and Merry picked up the receiver and dialled the Willises' number. Felix must have been waiting by the phone, for he answered at once.

'What's wrong, Felix?' Merry asked.

'Nothing. It's all right. There's nothing to worry about.'

'Is Rose OK?'

'She's coping. She's stopped working for Matt and she's

waiting to be transferred to a new job. It's not about her. It's me.'

'You?' Merry's voice sharpened.

'I got a letter this morning telling me to report to the Burns Unit at East Grinstead hospital tomorrow.'

'Oh!' Merry took a minute to digest the news. 'Well, that's good, isn't it?'

'Oh yes! I'm browned off with hanging around here. I mean, the Willises have been terrific and I've had a really good Christmas, but I can't go on sitting around doing nothing while other people fight the war. The sooner I get started on this treatment, whatever it consists of, the sooner I'll be able to get back on active duty.'

Merry resisted the temptation to tell him that whenever that time came it would be too soon as far as he was concerned and said instead, 'Pity the letter didn't come yesterday. You could have driven up to town with me.'

'I know. Sod's law, I suppose. Damn nuisance. We could have had a night out on the town.'

Merry smiled to himself. It was a measure of Felix's renewed self-confidence that he could contemplate such a thing. He said, 'How are you going to get to East Grinstead?'

'No problem,' Felix replied. 'They've sent me a rail warrant, and Jack Willis will drive me to the station.'

'Well, it's good that it's come at a weekend,' Merry said. 'I'll come and visit on Sunday.'

There was a fractional hesitation at the other end and then Felix said, 'I don't know what the rules are about visiting times and so on. You'd better wait until I can let you know. I'll ring you tomorrow from the hospital.'

'No,' Merry said. 'After tomorrow you won't be able to get me here or at the flat.' He explained briefly about his return to the base at Greenford and his intention to move. 'My new boss is going to be George Black. You've heard of the George Black who owns the Palladium? This is his son.'

'Black?' Felix queried. 'Isn't the man you work for now called Brown? Are you sure you're not getting involved with some undercover operation?'

Merry laughed. 'It is an odd coincidence, isn't it? But no, I'm sure they're genuine. Look, I'll ring the hospital tomorrow and get them to give you my new number.'

'OK,' Felix confirmed. 'Talk to you then.'

'Yes. Felix?' A pause. 'Take care.'

'I will. And you. 'Bye.'

As he put the phone down the corporal came over to him with a sheet of paper. 'This what you're looking for, sir?'

Merry glanced at it and saw that it was a letter from Ada Stevens and had her home address at the top. He copied it on to an envelope and wrote a brief note asking her to forward the enclosed letter to her son. He knew that she had not passed on Rose's address, as he had asked her to do when they met, but he hoped her possessive jealousy would not extend to Richard's friends. He folded his letter to Richard into the envelope, sealed it and put it into the 'Out' tray on the corporal's desk.

Back in the Taylors' flat he packed his few possessions, took a last look round, picked up his suitcase and closed the door carefully behind him.

By mid-afternoon he had found himself some reasonably cosy lodgings in a small hotel a mile or two from the base. As soon as he was installed, he rang the hospital at East Grinstead and left a message for Felix, giving the new number. All next day he hung around, trying to find things to occupy his mind and waiting for Felix's phone call. It did not come through until late afternoon.

'Sorry to be so late,' Felix said. 'I've been closeted with McIndoe – the surgeon.'

'It's all right,' Merry returned. 'How's it going?'

'OK. The chaps in the ward are a great bunch. There's a terrific atmosphere – more like a club than a hospital. And you should see the nurses!' He accompanied the remark with a low whistle.

'Should I?' Merry remarked dryly. 'Still, I'm glad you're in good company.'

'No doubt about that,' Felix responded. 'Mind you . . .' His tone changed. '. . . some of these boys . . . I thought I was bad, Merry, but some of them . . . And a lot of them have already been here for months and had four or five operations.'

'Well, then.' Merry tried to sound encouraging. 'At least it sounds as if you're a comparatively easy case. What does McIndoe say?'

'He was very positive. He seems pretty sure he can get the hand working again, and patch the face up so that I don't scare the horses. But it's not going to be a matter of weeks, Merry. He says it could take months, with breaks in between to let things settle down.'

'I'm sorry,' Merry murmured. 'I guess it's just something we'll have to be patient about. Now, when can I visit?'

'Well, that's it,' Felix said. 'Not just yet. McIndoe wants to operate tomorrow.'

'So soon! Well, I suppose it's better than hanging around.'

'Oh, definitely. I've done enough of that already.'

'What time is the operation?'

'First thing, I think.'

'So you ought to be out of the anaesthetic by evening. Can I come then?'

'Probably better not. I don't think I'll be feeling very talkative.'

'Monday, then.'

'No. The thing is, Merry,' Felix's voice had taken on a constrained tone, 'would you mind terribly not visiting for a while?'

Merry experienced an almost physical stab of pain. 'Why not?' he asked sharply.

'Well, I'm not going to be a very pretty sight for a while after the op.'

'Do you think I care about that?'

Felix's voice softened. 'No, I know you don't, bless your heart. You've proved that. But I do, you see. I've seen some of the men here who have been operated on recently and . . . well, I just think it would upset both of us. Do you mind?'

'Of course I mind,' Merry replied, but more gently now. 'I mind every day we're not together. But I'll respect your wishes. Just don't make it too long.'

'I won't, I promise.'

'I'll call the hospital tomorrow evening, just to check everything's gone OK.'

'Yes, if you like. But don't worry. I know I'm in good hands. I'll ring you as soon as I can – or I'll write.'

'Yes, do that. I'll be waiting to hear from you.' There was a silence and, unable to think of anything else to say, he added, 'Good luck. Sleep well.'

'You too. Goodnight.'

Merry rang off with a heavy heart. He could understand Felix's wish to spare him distress, but the prospect of an undefined period during which he would be unable to offer him any comfort or support in his ordeal depressed him deeply.

Merry spent a miserable weekend. The hotel, though comfortable enough, seemed to be populated entirely by deaf old ladies and he missed the lively company at the Willises' home. The weather was bitter, and the rubble-strewn streets all around offered few attractions. He tried to concentrate on ideas for the new show but there was little he could do until he met the musicians and other artistes who would be working with him. Anyway, his mind kept wandering to gloomier thoughts, either imagining what was happening to Felix or wondering how Rose was coping down in Wimborne.

Late on the Sunday afternoon he went to the phone and got through to the hospital at East Grinstead.

'I'm enquiring about Flight Lieutenant Mountjoy.' It still took a conscious effort to remember that in the RAF Felix was known by his real name, rather than as Felix Lamont, the stage name he had adopted when his father turned him out of the family home. 'He's in your Burns Unit and I understand he's being operated on today.'

'Are you a relative?' asked the cold, impersonal voice at the other end.

'No, just a friend.'

'Hold on a minute. I'll see what I can find out.'

A long pause. 'Are you there?'

'Yes, yes, I'm here.'

'Flight Lieutenant Mountjoy was operated on this morning. He's regained consciousness and he's as well as can be expected.'

Merry drew a deep breath. It was as much as he could hope for, he supposed.

'Thank you. Can you give him a message for me?'

'I'll see what I can do, but I can't make any promises.'

'Just tell him that Guy Merryweather phoned to see how he was, will you?'

'Guy Merryweather. All right, I'll try to see that he gets that message.'

Merry put the phone down and went to the local pub, which at least offered company.

4

Matthew Armitage turned up at the Willises' house on Sunday afternoon and asked to see Rose. It was a half-hour she would never forget. The stoic resignation of the other morning had vanished and had been replaced by abject grief. He begged her to change her mind, told her it did not matter to him that he could never be more than second best, promised her every luxury it was in his power to provide if she would marry him. Then, changing tack, he suggested that Richard had proved himself unreliable, that if he really cared for her he would have found a way of getting in touch with her, would not have put Christmas with his family before the need to seek her out. What, he asked, would she do if he had disappeared again and made no further attempt to contact her?

Rose could only repeat, again and again, that she was sorry for the pain she had caused him but that her decision was irrevocable, and it made no difference whether she saw Richard again or not. When she told him that she was being sent to work somewhere else he begged her to write to him, but she insisted that it would be better all round if he forgot her. He insisted that he would write to her and she told him, truthfully, that she had no idea where she was going. In the end he gave up and went away, leaving her shaking and exhausted.

On Tuesday Mrs Heatherington-Smythe arrived on her bicycle and slapped some papers down on the kitchen table in front of Rose.

'Well, there you are. That's the address of the farm you are being transferred to, there is a rail warrant and those are the instructions. It's taken me all weekend to sort out but that's what I'm here for, I suppose.'

Rose looked at the address. 'Montgomeryshire? That's miles away, isn't it?'

'Borders of Wales. North of Shrewsbury. That's what you wanted, isn't it? Somewhere well away?'

'But it's so far . . .' Rose protested. 'I shan't be able to see my family. I shan't know anyone.'

'Perhaps you should have thought of all that before you turned poor Matthew Armitage down,' Mrs Heatherington-Smythe snapped.

'When do I have to go?' Rose asked.

'Tomorrow. It's a dairy farm, so you'll be well qualified. The farmer's expecting you on the five thirty-six train. His name is Powell. He'll meet you at the station. Make sure you don't let him down!' She turned towards the door. 'Now, I must be on my way. I've got to get your replacement settled in.'

The front door banged behind her. Bet, who had been listening to the conversation, remarked viciously, 'Rotten cow! She's done it deliberately – sent you as far away as possible.'

'Don't call her a cow,' Rose said sadly. 'Cows are nice.'

It was dark and freezing hard by the time Rose got off the train at the little country station. It had taken all day, chugging and rattling across country, to get here. She had had to change trains twice, with long waits on windswept platforms in between, and the trains had been crowded, dirty and un-heated. Now her feet were like blocks of ice inside the enormous black boots, the sandwiches and thermos of tea prepared for her by Mrs Willis only a distant memory, and she was longing for a hot meal and a warm bed.

Very few people got off the train with her and they soon hurried off into the darkened streets of the little town. Rose looked up and down the empty platform. Then she carried her case to the exit and handed her ticket to the thin-faced man who stood there, muffled to the chin in a long overcoat.

'Someone is supposed to meet me from Hightop Farm,' she said. 'Do you know if anyone is waiting for me somewhere?'

The man sniffed and looked her up and down. 'Land Girl, are you?'

'Yes.'

'Where from?'

'London.' She had no inclination to go into further explanations.

He sniffed again. 'You won't last long, then.'

Rose straightened her shoulders. 'I've already worked on a farm down in Dorset. I know what I'm doing.'

'Oh-ah?' He looked at her mockingly. 'Not the same round these parts, though.'

Rose looked around the empty car park. There was no sign of anyone waiting.

'Do you think someone will be along soon?' she asked.

'Shouldn't think so,' the man replied. 'Old Bert Powell don't believe in wasting petrol.'

'But he's supposed to meet me,' Rose exclaimed, with rising desperation.

'Oh yes? Says who?'

Rose decided that it was futile to argue. 'How far is Hightop Farm?'

''Bout four mile. Straight up that lane there, then bear right along the cart track at the top of the hill.'

'Is there a bus I can get?'

'You won't find no buses going up there.'

'What about a taxi, then?' She calculated furiously and decided she could just about afford the fare.

'Haven't had a taxi hereabouts since Percy Dunn caught pneumonia last back end.'

'You mean I'm going to have to walk?'

'Looks like it.'

Rose looked at her heavy case and then at the dark, ice-bound road leading up the hill. There were a few houses and one or two shops, all shuttered for the night, and because of the blackout not a chink of light showed anywhere. There was not even a pub, as far as she could see. She thought wildly of taking the next train south, back to London, and wondered how long it would be before the authorities caught up with her. Then she reminded herself that there was a war on and she must do her bit towards keeping the country fed. She picked up her case and set off, on numb feet, up the lane.

It was after seven by the time she reached Hightop Farm, and by that time her arms and shoulders were aching, her feet were blistered and she was shivering with cold and exhaustion. In the darkness she groped her way across a yard cluttered with old bits of machinery and baulks of timber and eventually located the door of a low stone-built house. It was several minutes before there was any response to her knock.

Then the door opened to emit a pale gleam of light and a woman's voice said roughly, 'Well, you took your time! Get inside, before we have the Jerries using us for target practice.'

Rose found herself in a narrow, slate-floored hallway, facing a tall, bony woman with a red, weather-beaten face and sparse grey hair. She was holding an oil lamp, which she raised in order to inspect Rose.

'Well, you're a poor-looking thing, aren't you?' she commented. 'We'll not get much work out of you, I can see. You'd better come through.'

Stunned and miserable beyond words, Rose followed her into the kitchen. This too was lit by a lamp, set in the middle of a table cluttered with dirty dishes and covered with a stained and greasy oilcloth. The floor here was covered with linoleum that had been worn into holes and whose original colour could only be guessed at. An old black range gave off a feeble glow on the far side of the room, and in an armchair in front of it sat a thin, sandy-haired man of indeterminate age dressed in a collarless flannel shirt and a grimy waistcoat. A damp, unlit cigarette adhered to his lower lip and his half-open mouth displayed broken teeth stained yellow with nicotine.

'You're here, then, finally,' he commented, without rising.

'I thought I was going to be met at the station,' Rose retorted.

'And who's supposed to see to the milking while I'm off picking up namby-pamby girls from the station?' he enquired. 'You'll not be much use to me if you can't walk a couple of miles.'

'I've come a long way, and it's dark and cold and I don't know my way around yet,' Rose protested, and was furious to hear her voice breaking on the last words.

'Oh dear, oh dear! We are in a state, aren't we?' he mocked her. 'Better give her some supper, Mother.'

'We've had our meal,' the woman told her. 'I've got better things to do than keep food hot for people who might not turn up. But there's some cold pork under that dish there and bread and marge on the table. Help yourself.'

Rose dumped her case and moved to the table. The pork was mainly fat and the bread obviously several days old. She longed above everything for a cup of tea.

'Could I have a drink?' she asked hesitantly.

'Water in the jug,' was the laconic reply.

She ate what she could stomach and found a chipped glass, which was in need of washing. She went to the sink and was horrified to discover no taps.

'Where . . .?' she began. 'How do you wash up?'

'Water in the bucket there,' the woman said. 'Be careful how you use it. Remember it all has to be carried from the well.'

Rose rinsed the glass and drank. The water tasted oddly metallic.

'Right, then,' the farmer said. 'Since you're keen on washing up, you'd better tackle the rest of those dishes. I'm sure Mother won't object.'

Rose stood for a moment, poised on the brink of hysterics. Then anger came to her rescue. She said coldly, 'I'm sorry, Mr Powell. I'm a Land Girl. My job is to help out on the farm, not be a domestic servant.'

He looked up at her and for the first time she saw a gleam of interest in his pale eyes. 'Now then, girl, don't you get uppity with me,' he said. 'You'll do as you're bloody well told.'

For a moment Rose met his gaze. She no longer wanted to cry. Instead she was possessed by a grim determination that this man and his mother should not get the better of her.

After a few seconds he returned to his paper. 'Better show her her room, Mother. She'll have an early start in the morning.'

The woman took a stub of candle and lit it from the fire in the range. Rose followed her upstairs to a bare, icy box of a room with a narrow single bed. There was no carpet on the floor and the only other furniture was a washstand holding a jug and basin.

'This is yours,' Mrs Powell said. 'Make sure you keep the place clean. I've no time to be clearing up after you.'

Rose reflected that if what she had seen downstairs was anything to go by there wasn't much clearing up done anywhere in the house. Aloud she said, 'Where's the bathroom, please?'

'Bathroom?' The woman gave a hollow chuckle. 'You're not in the city now, you know. There's water in the jug there, and a pot under the bed. You fetch your own water from now on, and empty your own slops. Better get some sleep. You'll need all the rest you can get.'

She put down the candle and stumped off down the stairs.

Rose splashed her face with icy water, made a half-hearted attempt to clean her teeth and, much against her inclination, made use of the chamber pot. Then she undressed, shivering, put on her thick socks and her sweater over her pyjamas and crawled into bed. Alone and no longer bolstered by the need to keep up a brave face, she cried herself to sleep.

She was woken while it was still dark by a dull thudding that shook the bed and seemed to come from somewhere below her. She scrambled out of bed, still half asleep, convinced that they were in the middle of an air raid. On the landing she saw that there was a light downstairs in the hall and, peering over the banisters, made out the gaunt figure of Mrs Powell. She was holding a broomstick, with which she had been thumping on the ceiling below Rose's bedroom.

'What is it? What's wrong?' Rose asked, her voice still thick with sleep.

'Time you were up, my girl. The cows will want milking.'

Rose stumbled back to her room and looked at her watch. It was 5.30. She had got used to these early mornings while working for Matt, but the Willises' house had never been as cold and dark as this. Moreover, she had slept badly and felt now hardly more rested than when she had gone to bed. She went to the washstand. There was a film of ice on the water in the jug. She abandoned the idea of washing and, unable to face the thought of taking anything off, simply pulled on the rest of her clothes over her pyjamas.

Down in the kitchen Mrs Powell was raking out the fire in the range. Rose looked round hopefully for a hot drink but the kettle stood empty by the sink. The farmer's mother looked round and jerked her head towards the door.

'Cows are up in the top meadow at the end of the track. They know where to go. You'll find all the gear in the milking parlour.'

'Is Mr Powell up there already?' Rose asked.

'He'll be around when he's ready,' the woman replied. 'You're qualified, aren't you? No good to us if you can't manage a few cows on your own.'

Rose stumbled out into the first faint light of the winter dawn. She could just make out the low huddle of outbuildings that surrounded the farmhouse and the gate that led to a rutted track. She trudged over to it, noting that if the ground had not been frozen hard it would have been over ankle deep in mud and cow dung. The top field was about half a mile away and when she reached the gate a herd of a dozen cows was waiting by it, their coats rimed with frost and their breath steaming in the chill air. With numb fingers Rose unlatched the gate and let them pass her into the lane. She was no expert when it came to cows but it was not hard to see that, in comparison with the well-fed creatures she had looked after in Wimborne, these were a pathetic, sickly bunch.

She followed them down to the farm and watched as they shambled into the milking stalls. Like the Wimborne cows, each one knew which was her place and went straight to it. The shed was dark still and Rose had to grope around until she found an oil lamp and a box of matches, and it took her some time, in her inexperience, to work out how to light it. Then she began to look for the necessary equipment. She found buckets and a milking stool, but there was no sign of any cloths or any disinfectant for washing the cows' udders. She took a bucket out into the yard and found the well. Drawing water was harder work than she had imagined. She had just filled her bucket when the back door of the house opened and Powell came out, carrying a torch that gave a feeble glimmer of light.

'What you up to?' he demanded. 'You've not milked them cows yet.'

'I'm getting some water to wash them down,' Rose said.

He marched past her into the cowshed: 'You don't want to

bother with any of that nonsense. Get the job done, that's what matters.'

Rose watched in dismay as he seized a bucket and a stool, entered the first stall and sat down to milk. 'But it's not hygienic,' she protested.

'Hygienic be blowed!' was the reply. 'It's good enough for folks round here. We don't want any of your soft southern ways here, girl! Just get stuck in.' He looked up and she saw a glint in his eyes. 'You start with Bessie there, in the end stall.'

Rose soon found out why he had suggested Bessie. She was one of those cows that made it her business to make the milker's life as difficult as possible. First she swung her tail in a vicious swipe that caught Rose across the face and splatted dung into her hair. Then she attempted to kick the bucket over. But Rose had met difficult milkers before and Matt had shown her how, with patience, it was possible to change their behaviour. Rose guessed that Bessie resented the rough handling she got from Powell and instead of shouting at the cow she sat down calmly, leaned her head against her flank and began to sing softly. To begin with the cow refused to let down her milk and fidgeted restlessly but after a little she quietened and the milk began to hiss into the bucket in a satisfying rhythm. Shortly Powell finished his cow and came along the passage behind the stalls to see how she was getting on. Rose looked up serenely. For the first time in days she was beginning to feel warm as the body heat of the cows took the chill off the air in the shed, and she knew that she had scored a victory. He had come prepared to gloat and she had deprived him of that satisfaction. He gazed for a moment and then turned and stomped off to the next cow in the line.

If the lack of hygiene before milking had horrified Rose, she was no less disturbed by what went on in the dairy afterwards. When she reflected that this milk was going to be drunk by

children and nursing mothers and old people, she was seized
with impotent fury. Any protests or suggestions she tried to
make, however, were greeted with scornful derision, and she
soon saw that there was nothing to be gained. Powell was not
going to change his ways at the bidding of a slip of a girl from
the city.

Back in the kitchen Rose's nostrils twitched to the welcome
odour of frying bacon, but when she seated herself at the table
the plate put before her contained nothing but fried potatoes
swimming in bacon fat. On the side of the sink were two plates
already used and waiting to be washed up and on both of them
she saw telltale bacon rinds. Powell and his mother had had
their breakfast while she was fetching the cows down from the
field. There was a teapot on the table and Mrs Powell came
over from the range with a kettle.

'I'll just freshen this up for you,' she remarked.

The resulting brew was the colour of pale straw and tasted
of nothing but hot water. Of course, there was no sugar.

'I'll need your ration book,' the woman said.

'Yes, I'll get it for you,' Rose agreed, wondering gloomily
how much of her weekly ration she would ever see.

As soon as she had eaten Powell, who had been sitting by the
range smoking, said, 'You better get on and get that cowshed
mucked out.'

Rose had often helped Matt with the hard and heavy work
of mucking out but she had never had to do it on her own. For
the next hour she shovelled dung and straw into the barrow
and struggled across the rutted earth of the yard to the
midden. In order to empty the barrow she had first to push
it up a steep plank to reach the top of the heap. It took all her
strength to manoeuvre the heavy barrow into position, and
before long she was drenched in sweat, in spite of the low
temperature.

Towards the end she became aware that Powell was

watching her with a sly grin. 'You finding that hard work?' he asked sardonically.

'Yes,' Rose said curtly. 'Why don't you come and have a go?'

'I don't see no reason in keeping a dog and then barking myself,' he responded. 'I had a good lad to do that work until the army took him. You're supposed to take his place. If you can't do a man's work you'd better say so now. You're no good to me otherwise.'

It was on the tip of Rose's tongue to tell him that she couldn't and had no intention of trying, but something – pride, anger, fear of the consequences, she was not sure which – restrained her. She glared at him and turned to push the barrow back to the cowshed. As she went she heard him chuckle softly to himself.

5

On Monday morning Merry reported to Captain Black in Greenford. The Central Pool of Artistes was housed in an unpromising collection of draughty Nissen huts at one side of a windswept parade ground, but his welcome from George Black made up in warmth for the cheerless surroundings.

In response to Merry's formal salute and 'Lieutenant Merryweather reporting for duty, sir', he came round his desk and extended his hand. 'Welcome on board. I've heard great things about you from Basil Brown. And forget the "sir". We're very informal here.'

Black was a solidly built man with wavy hair and bright, humorous eyes, and Merry took to him at once. After some preliminary small talk he produced a list.

'I've been going round the units scouting for talent and these are the people I've pencilled in to work with you. See what you think.'

Merry scanned the list. Many of the names were unknown to him but several were familiar as stars in their own field, whether as cabaret artistes or band leaders or top-of-the-bill acts on the variety stage.

'Very impressive!' he said, handing the paper back. 'It's hard to imagine some of these people in the army at all.'

Black laughed. 'Too true! I think in many cases their units will be only too glad to get rid of them. They're a grand lot, bags of talent, but like all performers they all have their little ways, and most of them couldn't take an order if you presented it to them on a silver platter. You're the only officer in the group, so you'll be in charge, but you'll have to handle them with a lot of tact. I'm sure I can rely on you.'

Merry was reminded of his earlier experiences with the concert party he had taken to France, just before the German attack had swept him and his unit into the sea at Dunkirk, along with the rest of the British Expeditionary Force – or what remained of it. There had been some awkward characters in that, but he had been able to establish a good working relationship with them. Looking at the line-up of available talent he felt an unwonted surge of optimism. There were the makings of a really first-rate show here, if he could just get everyone pulling together.

It was as well for Merry that he had plenty to occupy his mind, since Felix resolutely refused to allow him to visit. They spoke on the telephone every few days and Felix assured him that the operation had been successful and he was quite recovered, but whenever Merry suggested that he might come down to East Grinstead he was requested to 'give it a few more days'. This went on until the end of the third week when, in answer to his routine request, Felix said unexpectedly, 'How about Sunday afternoon?'

At the appointed time Merry presented himself at the reception desk of the hospital and was directed to Ward 3, a hut set in the grounds some little distance from the main building. He approached it with a tightening in his chest, his body's normal reaction to any kind of stress. He did not know quite what he expected to encounter inside the hut, but he had seen Felix in the immediate aftermath of the crash in which he had been so badly burned, and in their telephone conversations Felix had hinted that some of the men in the ward had been even more terribly disfigured. Merry knew that for Felix's sake, if for no other reason, whatever he felt he must show neither revulsion nor pity. But he had doubts about his own ability to hide his reactions.

As he reached the door of the hut he was halted by the sound of a chorus of young male voices lustily singing a well-known hymn tune, 'The Church's One Foundation'. Merry hesitated, his hand on the latch. He had no wish to intrude on a religious service, and it was, after all, Sunday afternoon. Then he began to make out the words.

> *We are McIndoe's army,*
> *We are his Guinea Pigs.*
> *With dermatomes and pedicules,*
> *Glass eyes, false teeth and wigs.*
> *And when we get our discharge*
> *We'll shout with all our might:*
> *Per ardua ad astra*
> *We'd rather drink than fight.*

(There seemed to be competing versions of the last two lines. He thought he had heard correctly and recognised the motto of the RAF, but other voices opted for an instruction to the enemy to remove himself, in somewhat scatological terms.)

Grinning to himself, Merry pushed open the door and stepped inside. This was clearly no act of worship. At first sight, the interior of the hut reminded him not so much of a hospital ward as of the dormitory at his boarding school, except that it was a good deal warmer and pleasanter. In the centre a large black stove radiated heat and the beds, rather than the usual iron cots, all had normal wooden frames. The colour scheme too had departed from the institutional creams and greens in favour of warm pinkish tones. At one end of the room stood a piano, and at the other, incredibly, was a barrel of beer on a trestle. But it was the occupants who reinforced the impression of a senior boys' dorm at the end of term. A few of the men were lying quietly on their beds, reading or dozing, but the majority were up and dressed and there was a babble of laughter and chat. At the far end of the room some kind of mounted joust seemed to be in progress between four patients. Two of them, in wheelchairs, provided the horses while two more, mounted behind them, were trying to knock each other off with pillows, cheered on by a group of supporters on either side. It did not surprise Merry to see that one of the cavaliers was Felix.

It was a moment or two before anyone noticed his arrival, then a young man in the uniform of a pilot officer got up from a bed near the door and came over. At that moment Merry began to take in the faces around him. The young pilot greeted him with a friendly grin and an outstretched hand. He seemed unaware that his face lacked both lips and eyelids and that he appeared to have a new nose growing grotesquely from the middle of his forehead.

'Are you looking for someone?' he asked. 'Can I help?'

Merry forced himself to shake hands without dropping his eyes. 'I've come to visit Flight Lieutenant Mountjoy,' he said.

'Oh, right! He's over there,' the other man said, and then, raising his voice above the din, he called, 'Ned! Visitor!'

Felix turned, saw Merry, gave his mount a friendly pat on the shoulder and trotted up the ward. In the instant before they met Merry was able to register, with relief, that his face exhibited no such obscene protuberances. He understood then why he had been told to stay away.

'Merry! Good to see you!' Felix held out his left hand and Merry clasped it briefly between both of his own.

'How are you, Felix?'

'I'm fine! How about you?'

'OK. Cold. It's freezing out there.'

The words came automatically, meaning nothing. Their eyes did the speaking.

The pilot officer who had called him over said, 'Hang on. Why did you call him Felix? His name's Edward.'

Merry consulted his friend with a glance. Felix said, 'It's a nickname from before the war.'

'From school?'

'No, we used to work together.' Then, before he could ask any further questions, Felix went on, 'Let me introduce you to some of the gang.'

He took Merry round the ward, starting with the young pilot who had met him. If judged simply by the severity and the variety of deformities collected in that one room it might have seemed as desperate a collection of human misery as could be found anywhere in the world, but the overriding impression was not one of pathos and despair but rather of vitality and optimism. Again and again Merry was greeted with smiling eyes and good-natured quips, even from men whose pain was clearly only just held at bay by drugs.

Nevertheless it was a relief when Felix said casually, 'Fancy a breath of air?'

He fetched his greatcoat and they went out into the frosty twilight of the February afternoon. It was turning out to be another bitterly hard winter. Since Christmas, snow had fallen, turned to slush, frozen and then been covered by fresh falls. Occasionally there were days of brilliant sunshine but far more often they had days like this one of low cloud and fog.

Felix looked up at the sky. 'At least I'm not missing much. Nobody will be flying in this weather.'

Merry sighed. 'Do you still hanker to be up there?'

'Yes, I do,' Felix returned. 'There's nothing like it. It's quite literally "out of this world".'

'I'll stick to good old mother earth, thanks,' Merry said.

Felix looked at him. 'Got a cigarette? I left mine in my locker.'

Merry reached into his pocket and produced the silver cigarette case that Felix had given him for Christmas. Since then Merry had taken great pleasure in using it and reading the inscription engraved inside it. 'To Merry, in memory of 12 November 1940, from Felix. When in disgrace with fortune and men's eyes . . .' It was on the night of 12 November that they had become lovers, and Merry had not had to resort to his *Complete Shakespeare* for the rest of the sonnet.

> *When in disgrace with fortune and men's eyes*
> *I all alone beweep my outcast state,*
> *And trouble deaf heaven with my bootless cries,*
> *And look upon myself and curse my fate,*
> *Wishing me like to one more rich in hope,*
> *Featured like him, like him with friends possessed,*
> *Desiring this man's art, and that man's scope,*
> *With what I most enjoy contented least;*
> *Yet in these thoughts myself almost despising,*
> *Haply I think on thee, and then my state,*
> *Like to the lark at break of day arising*
> *From sullen earth, sings hymns at heaven's gate;*
> *For thy sweet love remembered such wealth brings*
> *That then I scorn to change my state with kings.*

Merry took out two cigarettes, put them both between his lips and lit them, then handed one to Felix. It was a gesture that might be explained, to a casual observer, by the damage to Felix's right hand, which made manipulating such things difficult. Only they both knew that Felix was perfectly capable of managing with one hand. They looked at each other through the cigarette smoke and Merry experienced the peculiar nervous flutter at the pit of his stomach that he always felt when he was close to Felix. He wanted desperately to reach out and embrace him.

Felix said, 'God, this is bloody! I wish there was somewhere we could go.'

'So do I,' Merry agreed. 'No chance, I suppose?'

'Not unless you fancy spreading your greatcoat in the shrubbery,' Felix responded caustically.

'No thanks,' Merry replied.

They grinned at each other. Merry said, 'You've got a new nose.'

Felix touched his right nostril self-consciously. 'It's not quite right yet. McIndoe says he can tidy it up later.'

Merry looked at him more closely. The nostril, as he said, was slightly bulbous and a different colour from the rest of his face, but before the operation it had been almost completely missing. Also, there seemed to be new skin at the corner of his eye, which was no longer dragged downwards in a permanent wink. But there was a fresh scar on his forehead.

'How is it done?' he asked.

'It's an amazing process,' Felix said. 'He takes skin from one part of the body and uses it to patch up the damaged bits. But the skin has to remain attached at one point until the graft has taken, otherwise it dies off. So he took a strip of skin from my forehead, twisted it round and shaped into a new nostril. Then, when it had developed a new blood supply, he snipped it off. I shall be able to comb my hair over the scar eventually.'

'Extraordinary!' Merry murmured. 'What next?'

'He's going to do something about the mouth – next week, probably. The main problem is finding skin that's the right type and near enough to use. It's not too bad for me. You'll have noticed that compared to some of these chaps I've been bloody lucky. Some of them have lost so much skin that it has to come from points much lower down on the body, so it has to be moved up in stages. He takes a strip, twists it round and reattaches it higher up, then repeats the process in a kind of leapfrog manner until he gets it to the right place.'

'That explains why some of those men had those peculiar tubes of skin growing out of odd places,' Merry said.

'The technical term is a pedicule,' Felix told him.

'Ah!' Merry chuckled. 'Yes, that was in the hymn.'

Felix laughed. 'You heard that, did you? That was the clean version. There are alternatives.'

'I can imagine,' Merry said dryly. Then he added, 'I must say, there's a fantastic atmosphere in there.'

'Isn't there?' Felix agreed. 'And it's all down to McIndoe. He is the most amazing man I've ever met. He's not only a brilliant surgeon, he's an incredibly clever psychologist too. He's realised that some of these chaps are going to spend months here, so he's insisted on making it as homely and informal as possible.'

'Speaking of that,' Merry cut in, 'is that really a beer barrel?'

'It certainly is! And it's replenished every time it runs out.'

'Doesn't that encourage some people to go over the top a bit?'

'Every so often. But sometimes a man just needs that. You've seen them, Merry. I thought I'd suffered but, my God, it's nothing to what some of them have been through. And everybody is sensible about the booze. They know they have to keep off it the night before they're due to go on the slab, and if they really abuse it it will have to go and then all the rest will suffer. It's just one small way of making life a bit more bearable. But that's not the end of it. McIndoe knows that these guys need rebuilding mentally as well as physically. He insists, for one thing, on having only the prettiest nurses on the ward. Apparently he interviews them personally.'

'It must be bloody hard for any girl to cope with what goes on in there,' Merry remarked.

'It is,' Felix agreed. 'But I've yet to see one of them crack. They're magnificent – and it's all down to McIndoe's example. Then there are other things. Take this, for example . . .' He flicked his fingers at the lapel of his uniform tunic. 'The authorities wanted to make us wear hospital blues – you know, those ghastly bright blue outfits that make you look like something out of a musical comedy. (No offence, old chap. I've got nothing against musical comedy in its right place, on the stage.) Apparently the lads took exception, and I don't blame them. After all, we're still RAF, even if we are temporarily grounded. So they burned the lot.'

'Burned them!'

'Yes, in the stove. But McIndoe stood up to the powers that be and nothing more was ever said.'

Merry laughed. 'He must be quite a character.'

'You can say that again!' Felix concurred. 'Apparently the RAF offered him a commission and a pretty senior rank, but he turned it down. This way he doesn't have to take orders from anyone and he can fight his corner however he sees fit.'

They had strolled as far as the main gate of the hospital. Merry shivered and glanced at Felix. 'I don't think you should be out in this.'

'Why not?' Felix asked. 'I'm not ill, you know.' Then he added, 'Tell you what. We could walk into town and get some tea in the hotel.'

'Is that permitted?' Merry enquired.

'Oh yes. Not only permitted but encouraged. That's another of McIndoe's master strokes. He understands that people like us need to feel that we're not freaks or pariahs.' He threw a sideways glance at Merry. 'Of course, I was lucky there, too. You taught me that, early on. If you hadn't given me the guts to go into pubs and places I should probably have hidden myself in my room and refused to venture out. Some of these blokes haven't had my good fortune. There are several whose girlfriends, wives even, have run out on them, unable to cope. Not all, of course. But even for them meeting strangers is a daunting prospect. That's where McIndoe's social cachet comes in.'

'How so?' Merry asked.

'Well, being a famous society surgeon who had done nose

jobs for a lot of very well-known ladies, he's extremely popular as a dinner guest among the local nobs. He's used that to educate people about what goes on at the hospital and to bring them on board. As a result we all get invited out for meals in homes round about. Then, he's talked to the local shopkeepers and publicans and persuaded them that we shan't drive their other customers away. As a result, all the chaps can wander around town when they're fit enough without feeling embarrassed or unwelcome.'

'That's wonderful,' Merry said with feeling. He remembered his own reactions at the sight of those maimed limbs and distorted faces, and could visualise the effect they might have on an unprepared public.

'That's McIndoe for you,' Felix replied. 'Doing wonders is all in a day's work to him.'

Merry felt a sudden, ignoble twinge of jealousy. 'You really think a lot of him, don't you?'

Felix grinned at him. 'To be honest with you, if someone told us he could walk on water I don't think any of us would be in the least surprised. You'll like him,' he added. 'You've got something in common. He plays the piano too – not like you, he's not a professional, but quite passably. He often comes into the ward after a long day in the operating theatre and spends hours playing, just to cheer everyone up.'

When they reached the hotel in the main street and made their way to a table in the lounge Merry had first-hand proof of what Felix had said. They were greeted warmly by the staff and several ladies taking tea nodded and waved cordially. As they settled themselves Felix said, 'Look, I've done nothing but talk about myself. How are things with you? How's the new show?'

For the next twenty minutes Merry entertained him with stories of the eccentricities of his little group of artistes. Eventually Felix said, 'So, how soon will you be ready to perform?'

'Another week, maybe,' Merry replied.

'And then what?'

Merry met his eyes and lifted his shoulders. 'Who knows? We could be sent anywhere.'

They were silent for a moment, both contemplating the prospect of a prolonged separation. Then Merry changed the subject. 'Oh, I knew there was something I wanted to tell you. I heard from Rose, finally.'

'You did? How's she getting on?'

'Not too well, it seems. She's been sent to a hill farm somewhere in Montgomeryshire and they're not treating her well. Reading between the lines, it sounds as though she's being worked to death and half starved.'

'That's terrible!' Felix said. 'What a bloody mess. Has she heard anything from Richard?'

'Apparently not. Come to that, neither have I. He seems to have gone to ground completely.'

They walked back to the hospital. Merry would have taken his leave at the door of the hut but Felix insisted that he come in and say goodbye to the others. Once inside someone remembered that Felix had told them that Merry played the piano and he found himself seated at the instrument. For the next half-hour, in response to various requests, he played everything from Chopin to Scott Joplin, while a crowd of grotesque, appreciative faces surrounded him and smiled encouragement.

After a while he became aware of a stir by the door of the hut and looked round to see a solidly built man in civilian clothes making his way towards him, exchanging good-humoured banter with the men he passed. It was easy to see, as they fell back to make way for him, that he was not simply respected by these young airmen in his care but loved and revered.

When Felix introduced Merry to him he said, 'So you're the

Guy Merryweather we've heard so much about! Good to meet you at last.'

Merry felt a warm surge of pleasure at the recognition that Felix had talked about him, but murmured self-deprecatingly, 'I don't know what you've heard, sir, but I promise you it isn't true.'

McIndoe laughed. 'Well, among other things I've heard that you're an accomplished pianist and I can vouch for the truth of that. Do go on playing.'

Merry shook his head. 'Oh no. It's your piano, I understand. I don't want to butt in.'

'Ever play duets?' McIndoe asked.

So they played duets until a very attractive nurse put her head round the door and said, 'Excuse me, Mr McIndoe. We're ready to serve the evening meal.'

Felix came to the door of the hut with him and they paused outside.

'Shall I come next Sunday?' Merry asked.

Felix shook his head. 'Better not, if I'm going on the slab again this week. I'll ring and let you know.'

'OK.' Merry knew better than to argue now. He reached out and squeezed Felix's arm briefly. 'Good luck, then. See you soon.'

'Thanks.' Felix smiled tightly and touched his sleeve in response. 'Take care. God bless.'

Merry turned away and walked quickly to where he had parked the Lagonda.

A couple of days later Merry was summoned to George Black's office.

'How soon is that show of yours going to be ready?' Black asked.

'Dress rehearsal on Friday,' Merry told him.

'Good. I'll come and have a look,' Black said.

The dress rehearsal having passed off without a hitch, the show was pronounced fit for performance and Merry was instructed to prepare for their first tour. To everyone's relief they found that their initial assignment was to entertain the various Royal Artillery batteries manning the defences around London. This meant that they could all remain in the various hotels and boarding houses where they had found digs, although it often entailed a long, cold journey back from some outlying suburb after the show. The days took on a regular pattern. They would clamber into the truck, which was already loaded with their props and costumes and the musical instruments, including an upright piano for Merry, and trundle away through the bomb-cratered streets to Northolt or Clapham or Mitcham or Gravesend. Once there they would unload and set up in whatever drill hall or scout hut had been earmarked for the occasion, run through a few items, sort out any problems with lighting – if there was anything other than the normal dim light bulbs – and then gather round a paraffin stove or something similar to eat the meal they had brought with them. Quite often the local WVS would be on hand with welcome urns of tea and extra sandwiches, and once or twice they were invited to a proper meal at the home of a local volunteer, but very soon it would be time to get into costume and put on their make-up.

The group consisted of four musicians – a saxophone, a clarinet, a double bass and Merry on piano; a couple of young men who had worked up a comedy act in the characters of two cockney housewives; a tenor who could also yodel; and a juggler. The show was simple. There were no special effects or big production numbers, but every individual act was good and they were invariably received with great appreciation. The job of constantly manning the guns surrounding the capital involved long stretches of boredom, shivering in sub-zero temperatures while waiting for the next air raid, and anything that broke the monotony was welcome. The only snag was that, all too often, just as the show was getting into its stride, the siren would sound and at least half the audience would leap up and race off to the gun emplacements. Sometimes the rest would head for the shelters, but more often than not they elected to stay where they were and take their chances. After six months of almost nightly bombardments Londoners were growing blasé. The streets might be full of rubble and the casualty lists ever longer, but during the day it was business as usual and at night they were determined to snatch whatever pleasure was on offer.

Wherever he went Merry encountered the same mood of determined cheerfulness. The threat of invasion had receded and the fighting was confined to North Africa and the Far East. With German bombers attacking the cities and German U-boats harassing the convoys that brought desperately needed food supplies, it had become a war of attrition. There was nothing to do but endure, until something happened to raise the siege.

6

Richard paid off his taxi outside the Northumberland Hotel with a twist of nervous anticipation in his stomach. He had no idea what to expect, but he was glad that something was happening at last. For the last few weeks he had existed in a kind of limbo, feeling that he belonged nowhere and had no purpose.

Initially he had been returned to his regiment, where he had been greeted ecstatically by his old comrades, who had heard nothing of him since he was left on the beach in the chaos of the evacuation from Dunkirk. But in spite of his pleasure at seeing them he found he could not reconcile himself to the tedium of army life. The endless training exercises, in preparation for the opening of a Second Front that would carry the battle back on to enemy-held territory, seemed to him pointless. Nor could he feel at ease with his old comrades. Previously he had been able to bridge the gap engendered by differences in upbringing and education, but now his experiences in France had finally set him apart from them.

All this faded into insignificance compared to the loss of Rose. Although nothing had ever been agreed between them, he had always assumed that when he returned to England she would be waiting for him. The discovery that she had committed herself to another man had left him bereft of the gyroscope that had kept him on an even keel for the last year. Without the prospect of a future with her he felt adrift. At the same time his thoughts kept returning to Chantal. In recounting his adventures to Rose's family and friends during that fraught discussion in the first minutes of the new year, he had not mentioned her part in his escape. Chantal was the French *soubrette* who had performed with them in the Follies, and she was now a dedicated member of the line that had taken him to safety. He was guiltily aware that his affair with her had been a betrayal of Rose and told himself that his rejection had been well deserved. But inextricably interwoven with that idea was the memory of Chantal herself, of her courage and generosity and her uncomplicated delight in sexual pleasure. She had always resisted any suggestion of a permanent relationship but, in spite of the dangers they faced, they had been very happy together, and now he longed for the warmth and comfort of her company. He worried constantly that she might have fallen into the hands of the Gestapo, and it compounded his sense of guilt that he had left her to face that danger while he had fled to the relative safety of England.

A spell away from the base for officer training came as a relief from routine, but when his promotion came through he felt even less at ease, in spite of the fact that he was welcomed in the officers' mess without apparent resentment. Toby Sandford, the young lieutenant with whom he had struck up an unspoken rapport during the chaotic days of their retreat, seemed genuinely glad to see him and would have been happy to make friends, but Richard was too absorbed in his own loss to reciprocate. The summons to meet some unspecified person in a particular room at the Northumberland Hotel had come like an order for early release to a prisoner.

He made his way through the sandbagged entrance into the foyer and reported to the front desk, where he was directed to the second floor. Entering the room, he stopped in surprise just inside the door. The room was completely bare of furniture except for two folding chairs and a trestle table covered with an army blanket. The blinds were drawn against the early winter dusk and a single, unshaded bulb shed a harsh light over the chairs and the lean, fair-haired man in the uniform of a major in the Buffs who rose to greet him.

'Richard Stevens?' The voice was uninflected, the clean-shaven face empty of expression.

Richard came to attention and saluted. 'Yes, sir.'

'Sit down.'

Richard sat and the major seated himself opposite. He had a folder on his knee, but it was closed.

'You were left behind at Dunkirk?' There was no attempt to put him at his ease, no casual small talk.

'Yes, sir.'

'How did that come about?'

Richard related the circumstances as succinctly as he could.

'And you were taken prisoner by the Germans and treated in one of their hospitals?'

'Yes, sir.'

'Were you treated well?'

'From a medical point of view, yes.'

'And from any other point of view?'

'I was a prisoner. I was treated as a prisoner.'

'But you have no complaints?'

'Not of my treatment in the hospital, no.'

'And your wounds? Does your leg give you any trouble now?'

'It aches a little when the weather is cold. It doesn't stop me from doing anything.'

'How did you escape?'

Richard related his escape from the ambulance and the circumstances that had brought him to the woodcutter's cottage occupied by Clothilde Jumeau and her son.

'*Et puis? Combien de temps avez-vous passé avec eux?*' The switch of languages was so completely unsignalled and the accent so perfect that Richard was caught momentarily on the wrong foot. He drew a quick breath and answered in French.

'*Quelques semaines. Peut-être un mois.*'

The inquisition proceeded, still in French. Richard told how he had been passed from safe house to safe house, but was careful not to give any names or the precise address of any of his helpers. He could not avoid, however, explaining the cover he had used for the last part of the journey, nor in what guise he had been able to cross the demarcation line into the unoccupied zone. The major looked at him, the only change in his expression a slight narrowing of the eyes.

'You passed yourself off as an Italian opera singer?'

'Yes.'

'And you made your way through France posing as half of a cabaret double act with this young woman, Chantal?'

'Yes. I told people that I had been working with an opera company in Belgium, which folded when the war broke out, and I was trying to earn enough money to get back to Italy to enlist.'

'And is this true? You trained as an opera singer in Italy?'

'Yes. I was there for three years.'

'And you speak Italian?'

'Yes.'

'Fluently?'

'Yes.'

'That would explain why you speak French with an Italian accent.'

'That was intentional. It made my story seem more genuine.'

The major gazed down for a moment at the unopened folder on his knee and then said, in English, 'Why do you want to go back to France?'

Richard thought carefully before he answered. He knew instinctively that any mention of his disappointment over Rose or his desire to see Chantal again would bring the interview to an abrupt and conclusive end. He said, 'I think I could be useful. More useful than I can be as an ordinary soldier.'

'Useful to whom?'

'To the people who helped me escape. I feel I owe them something. They are working in isolation at the moment, and it's costing them a lot of money to feed and clothe escaping prisoners. We should reimburse them somehow. And ultimately, useful to us, to our side. I came over the border with some airmen from a crashed bomber. They were totally lost. They couldn't speak the language, they had no idea where they were or how to behave. Obviously there are going to be a lot more like that, if we go on bombing Germany, and we can't afford to lose them. We need to support the French escape lines, and probably set up others, to get them back.'

The expressionless eyes scrutinised him for a moment longer, then the other man said, 'I'd like to talk to you again in a day or two. Today is Thursday. Come and see me again on Saturday at two p.m.' He rose and held out his hand. 'Good day.'

Richard shook hands and left. It seemed he was through the first round, at least.

He passed a lonely and aimless evening in the small hotel where he was staying, and an equally purposeless Friday. For reasons nobody could fathom the nightly bombing raids on London seemed to have tailed off, but the evidence of their destructive force was everywhere. Richard had never spent much time in the city and he knew no one there, now that he had lost contact with Rose, so he spent much of the day wandering the streets and marvelling at the fact that life seemed to go on almost normally in the midst of so much chaos.

On Saturday he presented himself as instructed to the same cheerless room and was confronted by the same enigmatic man, the only difference being that this time he was dressed in a tweed civilian suit. As before he launched without preamble into the business of the meeting.

'At this stage I usually have to point out to people that they are being recruited for a job which requires some very particular characteristics. I think you are already aware of the nature of what we are proposing, but I wonder if you have thought about all the possible ramifications. Could you jump out of an aeroplane, if required?'

Richard took a deep breath. He had been dreading this question. 'I honestly don't know,' he said at length. 'The idea terrifies me, but other people do it, so I suppose I can, if it comes to the push.'

His interlocutor nodded dispassionately. 'Have you ever killed a man?'

'Not to my knowledge. I've fired in the direction of the enemy. I can't say with certainty that I hit anyone.'

'Could you do it, if the need arose? Say a fellow agent was in danger and you had a suitable weapon.'

Richard imagined Chantal at the mercy of the Gestapo and nodded. 'If it was a German, or someone working for the Germans, yes. I've seen a bit of what they do to civilians.'

'And suppose you had nothing but your bare hands? Could you do it then?'

Once again Richard paused for thought. 'I think I could, yes. If the circumstances required it.'

The major nodded. 'I'm glad to see that you think before you answer. Some of the people I talk to seem to think that what is required is unquestioning heroism, a refusal to contemplate weakness. That may be all very well in a tank commander, but it is not what is needed in an agent in the field. In this case, discretion really is the better part of valour.' He paused and fixed Richard with his disconcerting stare. 'You realise that you will be placing yourself in extreme danger? If arrested, it is very unlikely that you would be able to claim the protection of the Geneva Convention. You would almost certainly be shot as a spy – and perhaps, indeed almost certainly, you would be tortured first. Are you prepared for that?'

Richard fought down the queasiness in his stomach. 'The French men and women who helped me risk that every day. I suppose I can do the same.'

The major nodded again and was silent for a moment. Then he said, 'I think we both need to sleep on this. It's a very big decision, for both of us.'

Richard felt a sudden surge of annoyance that he had come so far and still had to wait for a decision. 'You're not satisfied that I'm up to the job?'

'On the contrary, I think you are ideally suited for it. But it's not something you should rush into. Go away and think over all the implications – what you are going to tell your family, your girlfriend, for example. Then come back and see me tomorrow at the same time.'

Richard gave a passing thought to the question of whether this strange man ever took a day off, and said, 'Very well.'

'I need hardly point out, I presume, that you must not discuss this with anyone. Not friends or family, or superior officers. This is a decision you have to make completely alone.'

Richard nodded. 'Of course.'

The major rose and extended his hand. 'Till tomorrow, then.'

Back in his hotel room Richard felt a sudden urgent need for company. He knew he could not talk to anyone about the decision he had to make. He yearned simply for human contact, someone with whom to share a drink and a joke. He asked himself who he would choose, for preference, to spend that evening with, and the image of Merry's ironic grin came immediately into his mind. He remembered that Merry had told him that when he was in London he stayed at the Taylors' flat in Lambeth. Rose would not be there so there was no danger of bumping into her. She was down in Dorset with her Matthew, preparing for her wedding. There had been no sign of Merry when he went there looking for her before Christmas, but it was possible that he might be there now. At least it would be something to do. Anything was preferable to sitting around in this bleak room, contemplating the step he was about to take.

He took the Tube to Lambeth North and found himself in a darkened landscape, pockmarked with bomb craters. He remembered his first visit, a few weeks earlier. Then he had been buoyed up by excited anticipation, but as he stumbled along he was gripped by the fear that when he reached the address there would be nothing there but an empty, rubble-strewn space, like so many he had passed. It had been a great relief to find Taylors, the shoe shop, still standing, but it was boarded up and no one had answered when he rang the bell. He had been about to try one of the neighbours when the siren had sounded and he had been hustled down into a shelter by an air-raid warden. It was there that someone had told him the Taylors had left months before and no one knew where they had gone. The sickening despair that had gripped him then had been a mere foretaste, he thought as he picked his way along the dark street, of what was to follow.

This time there was no air raid and there were plenty of people about, hurrying home muffled against the bitter cold, and he found the shop and a door at the side that must lead to the flat. He rang the bell and waited but, as before, no one came. He looked at his watch. It was just after six. Perhaps Merry was working. He might come back later. On the far side of the street a door opened, giving a brief glimpse of a lighted interior from which came the sound of voices and the clink of glasses. Richard decided that he might as well wait in the warm.

In the pub he ordered half a pint of bitter and the landlord remarked, with friendly curiosity, 'Haven't seen you around here before, Lieutenant.'

Richard resisted the impulse to look over his shoulder for the officer who was being addressed and explained that he had been hoping to find a friend who was staying at the flat opposite.

'Oh, the Taylors? They haven't been there for months. Left to go to the country when the Blitz started.'

'Yes, I know,' Richard said. 'But they had a lodger, an army officer . . .'

'Oh, Lieutenant Merryweather! Mate of yours, is he? He's gone an' all. Well, nothing to keep him here now, is there? Know what I mean? Since Rose Taylor went away.'

Richard was not sure whether he wanted to laugh or cry at the thought that Merry was commonly regarded by the neighbours as Rose's 'fancy man'.

'He doesn't stay here any more?' he queried. 'When did he leave?'

'Oh, weeks ago. When was it, George?' The morose-looking man farther along the bar thus addressed looked up from his beer and shook his head. The publican went on, 'He came in one night, soon after Christmas it would be, and said he was moving so he wouldn't be in again. We were sorry to see him go. He used to come in some nights and play the old joanna for us. We had some right good old sing-songs.'

Richard finished his beer and declined the offer of 'the other half'. Stumbling back along the dark street, he felt that he had never been so alone, not even in France. His mother had forwarded Merry's letter but he had been too depressed to reply and there had been no mention of a change of address. He was not even sure of the address of the house where he had spent that disastrous New Year's Eve, since he had only reached it through a chance meeting with Merry. Now that Merry had moved, the last link with all those friends from his summer with the Follies was broken. There was only one person in the world, now, who offered him any chance of the companionship he craved, and that was Chantal.

The next day he reported to the bare room at the Northumberland and told the major that he had made his decision.

7

Rose dragged another bucket of hot water into her room and tipped it into the old tin bath. The water was still only about three inches deep and rapidly cooling in the chilly air. She contemplated going downstairs for another bucketful, but by the time she had lugged it upstairs the water already in the bath would be colder still, and besides, she didn't think that she had the strength to carry it. But the prospect of taking off all her clothes to sit in a lukewarm puddle was too daunting to contemplate. Shivering, she stripped off her thick sweater and her WLA uniform shirt and then the flannel pyjama jacket and the woollen vest she wore underneath and knelt beside the bath while she rapidly sponged her top half with the tepid water. When she had dried that part of her she put the sweater back on before removing the heavy corduroy breeches, the pyjama trousers and the flannel knickers that encased her lower half. Then she sat in the bath and hastily washed the exposed area. Her clean underclothes were on the bed but she shuddered as she put them on. In the unheated house it was almost impossible to get things dry and the thick garments remained perpetually damp.

She had not seen any sign of a bath until almost a week after her arrival at the farm. Until then she had made do with hasty strip washes in the icy water she carried up to her room from the well, and she had been uncomfortably aware of the stale-biscuit smell of her own body. Then, on the first Saturday evening, she had come into the kitchen to find Mrs Powell filling the tin bath, which she had set in front of the kitchen range, with buckets of hot water from the copper in the scullery next door. It had been snowing all day, a wet snow that filled the yard with slush and got into her boots and down the collar of her oilskin coat, and she felt chilled to the marrow of her bones.

'Oh, wonderful!' she exclaimed. 'A hot bath. Just the ticket!'

'Ah, I expect you can do with one,' the other woman agreed. 'You can take your turn after Powell and me.'

That was a disappointment but Rose could see the justice of it. It was not until later that the horrible truth came home to her. A screen was set up around the bath and Powell disappeared behind it and Rose could hear him splashing and grunting as she sat at the kitchen table trying to find some edible meat on a greasy piece of scrag-end of mutton.

When he eventually reappeared, looking very little cleaner than before to Rose's eyes, his mother stood up. 'You done, then? Right, I may as well have mine while there's still some heat in that water.'

With a sickening lurch in her stomach Rose realised that she was going to be expected to take her turn in the same water that had already been used by the other two. She thought of Powell's grimy neck, his hands ingrained with farmyard muck, the smell of sweat and dung that habitually emanated from him, and she knew she could not do it. When Mrs Powell reappeared and remarked tersely, 'All yours, girl,' she stood up.

'I'm sorry, but I'm afraid I'm not prepared to use the same bath water. I think I'm entitled to one bath a week, at least.'

'Oh, hark at Lady Muck!' exclaimed Powell, adding in a mocking falsetto, '*I think I'm entitled*. I'll tell you what, gal, you're entitled to what I decide to give you. That's all you're entitled to.'

Rose was about to protest when Mrs Powell cut in. 'It's up to you. You want fresh water, you'll have to empty this lot and refill it. There's water in the copper still – a bit, anyway.'

Powell grunted. 'OK. You want to spoil her, Mother, you go right ahead. No skin off my nose. I'm off to the pub.'

Wearily Rose hauled herself to her feet and fetched the bucket. By the time she had bailed out the dirty water and rinsed away the scum that clung round the bath, and then refilled it with what was left of the water in the copper, she was almost too exhausted to undress. But at least it was a relief to know that Powell had gone out. She knew she would not have felt safe taking her clothes off with him just the other side of the screen. Once she was in the water she was glad she had made the effort. The kitchen was warm and by the time she had finished bathing she felt comfortable for the first time since her arrival.

The bath did not appear again until the following Saturday, and when Rose dropped one or two hints mid-week about how much she would enjoy a bath she was met with a disapproving sniff and the phrase that seemed to have become a universal excuse for any sort of meanness: 'There is a war on, you know!' When bath night eventually came round again, however, it was taken for granted that she would get her own water and it seemed as though Mrs Powell had actually heated extra in anticipation. Rose's mother had sent her a parcel that contained, among other things, some scented bath cubes. She put one in the water and lay back, luxuriating in the perfumed steam and letting the hot water soak away the crippling aches in her back and shoulders. On the other side of the screen Mrs Powell was listening to the Light Programme, and for a moment Rose was transported back to the cosy kitchen of the Willises' house in Dorset. She closed her eyes and let herself relax.

A draught of cold air as the back door opened and closed

made her open them again. As soon as she did so she was aware, for the first time, that on the wall to one side of the range hung a mirror, spotted with age and misted with steam, but still reflecting with horrible clarity the image of Powell, mouth open in a leer, a yellowing cigarette butt stuck to his lower lip. And there was no doubt from the expression on his face that he could see her.

The next day Powell had come up behind her when she was mucking out the cowshed and put his hand on her breast. 'Nice little body you got there, girl. Didn't realise you was that well set up inside all them clothes!'

Rose swung round. She had a pitchfork in her hand and she levelled it quite deliberately at his groin. 'You touch me again and you know where I'm going to stick this, don't you!'

He backed off, grinning inanely and flapping his hands at her. 'Now then. There's no need to get on your high horse. Don't you know a compliment when you hear one?'

'I don't want your compliments,' Rose spat out. 'I'm here to do a job. Now just let me get on with it – or I'll report you to my supervisor.'

It was an empty threat. The woman who was supposed to be in charge of Land Army girls in the area had appeared once on her bike when Rose was working in one of the fields above the farm and shouted across the distance, 'Getting on OK?'

Rose had waved and started towards her but she had apparently taken the gesture as an affirmative and waved back. 'Jolly good! Must dash!' And before Rose could get close enough to speak she had mounted her bike and pedalled off down the hill.

However, the threat, or perhaps the pitchfork, worked with Powell, and he had not tried to lay hands on her again. So now, every Saturday night after the mother and son had finished, Rose lugged the heavy tin bath up to her room and then hauled up as many buckets of warm water as she could manage to fill it.

Powell's behaviour was not the only thing Rose wanted to discuss with her supervisor. There was the little matter of wages. Land Girls did not earn much, it was true, but Matthew had always been punctilious about paying her every Friday evening. Though she had handed most of it over to Mrs Willis for her keep, it had left her with enough to buy personal necessities and the occasional small luxury like a new lipstick or some talcum powder. On the evening of her first Friday at Hightop Farm she had waited for Powell to hand her what was due to her. When nothing was forthcoming she excused the lapse with the thought that she had not worked a full week and probably the difference would be made up in her next wage packet.

When the following Friday passed without any reference to money, she swallowed her natural reluctance to confront people and said, 'I was wondering about my wages, Mr Powell. I realise you'll want to deduct something for my keep, but I'd like to have whatever is owing to me after that.'

He put down his teacup and looked at her with the mocking grin she had come to hate so intensely. 'Wages, girl? What you want money for? You got your food and a bed to sleep in. Where you going to spend money round here?'

'I'd like to go into the village,' Rose said primly. 'There are things I need – personal things.'

'Oh-ah? When you planning on doing that, then?' he enquired in the same sarcastic tone.

'That's another thing,' Rose said, anger beginning to bubble to the surface. 'What about time off? I'm entitled to half a day a week, minimum.'

'Oh, here we go again!' he snorted. '*Entitled!* I'm entitled to this and that and the other thing. Let me tell you, Lady Muck, you can forget all that stuff. What am I entitled to, do you suppose? I might be entitled to some time off, too, but do I get it? Do I buggery!'

'But you can't keep me here like a prisoner!' Rose cried. 'And you do get a break sometimes. You go to the pub, don't you?'

'You want to come with me?' he asked, with a suggestive leer. 'I don't mind taking you, if that's what you fancy.'

'No, it's not what I want!' Rose exclaimed. 'I just want whatever money is owing to me and one afternoon to do some personal shopping. If you can't accept that I'll leave. I've had enough!' And she marched out of the kitchen.

What worried her more than anything was the thought that her period was due any day now. She had brought some sanitary towels with her, just to be on the safe side, but she knew she would need more. Somehow she had to get to a chemist's shop before long. She took out her purse and counted her pennies. She had just about enough to get through this month, but there was still the problem of getting to a shop. She thought of the long walk to the village and the longer haul back up the hill again. Since she had arrived at Hightop she had worked from the first gleam of the winter dawn until well after dark every day. There was no chance of getting to the village while the shops were open unless she could have some time off. She decided that, if Powell refused to change his attitude, she would simply have to walk out one afternoon and leave him to cope on his own.

In the event, it was Mrs Powell who came to her aid. She had been present when Rose asked for her wages, but had said nothing. The next Friday evening, however, when the meagre supper had been cleared away, she said, 'Now, son, it's time you gave Rose here what's owing to her. There's things she needs that aren't provided for her here.'

Powell grunted something unintelligible, but he groped in his trouser pocket and produced a handful of small change, from which he selected, after some fumbling and muttering, a two-shilling piece.

'There y'are,' he said, thrusting it at Rose. 'Now we're square.'

Rose felt that they were very far from 'square' but she decided to take what she could get while it was on offer. 'Until next week,' she said, pointedly, pocketing the money.

'And you better borrow my bike tomorrow afternoon,' Mrs Powell said, unexpectedly. 'It's a fair stretch into the village.'

The sense of release that Rose felt as she whizzed down the hill on the old bike the following day came as a surprise to her. It was ridiculous, she thought, that the prospect of a couple of hours off and a chance to look in one or two shops, where the goods on offer were likely to be limited even by wartime standards, should create such a sense of euphoria, but it was a measure of just how trapped and helpless she had been feeling. She made her essential purchases at the little chemist's shop and then wandered along the street. There were only a few shops and some of them were shut for the weekend, but the baker's shop was still open and in the window were a few hard, bright yellow buns. Rose spent the last of her money on one of them and started cramming it into her mouth before she was even out of the shop. It had all the worst characteristics she associated with what her mother always referred to disdainfully as 'shop cakes', accentuated by wartime rationing. It was dry and heavy and tasted of soda and dried egg, but Rose wolfed it down just the same. Then she turned to collect the decrepit bike and face the long ride back up the hill. Powell had told her to be sure she was back in time for the evening milking.

Suddenly her throat ached and her eyes pricked with tears at the prospect. She stood and looked behind her at the station. She would give anything, *anything*, to get on a train away from this place. The thought of going back to her mother and Bet and the Willises made her want to howl out loud. But she had

no money for a rail ticket, and anyway she knew that her
disappearance would be reported to the WLA authorities.
What the punishment might be for deserting her post she had
no idea. Soldiers could be shot, couldn't they? Surely they
couldn't do that to a girl in the Women's Land Army? But
whatever the consequences, it would certainly mean disgrace,
for her family as well as for herself. And how could she go back
to where she would be certain to encounter Matthew? She had
tried not to think about him since her arrival at Hightop Farm,
and mostly she had been so exhausted by the end of the day
that she had fallen asleep before any disturbing memories
could present themselves. It was better this way, she reasoned.
She had made her decision and now she must put up with the
consequences. She turned and began to pedal slowly up the
long hill to the farm.

The postman came only rarely to Hightop and when he did
Rose was usually too busy to notice him, but each evening when
she came in for supper she looked hopefully to see whether there
was an envelope by her plate. Her mother wrote regularly and
usually enclosed notes from Bet and scribbled postscripts from
the two little boys. Once a week there was a parcel. Rose had
tried hard not to suggest that she was going short of anything,
knowing how tight rations were for everyone these days, but it
had been impossible not to hint at the poor conditions and Mrs
Taylor was adept at reading between the lines. So the parcels
contained luxuries like Mrs Willis's home-made jam, carefully
repacked in a cleaned-out treacle tin to withstand the journey,
and biscuits bought with hoarded ration 'points'. When these
parcels arrived, Rose took them up to her room to open and sat
on the edge of the hard, narrow bed dipping biscuits in the jam
and stuffing them in her mouth as if they might be confiscated
before she could eat her fill. She had one or two twinges of guilt
when the first parcel came, wondering whether she should offer

to share the goodies with the Powells, but after the first week or two she did not give the idea a second thought.

Letters came from Merry, too, explaining that he was no longer living at the flat in Lambeth and giving news of Felix, but the one letter that mattered most never arrived. She had no doubt that Merry would have forwarded her own letter. He had told her that he had written to Richard himself, so he obviously knew his home address. The conclusion must be, then, that Richard had received her urgent plea to get in touch and had chosen not to. Rose's mind went round and round over these arguments while she milked the cows or shovelled manure. She tried to tell herself that there was no point in going on hoping for a letter, but she still entered the kitchen each evening with a knot in her stomach.

One day, however, she was delighted to find a letter from Sally Castle. Sally had been a member of the dance troupe to which Rose had belonged before the accident to her ankle cut short her career. Now with Babe Willis in the Wrens and Sally's sister, Lucy, in the ATS and Patricia doing war work in a munitions factory, she was the only one who was still involved in show business. Hearing from her was like hearing voices from another life, but at least it was proof that the other life still existed. They had kept in touch, intermittently, since Rose and her family left London, and she knew her friend was still working at the Windmill Theatre in Soho. She took the letter up to her room and opened it eagerly. Sally wrote in her usual slapdash manner and, as always, there was a special piece of gossip that she wanted to pass on. This time it was about herself. She had a new boyfriend, a Canadian pilot who had come over to fight with the RAF, and for several pages she waxed lyrical about his good looks and charming manners and his generosity – especially the latter. The letter was spiced with little anecdotes about the other artistes in the same show and some of her stories had Rose chuckling out loud.

When she came to the end she sat gazing down at the sheets of paper. For a moment she had been back in the warm, exciting, seedily glamorous world of the theatre, but now the reality of her own life came back to her. She looked at her hands holding the letter, and was suddenly aware that her nails were broken and dirty, her skin rough and chapped from constant immersion in cold water and the joints of her knuckles red and swollen. She raised her eyes and studied herself in the little mirror above the washstand. It was the first time she had really taken notice of how she looked since her arrival, and she was shocked by the stranger's face staring back at her – thin and drawn, with dark shadows under the eyes, her nose reddened by icy winds, the beginnings of lines forming at the corners of her eyes and mouth and the whole framed by lank hair in dire need of a shampoo and set. For a moment she could not think who this face reminded her of. Then she knew. 'If I stay here much longer I'm going to end up looking like Ma Powell,' she muttered aloud, and burst into tears. She flung herself down on the bed and muffled her face in the pillow, so that the Powells should not hear her despairing sobs. However bad she felt, she still had enough pride to be determined that they should never know they had reduced her to this state.

February had given way to March but there was no hint of spring. Up on the snow-covered hills the farmers struggled to save their new lambs and the cows at Hightop Farm grew scrawnier than ever. Rose had to carry water in buckets from the well for them to drink because the water in their troughs was frozen solid. She lugged bales of hay and shovelled manure until every fibre of her body screamed for a respite. Her muscles had developed over the weeks of hard labour until they stood out on her thin arms like knotted cords, but even so at times the weights she had to carry were almost beyond her strength. It did not help that she was always hungry. Her dancer's training had kept her slim, but now

there was not an ounce of spare flesh on her body and her hip
bones and shoulder blades stood out like those of the poor,
half-starved cows.

One evening she felt even more exhausted than usual and by
bedtime she had started to sneeze. Next morning her throat
was so sore that she could hardly swallow, but when Mrs
Powell banged on the ceiling in her usual brusque fashion she
crawled out of bed and dragged on her clothes. After all, the
cows had to be milked, and she knew that Powell would not
show his face until she had brought them down from their
pasture. By breakfast time she could hardly speak and her
head felt as if it were full of concrete.

'You've got a cold,' Powell remarked unnecessarily.

'Yes,' Rose croaked. 'I feel really bad.'

She had not expected sympathy, or any concession to her
condition, and she got none. Powell rose to his feet. 'Well, no
good sitting there like a dying duck in a thunderstorm. Work to
be done.'

By evening she had started to cough and her chest felt
tight and painful. She could not face the plate of greasy stew
Mrs Powell put in front of her and dragged herself up the
stairs to her room, where she fell into bed with all her
clothes on. Even so it was hours before she felt warm
enough to go to sleep, only to wake a short time later to
find her body bathed in sweat. That, in its turn, was
replaced by a bout of violent shivering and a sharp pain
under her ribs every time she took a deep breath. This time,
when the thumping began under the floor of her room, she
ignored it, and eventually Mrs Powell came up the stairs to
see where she was.

Rose croaked, 'I'm sorry. I can't get up this morning. I feel
really ill.'

For a moment the woman continued to glare at her. Then
she nodded briefly. 'I'll fetch the cows in.'

Later Rose heard Powell's voice raised angrily. 'If she's not up to the work she'd better shift out and we'll get someone who is. I'm not paying some namby-pamby girl to lie in bed while we do her job for her.'

She could not hear his mother's reply but a few moments later the back door banged as if he had gone off in a temper. All day Rose lay alternately shivering and sweating. Twice Mrs Powell brought her cups of tea and a dry cheese sandwich that she could not swallow. Then, towards the end of the afternoon, she came in with a packet of aspirin.

'Got these for you. May help,' she said laconically, and Rose realised with sudden gratitude that she must have cycled into the village specially to buy them. She took two and for a while she felt a little better, but by the following morning the pain in her chest was so bad that she could scarcely breathe and she guessed that her temperature was higher than ever.

Mrs Powell came into the room. 'You getting up, then?'

'I can't!' Rose whispered desperately. 'Mrs Powell, I really am ill. I think I need to see a doctor.'

The woman gave a brief, bitter laugh. 'You won't get no doctor to come all the way out here. Anyway, doctors cost money, and who's going to pay, I'd like to know? You bide there a bit longer. You'll be all right.'

Rose took two more aspirins and lay shivering and listening to the sounds from below. She was convinced that without medical help she would get worse rather than better. Would the Powells let her lie here until she died, rather than pay a doctor's bill? she wondered. If only her mother were here! The thought of how concerned she would be and how tenderly she would care for her brought the hot tears flooding down Rose's cheeks.

Slowly, as her tears subsided, a resolution came into her mind. If the Powells would not call a doctor to see her, then she must somehow get herself to a doctor. She rolled out of bed and realised that she was still wearing her clothes. With shaking hands she pulled on her boots and then, clinging to the banister for support, she made her way down to the kitchen. As she expected, it was empty. She sat at the table for a few minutes with her head in her hands, waiting for the latest wave of weakness to pass, and then got up and took her oilskin from its hook by the door. The cold air made her choke and for a minute the pain in her chest was so severe that she thought she might pass out, but then it eased enough for her to stagger to where Mrs Powell's old bike stood against the wall. Leaning on the handlebars for support, Rose pushed it across the yard and out into the lane. Once there, it was simply a matter of hoisting herself on to the saddle and letting gravity take over. Her teeth were chattering and her hands shook so much that she could hardly manage to keep a grip on the handlebars, but somehow she managed to steer the bike round the bends and twists in the lane without ending up in the ditch and cling on until the first houses of the village came into sight. She was aware of a group of women with shopping baskets standing in the lane and of the shocked expressions on their faces as she ploughed into them, then of nothing more.

8

Wanborough Manor was a mellow, red-brick mansion set in spacious grounds in a hollow below the ridge of the North Downs known as the Hog's Back. Richard studied it as he climbed out of the back of the army truck that had brought him from Guildford station, and it seemed to him to be redolent of country house parties, croquet on the lawn and bridge after dinner. He rang the bell with an odd feeling of dislocation. The woman who opened the door was about thirty, as near as he could judge, extremely attractive and well groomed and dressed in a uniform that he could not identify. Her voice and manner as she greeted him perfectly fitted the country house atmosphere. She might have been a society hostess welcoming an expected guest.

'You must be Richard Stevens. We've been expecting you. Do come in. My name is Marcia Venables.'

Richard shook hands and said, 'How do you do?' and Marcia went on, 'I'll take you up to your room. You've just got time to freshen up before tea. You'll meet all the others then.'

The room looked exactly as it must have done when the last house guest departed at the outbreak of war. The chintz curtains were, perhaps, a little faded and the candlewick bedspread slightly the worse for wear, but it was probably the nicest room Richard had slept in since he left home. The only snag was that it was bitterly cold. Central heating had never come to Wanborough and there were no longer either

the servants or the fuel to light a fire in the empty grate.
Richard glanced out of the window at a panorama of drooping
rhododendrons, their leaves weighed down by the frost. He
washed his hands at the basin in the corner, combed his hair
and made his way downstairs.

The sound of voices directed him to the open door of a long
sitting room, and again he experienced the strange sense of
stepping back in time. It was true that many of the men in the
room were in uniform, but apart from that the ambience was
that of a pre-war social gathering. There were several women,
too, all young and attractive and all in the same uniform as
Marcia Venables. Richard felt suddenly at a loss. His parents
had entertained in a small way, but he had no experience of the
country house 'set' and was unsure how to behave. Marcia
Venables saw him hovering uncertainly and came over.

'Richard, come in. Let me introduce you to our commandant. This way.' She led him over to a tall, thin man in civilian
clothes. 'Sir, may I present Richard Stevens? Richard, this is
Colonel Roger de Wesselow.'

Richard came to attention. 'How do you do, sir?'

De Wesselow stretched out his hand. 'Good to meet you,
Richard. It's ex-colonel, actually. The Coldstream Guards
pensioned me off several years ago. I was vegetating quietly
until they wheeled me out to take charge of you lot. Now, let
me introduce you to the staff and the rest of the students – if I
can use that term.'

Richard was introduced to several men in civvies, whose
precise function was not explained to him, and then to the little
group who were, presumably, being trained for the same sort
of operation as himself – whatever that might be. There were
two Polish airmen, whose highly eccentric English was eked
out with a great many expansive gestures. Then there was a
young man in civilian dress, who was introduced as Paul
Warren. After that he found himself shaking hands with a tall,

blond man in the uniform of a captain in the Coldstream Guards.

'Jeremy Clandon,' he said. 'Good to see another officer! I'd begun to think I was the only one.'

'What about them?' Richard asked, indicating the two airmen.

Clandon laughed. 'Don't qualify, old boy – on two counts. One, they're foreign and, two, they're air force. All mad bastards, that lot.' He gave Richard a look that made him uncomfortably aware of how new his officer's uniform was. 'Regular, are you?'

'I'm afraid not,' Richard replied stiffly. He had come across these over-confident types before and viewed them with a private soldier's distrust. 'I only joined up at the beginning of the war.'

'Seen much action, have you?'

'I was at Dunkirk. That was pretty active.'

'Really?' Clandon sounded impressed. 'Managed to get away, though.'

'No, as a matter of fact I was taken prisoner. I escaped.' Richard had no intention of going into details. 'How about you?'

'Stuck in Blighty with a bloody desk job! Bad show all round! That's why I volunteered for this lot. Heard they were looking for French speakers, so I put my name forward.'

'Do you speak French well?'

'Pretty well, actually. Mother thought it was a good thing, so I had a French governess from the age of three. Spent quite a lot of holidays there, too. Whole family's very keen on France, as a matter of fact. Not so sure about the bloody French, though. Not after Pétain and his mates caved in to Hitler.'

'No, quite,' Richard murmured, looking for a way of escape. Marcia came to his rescue, offering a plate of cucumber sandwiches, and while Clandon was being gallant to her he took the opportunity to move away. At one side of the room was a small, dark man in the uniform of a sergeant in the Royal Corps of Signals, who was looking very ill at ease. Richard introduced himself and he immediately put down his cup and came to attention.

'Sergeant Jack Duval, sir.'

Richard smiled at him. 'I don't think we have to be formal here, do you? After all, we're all in the same boat.'

'I don't know about that, sir,' the small man said unhappily. 'I didn't realise it was going to be all officers when I signed up for this. I don't honestly know what I'm doing here.'

'I think that goes for all of us,' Richard said, 'but I suppose we'll find out in due course. What did you think you were signing up for, as a matter of interest?'

'My CO said, you speak French, don't you, Duval? The army's looking for signallers who speak French. Well, I thought it sounded better than what I was doing, so I let him put my name forward.'

'Are you French?' Richard asked. 'I mean – the name . . .'

'My dad was born in Switzerland. My mum's French. He came over here to work as a chef at the Grosvenor Hotel. I was born in Balham, but we always spoke French at home.'

The conversation was interrupted by the colonel tapping his spoon on his teacup.

'Right, ladies and gentlemen! Pleasant as this is, I think it's time we got down to something more serious. If you'll all follow me into the next room I'll try to give you some idea what to expect over the next few days.'

The room had been stripped of its normal furniture and set up as a classroom. De Wesselow began by informing them that one purpose of the course would be to assess their level of physical fitness and to this end each day would begin with a cross-country run. Richard's heart sank. He had never particularly enjoyed games at school but cross-country runs had been his particular hate and the thought of turning out in the bitter cold before breakfast filled him with dismay. More importantly, he was afraid that his leg would not stand up to such a demanding test and that he might be turned down on that account.

De Wesselow was going on. There would be exercises in map-reading and others to test initiative and ability to work as a member of a team. There would also be training in the use of small arms and explosives.

After the talk there was a short break, 'to give them time to dress for dinner'. Suddenly Richard was back in the country house weekend. He went to his room and changed into mess kit, in which he always felt uncomfortably as though he were about to perform a role in *White Horse Inn* or some other light opera, and then found his way down to the drawing room. To his amazement, all the women were in long dresses.

Marcia approached with a tray of drinks. 'Sherry, Richard? Or would you prefer a Scotch?'

'I'd really rather have a dry martini, if that's possible,' Richard responded.

As Marcia went off to fetch his drink Jeremy Clandon came over. 'I must say these FANYs are amazing. You'd never think there was a war on, to look at them.'

'Fanny?' Richard queried. 'I thought her name was Marcia.'

Clandon laughed. 'No, F.A.N.Y. First Aid Nursing Yeomanry. It's about the most exclusive women's organisation there is. You practically have to have been presented at court to get in. But they're gorgeous girls, aren't they?'

'Yes,' Richard mumbled, embarrassed at his faux pas, 'they certainly are.'

Looking around the room he had to admit that Clandon was right. All the girls were attractive and beautifully groomed. That was, he thought, the right word. They had that glossy sheen that comes from wealth and social confidence. Among them, one stood out. She was a striking blonde, wearing a red dress that, to Richard's eye, was surprisingly décolleté. He couldn't put his finger on it, but somehow she didn't quite seem to fit.

After dinner, during which the conversation was steered on to neutral topics with no mention of the war, they all returned to the drawing room and someone rolled back the carpet while one of the girls wound up the gramophone and put on some dance music. The younger of the two Poles was the first on the floor, with the blonde in his arms, and he was rapidly followed by a couple of the younger staff members. Richard stood to one side, his sense of dislocation deepening with every minute. He remembered the flat in Marseilles, where he had sheltered with the good Dr Rodocanachi and his wife. There, too, Madame had dressed for dinner, keeping up appearances and trying, he supposed, to impart some sense of normality. Was that the purpose of this re-creation of pre-war society, or was there some deeper, more subtle objective behind it?

As he watched the dancers he felt a pain he had been trying to ignore twisting his gut. The sight of them brought back too vividly the memory of the summer tea dances at the Palace Hotel and Rose, light as gossamer, in his arms.

Marcia came over to him. 'You don't dance, Richard?'

He hesitated. 'I used to, but I'm not sure this leg will let me any more.'

'Does it give you a lot of pain?'

'No, no. It's just a bit stiff, that's all. I'm afraid I might be a bit clumsy on the dance floor.'

She laughed. 'Oh well, what's the odd dislocated toe between friends?'

Richard bowed to the inevitable. 'Well, if you don't mind taking the risk . . .'

'Why not? I've always been one for living dangerously.'

He led her on to the floor and was glad to find that nothing more stylish was required of him than a sedate shuffle around the restricted space. When the music stopped the other Polish airman whisked Marcia away and Richard, turning to pick up his drink, found himself face to face with the blonde girl.

'Good evening. I'm Laura. I can see you could really dance if there was a bit more space. Shall we?'

She was a good dancer and a pleasant companion, chatting easily about a variety of subjects, enquiring about his hobbies, his taste in music, generally drawing him out. To his surprise she even had a fair knowledge of opera. Yet he felt uneasy. She was a little too practised, too perfect. He was relieved when the dance ended and she excused herself and joined another group. Over the course of the evening he noticed that she made a point of dancing with everyone, even persuading a reluctant Jack Duval on to the floor. The only man with whom she had no success was Jeremy Clandon, who stood drinking by the bar, watching the dancers with something approaching a sneer on his handsome face.

Richard noticed that alcohol seemed to be available in unlimited quantities. He had accepted a brandy and soda on entering the room and made it last, in spite of invitations to 'drink up and have another'. Others, however, were not so abstemious. The two Poles seemed able to absorb large amounts without any appreciable change in manner, except that their English became more erratic and their gestures more extravagant than ever, and Clandon appeared to be knocking back whiskies as if the honour of the regiment depended on his keeping up with them.

At the first hint of dawn the next morning all delusions of gracious living were banished by the sound of a bell. Richard clambered out of bed and pulled on his PT kit, yawning and shivering in the inhospitable chill. Outside he joined the others, who mostly looked as sorry for themselves as he felt. Clandon was clearly nursing a hangover and only the two Poles seemed impervious both to the previous night's carousing and the icy early morning air. He was impressed, however, to discover that de Wesselow himself was to lead the run. The man must be over sixty, he reflected, and if he can do it, so can I.

For the first half-mile his leg held up well, but then the cramps started. By halfway round the course he had given up all hope of keeping up with the rest and was wondering whether he would make it back to the house. He eventually limped in to encounter the others already changed and heading for breakfast.

Clandon passed him on the stairs. 'Gammy leg, old chap? Hard luck!'

He smiled and passed on, leaving Richard mouthing something unseemly at his back.

The morning was spent learning map-reading with the aid of local Ordnance Survey maps, and after lunch they were sent out in groups of three on a kind of treasure hunt that involved bringing back various objects from specified locations identified only by the map coordinates. Richard was teamed with Jeremy Clandon and Sergeant Duval, a combination that he found extremely uncomfortable. Clandon made it obvious that he expected to take command and Duval, as a subordinate, was to be kept in his place. Initially it seemed that he was prepared to regard Richard as a social equal, but by the time they had established the fact that Richard did not ride and had no interest in hunting or shooting they were beginning to run out of conversation.

'I'm an Old Wykehamist myself,' Clandon pronounced. 'How about you?'

'Manchester Grammar,' Richard told him, and saw his lip curl.

'Grammar school boy, eh? Well, if you don't hunt or shoot, what do you do with yourself when you're off duty?'

'I sing. That's my profession.'

'Sing? You mean like this Yankee chappy – what's his name? – Sinatra?'

'No. Opera, mainly. And light ballads. Before the war I was with a concert party on the south coast.'

'You mean, on the stage?' Clandon stared at him for a moment with undisguised contempt. Then he turned away with a muttered 'Christ Almighty!'

Richard looked round and caught Duval's eye. 'How about you, Jack? Are you interested in music?'

Duval hesitated, looking at Clandon's back. Then he grinned. 'I've got a mouth organ – if you call that music.'

Richard grinned back. 'We'll have to get together some time and have a sing-song.'

Clandon turned. 'Can I remind you that there is a war on – and we have a mission to complete?'

The afternoon was overcast and the light was rapidly failing by the time they headed for their final objective, which involved crossing a river. It was not particularly wide but the winter rain had swollen it so that it almost filled the deep channel it had carved in the surrounding fields. Clandon, who had taken sole charge of the map, frowned at it for some minutes and then exclaimed, 'There's supposed to be a bridge. Bloody thing must have been washed away.'

'Are you sure we're at the right point?' Richard enquired.

Clandon looked at him with irritation. 'Of course we're at the right point. Are you suggesting I can't read the bloody map?'

Richard looked up and down the bank. 'I can't see any sign of a bridge. Surely there would be something left.'

'Well, there isn't,' Clandon snapped. 'Either the whole thing's disappeared or the fucking map's wrong.' He looked around him for a moment and then went on. 'Well, this is where we show initiative. We're not going to let a little thing like this stand in our way.'

'What did you have in mind?' Richard asked uneasily.

'Simple. We strip off and wade across. It can't be more than a few feet deep.'

'In this weather? You're crazy!'

'For God's sake, man! This is the army and there's a war on. You're not afraid of a bit of cold water, are you?'

'I'm not keen on catching pneumonia for the sake of a training exercise,' Richard said.

Clandon's eyes narrowed dangerously. 'Look. I don't want to have to order you. It won't go down well on your record.' He looked around him. 'Where the hell's Duval?'

Richard glanced round. There was no sign of the signaller. 'Gone for a slash, I imagine.'

'Well, he'll just have to follow on. Let's get moving before it gets dark.'

Richard watched in disbelief as Clandon started to remove his clothes. The temperature was close to zero and a light, icy rain was falling. The prospect of wading into the freezing waters of the river filled him with horror.

'Get your kit off, Stevens!' Clandon hissed. 'That's an order!'

Reluctantly Richard began to unlace his boots. As he did so Duval sauntered back from a small copse in a bend of the river. Richard straightened up and they both watched as Clandon waded into the water. He was up to his knees when Duval said, 'There's a bridge just along there, round the bend.'

Richard looked at him. He gazed back impassively and then they both turned to look at Clandon. They waited until he was up to his genitals in the icy flood before Richard called out, 'There's a bridge, Clandon. Just a bit farther along. See you on the other side!'

The trudge back to Wanborough Manor was accomplished in total silence, except for the chattering of Clandon's teeth.

*   *   *

Richard was relieved to find that the following day he was teamed with Paul Warren, the only civilian in the group and a much more amiable character. He learned that Warren was the son of an English engineer and a French mother, and had been brought up largely in Algeria, where his father worked in an oil refinery. He himself was a chemist by training and had been working on explosives at a government laboratory, which was why he had not been called up. Feeling that he was 'missing all the fun', in his phrase, he had finally managed to talk himself out of the lab and into an area where he felt his combined talents could be of more value.

A day or two later one of the civilian members of staff, whose function had not been explained, accosted Richard and asked him to come to his office 'for a bit of a chat'. Richard soon realised that he was talking to a psychologist. He spoke as freely as he could about his childhood and his schooling and about his training in Italy and his future ambitions. When it came to his experiences in France he was a good deal more circumspect, partly because he was reluctant to reveal anything that might endanger the people who had helped him, even to so apparently reliable a source, but largely because he was afraid that the psychologist would divine his feelings for Chantal and his true reasons for wanting to go back. About Rose and the debacle of New Year's Eve he said nothing at all.

The days began to assume a pattern. In the morning there were lectures or paper tests designed, presumably, to assess intelligence and aptitude for various kinds of activity. Later there were practical exercises. Richard found himself clambering up the large trees in the park and then sliding down a rope contraption, or learning to construct a raft out of old oil cans. He also practised firing various sorts of pistol and light machine gun and throwing hand grenades. After his time as a private soldier he was used to handling a rifle, but he had little experience of any other kind of weapon. It was a relief to find that he was a better than adequate marksman. He could see the point of the weapons training and even, after listening to the experiences of fellow escapees during his journey through France, of the raft-building exercise. He had met at least two men who had been forced to swim the Loire in order to cross from the occupied to the unoccupied zone. But the assault course was a source of intense frustration.

One morning, after landing painfully on his damaged leg for the third time, he got to his feet and turned on the sergeant-instructor who was yelling at him to carry on.

'Sod it! I've had enough of this. It's a bloody pointless exercise anyway.' And with that he marched back to the house, ignoring the torrent of threats that followed him.

When he was summoned to the commandant's office a couple of hours later he was still feeling intransigent.

De Wesselow studied him quietly from behind his desk. 'I gather you walked off the assault course this morning.'

'Yes, sir. I can't see any point in it. When – if – I get to France my cover will be as a singer. It isn't going to enhance my credibility to go swinging around in the trees like a chimpanzee.'

To his surprise he saw a fleeting smile cross the commandant's face. 'I take your point. But has it occurred to you that that exercise is designed to test things other than your ability to behave like an ape? Things like determination, fortitude in the face of physical risk or pain, the strength of character to carry on when the going gets rough?'

Richard felt the colour rise in his face. He met the CO's eyes. 'I've blown it, haven't I?'

De Wesselow pursed his lips. 'Not necessarily. There are other valuable characteristics. A bloody-minded refusal to submit to authority. An unwillingness to risk injury except in a case of necessity. Not desirable in the average soldier but perhaps invaluable in your line of country.'

'Then you'll give me another chance?' Richard held his breath.

'I see no reason not to.' De Wesselow rose, indicating the end of the interview. 'And we shall see you back on the assault course tomorrow morning, shan't we?'

'Yes, sir. Thank you, sir!'

From that day on Richard buckled down to every task he was given without complaint and found himself increasingly able to meet the demands made on him. Even the morning run became less of a struggle, as the muscles in his damaged leg grew stronger. He was never able to keep up with the front-runners, but at least he was no longer coming in half an hour behind them.

At dinner and afterwards, there was the sudden reversion to pre-war social niceties. Richard danced with the FANY girls and recognised, in an abstracted fashion, that some of them found him attractive and were puzzled, and maybe slightly hurt, by his distant manner. Every evening drink was freely available and more than once he was pressed by various members of staff to indulge in more than he was used to. The temptation to 'drown his sorrows' was intense, but he was afraid that if he once started he would not be able to stop. He guessed that this, too, was part of the assessment process and firmly refused the offers.

Not so Jeremy Clandon, who drank freely but could never be tempted on to the dance floor. Often Richard slipped away to his room early, to avoid further pressure, and mercifully he was usually so tired that he fell asleep at once, before the regret and loneliness that lurked at the bottom of his mind could rise to the surface.

One night he was preparing for bed when he heard shouting and the sound of furniture being knocked over. Opening his door, he realised that the noise was coming from a room on the other side of the passage, which was occupied by Lev, the younger of the two Polish airmen. He heard the young man shouting something in his own language, and then Clandon's voice, so slurred with drink that the words were indistinguishable.

As Richard hesitated, the door of the next room was thrown open and Stanislaw, the older Pole, rushed out and into his compatriot's. Richard crossed the passage to the open door and was shocked to see that, as well as the three men, Laura was there, wearing nothing but a pair of black lace briefs. Lev, too, was stripped to his underpants. He was shouting something in Polish to Stanislaw and, as Richard watched, the older man swung round and punched Clandon hard on the nose. Clandon staggered back and the Pole would have followed up his advantage if Richard had not stepped between them. It would have been enjoyable to see the supercilious Clandon getting his come-uppance but he had come to know and like the two Poles.

'Stan, hold on! I don't know what the hell is going on here, but you don't want to get yourself thrown off the course.'

Stanislaw checked himself, breathing hard, and as Clandon scrambled to his feet Richard heard de Wesselow's voice behind him.

'That's enough! Miss Franklin, you had better return to your room.'

Laura gathered up her discarded evening dress, without apparent embarrassment, and brushed past Richard on her way out.

Clandon drew himself up groggily. 'I want that man put on a charge for striking a superior officer!'

De Wesselow gave him a stony look. 'Go back to your room and report to me at reveille. We'll discuss the matter then.' He turned to Richard. 'Thank you, Mr Stevens. Your intervention was timely. You can go back to bed now.'

He stood aside and closed the door firmly behind Richard.

Others had come out of their rooms to see what the noise was about, and as Richard turned away he found himself face to face with Marcia.

He ran his hand through his hair, torn between exasperation and relief. 'Well, I don't know what all that was about. At least, I suppose I can guess. Poor old Laura! I suppose she's for the high jump.'

Marcia's lips twitched into a smile of amused disbelief. 'Not Laura! She was only doing her job.'

'Her job?'

'Oh, darling, surely you've caught on. No? She fooled you too? You didn't think she was really one of us, did you?'

'I don't know what you mean.'

'She's a . . . a courtesan, an escort – a high-class tart.'

'You don't mean . . .?' Richard stared at her. 'You mean she's here to . . . to seduce men on the course?'

'To see how susceptible they are to feminine wiles, yes. After all, where you're going – oh, I know we're not supposed to know what you're all being trained for, but we're not stupid – you don't want someone who'll spill the beans to the first beautiful girl who flirts with him, do you?'

'And if one of us succumbs to temptation . . .' Richard said, thinking of Lev, 'does that mean he's out on his ear?'

Marcia shrugged. 'Not always. I've seen some men survive. I think it depends on how he behaves. If he's discreet, doesn't talk too much – not even in his sleep – he might be let off with a warning.'

'Funny thing is,' Richard continued, 'I'd never thought Clandon was particularly susceptible. He never gave any sign of fancying Laura.'

Marcia gave a sigh and shook her head at him, as if he were a particularly slow child. 'I don't think the fight was over Laura, do you?'

'Not over Laura? Then why . . . You don't mean Lev?'

'That's my guess. Haven't you noticed how he keeps trying to get Lev into conversation, trying to prise him away from Stanislaw?'

Richard thought back. It was true that, after that first day, he had noticed Clandon spending time with the young Pole, offering to help with various tasks, telling him jokes. He had tried to view it charitably, telling himself that Clandon had a good side after all.

'So Clandon was drunk, and jealous, and barged in on Lev and Laura. What was Stanislaw doing?'

'Protecting his countryman's honour, I should imagine,' Marcia said.

Richard glanced at the closed door, from behind which he could hear the voices of de Wesselow and the two airmen. 'What do you think will happen to them?'

'Well, Clandon's had it. Much too unreliable. Don't know about the other two. We'll have to wait and see.' Marcia moved away. 'Better get some sleep. The CO won't be pleased if he comes out and finds us standing here gossiping.'

Next morning there was no sign of Clandon and the rumour quickly spread that he had been seen loading his kit into the truck that would take him to the station. Lev and Stanislaw, however, were still there, albeit somewhat subdued.

One evening Richard received a message that Colonel de Wesselow wished to see him.

'I thought you would like to know that you'll be leaving us tomorrow,' de Wesselow said.

'Leaving!' Richard exclaimed. He felt as though he had received a sudden blow to the stomach. 'Why? I thought I was getting on pretty well.'

'Very well indeed,' agreed the colonel. 'All the reports on you have been most favourable. That's why you're being moved on to the next stage. You'll get the official orders tomorrow morning. You're going to Scotland.'

9

In London Merry, like Rose, had succumbed to the rigours of the winter. For a chronic asthmatic, a regime of long journeys in unheated vehicles, interspersed with sessions in halls filled with tobacco smoke and the fumes of paraffin heaters, was a recipe for disaster. For several weeks he struggled on, relying more and more heavily on the pills that made his hands shake and his head sing, and trying to suppress the spasms of wheezing that threatened to interrupt his playing. Then one evening one of the company, looking for him to start the performance, found him hunched on a low wall outside the scout hut which was that night's venue, engaged in a painful struggle for every breath.

An air raid had just finished and all the emergency services were at full stretch, so there was no hope of getting an ambulance. Ignoring his protests, two of his colleagues loaded him into the back of the army truck and set off for the nearest hospital, leaving the rest of the company to struggle through the performance as best they could. The first hospital was inundated with casualties from the recent raid and so was the second. It was not until they had been touring the darkened streets for nearly an hour that they found an emergency department that would take Merry in, by which time he was almost unconscious.

For the next twenty-four hours he was aware of nothing except the endless struggle to get oxygen into his lungs. On the second day, he came round to a hazy realisation of where he was. Someone was bending over him with a stethoscope to his chest.

'What happened? What am I doing here?'

The doctor, an elderly man who looked grey faced with exhaustion himself, straightened up. 'I'm afraid it's pneumonia, old chap. But not to worry. It's not the death sentence it used to be. These new sulpha drugs work miracles in cases like yours. I'm afraid you're going to feel pretty rough for a while, but you'll pull through. You take my word for it.'

He was right on both counts. Merry did feel extremely ill for several days, but slowly he began to get better. He had to believe that that was the case, because the doctor and the nurses told him so, and it was true that he was able to breathe more freely and to sit up in bed from time to time. But the effects of the drugs were so debilitating that sometimes he wondered whether the effort of survival was worth making.

The first thing that came into his mind, when he was able to think coherently at all, was that he had not been in touch with Felix, who would be wondering what had happened to him. No one in the company, or at HQ, knew enough to contact him and let him know. Merry had visited him a couple of weeks earlier, and had found him more subdued than previously. The latest graft on his face had failed to take, so he was now faced with the prospect of going through the laborious business of raising another pedicule of skin from somewhere on his body to replace it. The only bright spot was the fact that McIndoe had also started work on his damaged right hand and he had demonstrated that he could now, with enormous effort and concentration, move two of his fingers. But Merry had noticed that the untouched side of his face was pale and his eyes were shadowed. The strain of being cooped up over weeks with other men who were in a worse state than himself, together with the effect of repeated anaesthetics, was beginning to tell.

All day Merry bullied and beseeched the busy nurses to get in touch with East Grinstead and pass a message to Felix, until in the end one of them came back to say that she had telephoned and had been put through to the ward.

'Flight Lieutenant Mountjoy says he's very sorry to hear that you're not well and you're not to worry about him. He says he's had another operation and he's fine – and he sent his love.'

Merry looked at the girl. There was no hint of surprise or suspicion behind her reassuring gaze. Obviously she found nothing unusual in that message. He managed a genuine smile and thanked her.

The days passed. Members of the company visited him and brought books and magazines, which he did not have the energy to read, and told him funny stories that did not make him laugh. Even George Black found time to come and reassure him that the show was going on without him. He had managed to find another pianist to take Merry's place, so there was no need to worry on that count. When he had gone Merry brooded gloomily on the thought that no one was indispensable and there had been nothing vital or unique about his contribution.

The news bulletins on the BBC Home Service, which were listened to in ritual silence, brought little to cheer him. In North Africa the Germans had taken Benghazi and encircled Tobruk, while in Greece the British Army was steadily beaten back, first to Mount Olympus and then to Thermopylae. Meanwhile the Blitz continued and more than once Merry and the other patients were wheeled or carried down into the cellars to shelter from a raid. The news that St Paul's had been damaged by a bomb brought furious exclamations all round the ward.

A letter arrived in the spiky scrawl that Felix had taught himself to write with his left hand. He sounded more optimistic. He now had some movement in all his fingers on the other hand and McIndoe had assured him that with time it could be improved still further. There was also more work to be done on rebuilding his face, but the surgeon did not want to operate again until he had had a chance to recuperate. He hoped to get some leave soon and go down to Wimborne.

There was another letter, forwarded from the hotel where he was lodging, in writing that Merry did not recognise. It was from Rose's mother.

> *Dear Merry,*
>
> *I thought you would want to know that Rose is in hospital. It seems that awful farmer has been working her to death in all sorts of weather and not even giving her enough to eat! I don't know how anyone can behave like that, but I think he ought to be shot. Apparently he and his mother wouldn't even call a doctor when Rose was taken ill. She had to bike three miles to the nearest village with a temperature of goodness knows what to get help.*
>
> *Anyway, she's in Shrewsbury General Hospital with pleurisy but, thank God, she's on the mend and the doctor says she should be able to come home soon. I know she'd like to hear from you, if you can spare the time to write. She's in Pasteur Ward.*
>
> *I hope you are keeping well. When are you coming to see us again?*
>
> *Yours ever,*
> *Elsie Taylor*

A few days after receiving that letter Merry was able to get out of bed and sit in the day room for a while. It was progress of a sort, he supposed, and a change of scenery was welcome, but the day room itself was a gloomy place full of an odd assortment of run-down furniture and with a view of untidy suburban back gardens in which the occasional crocus struggled for survival.

He was sitting there a couple of days later when a nurse put her head round the door and said, 'Visitor for you, Lieutenant Merryweather,' and in walked Felix.

Felix said jauntily, 'Hello, old chap. Thought the mountain had better come to Mohammed. How's it going?'

'Not too bad,' Merry answered automatically.

They looked at each other for a moment in silence, and then Felix said, in a different tone, 'My God, Merry, you look really rough!'

It was on the tip of Merry's tongue to retort, 'You're not looking so great yourself'. It was true. Felix's face was a patchwork of strips of skin that varied in colour and texture and what was left of his own natural complexion was pallid and unhealthy. He restrained the impulse and said instead, 'I've been pretty poorly, but I'm over the worst now – so they tell me.'

Felix drew up a chair and sat opposite him. They were both uncomfortably aware that there were three other patients in the room, all with nothing to do but listen in to their conversation.

'Cheer up,' he said. 'I had a word with Sister and she says you'll probably be able to leave here soon.'

'First I've heard of it,' Merry muttered.

Felix grinned at him. 'Come on, stop doing your Eeyore impression. She also says you'll need to go somewhere to convalesce.'

'No thanks,' Merry grunted. 'I've no intention of being stuck in one of their convalescent homes.'

'Don't be a clot,' Felix chided him. 'You can come down to Dorset. We can both go.'

'Oh!' said Merry, with the first flicker of optimism he had felt for weeks. 'Oh, I see what you're getting at.' Then the flame died. 'No. No, we can't. It wouldn't be fair.'

'Why on earth not?'

Merry fished in his dressing-gown pocket and handed Felix Mrs Taylor's letter. His friend's face hardened as he read.

'Poor Rose! I'd like to get my hands on that bastard! I'd push his teeth so far down his throat he'd have to stick a toothbrush up his arse to clean them!'

'Not if Mrs Taylor gets to him first,' Merry commented, with a shadow of his old ironic grin. 'He won't have any teeth left. But you see what I mean. We can't go and impose ourselves on them now. Once Rose comes out of hospital she'll need all their care and attention.'

Felix considered for a moment. 'I don't see why not. After all, we're not exactly helpless. Well, I'm not, anyway. And it might cheer Rose up to have company. She must need it, after all this.'

'Maybe,' Merry returned doubtfully. 'I'm not convinced.'

'Mrs T actually asks when you're going down to see them,' Felix pointed out. 'They want you to go.'

Merry sighed. 'OK. We'll do whatever you think best. I leave it to you.'

Felix looked at him tenderly. 'You are down, aren't you? Poor old Merry!'

They were silent for a moment, oppressed by the sense of being overheard. Then Felix said, 'Look, I'm dying for a fag. Is it OK if I smoke in here?'

''Fraid not,' Merry answered. 'If you want to smoke we'll have to go out in the corridor.'

Outside Felix took out his cigarette case and extracted two cigarettes. Merry stopped him with a gesture. 'Not for me. I've had to give up.'

'Really?' Felix frowned sympathetically. 'That must be bloody hard.'

'Not the way I've been feeling up to now,' Merry said, but he looked regretfully at the cigarette as Felix put it away. It was not so much the desire to smoke which suddenly assailed him, but nostalgia for the small gesture of intimacy that the lighting of cigarettes for each other had come to mean. He felt suddenly very tired and leaned against the wall as Felix lit up.

'One more thing,' Felix said, studying the glowing tip as if suddenly embarrassed. 'I was wondering – do you use the Lagonda much these days?'

'Not while I'm in here,' Merry replied with heavy irony.

'No, obviously. I mean, the rest of the time.'

'No, not a lot. We drive around in a truck.'

'Ah.' Felix looked up. 'In that case, would you mind if I had the keys back?'

'You're not thinking of driving yourself, are you?' Merry asked in alarm, remembering the last time Felix had attempted to control the powerful car.

'Look.' Felix held up his right hand. 'I can grip now. Watch this.' With great concentration he closed his fingers into a fist and then opened them again. 'See?' he added triumphantly.

'That won't be much good at fifty miles an hour,' Merry said sourly.

'I won't go fifty!' Felix said impatiently. 'Look, there are some of the other chaps whose hands aren't affected. They can drive without a problem. If we had the car we could get around a bit more. Get away from bloody East Grinstead!'

'Well, if that's what you meant why didn't you say so?' Merry snapped back. 'It's your bloody car!' Suddenly he felt a great wave of exhaustion sweep over him and the floor of the corridor seemed to tilt under his feet. He clutched at the wall and muttered, 'Look, I'll have to go back to bed. Sorry.'

'Christ!' Felix stubbed out his cigarette and grabbed Merry by the arm. 'What a selfish bastard I am. I should have seen you aren't fit to stand around. Come on, which way is the ward?'

Leaning heavily on Felix, Merry allowed himself to be led back to his ward. Felix put an arm round his waist to support him and for a moment or two they had an excuse for the physical closeness they both craved.

Felix helped him into bed and pulled the blankets up round his shoulders. Merry met his eyes. 'Join me?' he suggested softly.

'If only!' Felix replied, smiling.

A nurse hurried over. 'Is Lieutenant Merryweather all right?'

'No,' Felix said, turning his smile on her, 'he's a bit *under* the weather, actually – and not terribly merry, either.'

'Oh, you!' said the nurse. Then she looked at Felix properly for the first time and gave a small, involuntary gasp. Merry saw Felix's face tighten and wondered how many times he had to endure that reaction, or something worse.

'It's all right, Nurse,' he said. 'He only looks like this when there's a full moon.'

Felix chuckled and the nurse said, 'Oh, you!' again and blushed and hurried away to busy herself at the other end of the ward.

Merry caught Felix's eye. 'Sorry I was a bit short back there.'

'No, my fault,' Felix replied. 'I didn't think.'

'Look in the top drawer of my locker. I think the car keys are in there.'

Felix found them, but hesitated. 'I won't take them if you'd rather I didn't.'

'Don't be daft. I can't use it. It just worries me to think of you driving.'

'I'll let someone else drive,' Felix said. Then added, 'Most of the time, anyway.' And then, seeing Merry's expression, 'And I won't go over thirty. Promise!'

Merry sighed and resigned himself to the inevitable. 'OK, OK.'

Felix said, 'Look, I'll ring the Willises and see if they can cope with us as well as Rose. When do you think you'll be able to leave here?'

'God knows,' Merry muttered. 'You carry on. I don't want to spoil your leave.'

'No, I won't go until you can,' Felix said. 'And don't argue.'

'I haven't got the strength.'

'Good. I'll see you in a day or two and let you know what the arrangements are. You just concentrate on getting well.'

He paused, looking down, and then glanced round the ward. The nurses were all busy and the bed next to Merry's was empty. Felix put his fingers to his lips and laid them briefly on Merry's. Then he grinned and was gone.

IO

A little over a week later Merry found himself sitting beside Felix in the Lagonda, spinning through the Dorset countryside. Winter had finally relaxed its grip and the hedgerows were misted with faint green, while in cottage gardens daffodils flaunted themselves in odd corners that had escaped being cultivated for vegetables. Felix was actually driving at thirty miles an hour and whistling softly through his teeth. Ironically, the tune he had chosen was 'Keep Young and Beautiful', but there was a faint smile on his lips. Merry looked at him and at the countryside beyond and felt for the first time that being happy might not require too much energy after all.

At the Willises' smallholding they were greeted with a flurry of feminine concern as Mrs Willis, Mrs Taylor and Bet surrounded the car.

'Oh, you poor boys! You have been poorly, haven't you! Look at them, Elsie.'

'Never mind, we'll soon have them back on their feet. Good food and rest and fresh air, that's what they need. Put the kettle on, Bet, there's a love.'

When he could get a word in Felix said, 'How's Rose, Mrs Taylor?'

Rose's mother frowned and put her finger to her lips. 'Not too good,' she mouthed. Aloud she said, 'She's in the sitting room. Go on in and say hello. She'll be really glad to see you.'

Rose was sitting in a deep armchair with her feet up on a pouffe and a rug over her knees, and Merry was shocked to see how gaunt and pale she was. As soon as he and Felix entered the room she looked up and held out both her arms to them, and with one accord they crossed the room and knelt on either side of her.

She put an arm round the neck of each of them and exclaimed, 'Oh, am I glad to see you two! You're a sight for sore eyes, you are really!'

Felix gave a low laugh. 'Well, it's a long time since anyone said that to me.'

'But I mean it,' Rose said. She leaned over and kissed his good cheek. 'You know I do.' Then she turned her attention to Merry. 'Oh, poor Merry! You're so thin! You look really run down.'

'Well, you're not looking your best either, old thing,' Merry responded.

Rose sighed. 'I know. I've really lost my looks, haven't I?'

Merry took her hand from the back of his neck and kissed it. 'Not lost. Just temporarily mislaid.'

'Like the rest of us,' Felix added, and they all laughed, but the laughter was perilously close to tears.

Over the next weeks they slowly coaxed each other back to health, aided by the ministrations of the three women. Miraculously, fresh eggs appeared for their breakfasts and there was real butter for the home-baked bread at teatime and milky Horlicks before bed – to say nothing of main meals where the meagre meat ration was eked out with large quantities of fresh vegetables. And there was a steady procession of cups of tea, accompanied by little delicacies, throughout the rest of the day. Enough local farmers and shopkeepers owed the Willises a favour in return for fresh fruit or vegetables to make sure that the three patients went short of nothing, though Merry suspected that the other adults were sacrificing the few small luxuries that rationing allowed for their benefit.

To begin with, the three of them spent most of their time sitting in front of the wood fire in the sitting room. Then, as the weather decided to compensate for the terrible winter with an unseasonable spell of warm sunshine, they moved out to sit under the trees in the orchard, where the new grass was powdered with fallen plum blossom. Sometimes they read or dozed, and at one point Merry and Felix decided to teach Rose how to play chess, but they found that none of them could concentrate sufficiently to finish a game. Mostly they talked, pouring out the memories that still afflicted them. Rose described the horrors of life at Hightop Farm and Felix spoke for the first time of the traumatic scenes he had witnessed in the Burns Unit at East Grinstead. Merry, listening, realised that his experiences had been nothing compared with theirs and that the lassitude and depression he felt were simply the result of physical exhaustion and would pass as he grew stronger. He made it his role to lead the conversation into lighter channels, and little by little the three of them learned to laugh again.

Merry was ably assisted in his mission by Bet's two small boys, who were delighted to have 'Uncle' Merry and 'Uncle' Felix back again and totally impervious to Bet's admonitions to 'leave the gentlemen in peace'. Before long they were all passing the time between the boys' return from school and supper in hilarious games of Snap or Snakes and Ladders or Monopoly.

Merry noticed that during their talks and games Felix spent much of the time massaging his damaged hand.

'Is it hurting?' he asked.

Felix shook his head. 'No, it's not that. The physiotherapist told me that it might help to get it moving again.'

'Let me have a go,' Merry offered, reaching across.

Felix yelped as his fingers dug into the taut muscles. 'That's the trouble with you bloody pianists! You've got fingers like steel rods.'

Merry raised an eyebrow. 'Been holding hands with a lot of pianists, have you?'

'McIndoe plays, remember?' Felix said dryly.

He also had a rubber ball that he squeezed and released repeatedly until the sweat stood out on his brow with the effort. Merry watched until he could stand it no longer and then confiscated it for the rest of the day.

Rose's treatment by the Powells was a common topic of conversation for the whole family. On the first evening, as they sat at supper, Mrs Taylor remarked vengefully, 'I wish I could get my hands on that man! I'd teach him a thing or two!'

Merry said with a grin, 'I won't tell you what Felix threatened to do to him. It's not fit for ladies' ears.'

'Ladies be blowed!' Mrs Taylor retorted. 'If I ever get hold of him I'll soon show him I'm no lady!'

'I think he'll get his come-uppance anyway,' Rose remarked unexpectedly. 'The WLA woman told me she'd make sure that he didn't get any more Land Girls to help out. He'll have to do all the work himself from now on.'

Mrs Taylor sniffed. 'I wouldn't put much faith in that woman's word. I met her when I went up to visit Rose in hospital. "Ooh, Mrs Taylor!" she says to me. "I'm so sorry to find that Rose has been so badly treated!" I told her if she'd been doing her job properly she would have found out about it before there was any real harm done. Then she starts going on about how difficult it is to get round to all them outlying farms and how hard she has to work. "Not as hard as my Rose!" I said. That shut her up.'

'Well, anyway,' Rose put in mildly, 'I don't think the Powells will be in business much longer. I told her about the state of some of his cows. I'm sure some of them were sick and it could be TB. He's got no business selling the milk. If the inspectors go up there and check I'm pretty certain he'll be closed down.'

'Serves him right!' her mother exclaimed. 'A man like that shouldn't be in charge of animals or people.'

It was a sentiment that met with general approval.

It was not long before Rose brought up the subject that was hovering in the back of all their minds.

'I suppose you haven't heard anything from Richard?'

Merry shook his head sadly. 'Not a word. I wrote to him at his home address, as I told you, but I've no idea if the letter reached him. At any rate, there's been no reply.'

'No, he hasn't answered my letter, either,' Rose said. 'I suppose he's decided he doesn't want any more to do with us.'

'I don't understand it,' Felix commented. 'It doesn't seem in character to me.'

'I don't know,' Merry said. 'If he'd been building his hopes all the time he was in France it must have been a terrible shock to come home and find that Rose was engaged to someone else. Perhaps he just needs time to get over it.'

'But he knows now that she isn't marrying Matthew,' Felix pointed out. 'He does know that, doesn't he?'

'Of course he does,' Rose said. 'I wrote to him.'

'He could be overseas,' Merry suggested. 'Possibly in North Africa, or even Crete.'

'Oh, I hope not,' Rose said unhappily. 'It sounds from the news as though they're having a terrible time in Crete.'

The British Army had retreated to the island after the capitulation of Greece and was reported to be under heavy air attack.

'But it might explain why he hasn't written,' Merry said, trying to find some comfort for her.

Felix and Merry continued to share the big double bed in the Willises' spare room. When they first arrived Jack Willis caused them some alarm by suggesting that there should be some other arrangement, as they were both going to be there for some time. He even went so far as to begin negotiations with a neighbour for the loan of two camp beds, until they managed to convince him that they were perfectly comfortable and much preferred the double bed with its feather mattress. For the first few nights they were both too debilitated to be interested in sex, but happy to have the consolation of each other's physical closeness. Then, as they grew stronger, desire returned and they made love first with fierce, silent passion and then with lingering, luxurious delight, falling asleep, exhausted, in each other's arms.

One morning Merry was tying his shoelaces when he became aware of movement outside the bedroom door, which had been left ajar. Sam, Bet's younger boy, now six years old, was standing there. Felix was shaving at the washstand in the corner of the room and singing to himself as he did so. The song he had chosen was the anthem of 'McIndoe's Army', which Merry had heard being belted out in the ward on his first visit. He had just got to the last lines of the second verse.

> *'So guinea pigs stand ready*
> *For when your surgeon calls*
> *For if his hand's not steady*
> *He'll cut off both your . . .'*

'Ears,' interposed Merry sharply.

Felix turned from the mirror with a look of amused surprise and then saw the small boy in the doorway. 'Hello, Sam.'

'What's that song about?' Sam enquired.

'Guinea pigs,' said Merry and Felix with one voice.

Sam's face brightened. 'Auntie Enid says I might be able to have a guinea pig for my birthday if I promise to look after it.'

'That'll be jolly,' Felix said encouragingly.

Sam frowned. 'What's a surgeon?'

'Someone who operates on people – or animals in this case.'

Sam nodded wisely. 'Auntie Enid's Tibbles had to have an operation to stop her having kittens all the time.'

'Ah, well. There you are, then,' said Felix, turning back to the mirror.

'Why is he going to cut off the guinea pig's ears?' Sam demanded.

Felix turned back and cast a despairing glance at Merry. Merry's grin conveyed the clear message: 'You got yourself into this. Now you get out of it.'

'It's a sort of joke,' Felix improvised. 'Because guinea pigs don't have much in the way of ears. Like the one about what happens if you hold a guinea pig up by its tail.'

'Oh, I know that one,' Sam said disparagingly. 'Its eyes fall out.'

'Well, there you are, then,' Felix said again.

Sam considered for a moment. 'It doesn't rhyme,' he said finally. 'Calls and ears don't rhyme.'

'No,' Felix admitted with increasing desperation. 'I couldn't think of a rhyme.'

Sam nodded wisely. 'Rhymes are difficult,' he agreed. Then, 'Would you like me to see if I can think of one?'

'That would be very helpful,' Felix said humbly.

'OK.' The little boy turned away cheerfully and they heard him going down the stairs chanting to himself. 'Calls, falls, walls, stalls . . .'

Felix grabbed a towel and stuffed it in his mouth and Merry moved hastily to close the door.

'Do you think he'll ask his mum to help?' Felix said, when he could speak.

'It won't matter,' Merry answered, grinning. 'Bet's broad minded. I just hope he doesn't repeat it to his teacher.'

*   *   *

One afternoon, when they had been driven indoors by a shower, Felix, who was leafing through the pages of the *Illustrated London News*, suddenly exclaimed, 'Good Lord!'

'What?' Merry asked.

'Good Lord!' said Felix again, with greater emphasis.

'*What?*' Merry demanded.

Felix folded back the page he was reading and passed it over. 'Look.'

Merry saw a page of photographs. The theme was painfully familiar – London in the Blitz – but there was something about each image which arrested the eye; the position of a figure, an expression on a face, the particular angle of view. He looked over them and remarked, 'Yes, they're good, but why . . .?'

'Look at the name of the photographer,' Felix instructed.

Merry looked. 'Good Lord!'

'Quite,' agreed Felix.

Rose put down her book. 'What are you two going on about?'

Silently Merry passed her the magazine. She read, 'Photographs by Harriet Forsyth.' She looked at Felix. 'Sorry, I don't get it.'

'Oh, you must remember,' he said. 'You met her once, when you and Richard came to that dance at the Palace Hotel.'

'You don't mean *Lady* Harriet, your . . .' She stopped and Merry saw her flush. Harriet had been Felix's official girlfriend in the days when they all worked together in the concert party.

'It has to be,' Felix said. 'She was always mad on photography, had her own darkroom and all that.'

'I thought she'd joined the ambulance service,' Merry said.

'Yes, I thought so too. That's what she said in the last letter I had from her. But I suppose that doesn't stop her taking photos in her spare time.'

'And now she's turned professional,' Rose marvelled. 'Who'd have thought it?'

'It may be a one-off,' Merry pointed out. 'I suppose she had these pictures and she probably knows people who work for this sort of mag. It's the usual story – not what you know but who you know.'

'Come on, be fair,' Felix said. 'They really are good. I hope she has got her chance to make it as a professional. It's what she really wanted.'

Merry looked at him speculatively. After the way Harriet had behaved when Felix was shot down he could not understand why he should wish her well. As far as Merry was concerned she was a spoilt rich girl who had abandoned her lover because she couldn't face up to his disfigurement. It worried him that Felix was feeling so forgiving. Surely he couldn't still be carrying a torch for her? Then he remembered the previous night and banished the thought.

As they grew stronger Merry and Felix took to going for walks in the fields around Wimborne. They never walked up the hill towards Matthew's farm. Neither of them felt equal to an encounter that could only have resulted in embarrassment all round. One afternoon it was almost as warm as midsummer. The hedgerows were white with blackthorn and they walked under a constant shower of lark song from a cloudless sky, across which a formation of fighter planes was drawing parallel furrows of white vapour.

Felix cocked his head and watched them. 'Lucky buggers!'

Merry sighed. 'You really miss being up there, don't you?'

'So would you, if you'd ever flown,' Felix said. 'I can't describe how exciting it is. When you a fly a Spit especially. It's such a wonderful plane. You don't have to think "I move my hand to do this" or "I need to use my feet like this". You just think turn, dive, climb and it happens, as if the plane was part of your own body. It's the nearest thing to being a bird that it's possible to get.'

Merry shook his head with a sigh. It was impossible not to be caught up in his enthusiasm, but he felt impelled to remark, 'I think I see the attraction, but doesn't it occur to you that the main purpose of your being up there is to kill other human beings?'

Felix turned away. 'Only to stop them coming over here and killing innocent civilians.'

'Yes, I know that.' Merry's tone was conciliatory. 'And I admit the necessity of it. But should you look forward to it? Should it give you pleasure?'

Felix swung round. 'For God's sake, Merry, give me credit for some morals! Of course I don't get pleasure from killing! What do you think I am?'

They stared at each other, both painfully aware that they were on the verge of a damaging quarrel.

'I didn't mean that,' Merry protested. 'I just wonder why you're so eager to get back.'

'Because I don't like sitting around here doing nothing while other chaps are risking their lives to defend our country!' Felix snapped. 'Your trouble is you think like a bloody conchie!'

'Look,' Merry said desperately, 'I understand all that. I know I've never been in the front line so I've no right to criticise. I'm sorry. Forget I spoke.'

They walked on for a while in silence. Then Felix said, 'Look, sorry I snapped at you. You know I think what you're doing is every bit as important as any fighting soldier or airman. And you're absolutely right, of course. One shouldn't want to kill a fellow human being. The only mitigating factor I can offer you is that there is something about air combat that's different from trench warfare – something cleaner, more . . . more personal. It's you and him, one to one, and the outcome depends on your skill and speed of reactions against his, at any rate when it's a Spitfire against an Me 109. And there is a kind of chivalry about it. I know that sounds sentimental, but it's true. Oh, sometimes in a dogfight you don't know who you're shooting at or even if you've hit them, but there are times when you really begin to feel you know the other chap. You recognise his little idiosyncrasies, his strengths and weaknesses. It becomes like a medieval joust.' He stopped walking. 'There was one time . . . did I ever tell you about it?'

'Tell me what?'

'It was last summer, before I got shot down. I got into a dogfight over the French coast with a Hun in a 109 and we were so evenly matched neither of us could get a decent shot in. We climbed and dived and turned and rolled, used every manoeuvre in the book, but I couldn't catch him and he couldn't get me in his sights. I was so involved that I forgot everything else. God knows where the rest of the squadron were! Then I suddenly looked at my fuel gauge and realised that if I didn't break off at once I'd end up having to ditch in the Channel. I saw the Hun coming at me. He was so close I could see his face quite clearly and I thought I'd bought it. I don't know what came into my head but I waved at him and then pointed to my fuel gauge and went like this . . .' He drew his hand across his throat. 'And instead of shooting he waved back and pulled up so that he passed above me. So I put my nose down and made for the white cliffs of Dover like a bat out of hell. Then I suddenly realised he was following me and I thought, here it comes. Any minute now he's going to give me a squirt up the tail end. But nothing happened. I looked up and there he was, sitting on my tail a little bit above and behind me, and he stayed there until we got to the English coast. Then he gave a waggle of his wings and headed back for France.' Felix met Merry's eyes. 'Don't you see? He was seeing me home, protecting my rear and making sure I got back without having to ditch.'

'Very touching,' Merry agreed. 'But it could have been the same bloke who shot you down a few weeks later. And if you get back to flying again no doubt you will be trying to do the same to him.'

Felix turned away with a sigh and leaned his arms on the top rung of a stile.

'You're right, of course. War's a bloody awful business and there's no disguising the fact. But I have to go back. I can't forget that most of the men I served with last summer are dead now. Out of my old squadron I only know of three pilots who have survived. I'm one of the lucky ones, Merry. I feel I've got a debt to the rest of them. Does that make sense?'

'No,' Merry said, laying a hand on his shoulder. 'It's bloody nonsense. But I can understand it.'

The three weeks of Felix's leave were coming to an end. He was due to go back for another series of operations and then he had been promised that he would be sent to a unit that had been set up under McIndoe's auspices, where injured airmen were trained to manufacture some of the intricate parts for aircraft. This had the dual purpose of allowing them to feel that they were still contributing to the service and at the same time providing good practice in the fine motor skills they had temporarily lost. Felix commented that it would probably be deadly boring but at least he would feel he was being some use at last.

Merry had been told by George Black not to come back to work until he was completely fit, and he was tempted to stay at Wimborne for another week, but he too was beginning to feel guilty at remaining idle. Now that the weather had improved he felt sure that he could cope with the rigours of another tour. So it was agreed that he and Felix would travel up to London together.

When they explained their arrangement to Rose she nodded. 'Yes, you're probably right to get back to work. It's been lovely having you here, but we can't sit around doing nothing indefinitely, can we?'

'What are your plans, Rose?' Merry asked. 'Do you have any? Now that you've been invalided out of the Women's Land Army you're a free agent, I assume.'

He and Felix had been worried by Rose's state of mind. Physically, she was obviously much stronger than when they had arrived, but she still seemed lethargic and withdrawn.

Now, however, she raised her eyes and Merry saw a new determination in them. 'I've been thinking about that. I'm going back on the stage.'

Merry opened his mouth to speak and then shut it again. It was Felix who said, 'Attagirl! Good for you.'

'But what about your ankle?' Merry asked. 'I thought the specialist told you you could never dance again.'

Rose's chin lifted in a way Merry remembered from the old days. 'If I can work the way I did on that farm, climbing ladders, lifting bales of hay, tramping miles over rough ground, I'm darn sure I can learn to dance again.'

'So what will you do?' Merry asked.

'I'll go back to London, back to the flat, and I'll go and see my old dance teacher, Miss Levine. I'll start again from square one if I have to. I don't care if it takes a year, or more. I'll get there in the end.'

'Good for you!' Felix said again. He took out his wallet and extracted a card from it. 'Here. A chap in the ward gave me this in case I wanted some extra work on this hand. It's the address of a chiropractor in Harley Street. I know it sounds a bit offbeat, but the chap who gave it to me swears he's the gnat's pyjamas when it comes to damaged muscles and ligaments. Apparently, he went to him after he damaged his leg badly playing rugger before the war. If the ankle starts playing up again, why don't you go and see him?'

Rose looked at the card but did not touch it. 'Harley Street? You must be joking. I bet he costs an arm and a leg, never mind mending them.'

'Take it,' Felix said, 'and send the bill to me. I can afford it and I'd be happy to pay if it helps.'

Merry saw pride and gratitude fight it out on Rose's face. Then she took the card and kissed Felix on the cheek. 'You're a darling, Felix. Thanks. I won't forget this.'

'No need for thanks,' Felix said. 'Just let me see you up there, dancing, again.'

Merry watched this exchange with a sinking heart. He looked at Rose and saw the whipcord muscles in her thin arms and the slight roundness of her belly, due no doubt to her mother's efforts to 'build her up'. The heart-shaped face was still the same under the waves of dark hair, but its bone structure was sharper now, the cheekbones and nose more defined. The huge violet eyes seemed almost too large, and there were shadows under them and fine lines at their corners. There was no doubt that Rose was still a very attractive woman, but she had lost the delicate, almost fairy-like grace that he remembered from before the war. Merry was no connoisseur of feminine beauty but he had spent all his working life in the theatre and played for enough dance auditions to know what was required, and he doubted whether Rose any longer had the right looks to be selected for a chorus line.

They were packing on their last morning when Felix said, 'What will you be doing next, do you think?'

Merry shrugged. 'More of the same, I imagine.'

'I was thinking,' Felix went on, 'if you're going to be in the London area we might be able to get down to your place in Seaford for the odd forty-eight-hour leave occasionally.'

'It would be wonderful if we could,' Merry agreed, 'but I've no idea where I'll be from now on. Still, you never know. We could be lucky.'

After a moment's thought he felt in his pocket and produced a set of keys.

'Here. You might as well take these. I've got another set at the digs. If I can't make it, you might want to pop down for a night or two. Take some friends with you, if you like.'

Felix took the keys. 'Thanks. I might go down and check the place over for you – make sure squatters haven't moved in or anything. But I shan't take anyone with me. That would feel totally wrong.'

Their eyes met. 'Anyway,' Felix said, 'let's hope we can go together.'

They embraced, knowing there would be no later opportunity, and went down to make their farewells to the rest of the party.

II

'*Raus! Raus!*' The harsh German voice roused Richard from a deep sleep. He started up, screwing up his eyes against the light of the powerful torch that was being shone in his face.

'Up! Up!' the voice repeated in German, and rough hands hauled him to his feet.

'*Che cosa?*' Richard demanded in Italian. Then, switching to French. '*Qu'est-ce que vous voulez?*'

'Come!' was the only answer he received, and he was frogmarched out of the room and down the stairs. His captors led him across the hall and through a door that led to another steep flight of steps. The air smelt damp and faintly vinous. This had once been a wine cellar. At the bottom he found himself in a large shadowy space, in the centre of which was a single wooden chair, illuminated by the harsh light of an unshaded bulb. Beyond the circle of light he could just make out a table, behind which sat two figures in the uniforms of the SS. He was hustled over to the chair and thrust down upon it, while his two captors stood guard on either side.

'Name?' demanded a voice from behind the table, in German.

Richard was awake now and thought he understood what was happening but his still sleep-fuddled brain kept repeating the same phrase – *Stick to your story. Don't let them break your cover.*

'*Namen,*' he repeated as if translating the word to himself. '*Mi chiamo Benedetti – Ricardo Benedetti.*'

'Nationality?'

'*Italiano.*'

'Age?'

'*Ventiquattro.*'

'What are you doing in France?'

The questions were still in German. Richard puckered his face as if struggling to understand. '*Scusi?*'

'What are you doing in France?'

'*Non capisco.*' Then switching to French again, '*Je m'excuse. Je ne comprends pas l'Allemand.*'

A second voice, smoother and less hostile, spoke from out of the shadows, this time in Italian. 'What are you doing in France?'

'Ah!' Richard allowed an expression of relief to cross his face. 'I am a cabaret artiste. I sing.'

'Where do you perform?' enquired the Italian speaker.

'At the Café Bleu, at present.'

'If you are Italian, what are you doing singing in a French cabaret instead of fighting for your country alongside our glorious German troops?' demanded the first man, this time in French.

'I was with an opera company in Belgium at the outbreak of war. The company went bust. I had no money to pay my fare home. I had met a girl when the company played in Lille. I went to her for help. We formed the act so that I could earn enough to pay my fare back to Italy.'

'What is this girlfriend's name?'

'Henriette Gautier – but she calls herself Chantal.'

'Where do you live?'

'With her. Number eleven, Rue Montaigne.'

'Where do you come from in Italy?'

'Milano.'

'What address?'

'Via Pontaccio, twenty-five.'

He was beginning to feel very cold. Although the summer night was warm the air in the cellar was chill and damp and he was wearing nothing but pyjamas. He struggled to prevent himself from visibly shivering. The questions went on and on, sometimes in French, sometimes in Italian. 'Where did you go to school?' 'What is your mother's name?' 'Where was your father born?' Then, suddenly, in English, 'I don't believe you. You're lying.'

'*Che? Non capisco.*'

'You're an English spy.'

'*Je ne comprends pas. Qu'est-ce qu'il dit?*'

The Italian speaker again. 'You say you are a singer. Where did you train?'

'At the Milan conservatoire.'

'Who was your teacher?'

'Signor Alessandro Coretto.'

'If you trained at the conservatoire, what are you doing singing cabaret in a bar?'

'I told you. I needed money. It was the only work I could get.'

'He's lying. I don't believe a word of it. He's either a deserter or a spy.' The officer rose and came close to him. 'You might as well stop lying to us. We have already arrested your girlfriend and she has told us everything.' He laughed softly. 'She is a lovely girl, no? Such a shame to have to spoil that beautiful body – but we had to persuade her.'

'But she's done nothing!' Richard protested. 'Why are you doing this? We are innocent. We know nothing.'

The officer made a sharp movement in the direction of one of his guards and Richard almost fell off the chair under the force of a powerful open-handed slap across the face.

'Tell us the truth!' demanded the German voice. 'Why make things hard for yourself? This is only the beginning.'

'I have told you the truth!' Richard heard his voice break on the words. He was rewarded with another violent slap. He could feel his lip beginning to bleed.

'Please!' he begged. 'You must believe me. I'm just a simple entertainer. I don't know what all this is about.'

His interrogator turned to the two guards. 'Strip him!'

Richard was roughly jerked to his feet and stripped of his pyjamas. He felt at once embarrassed and acutely vulnerable, as if the flimsy covering had been some form of protection.

'Stand up on the chair.'

Slowly he climbed up.

'Put your hands above your head.'

He did as he was bid. The questioning went on. 'How long have you been in France?' 'What was the name of the opera company?' 'Where did you perform?' His arms were aching and he could no longer prevent his knees from shaking.

'You say you're a singer. Sing something,' the interrogator demanded.

'What? What do you want me to sing?'

'Anything. Let's hear you.'

'How can I sing like this?' He indicated his raised arms with a jerk of his head.

'Very well. Lower your arms. Now, sing!'

Richard's mind was whirling. What should he sing? One of the songs he had learned for his cabaret act with Chantal? Something from the repertoire he had used in the Follies? No, fool! Too English. Then it came to him, the theme that had been repeating itself over and over in his head ever since that terrible New Year's Eve. He took a deep breath and began to sing King Philip of Spain's aria from Verdi's *Don Carlos*. It was a bass solo, really, but his voice had always been at its best in the lower registers and recently it seemed to have dropped further.

'*Dormiro sol nel manto mio regal* . . .' 'I shall sleep alone in my royal robes.' The lament of a man betrayed in love.

The first notes came out husky and shaking. Then his

training took over and his diaphragm muscles steadied to control his breathing. Sombre, constrained, the voice of a man determined to retain his royal dignity in the face of unbearable loss, the measured tones marched on. In his mind he could hear the dark cello notes of the accompanying orchestra, leading him into the poignant main theme. The empty cellar amplified his voice, so that when emotion ultimately got the better of restraint the anguished cry filled the room: '*Ella giammai m'amo.*' 'She has never loved me!' Then came the final notes, sung on a sob: '*Amor per me no ha, amor per me non ha . . .*' 'For me she has no love.'

When the last note died away there was silence in the cellar. Then the chief interrogator turned to his colleague and said, in English, 'I think that will do, don't you?'

There was a movement behind the table and another light was switched on, illuminating the familiar features of the two men in German uniform. One of them pulled off his cap and ran his hand through his hair.

'Well done, Richard. Full marks. You can go back to bed now. Give him his pyjamas, Victor.'

Victor Maxim, the man who had slapped him and whom he had recognised some time earlier as his conducting officer, handed him the clothes and said, 'Sorry I had to rough you up a bit, old chap. But you have to know what to expect.'

'I'm not sure I needed the practical demonstration!' Richard mumbled, through rapidly swelling lips. He pulled on his pyjama trousers. The second 'officer' came over to him and held out his hand. 'Congratulations, Richard. You didn't put a foot wrong.'

Richard looked at the hand. He felt sick and he was still trembling uncontrollably. He shook his head and turned away. 'Oh, sod the lot of you!' he muttered, heading for the door.

Victor accompanied him back up to his room. 'Everyone goes through it, you know,' he said consolingly. 'They didn't give you a rougher time than anyone else. Anyway, you came through with flying colours. Well done.'

On his bedside table Richard found a mug of steaming cocoa and a large measure of brandy. Victor patted him on the shoulder. 'Drink up and try to get back to sleep. See you later.'

Richard swallowed the brandy and got into bed. He sipped the cocoa but his split lip hurt too much and he put the mug aside and lay down, curling himself into a fetal ball. So that was a taste of what he had let himself in for! But it was too late to pull out now.

Unable to sleep again, he went over in his mind the sequence of the mock interrogation. It had been hinted to him once or twice that he would be given some form of 'practice' in withstanding questioning by the enemy, but he had never imagined that the experience would be quite so realistic. 'Bastards!' he muttered to himself. 'I think they get a kick out of it.' But even as the words formed in his mind he knew it was not true. He had come to respect and trust the men who were preparing him for the role he was going to play. In retrospect, their rough handling had been neither excessive nor surprising. What did surprise him was his own reaction. It was true that he had realised what was going on and who his tormentors were quite early in the proceedings, but he had never expected things to get as nasty as they had done. For much of the time he had been genuinely frightened – initially that he would make some foolish blunder, but then as time went on at the lengths to which his interrogators seemed prepared to go. But he had not cracked. He had not betrayed himself in any way and the knowledge came as a relief. It was true that he still had no idea how much more pain he would have been able to take, and he had no illusions about the relative mildness of his treatment compared with the real thing. But at least he had maintained his cover story through some pretty intensive questioning, which would probably be enough to get him out of most situations.

The more he thought about it, the more amazed he felt that he, Richard Stevens, baritone and comedian's stooge from the Fairbourne Follies, was actually doing this. He could scarcely recognise the person he was now in the diffident boy who had first stepped on to the stage at Fairbourne two years earlier – or even in the young officer who had presented himself at Wanborough Manor in the last days of winter. Wanborough had begun the transformation, of course, but it was in Scotland that most of it had taken place. He still found it hard to credit the things he had learned to do there.

The instructions he was given when he left Wanborough took him to Arisaig, a remote area of the Western Highlands accessible only by a narrow road or a single-track railway, both of which were closely guarded and open only to those who carried special passes. He was housed in a gloomy old house called Garramor, full of dark corners and narrow, twisting staircases, and the contrast with the genteel atmosphere at Wanborough could not have been greater. Here he shared a room with Jack Duval and Paul Warren. The amenities were minimal and sanitary facilities so overcrowded that they were frequently forced to make use of an open window instead. But this was a minor inconvenience when set against the rigours of the existence they now endured.

These included an extension of the physical training begun at Wanborough – early morning runs, assault courses, survival skills. Next came further training with various kinds of fire-arms. This was very different from anything he had learned in the infantry. He was taught to be as quick on the draw as the hero of any cowboy film and to fire from any position and in any kind of light. It was not a question of marksmanship. It was a matter of dealing a lethal blow from close quarters and without hesitation. The old house and its grounds were full of booby traps and unexpected surprises in the shape of dummies dressed as German soldiers and the students were required to carry a weapon at all times and soon developed hair-trigger reactions.

They also learned how to handle various types of explosive and where to place charges in order to do the greatest damage. On the remote hillsides around Arisaig the sound of explosions disturbed no one, and they practised throwing grenades and blowing up old pieces of farm machinery. Later they were sent out to lay dummy charges on real targets such as piers and bridges. They were shown how to booby-trap a car, or bring down an unsuspecting motorcyclist with a length of wire stretched across a road.

But it was the training in unarmed combat which had the profoundest effect on Richard. He learned how to creep up behind an unsuspecting sentry and snap his spine with a sudden jerk; how to use a knife to kill quickly and silently; how to react if suddenly grabbed from behind. He knew what the effect would be of a chop with the side of the hand to various parts of the body and had been taught, though never allowed to practise for obvious reasons, a blow that could be guaranteed to kill an opponent. When he was interviewed in London – a long time ago it seemed now – he had been asked whether he could kill a man with his bare hands. He knew now that he had the technique and that, given the right stimulus, he would use it without pausing for thought. And the knowledge frightened him.

When this part of his training was over he had been sent south again, to Beaulieu, the country home of Lord Montagu. It was there that he finally learned the name of the organisation he was going to work for. To the outside world it was known as the Inter-Services Liaison Bureau, but to those within it, and to a few very highly placed outsiders, it was the Special

Operations Executive, whose mission was to encourage resistance in all the territories occupied by the Nazis. Richard
had been assigned to 'F' section, the branch responsible for
operations in France.

The head of 'F' section was Maurice Buckmaster, and from
time to time he came down from London to see how the
students were shaping up. On the occasion of one of these
visits Richard sought an interview with him.

'I appreciate the object of what we are being taught to do
here, sir,' he said, 'but I think in my case there may have been a
misunderstanding. I volunteered for this so that I could go
back and help the people who got me out of France last year. I
pointed out in my first interview that I thought it would
become increasingly important to return downed aircrew as
fast as possible and that we couldn't expect the French to go
on doing it without some back-up from over here. But the last
thing these *réseaux*, these escape lines, need is to draw attention to themselves by acts of sabotage or by distributing anti-
Nazi propaganda.'

'Are you telling me that you think you're wasting your time
here?' Buckmaster enquired.

'No, sir,' Richard replied. 'I think a lot of what I have
learned is extremely useful. I just don't want any misunderstanding about the role I hope to play when I get back to
France.'

Buckmaster subjected him to a long, impassive scrutiny.
Then he said, 'That is an operational decision, and not one
you will be required to make. But I can tell you that the
likelihood of your being returned to an area where your real
identity is known is remote. The security risk is too great.'

'But these are good people!' Richard said tensely. 'They
didn't betray me then and I'm sure they wouldn't if I went
back.'

'They might not wish to,' Buckmaster replied. 'But if the

Gestapo get hold of them they might. Everyone talks, sooner or later.'

Richard felt as if the ground had been swept from under his feet. 'But that's what I signed up for. If I can't go back there, I'm not sure I want to go on with this.'

Buckmaster looked at him with grim amusement. 'If you think that you can opt out now and be returned to your regiment, I'm afraid you are sadly mistaken. You know far too much. The only alternative you have is a spell in the "cooler". It's what we call an establishment we have set up in the far north of Scotland. Anyone who fails this course goes there and is occupied with useful but menial tasks until such time as their knowledge is regarded as having become obsolete. Would you prefer that?'

'No!' Richard swallowed hard and forced himself to think calmly. 'I have to respect your decision, of course. But isn't it worth bearing in mind that I already have good contacts among the people who run the escape line? It seems a waste not to make use of that.'

Buckmaster was silent for a moment. Then he nodded briefly. 'It's a valid point. I'll bear it in mind. OK, you can go now.'

The object of the curriculum at Beaulieu was to introduce the students to what was known as 'field craft'. This seemed to Richard much more relevant to the job he hoped to do. Some of it was second nature to him already, after several months on the run in France, though it was obviously new to many of the others. He had no need to be told how to distinguish between the Gestapo and the SS. He had learned that the best policy if asked for his papers was to be very matter-of-fact and to say as little as possible. The important thing was always to have a good reason for being where he was, and to produce it without hesitation. Now he was taught to study and memorise maps and directions so that he always appeared to know where he was going. Even looking the wrong way before crossing a road could give him away to an observant enemy.

It was not enough, however, to have acquired these basic survival skills. A successful agent needed more specialised techniques. He learned how to encode and decode messages and the importance of establishing a *boîte aux lettres*, a third person who would pass messages on without establishing a direct link between himself and the recipient. The students were also told how to recruit helpers among the local population. It was best to choose people who were either professionals or self-employed tradesmen who had good reason for moving around the area. Bakers, butchers, plumbers and other craftsmen probably had transport and permits to use it. Doctors, vets, priests would all have passes that allowed them to move around at night as well as during the day. Gamekeepers and poachers could also produce a convincing reason for being out after dark.

Above all, it was dinned into them that they must never, by even the slightest hesitation or mannerism, betray their true identity. They must live their cover story at all times. And they were warned that their greatest enemy would be loneliness and the desire to confide in someone. It might only be one person and that person might seem totally trustworthy, but nevertheless the temptation must be resisted. The most useful lectures on these topics were given by a very charming man with perfect manners and a fund of amusing stories. His name was Kim Philby.

It was when it came to establishing his cover story that Richard found himself in conflict with his mentors. His intention had always been to link up again with Chantal and resurrect their cabaret act. This seemed to his instructors to be too flamboyant and difficult to sustain. But his singing in the interrogation room had made an impression. One day, he was called into what had once been the elegant sitting room of the house, to be introduced to a small, wild-haired man who seemed to be in a very bad temper. Also present were the senior instructor, Major Skilbeck, and Victor Maxim. Victor came from a family that had extensive trading interests all through Europe. He had grown up in Paris and Vienna and was completely trilingual and had travelled extensively all over France. His present job was to act as Richard's personal coach and confidant.

'This is Dr Laslo Brodic,' Skilbeck said. 'He is Professor of Singing at the Royal College of Music in London.'

Richard offered his hand. 'I know you by reputation, sir. It's a great privilege to meet you in person.'

The little man greeted this overture with an ill-tempered snort. Richard guessed that he was not best pleased at being summoned from his lessons by the military for no very clear reason. It was obvious, however, that he had been briefed to some extent.

'You say you trained in Milan?'

'Yes, sir. I was there for three years.'

'Who did you study with?'

'Signor Coretto.'

'So. I have heard of Signor Coretto but not met him.' Brodic looked round the room. In one corner there was a grand piano, left behind by the previous occupants and much abused by the present residents. He headed towards it. 'You have your music?'

Suddenly Richard was transported back to the stage of the Pier Theatre in Fairbourne and heard Merry's voice issuing from the orchestra pit. *Got your dots, old boy?*

'No, I'm sorry,' he said. 'It's all stored away at home for the duration.'

Brodic snorted again. 'So, what are you going to sing for me?'

Unprepared, Richard floundered for a moment. 'What would you like me to sing?'

'My dear young man,' Brodic exclaimed irritably, 'how do I know what is in your repertoire? You are a bass, yes? Or a baritone?'

'A baritone. Well, bass-baritone.'

'Then you will know this, I presume.'

He struck up the opening bars of the Toreador's Song from *Carmen*. Richard felt a sudden sense of exhilaration. Of course he knew it. He had sung it often enough with the Follies. It had been a sure-fire success. He took a deep breath and launched in.

By the time he reached the end of the aria the little man's attitude had undergone a complete transformation. He raised his hands, palms upwards, and exclaimed, 'Bravo! Bravo! It is a good voice – an excellent voice. A little out of practice, yes, but the quality is there. Your tempi are erratic, phrasing needs attention, but you do Signor Coretto credit, my friend. But why have we not heard you in London? Where were you before the war?'

'In a concert party down on the south coast,' Richard told him.

Brodic looked scandalised. 'Concert party? What are you doing singing in concert party with a voice like that?'

'I was there because nobody wanted to listen to me in London,' Richard said, with a hint of bitterness.

Brodic threw his hands in the air. 'Ah, these English prejudices! But after the war everything will be different. Wait and see.'

Richard had his doubts about that but he did not voice them.

Brodic turned to the two instructors. 'Well, what do you want from me? This man has a voice. He can sing opera. Is this what you wanted to know?'

'Yes, that is basically it,' Skilbeck agreed.

'But he should practise more. Perhaps take some lessons with a good teacher,' Brodic suggested.

'That could be arranged. Can you recommend anyone?'

The little man considered for a moment. Then he said, 'I will teach him myself. Send him to me at the college twice a week.'

So from then on Richard took the train to London twice a week for his lessons and every afternoon he was excused from the normal training exercises for an hour to practise. It gave him a great deal of pleasure, but at the same time it awoke memories and dreams that he had firmly locked away for the duration of the war, if not for ever. It was not simply that his passion for opera and his ambition to sing it professionally were rekindled. Many of the arias he sung were ones he had performed with the Follies, and it was impossible to remember that summer in Fairbourne without remembering Rose. He had managed to shut his mind to her for the most part while he was at Wanborough and almost entirely during his time in Scotland, but now he found himself lying awake at night thinking about her. He imagined her busy with her new life on the farm and wondered whether she and Matthew were actually married yet. Once or twice he had an impulse to go to Wimborne and make a last-ditch attempt to persuade her to change her mind, but then reality reasserted itself. He was about to disappear into enemy-occupied territory with no guarantee of when, or if, he would return. He had no right to ask Rose to exchange the security of marriage to Matthew for that uncertainty.

He tried to distract himself with thoughts of Chantal, but there was little comfort there. He was plagued by the idea that she might already have been betrayed to the Germans, and his imagination conjured up agonising images of what she might be suffering at their hands. His mock interrogators' final ploy, that they had his girlfriend in custody and had 'persuaded' her to talk, showed that they had a greater insight into his mental state than he had given them credit for.

Once his cover story had been agreed his instructors left nothing to chance in making it as foolproof as possible. He could no longer sustain the excuse that he was on his way back to Italy to enlist. Instead it was decided that he should say that he had been wounded in the course of duty and discharged. A doctor examined the bullet scars on his leg and pronounced that they were sufficient to support his story. He was provided with documents discharging him on medical grounds and was assured that they were sufficiently good forgeries to pass scrutiny. Also it was suggested that in order to back up his story he should emphasise the slight limp he had been trying for months to eradicate. To this end he was provided with a shoe which, although apparently identical to the other in the pair, had a slightly built-up heel that made his gait uneven. He found it most uncomfortable to begin with but after a while his muscles adapted themselves.

Among the many other things they were taught was how to recognise when they were being followed and how to shake off their pursuer. Exercises were frequently carried out in Bournemouth, which was the nearest large town. One day, Richard was instructed to meet a stranger at a particular hotel and bring back a package he would give him.

At the station, in true Sherlock Holmes style, he took not the first or the second taxi in the rank but the third, and gave, not the name of the hotel, but a location in the centre of the town. From there he ducked into Plummer Roddis, the department store, and came out by a different door. He strolled along the street and stopped to study a window display, all the time watching the reflections in the glass. He had just about convinced himself that he was in the clear and could safely proceed to the rendezvous when he was shocked to hear a woman's voice hailing him shrilly by name.

'Richard! Hey, Richard! Over here!'

He looked across the street and froze. Sally Castle was waving at him wildly from the other side of the road. Luckily the traffic was heavy and she was unable to cross immediately. Richard looked around him. A few yards away a bus was just pulling away from a stop. He ran after it and leapt on to the platform, eliciting an irate expostulation from the conductor. A glance behind him showed Sally, now on his side of the street, staring after him and still waving, and he prayed that the bus would not be held up at traffic lights and allow her to catch it up. It was not until they had travelled a mile or so that he felt able to breathe easily. He got off at the next stop and took a taxi to the hotel.

Feeling distinctly shaken, he went to the bar and ordered a dry martini. Mercifully, from then on things started going according to plan. A middle-aged, mild-looking man came in carrying a golf umbrella, incongruous in view of the fine weather. He took a place beside Richard and ordered a beer.

Richard smiled and nodded at the umbrella. 'I see you believe in being prepared for every eventuality.'

His companion replied with a shrug, 'I can't bear to miss my round of golf and you never know when the heavens might open.'

It was the agreed exchange of passwords. They chatted for a few minutes and then the stranger finished his drink and said he must be on his way. Richard had set a briefcase down on the floor beside him and as he rose to leave the stranger picked it up, leaving his own identical one in its place.

Similar exercises were repeated again and again, until it became second nature for all of them to take evasive action in case they had acquired a 'tail'. Secret passwords, coded messages and dead-letter drops were a way of life. Finally,

Richard and Paul Warren were sent out to attach a dummy explosive charge to the car belonging to a senior army officer. This was their passing-out test. Two days later Richard packed his bags and headed north for a fortnight's leave.

12

Rose paused outside the door of her mother's flat in Lambeth and looked around her. It was almost a year since she had been home but the memory of that last day was still vivid. She could picture the bomb craters, still smoking from the raid of the previous night, and the detritus of familiar lives strewn over the pavement or hanging improbably suspended from what remained of walls. There had been no raids for three months now, and willow herb was flourishing among the ruins, but the street was noisy with people going about their daily business. Miraculously, the shoe shop and the flat above it were still standing, though the shop windows had been boarded up after a later blast had blown in the glass. She put her key in the lock and pushed the door open.

She was surprised to find a small pile of letters on the mat. Since Merry had given up using the flat they had asked the post office to forward all their mail. She collected them up and carried them upstairs. It was the first day of June, a warm summer afternoon, and the place smelt musty after being empty for so long, so she went round opening windows to air it. Then she sorted through the letters, which she had left lying on the kitchen table. Most were circulars or government propaganda, but she was puzzled to find one addressed to Merry in her own handwriting. It took a few seconds for the terrible realisation to dawn. It had been delivered after Merry left but before the Post Office had received the new instructions! She ripped the envelope and found another inside – the letter she had written to Richard at New Year and asked Merry to forward.

She sank down on a chair, propping her head on one hand, unsure whether what she felt was disappointment or relief. If Richard had never had the letter he must presume that she had gone ahead with her engagement to Matthew. He probably thought they were already married. On the other hand, it did explain why he had never replied. It dawned on her slowly that there might still be hope. She scrabbled in a drawer to find notepaper and composed a new letter, enclosing her original one and explaining why it had never reached him. *Of course,* she wrote, *this may be too late for you. You've probably put it all behind you and decided to forget me. I can't blame you if you have. But I want you to know that I've never stopped loving you and I would give anything to be able to go back to last New Year's Eve and make things turn out differently. Please, at least, write to me and tell me how you feel, now that you know the situation. I shall wait for your letter. With my love always, Rose.*

She addressed the letter to Richard, care of his parents, whose address she had got from Merry when they were all convalescing in Wimborne. Her heart was thumping and her throat was aching with something between laughter and tears as she carried it down to the corner of the street and posted it.

Rose spent the next day clearing up in the shop. There was plainly no hope of getting the glass replaced in the windows so she found a large piece of cardboard and painted BUSINESS AS USUAL on it and nailed it to the wooden shutters. Her work was interrupted frequently by neighbours dropping in to ask after her mother and sister and the two boys and to bring her up to date with the latest gossip, but by evening the broken glass had been swept away, the shelves and counters dusted and the remaining stock laid out as attractively as possible. It was meagre enough but shoes, like everything else, were in short supply. Feeling for the first time in a long while that she had achieved something, Rose went back up to the flat and cooked herself some tea. She was tired but she had no intention of sitting down to listen to the radio that evening. She had something much more important to do.

As soon as she had washed the dishes she put on her smartest dress. Admittedly it was two years out of date and had been worn to every party and dance she had attended in Wimborne, but everyone was making do with old clothes these days and she had washed and pressed it carefully. She did her face, too, though she had almost given up wearing make-up. Her hair needed cutting, but for now it would have to do tied back with a pretty scarf. Having made herself as presentable as possible she took a bus to the Levine School of Dance in Stockwell. This was where she had first learned ballet at the age of five and where she had become one of the star pupils by the time she was sixteen. It was from here that she had gone for her first audition – the audition that had got her her first professional job. Until the beginning of the war she had made a habit of going back to visit every autumn, between the end of the summer concert party season and the beginning of rehearsals for panto, but now she had no idea whether the school was still going. She was very relieved to see, when she got off the bus at the familiar stop, that the building was still standing and the sign announcing the school was still in place.

The Levine sisters were the daughters of a Jewish tailor who had come to England from Russia after the First World War. The younger, Sonia, had been a dancer in the corps de ballet of the Kirov opera house until anti-Jewish feeling had forced the family to flee. She taught all the senior classes. The elder, Irena, was the business brains of the enterprise who looked after all the administration and also taught the 'babies', the little tots of four and five who were learning their first steps. Sonia had seen Rose's potential early on and had offered to give her the private lessons her mother could not afford in exchange for her help with some of the juniors.

Rose slipped quietly in through the main door and stood listening. From the large room on her left came the sound of the same tinny old piano, hammering out the same inevitable Chopin waltz. How Merry would have winced! She moved closer until she could see into the room through the glass panel in the door. Some twelve or thirteen little girls in white tunics were lined up along the barre, arms and legs moving in time to the music, perfectly duplicated by their reflections in the long mirror.

'Plié, développé,' chanted a familiar voice as Sonia moved along the line, adjusting an arm here, pushing a leg higher there.

Rose waited until the barre exercises were over and the children were pausing for a breather, then she opened the door and went quietly into the room. Sonia looked up, for a moment irritated by the interruption. Then she recognised her visitor and opened her arms in an extravagant gesture of welcome.

'Rose! My dear little Rose! How lovely to see you!'

Rose went across and hugged her. She had always been slim, her high cheekbones accentuated by the tightly drawn back hair, but now she looked older, her figure gaunt rather than slender, the hollows under the cheekbones deeply shadowed. She had lost none of her old vivacity, however. For a few moments they exchanged brief enquiries about each other's health and family, then Rose was sent off to find Irena until the class was over. Irena, plumper than her sister and once apple cheeked, had also begun to sag and fade, but she was equally delighted to welcome Rose.

Once the class was over the three of them sat down to drink weak unsweetened coffee and swap stories. The sisters told Rose about the Blitz and their struggle to keep the school going, and she explained about the fall that had injured her ankle and the consultant's dismal prognosis. She went on to recount, in truncated terms, her experiences in the Women's Land Army. She did not mention her engagement to Matthew, nor Richard's sudden reappearance, and skated over some of the worst horrors of her time at Hightop Farm, but she said enough to have her audience exclaiming with distress.

'So, now, Rose,' Irena asked, 'what next?'

'Well,' Rose said, hesitating, 'that's partly why I'm here.' She took a deep breath and plunged in. 'The point is, that time at the farm made me realise that if I can work like that there can't be much wrong with my ankle. I want to dance again – professionally, I mean. I should never have given it up, I can see that now, but at the time it seemed the only thing to do. I know I'm horribly out of practice and I've developed muscles in all the wrong places, so that's why I've come to you. I want to come back to class again.'

The sisters looked at each other and Rose could see an unspoken doubt in their eyes.

'But Rose,' Sonia said, 'our oldest girls are only fifteen or sixteen. You would not want to come to lessons with them, surely.'

'I don't mind that,' Rose said. 'I realised that that would be the case. I don't care if I have to go back to the baby class. I just want to dance again.'

Again the sisters exchanged glances and Irena said gently, 'It is very hard, you know, to get back to the kind of standard you would expect of yourself, after such a long break. And you have been ill.'

'But if I'm prepared to work,' Rose said intently, 'surely I can get back into shape again. I'm not that old, after all, and it's only a year and a half since I last performed. And I'm perfectly fit again now.'

There was a short pause, and then Sonia said, 'Very well. We shall see what can be done. You had better come to me privately to begin with. Come next week, Wednesday, at half past eight. I shall be free then.'

Rose got up and kissed her warmly. 'Thank you so much. You really don't know what it means to me. I couldn't bear not to be able to dance again.'

They talked on for a while of other things, until Irena said, 'Rose, dear. You look tired and you have to get home in the blackout. The buses are not very frequent at this time of night, you know. I think you should go now.'

As the bus ground its way back through the darkened streets Rose hugged two thoughts to herself. She was going to dance again, and one day soon she would have a letter from Richard.

When Richard reported for duty on the last day in May it was with a mixed sensation of nervous anticipation and relief. He had not enjoyed his leave. All his old acquaintances were away in one or other of the armed forces or working extra shifts at the factory, so there was no one around of his own age. On the other hand, his mother had apparently decided that it was time he married and 'settled down'. Previously any suggestion of a romantic attachment had been greeted with a sniff and 'Plenty of time for all that nonsense later. You've got your way to make in the world'. Now she had changed her tune. Perhaps, Richard thought cynically, it had occurred to her that he might not survive the war, so she had better make sure of her grandchildren while the going was good.

Whatever the reason, he found that she had arranged a series of social events, 'because we want to make sure that you enjoy yourself while you're home', and at each of these he found himself being introduced, or reintroduced, to 'suitable' girls. He tried to be polite but did not want to give any of them a false impression of his intentions. He could tell that they thought him boring or 'stand-offish' and his mother did not conceal her growing irritation.

More difficult still were the mealtime conversations in which she recounted the wartime exploits of the sons of neighbours and friends. She had obviously extracted all the mileage she could out of his escape from France and his promotion to officer's rank and she wanted to know what he was doing now.

'I work for an outfit called the Inter-Services Liaison Bureau,' he told her. 'You know, making sure that the three services coordinate their efforts, don't get in each other's way and so on.'

'So it's a desk job, then?' she said, and he could see in her face the mingling of relief and disappointment – relief that he was safely away from the front line and disappointment that there was nothing there she could brag about to the neighbours.

'Not exactly,' he told her. 'It involves quite a lot of travelling. In fact, I may have to go away quite soon, so don't be surprised if you don't hear from me for a while.'

'Go away?' she asked. 'You mean, overseas?'

'Possibly.'

It was his father who came to his rescue. 'Nay, lass. Don't mither the boy with questions. He can't tell you where he's going. Security, tha knowst.' He tapped his finger against the side of his nose. 'Walls have ears, remember.'

It had been a relief when his leave came to an end. He had orders to report to Colonel Buckmaster at the headquarters of the 'Inter-Services Liaison Bureau' in Baker Street.

When he was settled with a whisky and soda and they had exchanged the usual courtesies, Buckmaster said, 'Well, you'll be on your way in a week or so, so it's time we filled in the details of what you're going to do.' Richard sat forward, his pulse quickening. 'First things first,' Buckmaster continued. 'You won't be parachuting in. The medics think that with that gammy leg of yours it would be too much of a risk.'

Richard felt a wave of relief. He had been dreading the information that his next assignment would be to Ringway aerodrome, near Manchester, to take the parachute training course.

'How am I going in then, sir?' he asked.

'You'll fly to Gibraltar for a start.'

'Then over the Pyrenees again?'

'No. We're going to try sending people in by sea. We've got a couple of Portuguese feluccas – kind of fishing boats – that we're converting for the purpose. You'll be dropped at night somewhere on the south coast. You'll get detailed instructions nearer the time. I think you said you have contacts in that area.'

'In Marseilles, yes.' Richard felt a surge of something close to triumph. He was going to get what he wanted after all.

'By this,' Buckmaster went on, 'you will have deduced that we are going along with your desire to work with the escape line that brought you out last year. Normally POW escapes and evasions by aircrew are dealt with by MI9, but it has occurred to us that we shall also need to be able to get agents out in a hurry if things go wrong. So we are setting up our own section, code-named DF, which will work in cooperation with MI9 where necessary. You will come under that section from now on.'

Richard nodded. It didn't matter to him who his nominal masters were in England.

'This means,' Buckmaster said, 'that as well as assisting the *réseau* that brought you out with money, intelligence, equipment or whatever you will also be required to set up a completely separate line for the use of our agents should the need arise. I emphasise the *completely separate*. No one in the existing *réseau* must know of the existence of this second line. You will need to establish safe houses and also lines of communication via couriers who can carry messages or if required accompany agents.'

'Are these agents going to be coming out over the Pyrenees,' he asked, 'or by sea from Marseilles?'

'Preferably neither,' Buckmaster said. 'It all takes too long and there are too many problems associated with getting them across the demarcation line. To say nothing of getting them out of Spain without being interned – and you know as well as anyone how uncomfortable that can be. Ideally we want to set up a much more direct route by sea. The Channel ports are too closely guarded so I want you to investigate the Brittany coast with a view to finding places where a small boat could put in without being seen and take men off to a larger vessel, possibly a submarine, lying offshore. That will be another important part of your job.'

'Understood,' Richard said. 'You mentioned money and equipment. How are those going to be delivered?'

'By parachute drops. You will need to find suitable fields in remote areas where containers can be dropped and then arrange to have them collected and hidden. You will be accompanied by a wireless operator – you'll meet him later – and he will keep in touch with London and let us know what you need. When a drop is imminent you will get a coded message via the *messages personnels* broadcast by the BBC. Is that clear so far?'

'Perfectly.'

'There is one more thing you can do for us. We are desperately short of up-to-the-minute information about conditions in occupied France. We need to know exactly what documents are required by ordinary people. We need examples of up-to-date ration books, for example. Also information about how easy or otherwise it is to move around. What is public transport like? Can you easily buy rail tickets? How often are papers checked? You know the sort of thing. And also, of course, any strategic information that might be of use to the air force – the location of major fuel dumps, troop concentrations, etc. You should be able to gather quite a lot of information as you move around.'

'That shouldn't be a problem,' Richard agreed. 'But how do I get it back to London? Basic information can be sent by radio, of course, but how do I get examples of ration books back to you?'

'When you have that kind of thing to transmit you let us know and a light aircraft, probably a Lysander, will land at an agreed point and you can hand the documents to the pilot. In a case of real emergency, of course, you can come out yourself that way. Whatever happens, we shall expect to exfiltrate you at the end of six months, so you can come back here for an extended debriefing. Now, what else . . .? Yes, code names. The members of your second escape line must not know you as Ricardo Benedetti. That is the name you will live under but to them you will be known simply by the code name Lucien. I suggest that you also abandon any suggestion that you are Italian and conceal your limp, as far as possible. Then, if anything goes wrong, no one should be able to say anything that might lead the Gestapo to you. And for further security you will have a second code name, which will be used in all radio communications with London. All F section operatives are known by the names of trades or professions. You will be Artist. Any questions?'

Richard thought for a moment. 'It all seems quite clear so far, sir. If anything occurs to me I assume I can come back to you?'

'Of course. You will get all this in the form of written orders in the next day or two, anyway. Now, you're going to need to be on hand for the next few days for various purposes so I've arranged some accommodation for you.' Buckmaster reached into a drawer and took out a Yale key with a label attached. 'It's a pleasant little flat. The address is on the label. Just move in and make yourself at home. No one will bother you. Do you have any friends in town?'

'No,' Richard answered without hesitation. 'No one.'

'Probably just as well. But we can't have you moping around on your own all day. I'll fix something up. There are some delightful FANY girls based in town. I'm sure some of them will be only too glad to show you around.'

Richard protested that he was really perfectly happy on his own, but Buckmaster brushed the comment aside and ushered him to the door.

'We shall meet again in a week or so. Meanwhile, someone will contact you very soon. Just remember, nothing of what we've discussed must go beyond these four walls.'

'I'll remember,' Richard promised.

He hailed a taxi and within a matter of minutes found himself unlocking the door of a flat in a block just off the Kensington High Road. He had no idea who it belonged to and the owner seemed to have left no clues in the form of furnishings or personal belongings. It was as impersonal as a hotel room, but the decor was pleasant and when he investigated he found the kitchen cupboards stocked with a variety of tinned goods and the cocktail cabinet in the lounge provided with a range of drinks not normally obtainable on the open market. Someone had even made sure that there was fresh milk and eggs in the fridge and a loaf of bread in a crock on the kitchen counter.

He unpacked and had a wash and was just debating with himself whether to go out for a meal or to make do with a boiled egg when the doorbell rang. He approached carefully and looked out through the spyhole in the door. A girl in FANY uniform was standing outside. Richard opened the door and saw a slim, attractive girl whose face seemed vaguely familiar.

At the sight of him her lips parted in a delighted smile.

'Richard! It is you! When they said Richard Stevens I thought, it can't be the same one. But it is! How lovely to see you again.'

Richard stared at her. There was something about her, but he could not for the life of him think where he had seen her before. His mind ran frantically over the FANY girls at Wanborough, but he still couldn't place her.

'I'm sorry,' he said hesitantly.

Her smile turned to a small, provocative pout. 'You don't remember me, do you? Well, it was a long time ago. Priscilla? Priscilla Vance?'

As she spoke she reached up and pulled off her uniform cap, revealing raven hair caught in a sleek chignon. Suddenly Richard recalled a slight figure tottering off the stage in tears, to a background of jeers and laughter from the audience.

'Good Lord!' he exclaimed. 'Priscilla! Of course I remember. I just didn't recognise you in that uniform.'

Priscilla laughed. 'I know, it is pretty dire, isn't it? But I suppose there are worse.'

'I think you look very smart,' Richard said gallantly. 'Look, please do come in. Can I get you a drink?'

'Thanks. I'd love a pink gin, if you've got one.'

As he poured the drinks Richard said, 'You said "they" said Richard Stevens. Who are "they"?'

'Oh, apparently Maurice Buckmaster rang my CO and said he'd got someone who needed entertaining for a day or two. When I heard the name I thought it might just be you, so I volunteered. I'm so glad it is you.'

'Well, so am I,' Richard responded, handing her a glass. 'I mean, glad you volunteered. Cheers!'

'Cheers.'

'Do you often get asked to entertain people who are at a loose end?' Richard asked.

'Oh, from time to time,' she answered. 'I mean, it must be hard, waiting around . . .' Catching a change of expression on

Richard's face, she hurried on, 'Oh, don't worry, I'm not going to ask you embarrassing questions. We're not supposed to know what's going on, of course, but most of us can make a pretty good guess. And I just want to say I admire you enormously.' She smiled at him beguilingly. 'There, now we won't talk about it any more.'

There was a brief silence. To break it Richard said, 'Are you still dancing – I mean, when you're not doing your bit as a FANY?'

She shook her head sadly. 'Not now. After that awful shambles at Fairbourne when I fell flat on my backside in the middle of my solo I thought I'd never be able to face putting on a pair of ballet shoes again. But when the war started and ENSA was formed I thought it would be a chance to "do my bit" and dear old Monty let me join a concert party he was putting together.' She paused and looked at him. 'But you must know about that. Didn't Rose tell you?'

'I haven't seen Rose since . . .' Richard began and then stopped himself. He didn't want to discuss New Year's Eve with anyone. 'Since before the war,' he concluded.

'Then you don't know it was my fault she had that dreadful fall and hurt her ankle so badly?'

Richard started. 'Hurt her ankle? I had no idea.' He checked himself again and took refuge in a half-truth. 'I'm afraid I've lost touch with all the old Follies crowd.'

'What a pity!' Priscilla said, and added with a shrug, 'But then, I suppose these summer romances never last, do they? Anyway, that was the last straw as far as I was concerned. As soon as that tour was over I hung up my dancing shoes for good.' She put down her glass and leaned forward. 'Talking of which, how is your career going these days?'

Richard shrugged. 'On hold, like everyone else's – for the duration.'

Priscilla's expression became quite intense. 'But you

mustn't look at it like that, Richard. Otherwise, when the war is over, you will have been completely forgotten.'

'Well, no one knew about me in the first place,' Richard pointed out, mildly amused by her seriousness. 'So that will be nothing new.'

'I'm not joking!' she told him. 'It's important. I've been giving this sort of thing a lot of thought lately. It may feel now as if the war will go on for ever, but one day it will be over and then the whole of the arts and music establishment will have to be rebuilt. It will be an opportunity to make a fresh start, with new faces and new ideas. And you have to be ready to take advantage of that.'

Richard looked at her with new interest. This was a different person from the rather flighty girl he remembered. 'You really are serious about this, aren't you?'

Priscilla paused and took up her drink again. 'When I gave up dancing and realised I was never going to be a great performer I looked around for some other way of being involved in that world. It occurred to me that if I couldn't perform myself I could at least encourage other people, people with real talent, and perhaps help some new ventures to get off the ground. You probably know my father left me pretty well off and now that I'm over twenty-one I can do what I like with the money. And dear old Uncle Lionel is always terribly supportive about anything I want to do, and he knows all sorts of useful people.'

'You're an angel,' Richard said.

She giggled. 'Thanks, and you're quite sweet, too. No, it's all right. I know what a theatrical "angel" is – but I'm trying to do more than just put up money for new productions. I want to bring people together, creative people with new ideas, so we can start something exciting and innovative.'

'What sort of thing do you have in mind?' Richard was interested now.

'It's all pretty fluid at the moment, but I can tell you one thing. I learned something from that fiasco at the Follies, and that is that ordinary people can't enjoy opera and ballet because they don't understand them. They don't have any opportunity to learn about them. So, one thing I want to do is make ballet and opera accessible to ordinary people by taking it out into village halls and schools and anywhere that has a stage.'

'There is the Carl Rosa company already,' Richard pointed out.

'Yes, but they can't cover the whole country. And they're a bit hidebound and traditional. Like I said before, I want our productions to be innovative.'

'*Our* productions?' Richard queried.

She relaxed and laughed. 'Oh, listen to me! Anybody would think I had an opera company ready to go. No, what I'm saying is, when the time comes and all you brilliant singers and dancers and musicians come out of the forces, I want there to be somewhere for you to go, somewhere where you can swap ideas and create the musical theatre of the future. And I want to be part of that. Does that sound terribly pretentious?'

'I think it sounds wonderful,' Richard said. 'It's what this country really needs.'

'And I want you to be part of it too, Richard,' Priscilla said. 'You have a wonderful voice. You mustn't waste it.'

He sighed and said quietly, 'Much as I should like to say yes I don't think I have to tell you why I can't make any plans for the future. It's quite possible I shan't be around at the end of the war.'

She leaned over and caught hold of his hand. 'You mustn't think like that. I know what you are doing is dangerous. But then, I could walk out of here and be blown to smithereens by a bomb. We just have to go on believing that we will be here when it's all over, and plan accordingly.'

'So what do you expect me to do?' he asked.

'I want you to meet some people,' she said. 'I'm sort of collecting them. Mostly young people, connected with music and the theatre – and some older ones too who want to see things changing. We've got a few days, I don't know how long, but at least I can introduce you to one or two people who will remember you when the time comes.'

'All right,' Richard said. He felt as if his life had taken a sudden, disconcerting change of direction. It seemed extraordinary to be talking like this when in a few days he would be in France, but he knew he would be a fool to turn down the opportunity.

'Good!' Priscilla exclaimed. 'Now, where are we going to dine tonight?'

Taken off balance by yet another sudden change of tack Richard murmured that he had been thinking of boiling an egg and then pulled himself together and added, 'But not any more. Where would you like to go?'

He did a quick calculation. He guessed that Priscilla was used to eating in some pretty exclusive restaurants but his pay had been mounting up while he was at the various training establishments and there had been little temptation to spend it at home in Didsbury, so he reckoned he could afford whatever she suggested for one night.

'They still do a pretty good menu at the Savoy,' she said. 'How about that?'

'The Savoy it is, then,' he agreed.

It was true that, within the constraints of rationing and the total shortage of any luxury items, the Savoy did a good job of disguising some fairly unpromising ingredients. Also, there was an orchestra and the dance floor was crowded with men and women, most of them in uniform. For the first time since those *thés dansants* at the Grand Hotel in Fairbourne with Rose, Richard found himself actively enjoying dancing. He was delighted to discover that his injury no longer bothered him and he had not lost the knack. In fact, he was aware that as they spun round the floor in a quickstep other dancers cast admiring looks in their direction.

At the end of the evening he delivered Priscilla back to her guardian's house in Mayfair and was able to say quite genuinely, 'Thank you. I haven't enjoyed myself so much for ages.'

13

Rose stood and looked at herself in the long mirror in the studio. In the unflattering black woollen tights and the simple practice tunic it was painfully obvious that what she had said to Sonia, half in jest, during their first conversation was all too true. She had developed muscles in all the wrong places. To make matters worse, three months of being cosseted by her mother and the Willises had replaced the weight she had lost at Hightop Farm, with interest. Her waist had thickened, her thighs were flabby and her shoulders would have looked more fitting on a navvy than a ballet dancer. Added to that was the fact that, in spite of three weeks of intensive practice at the studio and at home, she was still very unfit. The proof of that was the sweat that ran down her flushed face and her laboured breathing.

Sonia had been called away to the telephone, giving Rose a much-needed respite. She straightened up, rested one hand on the barre and raised one leg sideways. Once it would have required hardly any effort to lift it so that her foot was level with her shoulder. Now it was a struggle to get it past the horizontal. She lowered it again and looked at herself in the mirror. She had lost her 'turn-out' too. In spite of Sonia's constant prodding her feet refused to stay in fifth position and her knees were resolutely determined to face the front instead of pointing sideways. Rose leaned her head against the mirror and almost gave way to tears.

When Sonia re-entered the room, however, she straightened

up immediately and rubbed her arm across her forehead.
'Shall we try the adagio now?'

Sonia looked at her. 'Rose, dear, are you sure you want to go
on? You look all in.'

'I'm fine!' Rose insisted. 'I'll never get fit if I give up as soon
as I get a bit tired.'

She struggled on to the end of the lesson, aware that Sonia
was deliberately ignoring some of her mistakes, furious with
the body that refused to perform to her satisfaction.

Back at the flat she found a letter on the mat. It had been
redirected from Wimborne but a glance at the envelope
quickly destroyed any hope that it might be the longed-for
reply from Richard. The handwriting was unmistakably Sally
Castle's. Still, Sally was always good for a laugh, with her racy
gossip, and it was some weeks since Rose had last heard from
her. She took the letter up to the kitchen, put on the kettle and
sat down to read.

Sally rattled on in her usual exuberant manner about work
at the Windmill Theatre and the endless succession of young
men who seemed to be queuing up at the stage door to take her
out. *Mind you*, she added, *I'm getting a bit fed up with working
here. Six shows a day is no fun and the blokes in the audience don't
really want to watch the dancers. All they care about is ogling the
nudes. Still, it's work, and there isn't that much of it about these
days.*

Then came a paragraph that struck Rose like a blow in the
stomach.

*I managed to get a few days off, and Bill took me to
Bournemouth for the weekend. You remember Bill? He's the
dishy Canadian I told you about. OK, I know you don't
approve of that sort of thing but there is a war on, you
know, and who knows when you'll meet a nice chap again if
you don't take your chances when they're offered? Anyway,*

*we had a gorgeous weekend, staying at the Grand, no
expense spared! But a really weird thing happened while I
was there. I was doing a bit of shopping and I saw Richard!
He was on the other side of the road and I couldn't get
across because of the traffic but I shouted and waved and I'm
sure he recognised me but instead of waving back he looked
as if he'd seen a ghost! Then he jumped on a moving bus, as
if he was desperate to get away. Isn't that strange?*

Rose lifted her eyes from the letter. So, that was that, then.
Richard was in England, and clearly determined not to have
any contact with her. So much so that he would go to any
lengths to avoid speaking to someone who knew her. She
wondered whether Sally could have been mistaken. Maybe it
was just someone who looked like him . . . But she knew that
she was clutching at straws.

She put her feet into a bowl of salt water and whimpered
aloud as it entered the open blisters on her toes. She sat with
her head drooping and asked herself for the first time whether
the struggle was worth it. She reckoned that if she persisted she
could eventually get back to a reasonable level of fitness and
regain enough technique maybe to get her to Grade 5 or 6. But
she had passed them at fifteen and she knew only too well that
that level was a far cry from what was expected in the
ruthlessly competitive world of the professional dancer.
Would it not be better to give up now?

There was one simple fact that prevented her from adopting
that solution. If she gave up her ambition to dance again she
did not know what else to do with her life. True, she could
continue to run the shop. Her mother seemed in no hurry to
return to London and there was still enough trade to provide
her with a living. She could do some voluntary work to help the
war effort and wait . . . But for what? For Richard to write?
For all she knew he could be married to someone else by now.

And what about when the war was over? She had turned down her chance of marriage and a family and she was not going to fool herself that there would be another. Too many young men were being killed and the competition for those that survived would be intense. The only future she could foresee if she gave up her efforts to return to the stage was as an embittered old maid facing years of fitting shoes to sweaty feet.

She sat up and lifted her feet out of the water. 'I'm not giving up!' she said aloud as she dabbed them dry. 'I'll keep at it if it kills me!'

The days after his meeting with Priscilla were hectic beyond all Richard's expectations. Victor appeared the following morning, bringing with him his written orders, which he was instructed to memorise. He also brought a dapper little Italian tailor to take his measurements. The following day he returned with a shirt, tie and jacket of Italian style and, unbelievably, an apparently genuine Italian Army uniform. Richard was then whisked off to a basement room in some anonymous building that had been fitted out as a photographer's studio and had his picture taken, head and shoulders and full length, in both outfits.

At Victor's suggestion he also made a will. He had little to leave, except for whatever arrears of pay might be owing to him, some sheet music and a few small personal items. He bequeathed them all to his parents, but Victor pointed out, as gently as possible, that in these times of heavy bombing it was just possible that his parents might predecease him and he should name a residuary legatee. After some thought Richard added a sentence stating that in that event everything he possessed should go to a Mrs Matthew Armitage, née Rose Taylor, of Wimborne in Dorset.

Victor also handed him a packet of plain postcards.

'Write a few of those and address them to your parents,' he

said. 'We'll see that they are posted off at suitable intervals from various different places. You have told them to forward any mail to the Inter-Services Liaison Bureau, haven't you?'

Richard nodded and Victor said, 'We'll take care of anything that comes for you until you get home.'

Writing the postcards was one of the most difficult things Richard had been asked to do. It was very hard to think of cheerful, anodyne messages that would reassure them without giving any hint of where he was or what he was doing. On the first he wrote: *Just to let you know I am fine and everything is going well. I'm very busy and can't see much chance of leave for a while yet. Hope you are both well. Your loving son, Richard.* On the second he wrote: *Still very busy. Sorry I can't write at greater length. Everything is fine so don't worry about me. Give my regards to the family. Love, Richard.* On the third he put: *Just a line to let you know I'm OK. I still travel about a good deal so I'm not sure when I can get home again. I've made some new friends and taken up chess in my spare time. Hope you are both well. Love, Richard.* After three or four more in the same vein he gave up and hoped that those would be enough to last out until he got back – if he ever did.

While this was going on, Priscilla was pursuing her own plans for him. On the first day he received a telephone call inviting him to dine at the home of her guardian, Sir Lionel, and his wife. There he was introduced to an eminent conductor, a young man in naval uniform who was, he was assured, an extremely talented stage designer, and an Italian tenor who had fled the fascist regime of Mussolini before the outbreak of war. He was now working as a waiter in an Italian restaurant and expecting daily to be interned as an enemy alien.

When the meal was over Priscilla said, 'Richard, I've never forgotten you singing that beautiful duet from *The Pearl Fishers* with Franklyn Bell.'

'I only ever sang it once,' Richard pointed out.

'That's because Frank's voice simply wasn't up to it and he couldn't bear the thought that you were putting him in the shade. Do you still sing it?'

'I haven't sung it for years.'

'But you remember it?'

'Of course. It's not something you forget.'

'Then sing it with Carlo, for me – please! Maestro, you will accompany them, won't you?'

Richard embarked on the duet somewhat tentatively, hoping he could still remember the words and intensely grateful for the coaching he had received in recent weeks from Laslo Brodic. His misgivings soon disappeared as the music took over, and he was pleased to find that Carlo's voice was a perfect match for his own. When they finished, the whole company was lavish in its praise and Priscilla glowed with pride, as if he were her personal discovery.

He soon came to appreciate the force of her offhand remark that her guardian knew some useful people. The next day they lunched with a well-known impresario and dined with members of the Covent Garden opera chorus. For the first time Richard found he had an entrée into the kind of company he had always dreamed of keeping. Priscilla seemed to know everyone and to be very popular. Richard tried to suppress the uncharitable thought of the twin clichés that 'money talks' and 'it's not what you know, it's who you know'.

Whatever his doubts, the fact remained that he found he enjoyed her company more and more as the days passed. Towards the end of the week they went to the Savoy again and danced, and when they left it did not surprise him unduly to hear himself saying, 'How about coming back to the flat for a nightcap?'

Nor was he particularly surprised when she agreed. What did surprise him was her eager response to his kisses and the lack of resistance when he slid his hand into the front of her blouse. It was almost a year since he had said goodbye to Chantal and he had not been with a woman since, and he had the impression that Priscilla was at least as experienced as he was. It was only when they were in bed and he heard her small cry of pain that he realised she was still a virgin.

'Why?' he asked, stroking her cheek in the drowsy aftermath of passion. 'Why did you let me?'

She gazed at him with huge, dark eyes, the pupils dilated with satiety, and murmured, 'Because you're going away, and I don't know how much time we have together. And because I think I'm in love with you.'

He kissed her and held her close. She nestled against him and was soon asleep, but he lay wide eyed in the dark, overpowered by a sense of guilt. First Rose, then Chantal, and now Priscilla. Was he incapable of being faithful – or could he blame it all on the war and the prospect of imminent death?

Priscilla had hardly left the next morning before Victor appeared at his front door.

'You're on your way, old chap,' he said cheerfully. 'Pack all your gear. Buckmaster wants to see you before you go.'

At Buckmaster's flat they found their head of section waiting with a trim, dark-haired woman in the uniform of a squadron leader in the WAAF, who was introduced as Vera Atkins.

'You'll find a complete set of clothes laid out in the spare bedroom there,' she said briskly. 'Take off all your own things and put them in the empty suitcase. We'll take care of them till you get back. Make sure you take off everything and don't transfer anything from your pockets. No letters, no photographs, nothing. There mustn't be anything that could connect you with England. Victor will come in with you to make sure you don't forget anything.'

In the bedroom Richard found the Italian suit, together with a shirt and tie and underclothes, all of which were either made in Italy or had been made from Italian fabrics and had Italian makers' labels sewn into them. Even the shoes, which still had the artificial 'lift' built into them to exaggerate his limp, were Italian. On the floor beside the bed was a small case containing a spare set of underwear, pyjamas, a razor and toilet things, also of Italian origin. There was even a jar of the pomade that Italian men often used on their hair, the smell of which transported Richard instantly into the hot, crowded gallery of La Scala opera house in Milan.

He undressed, under the tactful but unwavering gaze of Victor, and put on the other clothes. Feeling in the pockets of the jacket, he found an old ticket for a bus on a route in Milan and a screwed-up sweet wrapper from an Italian confectioner. There were also a few shreds of tobacco, the smell of which was unmistakably French. Richard was amazed at such attention to detail, but found it undeniably reassuring.

He placed his own army uniform and the rest of his clothes in the suitcase, as instructed, and Victor handed him a large envelope in which to put his wallet and identity documents and various other small personal items. Then he nodded towards Richard's hand. 'That'll have to come off, I'm afraid.'

Richard looked at the gold signet ring he wore on the little finger of his left hand. It had been a twenty-first birthday present from his parents and was one of the few objects he owned of any value. After a brief hesitation he removed it, not without difficulty, and asked for a second envelope. When this was produced he wrote on it, 'Mrs Rose Armitage, née Taylor, to be handed to her in the event of my failure to return.'

Back in the living room of the flat Vera Atkins checked his pockets again and then handed him his new papers, one set in the name of Ricardo Benedetti, another for Lucien Du-frais. As well as the necessary identity documents and ration cards and his discharge papers from the Italian army there was a creased photograph of a middle-aged woman in a dark dress with her hair drawn back in a bun. On the back was written '*Al mio caro filio, Mamma*'. There was also an older picture of the same woman, with a man, obviously her husband, and a small boy who might very well have been Richard. He studied them in wonder and suddenly felt a lump in his throat. It was almost as if his own parents had been obliterated and these strangers put in their place. He swallowed and got control of himself.

Vera handed him a wallet containing both Italian and French money. 'This should keep you going until you meet up with your friends. It's a fairly substantial sum so try to hide it somewhere as soon as you find a place to stay. You'll have to think up a plausible reason for it in case you're stopped and searched.'

'I'm supposed to be supplying the *réseau* with funds,' Richard said. 'What about the money for that?'

'You'll get that in a parachute drop,' Buckmaster said, 'as soon as your wireless operator lets us know the place. It's far too risky for you to carry that sort of sum with you into the occupied zone.'

'What about this wireless operator?' Richard enquired. 'When do I meet up with him?'

'He'll travel separately. Safer that way. In fact, he's going to be dropped in by parachute to northern France. You need to give us a rendezvous and a recognition code so he can get in touch. Any suggestions?'

Richard thought. 'Tell him to come to the Café Bleu – Lille, Rue de la Paix. Tell him to ask the waiter if the cabaret singer who wears the red shirt is still performing there. If the waiter says yes, that means I've arrived and everything is OK. In that

case, he should send me a note saying I owe him some money –
fifty francs – to settle a bet. Then I'll contact him.'

'Got that, Vera?' Buckmaster asked.

Vera was taking rapid notes in shorthand. 'Yes, got it.
That's all, I think,' she said.

'One more thing.' Buckmaster reached into his pocket and
produced a small box, which he handed to Richard. Inside was
a pair of gold cufflinks set with onyx. Buckmaster said, 'You'll
find they are Italian-hallmarked and were made by a jeweller in
Milan. You might find them handy to pawn, if you get short of
cash. Otherwise they're yours to keep. A little token of thanks
from the government. The stone in one will open. Try it.'

Richard fiddled with the links for a moment and the onyx in
one swung back with a little click to reveal a small cavity. In it
was a little yellow capsule.

'It's what we call an L-pill,' Buckmaster said. 'L for lethal. It
contains cyanide. If you bite it death follows in seconds. If it is
swallowed it takes several hours to dissolve in the stomach.
You can safely carry it in your cheek for a period of seven or
eight hours if the need arises. We can be sure of that because
some of our boffins have slept with one in their mouth to prove
it. I'm not advocating that you should make use of it, but if the
situation arises where you feel that there is no other way out
and that a quick exit is preferable to whatever else is in store,
it's there. All right?'

Richard contemplated the capsule for a moment. Suddenly
he was face to face with the fear he had been trying to suppress
since his first interview in that bare room in the Northumberland Hotel. He drew a deep breath, clicked the hidden
compartment shut and inserted the cufflink into his shirt-
sleeve.

'All right,' he affirmed. 'Is that all?'

In the street outside a surprisingly opulent car was drawn up
to the kerb with a FANY driver behind the wheel.

Buckmaster shook his hand. 'Good luck, Richard. I'll have a large whisky waiting for you when you get back.'

Richard gave him a lopsided grin. 'Make it a dry martini,' he said.

He got into the back seat, with Victor beside him. Before long they were heading north, into the open fields of Bedfordshire. It was only then that Richard remembered he had not said goodbye to Priscilla.

14

Merry had spent the summer touring remote outposts in Scotland. He had never visited the area before and the austere grandeur of the scenery at once soothed and exhilarated him. There was little evidence of enemy activity and sometimes, leaning on the rail of a ferry heading for one of the islands, or nursing the old lorry along the edge of a loch, he was almost able to forget the war. His company, made up of familiar friends together with a few new faces, was talented and the bored soldiers they performed for were for the most part almost comically grateful for any form of entertainment. After the shows there were convivial dinners in the mess and late-night, alcohol-fuelled exchanges of stories around the bar. And occasionally there were precious moments of solitude and repose when he could drink in the beauty of his surroundings. But the routine of travel, unload, rehearse, perform, sleep and load up again to move on was gruelling, and by midsummer he was very tired.

Exhaustion made him more aware than ever of the nagging pain of separation from Felix. They wrote regularly, although the vagaries of the post and the constant change of location meant that Merry tended to receive the letters in batches at irregular intervals. Worse than that was the awareness that everything they wrote might be read by the censor. Merry appreciated the need for security, but he resented the fact that, while other men could include extravagant expressions of love in letters to wives and girlfriends, he and Felix had to restrict themselves to the language of casual friendship. As the weeks passed he could not suppress the feeling that the bond between them was slowly loosening.

Felix wrote that his most recent operation had been a success and that he now had almost full use of his right hand. Later he wrote from the workshop established by McIndoe to say that the work was tedious but that at last he felt he was being of some use and the constant exercise of the atrophied muscles was bringing results. Then came the letter Merry had dreaded.

> *Wonderful news! I'm back on the active service list! Not flying, of course, that would be too much to hope for at this stage, but I'm being posted to a squadron as intelligence officer. (All right, no nasty cracks about the gulf between intelligence, human, and intelligence, military – I've heard them all before.) Of course, it's not the same as being up there at the sharp end, but at least I shall be back with a fighting unit again and able to make a contribution. And who knows, I might be able to persuade someone to let me get back into one of the old kites again, just to get the feeling of the air under my wings. I can't tell you where I shall be, of course, but when you get back to London we must meet up for a drink.*

Merry laid the letter down and gazed unseeingly at the walls of the small room he had been allotted. He did not know whether to feel pleased for Felix or sorry for himself. It was what Felix desperately wanted, he knew, but it meant that he was no longer in the comparative safety of the hospital or the work-shop, under the protection of the Red Cross, but on an airfield that was probably subject to daily bombing by the Luftwaffe. And as for the thought of him being allowed to fly again . . .! He could only hope that his superior officers would have more sense than to let him near the cockpit of an aeroplane, but no one knew better than he did how persuasive Felix could be when it suited him.

News from the front was not encouraging. In the Western Desert the army had lost ninety-one tanks in the abortive 'Operation Battleaxe'. Malta was under siege and all attempts to reach the island were frustrated by the German and Italian naval and air forces. Then, on 22 June, Merry heard cheers coming from the group of men clustered around a radio. Hitler, for some reason no one could fathom, had invaded Russia. This meant that the Nazis would now have to fight on two fronts and Winston Churchill was quick to capitalise on the situation by offering aid to the Russians.

In the middle of July Merry received a large envelope addressed in Felix's handwriting and labelled 'Photographs, please do not bend'. Shaking out the contents he discovered two pictures. The first was cut from a newspaper and showed a group of airmen standing by a Spitfire. Felix was among them, but his uniform cap shaded his face and in the blurred newsprint the scarring hardly showed. The second picture was obviously a posed studio portrait and showed Felix full-face and without a hat. Merry peered at it closely, unable to decide whether it was just clever lighting or whether McIndoe's surgery had been far more successful than he had ever thought possible. Either way, the effect was remarkable. The photographer had managed somehow to suggest that the scarring enhanced Felix's good looks rather than detracting from them, as if the damaged side of his face provided a romantic counterpoint to the undamaged side, which might, if repeated, have seemed too bland in its perfection. But it was the expression on Felix's face which made the breath catch in Merry's throat. He was gazing straight into the lens of the camera, his eyes dreamy and a faint smile touching his lips.

Merry unfolded the accompanying letter and read:

A really extraordinary thing has happened. A couple of days ago the CO called me in and told me that the Air Ministry was sending a photographer down to take pictures of the squadron. You know the sort of public relations exercise that these people are so fond of – our brave boys, etc., etc. There were to be pictures of ground crew readying the planes and pilots about to take off and so on and also studio portraits of all the officers. The CO, being a decent sort of cove, thought I might find that a bit embarrassing and offered to give me 24 hours' leave if I wanted it. Well, I thought it over and eventually decided that the public ought to see the less glamorous side of the picture – not just the Brylcreem boys but a hint of the price some of us are paying to keep the Luftwaffe off their backs. So I said I'd stay around and have my pic taken with the rest.

Now I come to the really amazing bit. I was in the mess, having a drink with some of the lads before lunch, when in comes the CO with the photographer and – you've probably already guessed – it was none other than Harriet. Well, I couldn't duck out at that point so I just had to stay and brazen it out and I must say she behaved extraordinarily coolly. The CO took her round, introducing her, and as you can imagine the chaps practically had their tongues hanging out. She was always a looker and she's improved over the years if anything. By the time they got to me I knew she'd already spotted me so it wasn't a total shock and she just smiled and held out her hand and said, 'We've already met. How are you, Ned?' Pretty acute of her to remember that I'm Ned in the RAF, after calling me Felix for years, don't you think?

Well, of course, that sealed it. The CO looked mightily

relieved — looking after the fair sex isn't exactly his cup of tea — and handed her over to me for the rest of the day. I must say, I think on the whole we both handled it pretty well. Of course, all the others were dying to chat her up so there wasn't any difficulty about making small talk over lunch, but then I had to take her over to the room we'd set aside for the portraits and generally take charge of wheeling in the next customer and smoothing out any wrinkles. I have to hand it to her, she is very professional and very good at putting people at ease. Even some of the pimply youths who pass as pilot officers these days should come out looking reasonably human. Anyway, she decided to keep me to last and when we'd got through the rest and were on our own she apologised very nicely for dumping me when I was in the hospital. She said, quite reasonably I thought, that she was very immature then and simply had never had to cope with any unpleasantness and didn't know what to do. And she pointed out that if she hadn't been so fond of me it wouldn't have been so difficult. Anyway, we agreed to let bygones be bygones and I asked if I could take her to the local for a drink when she had finished. She said she had to get back to town for dinner with an old family friend but we've agreed to keep in touch. I'm glad we've met up again and sorted things out. I suppose it has been niggling away at the back of my mind and now I can forget about it.

Merry laid the letter on his table and pressed his thumb and forefinger into the corners of his eyes. It had been a trying day. He had greeted Felix's letter as a welcome oasis of comfort before getting ready for the performance – and now this!

He took up the sheet of paper and looked through it again. Certain phrases might have been written in red ink, to his eyes.

She was always a looker and she's improved over the years if
anything . . . I must say, I think on the whole we both handled it
pretty well . . . she apologised very nicely for dumping me when I
was in the hospital . . . we agreed to let bygones be bygones and I
asked if I could take her to the local for a drink when she had
finished . . . I'm glad we've met up again . . .

He turned back to the photograph. It was clear that Felix
was contemplating something that gave him great pleasure. He
was looking straight at the camera and behind the camera was
– Harriet Forsyth! Merry gazed at the picture for a long time,
then he put it carefully back in the envelope. A memory came
back to him from learning Morse code during a brief stint as a
Boy Scout. *Dot-dash-dot* – the letter R for Roger. *Message*
received and understood!

Returning to his temporary base at Inverness a month later,
Merry found that at last the long-awaited order had arrived
summoning him and his company back to London and
granting them two weeks' leave. He wrote to Felix, asking
whether there was any chance that he might be able to get
away and suggesting that they spend the time at the house in
Seaford. On the train south he struggled with the thoughts that
had been haunting him since he received the photograph. In
vain he told himself that he was being stupid, but the knowledge that Felix was seeing Harriet again brought back too
many painful memories. For a whole summer he had watched
in bitterness and frustration while Felix paraded her as his
mistress. Now he was terribly afraid that he might be yielding
again to the pressure to conform. Harriet was, as she always
had been, a 'catch', beautiful, aristocratic and rich, the perfect
consort for the Hon. Edward Mountjoy, and Merry knew that
part of Felix still longed for acceptance in the conventional
world in which he had grown up. Had he decided now that
that was, after all, the path he wanted to follow?

As soon as he walked into his office in London, the phone rang. It was Felix.

'I've managed to wangle a week's leave. I'll meet you at the house tomorrow afternoon.'

He sounded pleased but there was something else – a suggestion in his voice that he was keeping something back. At least, so it seemed to Merry's hyper-sensitive ear through the crackle of a poor line.

'Is everything all right?' he asked.

'Absolutely tickety-boo,' Felix assured him exuberantly. 'See you tomorrow.'

The next morning Merry had an interview with George Black before starting his leave. The one-time impresario greeted him genially.

'Congratulations, old man! I've heard nothing but good reports from Scotland. *Definitely a cut above the usual standard – thoroughly professional – highly entertaining.* I'll spare your blushes but that's a sample of the sort of reaction we've been getting.'

Merry gave him one of his self-deprecating smiles. 'I'm glad we went down all right. The lads worked pretty hard. Mind you, up there I think they'd have been delighted with a troupe of performing fleas.' He paused and scratched his neck ruefully. 'Or perhaps I mean midges.'

Black chuckled. 'Anyway, it's good to have you back. Now . . .' He seated himself behind his desk and became business-like. 'About the future. Bearing in mind the problems you experienced last winter, how do you fancy spending this one in sunnier climes?'

Merry's stomach turned over. 'You're sending us overseas?'

'Time some of the lads at the front had a bit of first-rate entertainment, don't you think?'

'Where?' Merry said, unthinkingly.

Black tapped his finger against the side of his nose. 'You

know I can't tell you that. All I can say is you'll need to draw tropical kit before you leave.'

Merry did a quick mental survey of the current battle-grounds. North Africa, the Middle East, the Far East – all would be classed as tropical. It could be anywhere. He said, 'I imagine we'll be gone for some time, then.'

'Several months, I'm afraid,' Black agreed. 'But that's war for you. These two weeks I'm giving you now will be embarkation leave. You sail at the beginning of September, so you'll have about a week to get yourselves organised.'

'Am I taking the same company?' Merry asked, trying to put his mind to the practical implications.

'By and large, with one or two additions.'

'A week's not long to rehearse new routines. We really need a change of programme. We were all getting pretty stale.'

'That won't be a problem,' Black said. 'I'm sending you on a nice sea cruise to start with. You'll have plenty of time to rehearse on board ship.'

Merry broke the news to his company, receiving varying reactions, and then grabbed his case and headed for the station. He felt sick with foreboding. The thought that now he was going to be separated from Felix for an even longer period only compounded his anguish. He knew he could cope with loneliness, he had learned that through bitter experience, but he was less sure about Felix, who had always been blessed with the talent for easy popularity but who was, at base, more needy and insecure. Even if nothing had happened yet it would be so easy for him to drift back into his old relationship with Harriet. He ended the journey in a mood of stoic resignation, prepared to face the worst.

The first thing he noticed when he got out of the taxi was that the garden, which when he had last seen it had pre-sented a picture of sad neglect, had been tidied up. The lawn had been mown, the roses pruned, the errant fronds of wisteria around the door and windows had been cut back and the flower beds weeded. There were even one or two bright patches of annuals, marigolds and antirrhinums. He wondered who was responsible. Presumably Mrs Pierce, the woman who came in once a week to air the place and check that there was no damage, must have taken it upon herself to engage a gardener and would present him with the bill in due course.

As he opened the gate Felix appeared at the front door in his shirtsleeves and waved, but instead of coming to meet him he stepped back into the hallway. Merry followed him in, momentarily blinded by the change from bright sunlight to shadow. He dropped his suitcase on the floor, heard the door close behind him and turned into an embrace so passionate that it banished all suspicions.

When his mouth was free again, Felix murmured in his ear, 'Oh God, I've missed you! This summer seems to have gone on for ever.'

Merry could only hold him and bury his face in his hair and mumble, 'Oh, Felix! Thank God! Thank God!' After a little he added, 'Shall we go straight upstairs?'

To his surprise Felix drew back. 'Later. Soon. I expect you could do with a cup of tea, couldn't you?' He was sidling round him, moving towards the kitchen door. 'Go in the sitting room. I'll put the kettle on.'

Merry looked at him. There was a familiar expression on his face – a sense of excitement and a glint of mischief, as if in anticipation of some elaborate practical joke. He opened his mouth to protest that he didn't want tea at that moment, and then closed it again and went into the sitting room as he was bidden. The first thing that struck him was that the furniture had been moved. The settee had been pulled across in front of the empty fireplace and the table that had once stood in the bay window was now over against the wall, where his old piano used to be. And the piano was . . . nowhere to be seen. Then he turned his head and there, in the bay, its polished mahogany surface reflecting the play of light and shade from the garden outside, stood a baby grand.

'What the . . .?'

Felix was standing in the doorway. 'It's a piano,' he said helpfully.

'But how did it get here?'

'Two men brought it in a van.'

'But you can't have . . . you haven't *bought* it, have you?'

'Well, I didn't steal it, if that's what's worrying you. Oh, by the way, I gave the old one to the village hall. I hope that's all right.'

'God help the village hall,' Merry commented. 'But *why*, Felix?'

'Because you always refused to play the old one as it wouldn't stay in tune,' Felix said. 'I asked Boosey and Hawkes months back to keep their eyes open for something decent and a couple of weeks ago they got on to me and said there was an old dear in Tunbridge Wells that wanted to get rid of this one, so I told them to bring it straight over. I hope it's OK. They say it's a good one.'

Merry moved towards the instrument. 'Felix, it's a Bechstein. Of course it's good. But you can't just buy me something like this.'

'Why not?' Felix came farther into the room. 'It's your birthday next week, isn't it? Think of it as a birthday present.'

'My birthday?' Merry queried, astounded. 'Yes, but how did you know?'

Felix laughed. 'Two years ago you stood us all drinks after the show to celebrate. Don't you remember?'

'Yes, but I'd no idea you did.'

'Oh, I made a note of it,' Felix said, smiling.

Merry looked again at the piano and said painfully, 'But I can't accept something like this, Felix. It's far too expensive.'

'But you know I can afford it,' Felix said, 'thanks to Auntie Betty's little legacy. And it'll give me pleasure too. Now I can insist on a private command performance every evening.'

'But it isn't fair,' Merry continued to protest. 'I could never give you anything to match it.'

Felix came to him and laid his hands on his shoulders. 'My dear old Merry, you cancelled all possible debts between us in ten minutes last November, when you gave me back a reason for living. That's worth any number of pianos.' He kissed him briefly. 'Aren't you going to try it? I had it tuned and the old guy who did it said it had an excellent tone.'

Merry sat down on the piano stool and ran his fingers over the keys. The tone, as predicted, was superb – mellow and rich, almost indistinguishable from a full-sized grand. He played a rising fountain of arpeggios.

Felix grinned, satisfied. 'I'll make the tea.'

Merry let his fingers wander until they found their way into Liszt's 'Liebestraum'. When he had finished Felix was standing in the doorway again. He was holding a bottle of champagne and two glasses.

'I changed my mind about the tea,' he said. 'Shall we take these upstairs with us?'

In the bedroom Felix uncorked the champagne and handed Merry a glass.

'Welcome home. It's wonderful to see you.'

'And you,' Merry replied fondly, and added, 'And while we're talking of seeing . . .' He took Felix's chin and turned his face to the light from the window.

Harriet's camera had not lied. The grafts had knitted together and the scarring between them had faded to white lines. The right side of Felix's mouth was no longer pulled up and the corner of the eye pulled down in a permanent leer, and both nostrils were more or less symmetrical. The result was not perfect and never would be, but a casual glance would not provoke the sort of shocked reaction they had seen from that young nurse.

'Well?' Felix asked.

'It's amazing!' Merry replied. 'I would never have believed the results could be as good as this a few months ago.'

Felix nodded happily. 'McIndoe's done a good job, hasn't he? He's as pleased as Punch. I'm his star exhibit.'

'Well, he had a pretty good model to work from,' Merry commented.

Felix shrugged slightly and his face clouded. 'More importantly, I still had plenty of skin left for him to work with. Some of the others . . .' He left the sentence unfinished.

Merry said softly, 'I know. But let's not think about them just now.'

'No, you're right.' Felix raised his glass and smiled. 'We've got a whole week together and we're not even going to think about the bloody war!'

'I'll drink to that!' Merry agreed.

Over dinner that night – meat-and-potato pie left by Mrs Pierce, washed down with a bottle of claret from Colonel Merryweather's dwindling cellar – Felix said, 'Well, how was Scotland?'

'Bloody awful most of the time,' Merry replied. 'It rained almost every day and when the rain stopped the midges came out.'

'Ah,' Felix said. 'I remember the midges.'

Merry looked at him. 'You've been to Scotland?'

Felix dropped his gaze, his tone non-committal. 'Once or twice.'

Merry was tempted to ask for details but he restrained himself. He knew from experience that it did not pay to probe for details of Felix's former life. Instead he said, 'I'm being unjust, actually. Some of the time it was wonderful. The scenery is superb, of course. And we did have our lighter moments.'

Felix's face brightened. He was always eager for amusing anecdotes. 'Go on.'

'Well, I suppose the funniest was when we played to an artillery company based right up in the far north-west. It was miles from anywhere and it had been raining all day, as usual. When we got there the whole base was a sea of mud. We couldn't get the truck anywhere near the mess hut where we were to perform and half a dozen squaddies had a hell of a job manhandling the piano along a trail of half-submerged duckboards. Anyway, they managed it in the end and we had a quick run through and then we were invited to eat in the officers' mess while the other ranks had their dinner. So, after the meal, there we were, all ready to start the show. What I hadn't noticed was that there was a pond just behind the mess hut and it must have been full of frogspawn a week or so back. I sat down at the piano to play the opening number and when I opened the lid the keyboard was covered in tiny froglets. The silly buggers had been down to the pond and filled the piano with them.'

Felix was crowing with laughter. 'Go on! What happened?'

'Well, you can imagine the chaos. The frogs went jumping all over the place. The chaps in the front rows were trying to catch them, the ones at the back were on their feet trying to see what was going on, officers shouting orders and my company corpsing themselves with laughter. Order was restored eventually and the show went down really well. But I think the bit the audience enjoyed most was the unrehearsed opening!'

'But the piano still played?'

'Fortunately. At least the squaddies had had the sense not to put the water in with the frogs.'

Felix sat back and took out his cigarette case. He offered it to

Merry, and when he refused with a regretful shake of his head he took out a cigarette and lit it. 'Any other incidents?' he prompted.

Merry watched him smoke for a minute, then leaned across and took the cigarette out of his mouth. He treated himself to a couple of luxurious drags and handed it back. Felix drew on it once, then stubbed it out.

'Sorry. It's not fair of me to smoke when you can't.'

'There was one other thing,' Merry went on. 'It's funny to look back on, but it was a bit nerve-racking at the time. Did I tell you that one of the acts is a female impersonator? Lad called Clive Crawley. Not much to look at normally, and straight as a die, but when he gets his slap on he makes an extraordinarily attractive woman. Not your pantomime dame, something much more sophisticated. He does an amazing impression of Marlene Dietrich. You probably haven't noticed, but that kind of act is incredibly popular at the moment.'

'Stands to reason, I suppose,' Felix said. 'All those chaps shut up together without female company.'

'That's just the point. Of course, it's absolutely forbidden for any of the cast to leave the base in costume, but on this particular occasion they took it into their heads to smuggle Clive out in full drag and take him to the local pub. There were quite a few off-duty soldiers in there and a really bizarre situation developed with them flirting with Clive as if he was a real girl and him playing up to them in return. Apparently it was all quite good natured to begin with but then things turned nasty. Two of the squaddies started to quarrel about who was going to see Clive home. My lot waded in to protect Clive and a full-scale fight developed. Next thing, the Redcaps arrive, summoned by the landlord, and the whole lot are hauled off to the clink. I had a hell of a time talking my lads out of trouble, as you can imagine.'

Felix chuckled. 'I see your point. Makes a good story, but not easy to live through at the time.'

'Anyway,' Merry said. 'How about you? Are you happy with your new squadron?'

'Oh yes, great lot of chaps.' Felix sighed. 'It's good to be back in harness but I have to admit it is a bit like giving a kid the run of a sweet shop and then telling him he mustn't touch the sweets. I'm just not cut out for flying a desk.'

'But someone has to do that sort of job,' Merry pointed out consolingly. 'Someone has to coordinate operations, collate intelligence, that sort of thing.'

'I know,' Felix said. 'But I hate being a penguin.'

'A what?'

'It's what the pilots call the desk wallahs. Penguin – calls itself a bird but can't fly. Get it?'

Merry reached across and gripped his hand sympathetically. 'Poor old Felix! Here . . .' He picked up the bottle and refilled their glasses. 'Drink up. We agreed not to talk about the war. Remember?'

15

Richard stood at the rail of the felucca and strained his eyes to make out the contours of the Mediterranean coast of France. It had been sixteen days since he had left London. The car had taken him to the RAF airfield at Newmarket Heath, where he had said goodbye to Victor and climbed aboard a single-engined Lysander plane. This had taken him to Portreath, in Cornwall, where he had transferred to a Whitley bomber for the flight to Gibraltar. It was his first experience of flying and he was glad to find he did not suffer from airsickness. Nevertheless, the Whitley was not designed for carrying passengers and, with the ever present threat of enemy aircraft at the back of his mind, he was relieved to disembark into the sudden heat of a Mediterranean afternoon.

He was met by a familiar face, a man he knew only by his SOE code name of 'Monday'. He was the diplomat who had smuggled him across the border from Spain in the last stage of his escape the previous year.

'Bloody hell!' Monday said in greeting. 'I thought we'd got rid of you last December. Talk about out of the frying pan and into the fire!'

Gibraltar was as he remembered it, a brilliant and comparatively luxurious contrast to embattled Britain. On his first visit he had been amazed to find that there were no blackout restrictions and at night the streets blazed with light. It was explained to him that, since Spain was neutral and therefore had no need to fear bombing, to have plunged Gibraltar into darkness would simply have made it easier for enemy aircraft to identify. He was entertained generously for two days but found himself growing increasingly impatient. The waiting had gone on long enough.

Eventually, he was taken after dark to the harbour, where a small fishing boat was tied up to the quay. The skipper was a large, blond Polish naval officer with a charming manner and a buccaneering disposition. He explained to Richard, in the course of the voyage, that after the fall of Poland he had offered himself to the British naval command as a 'freelance' and had come to Gibraltar initially to attempt the rescue of a number of his compatriots who had been interned by the Vichy government in French Morocco. The use of the felucca as an undercover means of transporting agents and other escapees had followed naturally from that.

The voyage had taken ten days, during which time the felucca had been repainted and decked out with different flags three times. For the first four days the weather was appalling and Richard had spent half his time clinging to his bunk in the tiny cabin he shared with the captain and the other half hanging over the side. After that the wind dropped and they entered calmer waters and he was able to relax and enjoy a last few days of relative safety. Now the coast of France was in sight and tonight he would be put ashore to fend for himself. He went below and changed out of the rough, deck-hand gear he had been lent for the voyage and into the respectable Italian suit.

By the time darkness had fallen the little boat was lying off a stretch of rocky coast between Cannes and Juan-les-Pins. Here the Alpes Maritimes dropped sharply to the sea and there was only just room for the road and the railway line between the mountains and the coast, but on a small promontory two villas had been built, both painted white, and they served as landmarks for the rendezvous. As the appointed hour approached Richard studied the shoreline tensely through his field glasses. Dead on time a light flashed from the shore, giving the pre-arranged recognition signal. An answering light flickered from the ship and then a rubber dinghy put off, crewed by a single rower. A few minutes later it reappeared, this time with three occupants. Two young men in ill-fitting suits scrambled aboard the felucca. From their strained expressions it was not hard for Richard to guess where they had come from.

'RAF?' he asked in English. 'Come down one of the escape lines?'

'Yes,' responded one, breathlessly. 'Who are you?'

'Doesn't matter,' Richard said. 'Don't worry. You're in good hands now.'

They exchanged a brief handshake and he clambered down to take their place in the dinghy.

Some yards from the beach the man rowing, a compatriot of the captain's, stopped and leaned on his oars. 'There are too many rocks from here on. You'll have to wade the last bit.'

Richard rolled up his trouser legs and tied his shoes round his neck by the laces. He climbed out of the dinghy and his companion handed him his suitcase.

'They're waiting for you. Good luck!'

They shook hands and Richard turned and began wading towards the shore. The rocks were slimy with seaweed and he had great difficulty keeping his footing. Once he stepped into a crevasse between two boulders and soaked his trouser leg up to the thigh. By the time he finally struggled on to dry land he wished he had taken his trousers off altogether and come ashore in his underpants.

Three dark figures stepped out from the shadow of a large rock. '*Vous avez apporté les cigarettes pour ma grandmère?*' the leader enquired softly.

'*Non, mais j'ai les saucissons de Pierre,*' Richard replied

The man offered his hand. '*Bonsoir. Je m'appelle Jean-Claude. Bienvenu en France.*'

'*Lucien,*' Richard said in response.

The other two were introduced as Raoul and Denis. The three led him under the main road by way of a large culvert and in through the rear door of a house on the far side. It appeared to be unoccupied and empty of furniture, but Jean-Claude produced glasses and a bottle of rough red wine and they drank to victory and death to the Boches. Richard had been told before he left Gibraltar that the men in the reception committee were not in any way connected with the *réseau* that had brought him out of France, which he intended to rejoin, so he was careful to say nothing about his mission and refrained from asking any questions about their organisation. What he did not know, he could not afterwards give away.

After some desultory conversation about the war in general his host handed him a blanket. 'Try to get some sleep. We will take turns to keep watch. It isn't safe to move until daylight.'

The next morning, after a breakfast of dry bread and ersatz coffee, Denis appeared pushing an ancient bicycle.

Jean-Claude said, 'Go with him. He will take you to the railway station. You have your papers?'

Richard unwrapped the documents from the waterproof pouch in which he had carried them ashore and tucked them into the pocket of his jacket. Then he strapped his case to the carrier of the bicycle, shook hands with the other two members of the reception committee and followed Denis down to the road. They took turns to ride the bike, which clanked and wheezed with every stroke of the pedals but somehow kept going until they reached their destination. At the station Richard said goodbye to his guide and carried his case into the booking hall. His heart was thumping as he approached the counter but the booking clerk scarcely looked up when he requested a single ticket to Marseilles. Nevertheless, he spent ten nervous minutes on the platform. He had not forgotten how he and his travelling companion had assumed that they had aroused no suspicions when they had bought tickets in Spain, only to be arrested as they were about to board the train. This time, however, there were no problems, and by midday he was getting out in Marseilles.

The police were checking the papers of everyone going through the barrier and Richard knew this would be the first big test. Although Germany and Italy were allies he did not know what the attitude of the Vichy police would be towards a non-national, particularly someone of military-service age. After a brief scrutiny, however, the gendarme handed him back his papers and waved him through. Richard took a deep breath, hoped his relief did not show in his face and walked out into the street.

Immediately he was assailed with a feeling of intense nostalgia. These were the streets he had walked with Chantal. The same tall grey buildings, the same harbour crowded with masts, the same tang in the air of salt water and fish and the scent of herbs wafted in from the mountains. He was tempted to go and book into the same hotel, but caution told him that that might give rise to unwelcome questions, so he found another small, unpretentious place near the harbour where the desk clerk handed him a key after only the briefest glance at his papers. Once in his room he unpacked his essential needs and then found his way to the bathroom, where he washed and attempted to sponge the salt stains from his trouser legs. Having spruced himself up as much as possible he set off to undertake the next part of his plan – a plan that he had not divulged even to his superiors in London, since he expected that they would regard it as far too risky.

Walking briskly, he headed for the Hôtel Louvre et Paix, the headquarters of the German–Italian Armistice Commission.

In the foyer men and women in both nations' uniforms were coming and going. Talk about into the lion's mouth, Richard thought as he approached a desk manned by an Italian soldier.

'Excuse me,' he said meekly, in Italian. 'I wish to see Captain Parigi.'

He knew he was taking a chance. The previous October, on the run from the Germans and masquerading as a cabaret singer, he had encountered Parigi, who was, in civilian life, the répétiteur with the Bologna Opera. Parigi had recognised a trained voice and Richard had fallen back on the story of the failed opera company. To his dismay, he had then been invited to sing for Parigi and his friends at the Italian's birthday celebrations, and only the arrival of orders for the last stage of his escape had prevented him from having to fulfil the engagement. Chantal had offered to deputise for him but he had no way of knowing how she had been received. What Parigi's attitude would be now he could not be sure, but he had warmed to the little man on their first meeting and judged that he would not bear malice for his disappointment.

The soldier checked his papers and directed him up to the first floor, where a female clerk asked him his business. He told her about the missed engagement and said he wanted to apologise to Parigi in person.

The woman looked as if she would like to have sent him packing, but apparently thought better of it and spoke into a telephone. A moment later an inner door opened and the plump, rubicund figure of Massimo Parigi bounded into the room. Seeing Richard, he beamed and came forward, extending his hand. 'Benedetti! My dear boy, I'm delighted to see you again. But what has happened? Why are you not in uniform? I thought you had returned home to enlist.'

Richard produced his carefully prepared story about the accidental wounding and ended, 'I want to apologise, signor, for letting you down last year. I felt bad about it, but the chance came up to get back to Italy and I felt I had to take it.'

'And the lady in question was beautiful, no?' Parigi said with a twinkle. 'Oh, don't worry, my boy. I heard all about it from your lovely companion. But how could you leave such a charming girl? The alternative must have been an exceptional woman – or exceptionally rich, perhaps?'

The tone was jocular but Richard attempted to look suitably chastened. 'It was a terrible mistake, signor. Chantal and I had quarrelled and I wanted to pay her back. I see now that I was a fool. That is why I have come back to France.'

'To look for her?'

'And to resume our partnership,' Richard assented. 'Now that the army does not want me I must earn my living somehow, and there is no work for opera singers in Italy at the moment.'

'Ah-ha!' Parigi nodded. 'So! You have not come purely to apologise to me.'

'Not solely, signor,' Richard admitted. 'But if I can, I should like to make up for last year.'

'You will sing for me?'

'If you still wish it.'

'It would give me the greatest pleasure. How long are you staying in Marseilles?'

'I don't know. A few days. I want to go north to find my girlfriend. But I need a pass to cross into the occupied zone. If you could help me with that . . .?'

Parigi laughed and winked. 'A quid pro quo – your fee for the performance? Well, why not? I'm sure it could be arranged. Are you free tomorrow evening?'

'I am at your service, signor.'

'Good. I shall invite a few friends for dinner and some entertainment. Come at about eight thirty. Then we will see what can be done about getting you a pass.'

Richard thanked him and left the hotel. He felt almost light headed with relief. He had not expected Parigi to receive him so genially or to agree to his request so easily. To calm himself he went and sat at a pavement café and drank a cup of the wretched brew that passed for coffee. His triumphant mood was succeeded after a little by a sense of something approaching shame. He genuinely liked the plump little man and recognised in him a kindred spirit, one for whom delight in music transcended all national boundaries and animosities. Two years earlier, he would have thought a chance meeting with the répétiteur of the Bologna Opera and the opportunity to sing for him the biggest break of his career. It hurt him to deceive a man who was so transparently honest and amiable.

He paid for his coffee and set off to walk across the city to the tall block of apartments to which Chantal had directed him on his first visit. He climbed the stone stairs to the second floor and rang the doorbell labelled 'Dr Rodocanachi'. The same elderly maidservant as before answered the door and he saw at once that she remembered him.

'I should like to see the doctor, please,' he said.

She stood aside for him to enter and then, instead of showing him into the waiting room, led him silently through to the sitting room at the rear of the flat. The room was empty, the lace curtains closed across the windows, as he remembered them, to frustrate the prying eyes of nosy neighbours. Madame Rodocanachi's piano stood in the corner. He remembered how one of the young pilots who had been hidden in the flat had been told off for playing a popular song on it, because it was something that she would never have played herself. He wondered whether there was anyone hidden here now.

The door opened, but instead of admitting the doctor a slight, dark man who was a stranger to Richard came in.

'Clémence says you have been here before,' he said in

French, without preamble. He spoke softly, with a cultured accent, and yet the voice carried an unmistakable authority.

Richard hesitated and then decided he had to take a calculated risk. If this man was known to Clémence he was also, presumably, known to the doctor and his wife.

'I was here a year ago,' he admitted.

'Why have you come back?'

'Look,' Richard said, 'I'm sorry, but I don't know who you are.'

'And I don't know you,' the other man returned, 'which is more to the point.'

At that moment Dr Rodocanachi came in and Richard was struck by how much older and greyer he looked, although it was less than a year since they had met before.

'*Mon Dieu!*' he exclaimed. 'What are you doing back here, after all this time?'

'You know him?' the other man said.

'Of course. We passed him down the line last autumn. I thought he had got clean away.'

'So I did,' Richard said quickly. 'I reached England in time for Christmas. I have come back to help you.'

'To help us?' queried the stranger.

The doctor said quickly, 'I should introduce you. This is Pat O'Leary. Pat, this . . .'

'Ricardo,' Richard put in quickly. 'Ricardo Benedetti.'

O'Leary eyed him narrowly and nodded a greeting. 'Ben-edetti.'

For his own part Richard did not believe for a moment that the Irish-sounding name was his real one. He spoke perfect French and there was nothing in his dapper appearance that looked in the least Irish. However, the last thing he wanted to do, in the circumstances, was to question another man's alias. So he offered his hand and murmured the conventional '*Enchanté*'.

'So,' said O'Leary, 'what are you doing here?'

As briefly as possible Richard explained his purpose in returning to France. 'I have to go north as soon as possible,' he went on. 'There are contacts I have to make there. But I wanted to make sure that the *réseau* was still operating and intact before I did anything.'

O'Leary, who in spite of his quiet manner seemed to have taken charge of the conversation, said, 'Yes, it's still intact, at the moment. Who knows how long that will last?'

Richard took a deep breath and asked, 'Have you heard from Chantal lately?'

'But yes!' exclaimed the doctor. 'She is here, in Marseilles. Did you not know?'

'In Marseilles?' Richard exclaimed. 'No, I didn't know. How could I? Is she all right?'

'She is very well,' the doctor reassured him. 'But she is a brave girl and takes such risks. She has just brought three more men down from the occupied zone.'

'I should like to see her,' Richard said. 'Do you know where I can find her?'

'You know that we never reveal addresses,' O'Leary told him reprovingly.

'But I will tell you how to contact her,' the doctor began, but O'Leary silenced him with a rapid gesture. At that moment they heard the doorbell ring and Richard sensed the tension in the room as they all waited to see who it was. To his relief the tall, kilted figure of Ian Garrow, the officer from the Seaforth Highlanders who had turned down the chance of being repatriated in order to stay and help others to escape, strode into the room.

He stopped short, staring at Richard, and exclaimed, 'What the hell are you doing here?'

Once again Richard explained his mission and Garrow burst out, 'Well, thank God someone has taken notice at last!

I've been sending back messages for the past year saying we need some back-up. Now, what can you do for us?'

Richard outlined the plans for the arrival of his radio operator and the expected parachute drop of money to help fund the line. Garrow seemed satisfied and Richard sensed that O'Leary had relaxed now that he had been vouched for by a second person. Briefly, for his benefit, Richard told the story of his escape and his first encounter with Chantal at the café in Lille. 'I really do want to contact her,' he finished. 'Please tell me where I can find her.'

Garrow and O'Leary exchanged glances and Garrow nodded. O'Leary said, 'She will be waiting for any messages to take back with her. The rendezvous is in the little park near the Avenue Foch. She will be sitting on the third bench from the gate and the recognition signal is "Have you seen a small white dog?" To which she will answer, "Does he have a spot over one eye?"'

'When will she be there?' Richard asked.

'At six o'clock this evening.'

As he prepared to leave shortly afterwards O'Leary drew him to one side and said quietly, 'Did you come across Paul Cole when you were in Lille before?'

'Yes,' Richard answered. 'He organised my escape.'

'What did you make of him?' O'Leary asked.

Richard hesitated. 'He seemed to have everything pretty well sewn up.'

'But as a man?'

'I don't know. He was very friendly, very efficient, but . . .'

'But?'

'There was something about him that struck me as phoney. I couldn't put my finger on it. Just a feeling, you know?'

'Ah!' O'Leary exclaimed with satisfaction. 'That is exactly my impression too. Ian thinks I am wrong and I know a lot of the men he has brought across the demarcation line won't hear a word against him, but somehow he makes me uneasy. For one thing, he always seems to have far more money to flash around than you would expect. I've given him some quite large sums that we've collected here to fund the line and I can't help wondering . . .' He left the sentence unfinished.

'What do you want me to do?' Richard asked.

'Nothing at the moment. Just keep your eyes open. If you think there is something wrong send me a message with someone reliable – someone like Chantal, for example.'

A few minutes before six Richard entered the little park. Some children were playing on swings, watched over by mothers or nursemaids, and there were a few adults sitting or strolling, enjoying the cool evening air before going home to dinner. He saw Chantal at once, her head with its bright helmet of chestnut hair bent over a newspaper. For a moment he hesitated. He had not expected to meet her for the first time in such a public place and he was afraid that in her surprise she might give him away. In the circumstances, however, there was nothing for it but to rely on her ingrained caution and her actress's ability to improvise. He walked up to her and cleared his throat.

'Excuse me. Have you seen a small white dog?'

She looked up and the colour drained from her face. He went on quickly, without waiting for the specified response, '*Chérie*, forgive me! I have come back. I should never have left you for that other bitch!'

She rose to her feet, staring at him as if she suspected that he was some kind of hallucination. Then he saw a gathering glow of fury in her amber eyes. A second later she drew back her hand and slapped him hard across the face.

'*Cochon!* How dare you ask me to forgive you after you went off with that Italian whore! What are you doing here, anyway? Why aren't you in the army?'

'The army don't want me,' he said humbly, his hand to his stinging cheek. 'I was wounded. See, I limp . . .' and he jogged from foot to foot in illustration.

'So now you come crawling back to me! Do you expect me to take you back, after all this time?'

'*Cara mia*,' he pleaded, beginning to wonder how much of her reaction was a brilliant piece of acting and how much was genuine, 'I am at your feet! For months I have thought only of you. Please, give me another chance!'

Suddenly her eyes were full of tears and a second later she was in his arms. He held her tightly, burying his face in the bright hair and feeling the familiar way her body moulded itself to his. This was what he had dreamed of all through his training. This was what had brought him back to France.

She lifted her face to his and whispered, 'I thought I should never see you again.'

'I thought the same,' he answered. 'I couldn't bear it. That's why I had to come back.'

They kissed and the taste of her mouth, the smell of her skin, set his pulses racing. She murmured, 'I am in the same hotel. Come back with me.'

'Soon,' he whispered. 'But first we must talk.'

'Here?' she asked. 'Why not at the hotel?'

He drew her down on to the seat and put his arms round her. To anyone watching they would simply have seemed like two lovers making up after a tiff. 'It's safer here,' he said. 'No chance of hidden microphones.'

She stared at him. '*Chéri*, why are you here? I thought you had got away. I thought you were safe at home.'

'So I was,' he answered. 'But then I realised I couldn't stay there while you and the others risked their lives, so I came back.' Holding her and whispering in her ear as if he were murmuring words of love, he explained his mission and what he hoped would be her part in it.

'And Rose?' she asked. 'What has happened to Rose?'

He looked away. 'Rose has married someone else,' he said. 'That's all over. It's you I want to be with, Chantal.'

She put her hand against his cheek and forced him to look up, and he knew that she had seen the lie for what it was and accepted it. '*Mon pauvre petit!*' she whispered, and kissed him again.

They went back to her hotel, to the same room they had shared a year before. He watched as she took off her clothes and held out her arms to him. Her arms and shoulders were tanned gold by the sun, her breasts and belly white as marble, and she was totally unashamed by her nakedness. He went to her and cupped her breasts in his hands, then bent and kissed them. She wound her arms round his neck and pulled him against her, her fingers twined in his hair, and he stroked his hands over the lithe muscles that moved below the velvet skin. Suddenly a flood of images surfaced in his memory. Chantal swimming off the beach at Fairbourne, her easy, economical strokes making the splashing of Sally and the rest look childish; Chantal in her tiny, immaculate house, naked in his arms, the woman of experience seducing the inexperienced youth.

He pressed his face into the angle of her neck and breathed, 'You are magnificent! I've missed you so much!'

She kissed him and then drew back, looking into his eyes. 'And I have missed you, *chéri*. Since you left there has been no one else – and for me that is unusual, no?'

'No one?' He searched her face. It had not even occurred to him to wonder whether she had had other lovers since they parted, but now he realised that it would have been quite in character if she had gone to bed with any of the escaping airmen she found attractive. He remembered, too, that he had not been faithful. He kissed her again and whispered, 'Let's not waste any more time.'

That night they did not go out, even to eat. At one point

Chantal went downstairs and spoke to the landlord and came back with bread and cheese and a bottle of wine and they picnicked on the bed. The rest of the time they lay in each other's arms, either dozing or making love. Waking next morning, Richard suddenly found himself thinking of Priscilla. Whatever had possessed him, he wondered, to seduce her? Not that it had really been a seduction. She had been as eager as he was. But was she now waiting for him, expecting him to return and . . . and what? Pick up where they had left off? Marry her? He remembered the plans she had made for him for after the war, the people she had introduced him to. At the time it had all seemed so reasonable, so appealing. Now it struck him as bizarre. He looked at Chantal, asleep beside him, her flame-coloured hair spread over the pillow. He knew that she would never expect a proposal of marriage from him. She had made that quite clear from the start. He could not begin to envisage what the future might hold for either of them. He knew only that for now, at least, he belonged with her.

That evening he dressed and shaved carefully and set off for the Hôtel Louvre et Paix. Massimo Parigi was waiting for him in a private dining room in the company of a dozen or so officers, both Italian and German. Richard's heart was pounding, but he had prepared his programme carefully: Figaro's aria '*Non piu andrai*' from *The Marriage of Figaro*, which he thought had a suitably militaristic tone; Don Giovanni's serenade '*Vieni al fenestra*' for the romantically inclined; and the aria that had become his personal theme tune, '*Dormiro sol*' from *Don Carlos*. Parigi, as he had anticipated, turned out to be a consummate musician and a sympathetic accompanist, and the three songs were greeted with enthusiastic applause, though Richard guessed that some of the German officers would have preferred Wagner.

Parigi would have detained him to join the others for drinks but Richard felt he had risked enough for one night and begged to be excused, on the pretext that he had been travelling for several days and was very tired.

As he left Parigi held out an envelope. 'Your pass. I think you will find everything is in order.'

'Thank you, signor,' Richard said. 'I'm very grateful.'

'No, it is I who am grateful to you,' the captain responded. 'It has given me great pleasure.' He felt in his pocket and produced a silver card case. 'Take my card. When this terrible war is over, come and see me. We shall need to rebuild the opera company and I think I can be sure of finding you a place.'

Richard looked at the card and felt a sharp stab of regret. If only it were possible! To sing with the Bologna Opera would have been an opportunity in a thousand. He shook hands, thanked the amiable little captain again and set off back to his hotel.

16

The week of Felix's leave stayed in Merry's memory as an idyll comparable to the one they had spent together the previous November, when they first became lovers. The only difference was the weather. It had been a perfect summer and the late August landscape was mellow and sun drenched. They wandered the lanes and fields or lounged around the garden, soaking up the sun.

On the first afternoon Merry remarked, 'By the way, do you know who is responsible for tidying up the garden? I must owe them some money.'

Felix grinned. 'I'll send in my bill.'

'You did it?'

'Yes. I've been coming over in my free time pretty often and I couldn't bear to see the place looking so uncared for. I've enjoyed working on it.'

'It's extremely noble of you,' Merry commented. 'And you've done a wonderful job. I had no idea you were interested in horticulture.'

'I'm a country boy by upbringing, remember?' Felix pointed out.

Merry recalled his one, clandestine visit to Malpas Hall – a visit he had never mentioned to Felix. He remembered the sweeping grounds, at that time largely given over to growing vegetables. It was not hard to imagine them as they used to be before the war, or the small army of gardeners that must have been needed to keep them up.

'I can't somehow believe that you ever had a great deal of hands-on experience at home,' he commented.

'Well, it was at school mostly, I suppose,' Felix admitted. 'We all had a small plot where we were allowed to grow anything we liked. I used to spend as much time there as possible. The garden plots were next to the tennis courts and I had a terrible crush on the captain of the first team.'

'Was it reciprocated?' Merry asked. By unspoken consent they had never discussed their previous relationships but he could not resist the question.

'Not a chance!' Felix chuckled. 'I was far beneath his notice.'

'He must have been blind, then,' Merry said, secretly and unreasonably relieved.

There was only one cloud over Merry's happiness, and that was the knowledge that sooner or later he had to tell Felix that he was going abroad. He put it off on the pretext that he did not want it to spoil the one complete week they had together, but on the night before Felix was due to go back on duty he could keep it to himself no longer. As they sat over dinner he said, 'Felix, there's something I have to tell you.'

Felix looked at him for a moment. Then he said, 'You're being sent overseas, aren't you?'

Merry gaped at him. 'How did you know?'

'I didn't. It was a guess. I just knew there was something you weren't telling me.'

Merry remembered how he had suffered from exactly that impression and felt ashamed. 'I'm sorry. I should have come straight out with it, but I didn't want to spoil the mood.'

'So this is embarkation leave?'

'Yes.'

'When do you go?'

'The beginning of next month.'

'I suppose you've no idea where?'

'None at all. Except that we've been told to draw tropical kit.' He grinned ironically. 'So that probably means they're sending us to the North Atlantic.'

'Very likely.'

They looked at each other in silence. Then Felix said, 'You'll be away for a long time, then.'

'It looks like it,' Merry agreed heavily.

Felix reached across the table and took his hand. 'I guess it's no worse for us than for thousands of other couples.'

'Except that they can write to each other and say what they're really feeling.'

'I know.' Felix sighed. 'It's hell knowing that everything you write is going to be read by the censor. Our private lives are none of their bloody business. It's got nothing to do with national security.'

'No,' Merry said bitterly. 'We just happen to be breaking a bloody stupid law, that's all.'

Felix made an effort to lighten the mood. 'Oh well. Look on the bright side. I might be posted overseas too. We could end up in the same theatre.'

Merry laughed in spite of himself. 'It's a funny phrase, that. You mean "theatre of war", of course, but my immediate thought was that we might both end up playing the Palace Theatre, Benghazi.'

'Some hopes!' said Felix, laughing in return. 'Anyway,' he went on, 'I've got a little surprise too. Tonight doesn't have to be our last. I'm stationed at Wittering. It's only an hour's drive in the Lagonda and I've got a living-out pass. I'll be able to get home most nights while your leave lasts.'

'That's wonderful!' Merry exclaimed. Felix had called this 'home'. He hugged the word to himself.

Later that night, on their way to bed, Felix said, 'By the way, what did you think of that photo I sent you? Harriet sent it to me because she said it was "too intimate" to use for publication. I didn't know she was taking it. I thought she was still fiddling around with exposure meters and what not.'

Merry recalled vividly the look on Felix's face in the picture. He could understand why Harriet had called it 'too intimate'. 'What were you thinking about?' he asked.

'You, of course, you clot! I was thinking how amused you would be when I wrote and told you what was happening.'

'Amused!' Merry exclaimed involuntarily.

'You weren't amused?' Felix searched his face.

Merry looked away. 'It wasn't the first emotion that came to mind.'

'I don't see . . .' Felix began, puzzled. Then, with dawning comprehension, 'You didn't think . . .? Surely you didn't imagine . . .?' Abruptly he reached out and grasped Merry's shoulder, forcing him to face him. 'Merry, you didn't think that I could ever take up where I left off with Harriet, did you?'

Merry could only shrug helplessly.

'You actually worried that I might be two-timing you with someone else? With Harry, of all people!'

His eyes were angry and Merry felt suddenly ashamed. 'I'm sorry! But you were so far away, and I couldn't write what I wanted to say. I just felt somehow . . . disconnected, helpless. After all, you and she were very close once.'

'Once! When I was trying desperately to prove that I was something I'm not, and never can be. And it wasn't Harry who stood by me and made me feel that I wasn't something pitiable and . . . and revolting. How could you believe that I might drop you for her?'

'I couldn't help myself. I knew I was being ridiculous and unjust, but I couldn't stop.'

Felix looked at him for a moment longer, then his eyes softened. 'You've been torturing yourself, haven't you? And all over nothing.' He shifted his hand so that his fingers curled around the back of Merry's neck. 'You mustn't do it, Merry. You mustn't doubt me. We're going to be apart for a long time. It will be bad enough, but I can't bear the thought that you might be torturing yourself worrying that I'm going to leave you for someone else. I told you right at the start. This is it, as far as I'm concerned. "Forsaking all others – till death us do part . . ." The full works. You have to believe that.'

Merry put his arms round him. 'I do,' he said. 'I knew the moment I got back what a fool I'd been. I won't make the same mistake again. Promise.'

'Come to bed,' said Felix.

Later, when they lay exhausted and satiated, Merry made to shift his weight off Felix's prone body but found himself held back.

'Don't move.'

'I'm squashing you.'

'I don't mind. I like the feeling – as if our two bodies are melting into each other.' After a moment Felix went on, 'Did you ever read Plato?'

'Naturally. For people like us Plato was a merciful revelation, wasn't he?'

'Thank God for a classical education! Do you remember that passage in the Symposium where Socrates's disciples are all trying to define perfect love?'

'I think so.'

'Agathon, I think it was, told this story. Once upon a time human beings had four arms and four legs and two of everything else but some jealous god came down and smote them in half and since then everyone has been trying to find his other half. When that happens, if you're ever lucky enough, that's perfect love.'

Merry smiled in the darkness. 'Yes, I remember.'

Felix moved his limbs lazily. 'Well, look. Four legs, four arms, one body. We're one of the lucky ones.'

'So lucky!' Merry murmured, drifting on the edge of sleep. 'So lucky . . .'

The next day dragged. Felix had to leave early to be back on station by eight o'clock and Merry wondered around in a drowsy stupor for most of the morning. Then, in the afternoon, he pulled himself together and began the task of putting his affairs in order. There were still things belonging to his father that needed to be disposed of and some paperwork to be attended to. In the process Merry opened a locked drawer and found that it contained his mother's emerald-and-diamond engagement ring and several other small items of jewellery that he dimly remembered her wearing. He sat for a long time turning them over in his hands and wondering why his father had kept them locked away all these years.

Felix came home full of bounce and with a selection of amusing anecdotes to recount but Merry sensed an edginess behind his good humour.

'Had a hectic day?' he enquired.

Felix shook his head. 'No, not really. That's the trouble. Too much waiting around. There isn't a lot for our boys to do at the moment. The night-fighter squadrons have got most of the action, escorting the bombers over to Germany. Our chaps fly regular patrols, of course, and every now and then they come across a few Me 109s and have a bit of a scrap, but most of the time there's nothing doing. I'm bored, to be honest.'

'That's fine,' Merry told him. 'Bored is good. If you were finding life exciting I'd be worried.'

The next day Merry made an appointment with his solicitor and made a will. He had no close relatives and no expectation of ever having children, so he simply left everything to Felix, allowing the solicitor to draw whatever conclusions he liked. There was only one exception. After some thought he added an extra bequest, leaving his mother's jewellery to Miss Rose Taylor of Lambeth.

Thinking of Rose brought a new idea to his mind. He had heard from her some time previously saying that she had moved back to London and reopened the shop and it occurred to him that, rather than wait around all day for Felix, he could take the train up to town and go and visit her. The following morning he walked into the shop just as Rose was fitting a pair of Clarks sandals on a particularly obstreperous small boy.

Rose jumped to her feet and greeted him with a hug. 'Merry! How lovely! Why didn't you let me know you were coming?'

'Sorry,' Merry said, torn between embarrassment and amusement at the expression on the face of the small boy's mother. 'Spur-of-the-moment thing, you know.'

Rose squeezed his hand. 'Well, it's lovely to see you. Hang on just a minute, can you, while I finish seeing to this customer?'

The small boy and his mother found themselves packed off in remarkably short time with the assurance that there were positively no other shoes in the shop that he could try on and they had better take the ones he was wearing because stocks were very low and there was a war on, or had they forgotten. As soon as they were out of the shop Rose locked the door and turned the notice on it to CLOSED.

'People will get the wrong idea,' Merry pointed out.

Rose laughed. 'Who cares? It'll be all over the street in ten minutes anyway, if I know Mrs Jones. Besides, everyone thinks you're my fancy man, ever since you stayed here before. Come on up to the flat and I'll make us a cup of tea.'

Watching her as she put the kettle on Merry said, 'You look well, Rose.'

She threw him a glance. 'Do I?'

'Definitely. Last time I saw you, in Wimborne, you were still terribly thin.'

'And now I'm much too fat,' she responded.

'Rubbish!' he said. 'You don't look fat to me.'

Rose sighed. 'Oh, I am, Merry. I can hardly bear to look at myself in my dance clothes.'

'So you stuck to your plan, then?' Merry queried. 'You're dancing again.'

Rose turned to get cups from the cupboard. 'Well, I'm going to class.'

'Still? Is that really necessary?'

'Absolutely. My technique's gone to pot completely and I'm hopelessly out of condition. I wouldn't stand a chance of passing an audition at the moment.'

'Rose,' Merry said hesitantly, 'are you sure this is what you want?'

'Why is it,' Rose demanded, 'that everyone assumes that for a woman a career is just a stopgap until she gets married? If you hadn't had the chance to join Stars in Battledress, would you have given up playing the piano?'

'No, of course not. Music's my life, it always has been.'

'*And dance is mine!*' Rose told him, with passionate intensity. 'Ever since I was a little girl, it's all I've wanted to do. I should never have given it up in the first place. That surgeon didn't know what he was talking about. I expect Sally could have got me a job at the Windmill, if I'd asked.'

'Well, there's nothing to stop you now, is there?' Merry asked.

Rose poured boiling water from the kettle and brought the teapot to the table. She sat down with a sigh, all the fire suddenly gone out of her.

'Only the fact that I can't do it any more. I've been going to classes for weeks now, and practising at home, but I just can't make my body do the things it used to do. You're so lucky, Merry. You'll be able to go on playing until you're ninety, but once a dancer lets herself go that's the end.'

'I suppose,' Merry said, searching for words of comfort, 'that a dancer's career is always much shorter than a musician's, in the nature of things.'

'Specially for someone like me,' Rose said bitterly. 'No one wants to look at a chorus girl once she gets past the age of thirty. But I'm only twenty-two, Merry! I'm not over the hill yet!'

Merry leaned across the table and took her hand, and saw that her huge violet eyes were full of tears. 'Of course you're not. You're still young and very lovely. You mustn't give up. It will come back.'

To his great distress she suddenly bowed her head and burst into sobs. He moved swiftly round the table and perched on the edge of it to put his arms around her.

'Don't, Rose! Please don't. Things can't be that bad. What is it?'

She buried her face in his shirt front and continued to weep for a few minutes, then pulled herself together and sat back, sniffing.

'Don't take any notice. I'm just being silly. The least little thing seems to set me off these days. It's having no one to talk to, I expect.' She looked up at him, her eyes still swimming. 'It's just that I don't know what I'll do with myself if I can't go back to dancing.'

He stroked her hair back from her damp face. 'You mustn't let it get you down. None of us knows what's round the corner these days. We just have to go on from day to day and make the most of every little moment of happiness. You never know, you could go out of your door tomorrow and bump into some fabulous bloke who you've never even dreamed of and fall madly in love. This time next year you could be married with a baby.'

Rose smiled ironically. 'There you go again! Why do men always think that marriage is the answer to everything for a woman? Anyway,' she sighed and shook her head, 'you know that isn't likely to happen. There's only ever been one man for me.'

'How can you be so sure?' he asked.

She looked at him. 'I don't know how you of all people can ask me that. There's only ever been one man for you, hasn't there?'

Merry felt himself flush slightly. It was the nearest they had ever come to openly discussing his relationship with Felix, but he nodded. 'That's true.'

'How is Felix?' Rose asked.

'He's well. We've just had a week's leave together. We've been down at my place in Seaford.'

Rose smiled at him. 'I'm glad. Give him my love, will you?'

'I will.' He straightened up. 'Come on, drink your tea. It'll be cold.'

Rose sipped her tea and after a moment she said, 'Now tell me what you're doing. Where do you go next?'

He explained that he was on embarkation leave and she stared at him in horror.

'Oh, and there I was moaning about my troubles, and you're going overseas! Oh, Merry, I am sorry.'

'Nonsense,' he said. 'I don't particularly want to go, but it could be worse. After all, I get on well with the rest of the company and an ocean cruise followed by a chance to see foreign parts isn't an opportunity I'd have had working for Monty Prince, is it?'

Rose leaned across and kissed him. 'Dear old Merry. You always cheer me up!' She looked at the clock. 'It's gone twelve! I'll see what I can rake up for lunch.'

'You will not!' Merry told her. 'Go and powder your nose. We're going up west for the best lunch we can find. And then, as it's a Wednesday, do you think there's any chance of getting in to a matinée?'

Rose's face lit up. 'A show? Oh, Merry, that would be lovely! That's just what I need.'

'Well, get your hat and we'll see what we can do,' he said, pleased at the change in her.

In the event, they had a rather indifferent lunch in a pub on Oxford Street, but good food was almost unobtainable wherever you went. Afterwards, they managed to get tickets for *The Dancing Years* at the Adelphi and for two hours were transported back to the magical world they had inhabited so happily two summers previously.

When the show was over Rose insisted on accompanying Merry to Waterloo Station instead of allowing him to see her home, knowing that he was anxious to get the train back to Seaford and Felix. Like every mainline station in London, Waterloo was crowded with men in uniform, some being ecstatically greeted by wives and girlfriends, others making tearful farewells.

Rose tucked her arm into Merry's. 'Ooh, I feel ever so posh, being escorted by an officer. I bet everyone thinks I'm your girlfriend.'

'Well, I should be very flattered if they did,' he replied gallantly. 'You're definitely the prettiest girl around.'

At the barrier he kissed her chastely on the cheek and said, 'Keep your pecker up, love. It'll all come right in the end.'

'Let's hope so,' she answered. 'Take care, Merry. And write as soon as you can.'

'I'll send you a dirty postcard from wherever it is I end up,' he promised.

After dinner Merry sat down at the piano as usual but instead of playing Chopin or Beethoven he began fingering out a melody by ear.

'What's that?' Felix asked.

'It's one of the numbers from the show we saw this

afternoon,' Merry answered. 'Typical Ivor Novello. You know, he can't sing but he always writes himself a number that he can half sing, half speak through. This one stuck in my mind. I can't remember the lyrics exactly, but it's something about wishing he could express himself as clearly in words as he can when he plays the piano.'

Felix had come to stand behind him, his hands on his shoulders. 'You don't need words – or a piano, come to that. But, speaking of words, and the difficulty of communication, I've been thinking about this problem of letters being censored and I think I've had a brainwave.'

'Oh?' Merry said doubtfully. 'It's no good inventing some kind of code. That'll have the censor on our necks straight away.'

'Nothing as complicated as that,' Felix assured him. 'It just struck me on the way home. What we have to do is invent a girlfriend for you.'

'*A girlfriend!*' Merry queried in astonishment.

'Yes. Listen. You are having a crazy affair with this imaginary woman who happens to be married. You can't write to her directly for fear of her husband finding out, so you have to pass messages through a mutual friend – i.e. me.'

'Oh.' Merry gave a long whistle of comprehension. 'I get it! Something along the lines of "give Mary my undying love and tell her I miss her terribly".'

'Well, it's not exactly great poetry, but you have grasped the general idea,' Felix conceded with a grin. 'Though I thought we might call her Felicity.'

'Isn't that a bit too obvious? The censor might get suspicious.'

'Stuff the censor. He can't prove anything. Like I said, our private lives are none of his business. Anyway, you always address me as Ned when you write.'

This was true. Merry had adopted the use of Felix's real name in his letters in order to avoid confusion.

'All right.' A slow smile spread across Merry's normally grave features. 'Felicity it shall be. I shall enjoy writing to her.'

'And I, of course, shall be happy to send you her replies,' Felix said, grinning back.

Felix managed to get some time off on the last morning so that he could drive Merry to the station. While he packed Merry said, 'I suppose you're still trying to get back into the air.'

'Yes, of course.'

'And I imagine it isn't the slightest use for me to ask you not to?'

Felix shook his head slowly. 'It wouldn't be kind of you.'

Merry sighed. 'No, I suppose it would be like caging a wild bird. But for God's sake don't try to push yourself too far. You don't have to prove anything to anybody.'

'Only to myself,' Felix said soberly.

'What, in heaven's name?' Merry demanded. 'After everything that's happened, what can you possibly need to prove?'

Felix did not answer for a moment. Then he said, 'Perhaps that I deserve to still be alive, when so many of the others are dead.'

'Oh, Felix!' Merry looked at him in despair. He went to him and put his arms round him. 'Some of us have to stay alive, otherwise their sacrifice makes no sense. That's our duty to them – to survive.'

Felix smiled at him. 'Perhaps you're right. Anyway, I don't know what you're worrying about. You're the one who is off to the battle front. I'm staying safely at home in good old Blighty.'

'Nonsense!' Merry replied. 'The only way I'm likely to get near a battle front is if I let Chubby Hawkes do the map-reading. I'm going to have a nice ocean voyage. I've always been told that's very good for the health.'

'Well, at least you shouldn't end up with pneumonia this year.'

'No, true. Scurvy perhaps, but not pneumonia.'

They both spoke with an artificial brightness, but both knew that behind the words was one unspoken thought, which could be summed up in a single phrase – U-boats. Merry turned away and closed his suitcase. There was nothing else to do but take a last look round.

Felix said, 'Remember, you made me a promise.'

'Not to doubt?' Merry nodded. 'Don't worry. That's one promise I shall definitely keep.'

They embraced for the last time and went down to the car. At the station they stood awkwardly, trying to make conversation, and Merry was relieved when the train came into sight. As the engine hissed past them Felix gripped his elbow and said, 'Take care. Write as soon as you can.'

'I will. And you take care too. No silly stunts!'

'Chance would be a fine thing!'

'Promise me! Don't take any unnecessary risks.'

'Yes, all right. I promise.'

Merry climbed into an empty carriage and lowered the window. Felix looked up at him and his eyes were wet. Merry reached out impulsively and laid a hand against the side of his face. Then the whistle blew and the engine gave off a volley of steamy snorts and began to move. Merry waved and Felix waved back, then suddenly, surprisingly, came to attention and saluted and stood like that until a bend in the line hid him from view. Merry pulled up the window and collapsed on to the seat. He felt as if someone had punched him in the stomach and for a moment he thought he was going to be sick. Then the tears came.

17

Richard was dressing for his first cabaret spot at the Café Bleu when the waiter, Gaston, appeared at the door of the tiny dressing room he shared with Chantal. They had been back in Lille for two weeks and the proprietor had made no difficulties about employing them as a double act. After all, they had been a success the previous year and had brought in a lot of customers, especially the German officers who had more money to spend than the locals.

'There's a character out front who says you owe him money,' Gaston said abruptly.

Richard looked up sharply. 'Who is it?'

'Didn't give his name, but he gave me a note for you.'

Richard took the slip of paper and read, *You still owe me that fifty francs, you hound! Don't think I'm going to let you get away with it. Henri.*

'Did he ask for me by name?' Richard enquired.

'No. He said the singer in the red shirt.'

Richard nodded. He was wearing the famous red shirt at that moment. Chantal looked across at him from her position by the mirror and raised her eyebrows. Richard said easily, 'Don't worry. I know what this is about.' He turned to the waiter. 'Where is he?'

'The table by the door. I'll show you.'

Gaston led him to the door that gave access to the main part of the café and pointed. 'There. The little bloke drinking pastis. Recognise him?'

'Oh yes,' Richard said. 'Yes, I know him.'

Amazingly, it was true. Sitting by himself, dressed in the blue overalls and beret that were the working uniform of almost every Frenchman, was his old friend from Wanborough and Arisaig, the sergeant from the Royal Corps of Signals, Jack Duval. Richard gave Gaston a look of resigned amusement and said, 'I'd better go and speak to him, otherwise he'll probably interrupt in the middle of the show.'

As he threaded his way between the tables he wondered whether Jack had any idea who he was about to meet and what his reaction might be. He need not have worried. Jack looked up and saw him when he was still some way away and his dark face broke into a broad grin. As Richard reached him he rose and extended his hand. 'So, *mon ami*, you have not forgotten your old friend Henri Lebrun?'

'How could I forget?' Richard asked, shaking hands. 'How are you, you old rogue?'

They sat down and Jack/Henri called to the waiter to bring another glass of pastis for his companion. For a while they kept up the sort of casual chatter that two old friends might be expected to exchange, until Richard said, 'I'll have to leave you for a bit. I've got to go and do my turn. I'll come back afterwards. Just sit tight.'

Heading back to the dressing room he felt a sense of relief. He had begun to worry that his promised radio operator had either mistaken the rendezvous or been picked up by the Germans. Things were working out. He had not been idle since his arrival in Lille but he had begun to feel that any information he might gather was going to be useless unless he had some means of communicating with England. Now, he told himself, work could begin in earnest.

In the dressing room Chantal said casually, 'Is that the man you were expecting?'

'Yes,' he said briefly. 'I'll introduce you after we've done our act.'

He kept his promise, introducing the new arrival simply as Henri. Even with her he stuck carefully to the instruction impressed on him at Beaulieu not to give out any information other than what was strictly necessary. The less any of them knew about the identities of other members of the *réseau*, the less chance there was of the Gestapo being able to force the information from them. She, for her part, adopted her usual role of the flirtatious charmer, and he could see that Jack was completely captivated by her. They drank a bottle of wine together, and as closing time drew near Richard suggested that he come back to their place for a nightcap.

At the apartment Richard said, 'It's all right. You can relax. Chantal is one of us.'

They were still speaking French, and indeed it would not have occurred to him to revert to English. It had become the language of another life, another world. Now he spoke only French or Italian.

Duval said, 'Is this place secure?'

'Yes, we've checked it out thoroughly.' He grinned at Duval. 'It's great to see you. I wasn't expecting a familiar face.'

'I was,' the little sergeant said. 'As soon as they said "the singer in the red shirt" I knew it had to be you. By the way, what do I call you?'

Richard told him and briefly explained his cover story. In exchange Duval told them that he was posing as a mechanic from the Ardennes who had lost his home and his job when a British tank shelled his village during the German advance the previous summer. He had been in Lille for three days and had already found a job with a local garage and a room in the house of an elderly lady.

'She appears to be almost completely deaf,' he said, 'and, what's even better, she's told me that I must do my own cleaning because she can't manage the stairs up to the top of the house, so there's no chance of her happening to come in while I'm transmitting.'

'Ideal!' Richard said. 'I assume you had no trouble getting here?'

Duval grinned. 'None at all. I just dropped in, so to speak. By the way,' he added, 'I've already made contact to let them know I've arrived safely. London wants to know if you're OK and if you've found a suitable DZ.'

DZ stood for dropping zone, where supplies or people could be dropped by parachute. It had been one of the first things Richard had investigated. He told Duval that he knew of just the place and could also muster a group of trustworthy people to act as a reception party.

'But tell them I've got documents to send back,' Richard said. 'The plane will need to land.'

'I'll need a code phrase for the BBC,' Duval said.

Richard thought for a moment and said, 'Monty's dog has no nose.'

Chantal, listening, suppressed a giggle of recognition. The 'my dog ain't got no nose' gag was one Richard had had to endure when he had acted as Monty's straight man in the Follies. Duval looked askance at the two of them and shrugged. 'OK. You're the boss. Two days after we hear that we can expect the drop.'

From then on 'Henri' formed the habit of dropping in to the café most evenings for a pastis, and usually, after they had finished their act, Richard and Chantal would have a drink with him. One evening they were joined unexpectedly by Paul Cole.

The ginger-haired captain was in his usual exuberant form, greeting all his acquaintances with cheerful bonhomie and giving Chantal a smacking kiss. Richard wondered, not for the first time, what it was about this man that set alarm bells ringing at the back of his brain. He had made contact as soon as he arrived in Lille and it had been necessary to trust Cole with the truth about the reason for his unexpected reappearance, but Richard felt that he had not been welcomed with quite the enthusiasm he expected. When he commented on that impression to Chantal she had replied with a shrug, 'Paul is a loner. He likes to run his own show. I expect he thinks you will try to take over, or at least that he is going to get a lot of interference from London.'

'I don't see why he should regard it as interference,' Richard commented. 'Down south they are crying out for a bit of help and recognition.'

There was, however, no denying the fact that Paul ran a very effective operation and Richard told himself that one must make allowances for the sort of buccaneering spirit that would be prepared to undertake such a risky business. Yet he still could not bring himself to like the man or to forget Pat O'Leary's warning. He was careful to give no hint that Duval was anything other than a casual acquaintance.

After Duval had said goodnight, Paul confided to them in a low voice that he was expecting a new 'customer' to arrive within the next day or two. 'I'm sure Chantal will be happy to entertain him,' he added with a smirk.

'What password will he give?' Chantal asked.

'The poor sap doesn't speak a word of French so he's posing as deaf and dumb,' Cole replied. 'He'll sit at the usual table, in the corner, and he'll have a note asking for a beer. He's been told that his contact will bring him a bottle of red wine instead. OK?'

It occurred to Richard that his presence would necessitate a change in the procedure by which Chantal had previously made contact with escaping British servicemen. She could no longer simply 'pick them up' in the guise of indulging a voracious sexual appetite – or at least, he could not be seen to accept the situation. Some new formula would have to be devised.

When they were alone Chantal said, 'Why didn't you tell Paul that Henri is one of us?'

'Because I don't think there is any reason for Paul to know anything about him,' Richard said. He was tired and his tone was a little sharper than he intended.

'But he's in charge of the *réseau*,' Chantal exclaimed. 'We can't keep him in the dark. Why don't you trust him?'

'I don't know! There's just something about him. O'Leary doesn't trust him either.'

'But he has taken so many men south, and risked his life to do it! How can you not trust him?'

Richard sighed and shook his head. 'I don't know, Chantal. I know it's not logical and lots of people wouldn't agree with me, but I just have this feeling that he's not what he pretends to be. Anyway, Henri's part of my team. It's nothing to do with Paul. You know the principle. You don't tell anyone anything they don't have to know.'

She shrugged and turned away. 'You are becoming paranoid, *mon cher*. All this training in England has twisted your mind.'

'Have it your own way,' he said.

For the first days after they were reunited they had both lived in a kind of sexual Eden, able to banish all anxieties about the outside world as soon as they were alone together. But now the strain of living a double life was beginning to make itself felt and Richard found himself oscillating between intense desire and a sense of frustration. Chantal was a free spirit who could not be tied down. He had always known that and had thought that he accepted it, but now he was beginning to realise that it was not enough.

He said, 'How are we going to deal with this new "customer" when he shows up? You can't just pick men up like you used to.'

'Why not?' she demanded.

'Well, because it would look bloody funny to everyone who knows us. What am I supposed to do — act as your pimp?'

She swung round and stared at him with cold anger in her eyes. 'Do as you please, *mon ami*! I shall do what seems necessary. You can act the jealous lover if you like. You are good at acting, after all!'

He got up and went to her, suddenly desperate for a reconciliation. 'But don't you see, *chérie*? I wouldn't be acting. I can't just stand by and watch you flirting with another man.'

She looked at him for a moment and then burst out laughing and flung her arms round his neck. 'Oh, *mon pauvre petit*, it's not as if I am going to take these men to bed! Yes, I did it with you, when you first came to the café, but that doesn't mean I do it with all of them. We were already old lovers, *n'est-ce pas*?'

He kissed her but then forced his mind back to the problem. 'But how are we going to play it now, *chérie*?'

'Well,' she gave him a mischievous smile, 'let us put on a little performance for the benefit of the others, if you like. I will flirt, you can be jealous, then there is a big reconciliation and we all get drunk and go home together.'

'That really will get the tongues wagging!' Richard said, laughing. 'But there's a snag. Our customer doesn't speak a word of French.'

Chantal pursed her lips and put her head on one side. '*Dis donc, mon cher*. It is possible to flirt without the use of words, *n'est-ce pas*?'

Richard shrugged. 'As long as our friend has the sense to keep his mouth shut, I suppose it's as good a scheme as any.'

The next evening, when they went out to begin their act, they both paid particular attention to the table in the corner, but it was unoccupied. The following night they saw him as soon as they made their entrance. Tall, blond and square jawed, he looked like the archetypal product of the English public school. Just possibly he might have been German, but never French. To make matters worse, instead of keeping his head down and trying to be inconspicuous, he was sitting erect and gazing about him as if he were in his own local pub. Already he was attracting curious glances from the regular clients, and as usual there were two tables of German officers placed near the stage area.

When they had finished their number and got back to the dressing room Richard burst out, 'Bloody idiot! Hasn't he got any sense at all?'

'We'll have to get him out before people start asking questions,' Chantal said. 'We can't sit and drink with him. It would be asking for trouble.'

'I've got it!' Richard said. 'Remember what you said about acting jealous? Well, go out and do your solo, take him the red wine and start flirting – and be prepared for fireworks.'

Chantal began her song. It was a regular feature that during this number she moved from table to table, taking a cigarette from one man, leaning across to another for a light, stealing a sip from someone else's glass, and usually Richard pretended indifference and flirted with one of the waitresses. Tonight, however, he made it clear from the start that he was in no mood for flirtation, standing with his arms folded and watching Chantal with burning eyes. In the corner of his field of vision he could see the Englishman, watching proceedings with open fascination, apparently completely unaware of danger. Chantal took a bottle of red wine and a glass from the bar and carried it over to him. Perching on the edge of the table, her long, silk-clad legs provocatively crossed, she leaned over and poured him a glass of wine, murmuring huskily, '_Dis donc, chéri, tu veux boire du vin rouge avec moi?_'

There was a general chuckle from around the room. This

was all part of the act and the regulars enjoyed the embarrassment of the unsuspecting newcomer, but Richard was already
on his way over to the table. Flinging a chair out of his way, he
pounced on the young airman, who was goggling up into
Chantal's face like a Labrador puppy about to roll over to have
its tummy tickled. Seizing him with one hand by the collar and
clamping the other over the lower part of his face, effectively
preventing him from uttering anything more than a startled
grunt, Richard hauled him to his feet, at the same time
berating him in gutter Italian. The onlookers cheered deri-
sively, but out of the corner of his eye he could see the
proprietor of the café and Gaston, the waiter, heading rapidly
in their direction.

Having got the Englishman to his feet Richard became
uncomfortably aware that he was a good half-head taller than
himself and built like the proverbial brick privy. If he chose to
fight back it would be an unequal match unless he, Richard,
used some of the techniques he had learned at Arisaig, which
would of themselves give rise to awkward questions. Fortunately his adversary was so taken aback by the sudden
onslaught that he put up very little resistance and almost at
once Gaston and the proprietor were upon them.

'Out!' shouted the proprietor. 'Out before we have any
more trouble.'

A few seconds later they were both forcibly ejected on to the
street, accompanied by a chorus of cheers and catcalls from
inside. Richard shifted his grip, yanked the other man to him
and said into his ear, in English, 'It's all right. Pretend to
struggle but let me get you round the corner into the alley.'

To his credit, the airman reacted at once without further
prompting and the two of them wrestled their way into the
dark shadows of the alley. Richard pushed him against the wall
and put a hand over his mouth. With his mouth still close to his
ear he hissed, 'You bloody idiot! You're about as conspicuous

as an elephant in a herd of sheep. Stay quiet, for God's sake, and do as I tell you.' He let go and the other man stared at him in silence, panting slightly. Richard looked around him. No one had followed them out. 'Stay here and don't move,' he instructed. 'I have to go back in but in a moment the girl will come out. Go with her and do as she tells you. Understand?'

The other nodded and Richard left him leaning against the wall and returned to the café. Chantal was standing by the bar, looking defiant. He went over to her and grabbed her by the wrist.

'All right, go on!' he yelled, dragging her towards the door. 'Go and find your fancy man, if that's what you want. Just don't come crawling back to me when he's finished with you.'

He pushed her through the door and jerked his head towards the alley. She stared at him for a moment, then drew herself up, tossed her head and jerked a raised middle finger upwards. Then she turned and sauntered into the alley.

Richard went back into the café, ordered a brandy and made himself sufficiently unpleasant to be left alone to drink it. He waited until enough time had elapsed to allow his temper to cool and for the owner to bully him into singing his final number, and then changed his clothes and headed for the flat.

He found Chantal and the airman sitting cosily over cups of what passed for coffee and apparently quite at ease with each other. The young man rose as he came in and extended his hand.

'Peter Cornwallis – Flying Officer. I gather I was in a bit of a tricky situation back there. Thanks for getting me out of it.'

'Benedetti,' Richard said. 'Ricardo. Hasn't it occurred to you that you stick out like a sore thumb among the locals?'

'He can't help that!' Chantal pointed out. 'It's not his fault that he's tall and fair.'

Richard said nothing. It was, of course, a valid point, but he still felt unreasonably angered by the airman's insouciant attitude.

'I say,' said Cornwallis, 'your English is frightfully good! I thought you were English.'

'I'm Italian,' Richard said shortly, 'but I don't support Mussolini or the Nazis. That's why I'm prepared to help you.'

They explained to their guest that he would have to stay hidden in the flat until papers could be prepared for him that would allow him to travel with reasonable safety and that then someone would accompany him south.

'Good show!' he commented. 'How long is all this going to take?'

'Several days to get the papers,' Richard told him. 'Then you'll have to wait for someone to take you to Marseilles. After that it can take a week or more to get you across the Pyrenees and hand you over to our man in Madrid. Then you'll have to wait again for transport to Gibraltar and a ship home.'

'You're talking about months!' the young man exclaimed. 'Isn't there a quicker way?'

'You could try swimming, I suppose,' Richard said sourly.

'It's just that I've got a very particular reason for getting back in a hurry,' Cornwallis went on with a winning smile. 'The fact is, just the night before I took off I got engaged to an absolutely gorgeous girl. I wouldn't want her to think I'd changed my mind!'

Richard looked at him for a long moment. How was it possible, he wondered, for anyone to be so completely self-centred?

'Perhaps someone should tell her there's a war on,' he grunted finally.

The next day Richard and Chantal reappeared at the café as if nothing had happened and made it quite clear from their behaviour that the interloper had been seen off and that they were reconciled. In point of fact, of course, Peter Cornwallis had spent the night on the couch in Chantal's living room and had passed the day prowling up and down like a caged animal. Richard took him to the photographer they always used for this purpose and got the necessary pictures for his identity card and other documents. For the rest of the time he and Chantal had tried to occupy him with games of cards or chess, but it was clear he was not going to be an easy guest. When they told him that they would have to leave him alone for the evening he immediately wanted to know why he couldn't come with them.

'You can tell them we're all friends now, can't you?' he demanded.

'And what will happen if the police ask for your papers?' Richard enquired.

'You can tell them I lost them when I was bombed out,' was the reply. 'That's what Jeanette told them on the train here.'

'Well, you were lucky they believed her,' Richard told him. He had never met the girl who went by the name of Jeanette but he knew her by reputation as another intrepid member of the *réseau* who regularly risked her life to conduct escapers from the Brussels area down to Lille. It infuriated him to think how close she had come to discovery and how casually Cornwallis accepted the dangers being undergone on his behalf. 'Anyway,' he said, 'we're not risking that again. You'll just have to stay here and keep your head down.'

When they got back from the café later that night Cornwallis was sprawled on the sofa. He had drunk a bottle of wine and finished off the cognac that Chantal was carefully hoarding for emergencies and was as sulky as a spoilt child denied a treat.

The following day Richard set off for Abbeville to visit the gentle-mannered priest who kept a printing press in his back room and had turned himself into an expert forger in the interests of aiding escaping servicemen. He took with him the photographs of Cornwallis and left Chantal to 'babysit' the young airman in his absence. He was glad to have an excuse to visit the ábbé. He had come to the conclusion that, if he was to set up the independent network for escaping SOE agents that he had been commissioned to create, he must involve one or two trustworthy people who might suggest possible contacts. And there was no one he trusted more than the Abbé Carpentier.

Once the matter of the papers for Cornwallis had been dealt with and they were sitting over a glass of Calvados in the priest's living room he made an oblique approach to the subject.

'Did you know, Father, that when I was escaping myself I was sheltered for a while by a convent of Poor Clares?'

'I know the place you mean,' the priest answered. 'I didn't realise that you had stayed there.'

'I admired the courage of the mother superior,' Richard continued, 'as I admire yours. Would you say that most of those in holy orders would take the same position?'

'I cannot see how it is possible to be a Christian and not hate the Nazis,' the priest said. 'But there may be those who feel that it is better to oppose them by means of prayer than by becoming actively involved.'

Richard met his eyes and saw that they both knew what they were talking about. He said, 'As the war goes on, there are going to be more and more men – and women too perhaps – who need help in evading capture. I have been instructed to look for safe houses where they might stay – particularly between here and Brittany. Perhaps you are aware of fellow priests or religious houses that it might be worth my while to visit?'

The priest studied him gravely for a moment. Then he said, 'I cannot give you any guarantee of what reception you will get, except that you will not be betrayed to the authorities. But I can give you three addresses where you might find a sympathetic ear.'

He got up and went to a desk in one corner of the room and, after a moment, returned with a slip of paper on which he had written three addresses.

'You must memorise these. I cannot let you take the paper away.'

Richard nodded. 'Of course.' He studied the addresses for a while, until he was sure that he had committed them to memory. It was an exercise he had practised many times at Beaulieu. Then he handed the paper back to the ábbé and watched while he lit a match and reduced it to ashes and scattered the ashes among the dead coals in the fireplace. Shortly afterwards he thanked the priest and took his leave to head back to Lille.

As he approached the apartment he could hear voices and laughter and when he entered he found Chantal and Peter Cornwallis sitting opposite each other at the table with various strips of paper between them. Both were flushed and bright eyed.

'You two look as if you're enjoying yourselves,' he remarked, and it was an effort to keep his voice neutral.

'I am teaching Peter French,' Chantal said.

'We've been playing a sort of daft game of consequences,' Cornwallis added cheerily. 'It's good fun!'

Richard looked at them. Could an innocent game have produced the flush on Peter's cheeks, the glint in Chantal's eyes? 'Really?' he said dryly, adding, 'Your papers will be ready in two days.'

'Good-oh!' the boy exclaimed. 'Does that mean I can get on my way as soon as I have them?'

'Not necessarily,' Richard responded. 'We still have to work out how you are going to travel and where you're going to cross the demarcation line.'

'That shouldn't be a problem, should it? Once I have the right papers?'

Richard looked at him despairingly. 'And suppose you are questioned at the checkpoint?'

'I play dumb, like before.'

'Look,' Richard said, beginning to lose patience, 'the patrols along the demarcation line are German soldiers. They're a very different matter from your average French gendarme, who either actively sympathises or doesn't want to get involved. If these chaps are even faintly suspicious they are quite likely to haul you in and rough you up – and I'd like to see how long you can keep up the deaf-and-dumb act under that sort of treatment.'

'So what am I supposed to do?' Cornwallis asked sulkily.

'Be patient and wait till we work out the best way to tackle the problem. And try to bear in mind that if it all goes wrong it won't only be you who gets arrested. And while you may just have a chance of being held under the Geneva Convention and sent to an ordinary POW camp, whoever is travelling with you is likely to be shot.'

His tone was brutal and Cornwallis ducked his head and muttered defensively, 'OK, OK!'

Chantal got up and came to Richard, slipping an arm round his neck. 'What's wrong, *chéri*?'

'Nothing,' he said tersely, avoiding the embrace. 'I'm tired, that's all. Is there anything to eat?'

'Naturally.' She studied his face for a moment. 'Did you think we would have eaten without you?'

He shrugged and turned away.

Later, when they were getting ready to go to the café for their nightly performance, Chantal said, 'Why are you so hard on Peter?'

'Hard on him? I'm risking my neck to get him back to his precious fiancée. Isn't that enough?'

'But you can hardly bring yourself to speak a civil word to him. Why?'

It was a moment before Richard answered. 'The man's an idiot,' was all the explanation he could think of.

'So?' she responded. 'Perhaps he is not all that bright. But we cannot all be highly intelligent, highly trained agents like you! He is alone in a foreign country and he is frightened.'

'Then I wish he'd act that way, instead of behaving as if he was at home in his own back yard!' Richard exclaimed. 'He's a spoilt kid. It'll do him good to find he can't always have everything his own way. And I don't regard myself as "highly intelligent" or any of that crap! I just have a modicum of common sense.'

It was Chantal's turn to shrug. '*Eh bien, mon brave*, if that's how you feel. I feel sorry for the boy. He needs someone to console him.'

'Yes!' he flashed back at her. 'And I know what your idea of consolation consists of!'

For a moment he thought she was going to slap him, then he saw her face tighten and close. 'Very well. Think what you like. I shall do as I please.'

'As usual!' he snapped, but she refused to be drawn any further.

That night they were both aware that their numbers lacked the essential magic that had made them so popular with the habitués of the Café Bleu.

When they got back to the flat it was empty. Their irritation with each other was instantly forgotten as they searched the rooms and found no sign of Cornwallis.

'Nothing has been disturbed,' Richard said tensely. 'If the Gestapo had been here they would have searched.'

'Unless they are waiting for us to come home,' Chantal said.

They stared at each other and Richard felt panic rising in his throat. Should they leave now while there was still a chance of getting away? Or was it better to stay here and hope for the best? If the Gestapo had lifted Cornwallis it would not take them long to establish his identity, or at least his nationality. There would be no way of explaining his presence in their flat.

In the silence they both heard footsteps mounting the stairs. Richard moved to the door. 'One man!' he breathed. The steps were heavy, with no attempt at concealment. They came to the door and the bell rang – a long, insistent peal. Richard reached into his pocket. Hanging from a specially made loop inside his trouser leg was his .32 Colt. He had never yet fired it at a living target but now he took comfort in the familiar feel of the butt. He stepped aside, so that the open door would conceal him, and nodded to Chantal. She took a deep breath and undid the lock.

Peter Cornwallis half fell into the hallway. It was immediately apparent, from the smell of him if from nothing else, that he was very drunk.

'Glad you're back,' he mumbled. 'Suddenly realised I don't have a key.'

Richard released his grip on the gun and grabbed him by the arm.

'You bloody idiot!' he exclaimed. 'Do you want to get us all killed? Where the hell have you been?'

Cornwallis pulled himself upright and shook off Richard's hand. 'Went out for a drink,' he said, in injured tones. 'Nothing left here to drink. You wouldn't take me with you. Couldn't sit around on my own all evening.'

He marched into the sitting room and flopped on to the sofa. Richard and Chantal gazed at him, and then at each other.

'You are right, *mon cher*,' Chantal said. 'The man is an idiot.'

'How did you manage?' Richard asked. 'You don't speak a word of the language.'

'Yes I do,' Cornwallis returned, grinning stupidly. '*Une bière, s'il vous plaît*. See? Chantal taught me that yesterday.'

'And you've been going round saying that?' Richard demanded. 'Where? Where did you go?'

But Cornwallis's short interlude of lucidity was over and they could not get any further sense out of him. Before long he lay back on the sofa and began to snore loudly.

'What do we do?' Chantal asked.

'If anyone had followed him they would be here by now,' Richard said. 'Put the light out.'

When the room was in darkness he lifted a corner of the curtain and studied the street below. There was no sign of anyone. He watched for a long time, straining his eyes for any sign of movement in a shop doorway or any of the windows opposite. Finally he turned back into the room.

'We may have got away with it. But we daren't relax too much. Pack a small bag in case we have to move in a hurry and open the back window on to the roof.' He had established early on that it was possible to leave the flat by clambering over the roofs of adjoining buildings and then descending a fire escape. It was a slim chance, but better than nothing.

When Chantal came back he said, 'You get some sleep. I'll keep watch.'

She hesitated and looked at the clock. Then she said, 'At four I will come and relieve you.' They looked at each other in the faint light from the window and then she put her arms round his neck. 'You were jealous, *chéri*? Of that?'

He held her for a moment. 'Yes. I couldn't help it.'

'There was no need. Do you believe me?'

He met her eyes and nodded. 'Yes, I believe you.'

Her mouth was soft, sweet as ripe fruit, and he was tempted for a moment to forget his vigil. Regretfully he pushed her away and murmured, 'Try to get some sleep.'

He did not really expect that she would wake to keep her

promise but just before four she appeared, yawning, and put on the kettle to make coffee for them both. Then she kissed him and said, 'Now it is your turn to sleep.'

When he woke she was dressed and administering coffee to a haggard and shaky Peter Cornwallis. He looked up as Richard arrived.

'Gather I behaved like a bit of a clot last night.'

'You could say that,' Richard agreed dryly.

The boy looked up at him with an expression of humble entreaty. 'Can we skip the lecture – please? I've had it all already from Chantal.'

Chantal said, 'It is true, *chéri*. I think he understands now how very foolish he has been.'

Richard stood over Cornwallis, his hands thrust deep into his pockets. 'We could all have been in the hands of the Gestapo by now, thanks to you. It's pure luck that we're not. I can only assume that the people who saw you and heard you last night are anti-Nazi and chose not to give you away, but they could just as easily have been *collaborateurs*. If you disobey orders again, even in the smallest detail, I shall wash my hands of you and you will have to find your own way home. In fact, I might hand you over to the Germans myself, to prevent you putting any other lives at risk. Understood?'

'Understood,' Cornwallis agreed humbly.

That evening Jack/Henri showed up at the Café Bleu again and when Richard joined him he said quietly, 'By the way, Monty's dog has no nose.'

'Tonight!' Richard said. 'You heard it tonight?'

'After the six o'clock bulletin.'

'That means the drop is set for the night after next.'

'Provided we get the confirmation. Can you organise the reception party?'

'Yes, leave that to me.' Richard's mind was working quickly. 'They're definitely going to land to pick up the documents?'

'That's what I asked for.'

'Can you get on to London again? Tell them there will be a passenger to collect as well.'

'A passenger? You're not going back, are you?'

Richard smiled at him reassuringly. 'No, don't worry. I'm going to stick around. But there is someone I want to get out of the way as quickly as possible, before he does any more damage.'

Cornwallis was sitting where they had left him when they got back to the flat, staring gloomily into space.

Richard grinned at him. 'Cheer up! You may be on your way sooner than you think.'

Then he led Chantal into their bedroom and made love to her noisily enough to be heard in the next room.

18

Rose completed a series of steps prescribed by her dance teacher and stood aside to watch the other girls in the class perform the same exercise. Sonia kept up a volley of comments as each took her turn.

'The leg higher in the arabesque, Jacqueline! Mary, what are you doing with your arms? Peggy, the pirouettes are supposed to be *en place*. You are wobbling all over the floor!'

It struck Rose that Sonia had made no such criticisms of her efforts. All she had said was 'Excellent, Rose. Well done'. After months of hard work, going to class three evenings a week and getting up at seven to put in an hour's practice before she opened the shop, she had finally recovered her technique to the point where she could show the senior class how it should be done.

When the class was over Sonia called her. 'Rose, hang on a minute, will you, dear? I want to have a word.'

As soon as the other girls had gone Sonia said, 'Rose, you remember how you used to teach the little ones sometimes, when you were a student here?'

'Of course I do,' Rose replied. She was puzzled because this time around she had insisted on paying for her classes out of the money she earned in the shoe shop.

'I was wondering,' Sonia said. 'The classes are getting a bit too much for Irena. She has arthritis in her knee, you know, and she really can't demonstrate properly. I haven't got time to fit them in so it occurred to me that perhaps you might be prepared to take them over. There are four classes but it would only be twice a week – two on Wednesday afternoon and two on Saturday. And I should pay you, of course. It would more than cover the cost of your own classes. What do you think?'

Rose hesitated. The extra money would be useful, certainly, and she had enjoyed teaching the little ones. Wednesday afternoons were no problem as it was half-day closing and on Saturdays – well, if people wanted shoes they would just have to come to the shop in the morning. But still she was unwilling to commit herself. It was the middle of October. In a few weeks' time auditions would start for Christmas pantomimes and Rose had made up her mind that this year she would be back at work as a professional dancer. There would not be so many pantos this year, and they would probably be less lavish, with smaller casts and fewer dancers, but there was still a chance. After all, she reasoned, a lot of girls were away in the forces or working in factories. The competition might not be as fierce as usual – and anyway, she had never had trouble getting work before. Now this request of Sonia's put her in an awkward position. She had decided not to mention that she intended to audition, because she had the feeling that Sonia would try to dissuade her; but she did not want to start the classes and then let her down after a few weeks if she got a job. On the other hand, she could think of no good reason for refusing.

In the end she said, 'I'll have to think about it, Sonia. I'd like to do it and it's sweet of you to ask me, but there's the shop to think of. I'm not sure if I can manage both. Can I sleep on it?'

'Of course,' Sonia replied. 'But let me know soon. If you can't manage it I may have to employ someone else.' She paused and added, 'Have you ever thought of taking your teacher's certificate?'

'No,' Rose said, taken by surprise. 'Why?'

'Well, surely, you would rather have a career as a dancing teacher than spend all your life working in a shoe shop?'

Rose looked at her and then stared hard out of the window. Sonia had made up her mind that she was never going to dance professionally again. Had she just assumed that, or did she genuinely think that she would never be good enough? Tears stung the back of her eyes.

'I don't know,' she said hastily. 'I've never thought about it. I have to go now. I'll let you know tomorrow about the classes.'

Sitting by herself when she got home, Rose tried again to face up to the future. If it was true that she could never regain the skills that had once ensured her a reasonably secure career – as secure as any career in the chancy business of the stage could ever be – then what was the alternative? It was true, as Sonia had said, that the idea of becoming a teacher was more attractive than staying in the shop. She tried to imagine herself at Sonia's age, with her own dancing school. After all, she reminded herself, even if her stage career had not been interrupted she could not have gone on for ever. She had always assumed that long before the time came when she had to give up dancing she would be married. Now she must think again. She decided that she could not afford to turn down Sonia's offer.

Merry's ship sailed from Liverpool as part of a convoy at the beginning of September. For the first few days he was as sick at heart as the majority of the passengers were sick to their stomachs, while the ship battled across the Bay of Biscay. The realisation that he did not suffer from seasickness did something to restore his spirits, and as the days passed he began to enjoy what George Black had predicted – a pleasant ocean cruise. The vessel was a passenger liner converted for use as a troopship, crowded with men from a number of different units. While conditions for the men were cramped and the facilities basic to say the least, the officers' accommodation retained at least some hint of former luxuries. Merry had a cabin to himself and was made welcome in the wardroom, where he found congenial company and an unlimited supply of pink gin, his favourite tipple. More importantly, the sea air, unpolluted by pollen or exhaust fumes, suited him so well that he was scarcely troubled by his asthma.

It was not long before the illusion of a pleasure cruise was rudely dispelled. Twice the convoy was bombed and strafed by enemy aircraft and later in the voyage they were attacked by U-boats and one ship in the convoy was sunk. Merry watched as the boats lifted survivors from the water and felt cold sweat break out on his brow. It could so easily be their turn next.

After this, however, the voyage proceeded smoothly, and it was pleasant to feel the power of the sun strengthening day by day. For long periods it was almost possible to forget the war completely. This was particularly true once it became clear that they were not heading east into the Mediterranean, and they all settled in for what was obviously going to be a long trip.

Early in the voyage Merry had negotiated the use of what had once been the liner's ballroom every morning for rehearsals. Once most of his company had got their sea legs he called them together for an initial discussion. Looking around as they assembled, he was encouraged by the sight of familiar faces. Some of them had been with him in Scotland, some for even longer. They were a talented and versatile bunch. There was Clive, the female impersonator who had caused such havoc in the Scottish pub, and Ronnie Davies, a Welsh tenor with the physique of a rugby player and a repertoire of sentimental ballads. Then there was the band, all old friends and thorough professionals. There were four of them, and between them they could play a surprising variety of instruments, giving Merry plenty of scope for his talents as an arranger. Among them were Dave Shadwell, the saxophonist who had caused such a furore in the early days at Greenford, when he had offered an officer his telephone number instead of his service number, and Chubby Hawkes, one of the best-known trumpeters on the civilian jazz circuit.

There were new faces, too. Some of the old crowd had dropped out, for various reasons, and Merry had conducted hasty auditions before leaving London. Six-foot-two Ray Short and his partner, Wally Levine who, for the purposes of the act, had changed his name to Walter Long, formed a cross-talking double act which they always concluded with a chorus of 'Bless 'em All'. They had an irreverent attitude and a knack for picking on the idiocies of army life that he knew would go down well. Then there was the youngest member of the group, a lad of nineteen called Tom Dyson, who tap-danced in a very creditable imitation of his hero, Fred Astaire. He was a good-looking boy, slim and dark haired, with large blue-grey eyes fringed with long lashes.

Once they were all assembled Merry began. 'Right, chaps. I hope you're all over your collywobbles and ready to start work. It's good to be working with so many old friends again but as you will have realised we have some new members, so for their benefit I'd like to go over a few ground rules before we start. The most important one is this. We're all professionals and we respect each other's work. We know that what matters is the show and in that effort we are all equal, irrespective of rank. So, within these walls, we're on Christian-name terms and you can call me Merry. But like it or not we are all serving soldiers so outside this room we have to respect military discipline. Which means that in front of other people you will treat me as you would any other officer. Understood?'

There was a murmur of agreement from the old hands. Merry looked at Wally and Ray. They nodded and Wally said cheerfully, 'Right you are, boss. Whatever you say.'

'Tom?'

'Yes, *sir* – Merry.'

The words were unexceptionable but there was something about the intonation, and the way the large eyes sought and held his own, that set alarm bells ringing at the back of Merry's mind.

Dave said, 'Before we go any farther, the lads and I have been thinking about a name for the company and we've come up with an idea. We think we should be called Guy Merryweather and his Merry Men.'

There was a ripple of applause and murmurs of approval but Merry felt himself blush. 'No, no! That's far too personal. It makes me sound much too egotistical.'

'I don't see why,' Dave said. 'Lots of bands are known by the bandleader's name.'

'Well, we're not a band. It wouldn't be fair on the others.'

'Merry, dahling!' Clive protested. 'You're much too modest.'

'Tell you what,' Ronnie put in. 'Why don't we just call ourselves the Merrymakers? Then it's not so personal.'

There was such a consensus of approval for this that Merry felt it would be churlish to disagree. 'OK. Now let's get down to work. I want to sort out the music first so we can copy out band parts if necessary. Ronnie, got your dots?'

He seated himself at the piano and the tenor came forward and handed over several sheets of music. Merry glanced through them and turned to Clive. 'How about you? Are you sticking to your Marlene Dietrich number?'

'Thought I might branch out and do a Judy Garland.'

'"Somewhere over the Rainbow"? OK, that's no problem. We all know that. Now, Tom. What do you need?'

The boy unwound himself from his chair and came across to place the music on the piano, and in doing so his arm brushed Merry's shoulder. 'This, if it's OK with you, Merry.' The words were spoken close to his ear and for a moment his face was almost against Merry's cheek. The alarm bells were sounding loud and clear now. There was a time when Merry would have responded to such an open invitation. But not any more – and certainly not in the present circumstances.

From then on, all through rehearsals, he was aware of Tom's puppy-dog eyes following him, and whenever possible the boy was at his side, handing him things, offering quite unnecessarily to turn over while he was playing, making physical contact at every opportunity. Merry responded by being as curt and distant as the situation would allow, but Tom seemed unable to take the hint.

The first public performance of the new show took place just before their arrival in Cape Town and was greeted with prolonged applause and demands for encores. The next morning, however, Merry was asked to attend the commanding officer in his cabin.

'Good show last night, Merryweather. Greatly appreciated by the men. That female impersonator – remarkable. Can't say I like that sort of thing myself but the men seem to enjoy it. I suppose he's a raving poofter?'

'As a matter of fact he has a wife and two kids in Sidcup,' Merry said.

'Really? You amaze me. Just one thing. Those two comics – Push and Shove or whatever they call themselves . . .'

'Long and Short.' Merry knew what was coming.

'That take off of Major Warrington went a bit too far. Bad for discipline, what? Can you have a word?'

Merry stifled a grin. Wally and Ray had an unerring ear for mannerisms that struck them as absurd and an instinct for which officers were less than popular with their men, and last night they had lampooned the major, to hoots of delighted laughter. 'I'll speak to them, sir. It wasn't in the original script.'

Wally and Ray looked duly contrite when admonished, but it did not stop them from taking the mickey out of another officer the following evening.

In spite of that, they were asked to put on regular performances to entertain the troops until they arrived at their final destination. Where that might be was still a mystery and a number of the more enterprising soldiers were taking bets, with Singapore a clear favourite.

Merry related most of this in a long letter to Felix, though he forbore to mention the minor embarrassment of Tom's attitude. He concluded with a final paragraph.

> *As you know, there is someone I should like to write to, but I could never say the things I want to say for fear of it being seen by the wrong person. However, I know I can rely on you to relay the message. F. is present with me continually, like a beautiful leitmotif, even when my conscious thoughts are occupied elsewhere. Sometimes it is a piece of perfect background music, enhancing my pleasure in the good moments and consoling me when things are not going so well. Sometimes it swells to a great crescendo and nearly breaks my heart with longing and at others it is a gentle lullaby that soothes me off to sleep. At all times I should be totally bereft without it and my life would be as flat and insipid as a silent movie without its musical accompaniment. I'm sure you will understand what I mean.*
>
> *My enduring love to F.*
> *Yours, as always,*
> *Merry*

Meanwhile, Felix had problems of his own, of a slightly different kind. Since he had joined the squadron some of the younger pilots, to whom he was already a hero, had been disturbed by his apparent lack of what they termed 'social life', by which they meant female companionship. From the occasional hint, tactful or otherwise, he gathered that they had decided that his disfigurement had destroyed his confidence and that it was their duty to convince him that there were plenty of attractive girls who would be only too happy to be seen on the arm of a Battle of Britain hero, scarred or not.

Felix therefore found himself being constantly ambushed by introductions to pretty girls. Pilots who had sisters invited them down to stay in a local hotel and presented them when Felix came in for a drink in the bar. Men would suggest a game of tennis, which Felix had taught himself to play left-handed, and he would find that he was playing mixed doubles. Even the CO's wife got involved and insisted on inviting him to dinners at which he was always paired with an unattached girl. He was always polite. The girl in question would be treated to his undivided attention for the duration of whatever function was in progress, bought drinks and made to laugh at his jokes and then walked or driven home, as appropriate. But at the crucial point she would receive a platonic kiss on the cheek and a murmured 'Goodnight, and thank you for a lovely evening', and be ushered to her front door. He could only hope that she would not spend the next days waiting in vain for a phone call.

As his friends became more desperate Felix found the joke beginning to wear a bit thin. In the end he decided that the only way to discourage these unwanted attentions was to produce a girlfriend of his own. That was when he thought of Harriet. They had kept in touch since the episode of the photographs and he had taken her out to dinner once or twice. So the next time he was invited to a party he asked her to join him. Naturally, his fellow officers remembered the beautiful photographer and he saw looks of comprehension being exchanged as he entered the room with her on his arm. So that was the secret Ned Mountjoy had been keeping all this time! They might have guessed!

Harriet had booked a room in a local hotel, and when the party was over Felix drove her back there. As they drew up outside she said, 'I'd ask you in for a nightcap but I have a feeling the management wouldn't approve.'

'Probably not,' he agreed, 'and anyway I have to get back to the station.' But he turned off the engine and sat silent for a moment. Then he drew a deep breath and went on, 'Harry, there's something I have to talk to you about.'

'Oh?'

Felix folded his hands on the steering wheel and fixed his gaze on them. 'The thing is, I led you up the garden path before. I don't want to do it again.'

'Led me up the garden path? I don't know what you're talking about.'

'When we were together before the war – and later, until I got shot down – I wasn't being honest with you. I led you to assume that . . . that there was a future for us, as a couple.'

'Just a minute.' Harriet laid a hand on his arm. 'I was the one who let you down, not the other way round. You don't have anything to feel ashamed of.'

'That's the point,' Felix said. 'There is something. You see, all that time I was . . . was sailing under false colours, if you like. Pretending to be something I'm not.'

'Well, I knew that! We grew up together. I've always known who you really were.'

'No, I don't mean that,' Felix said. He was struggling for words. 'I mean something much more fundamental and personal than that. It doesn't matter whether I'm called Felix Lamont or Ned Mountjoy, I've got no right to lead you – or any woman – to think I'm offering a permanent relationship.'

Harriet was silent for a moment and then she said, 'Are you telling me that what happened in Cambridge wasn't a one-off, a momentary aberration that only happened because you were drunk?' Felix nodded silently and she added, almost under her breath, 'You know, I think I always knew that, somehow.'

'You knew that I'm what the rest of the world calls queer, bent, a fairy, a poofter?' His tone was bitter.

She touched his arm again. 'Don't! I can't bear to hear you calling yourself those horrible names! I know you! You're brave and honourable and kind and . . . and straight!'

He squeezed her hand briefly. 'Thank you, Harry. It's sweet of you to take it like this, but the fact is I wasn't being straight or honourable with you. The only mitigating circumstance I can claim is that I was deceiving myself as well. I genuinely convinced myself that we could make a go of it.'

'Until I let you down,' she said. 'I behaved abominably in that hospital and I've never forgiven myself. But I suppose the fact is, if I'd really loved you I'd have stuck by you.' She looked at him. 'Merry did. Is that what happened?'

'In a way,' he replied. 'But I don't want you to think it was in any way your fault. I suppose if you'd stuck around I might have gone on kidding myself a bit longer. But I doubt it. The fact is that lying there in that hospital bed I realised what it was I really wanted – needed – and who it was.'

'And it wasn't me,' Harriet said. 'Well, it's justice, isn't it? Merry got what he deserved. Only the brave, etc., etc. Are you and he still . . . together?'

Felix gave a rueful smile. 'When this bloody war lets us be. At the moment he's on a ship somewhere so God knows when we'll see each other again.'

'But you are happy, with him?'

'Oh yes. When I'm with him I'm as happy as . . . happier than I ever expected to be.'

'Then I'm pleased for you,' she said. 'It's all worked out for the best, hasn't it?'

He looked at her. 'You really are very sweet, Harry. Can I ask you something? Is there anyone . . . do you have anyone special at the moment?'

She shook her head. 'There doesn't seem to be much point in getting involved with anyone as long as the war goes on.'

'Then, can I ask you an enormous favour?'

'What?'

'Well, I have a problem with the other chaps in the squadron.'

'You think they suspect?'

'No, not that. I think I'm pretty secure there at present. But they've made up their minds that I'm suffering from a broken heart or something. They keep trying to pair me off with every available woman under forty in the county. I need someone to . . . to . . .' He trailed into silence.

'To pose as your mistress?' Harriet suggested.

'Something like that.'

'And you want me to do it?'

'Well, girlfriend anyway. But I wouldn't want to get in the way if there was someone else.'

'I've told you, there's no one else.'

'So, what do you think?' He paused and drew a long breath. 'Believe me, Harry, I hate all this subterfuge. I wish I could stand up and proclaim my real feelings. I wish I could,' he gave a brief, ironic smile, 'I wish I could "make an honest man" of Merry! But the fact is, I'm breaking the law. I don't want to end up like poor bloody Oscar Wilde!'

'Yes, I can understand that,' she said. 'It's rotten for you. I'd like to help if I can.'

'You're a brick, Harry! You're sure it won't be too much of a bore?'

She gave a brief, tight laugh. 'Oh, being around you, Felix, can be described in a lot of ways but boring is not one of them! Or should I be calling you Ned?'

'Whichever you find most comfortable.'

She sighed. 'That's the trouble. I don't know. I don't know if I'm talking to Ned or Felix.'

He nodded and looked away for a moment. 'I can understand that. Sometimes I feel like two different people.'

'It's all a bit of a mess, isn't it?' she said sadly. 'When we were growing up you were just a friend – someone to go out riding with and play tennis with and all that. Then, when we got a bit older, I thought perhaps it might be more than that. But when that terrible business happened at Cambridge and your parents treated you so abominably I just wanted to help in any way I could.'

'And you did,' he answered. 'Don't think I've ever forgotten how you stuck by me then. We've always been good friends, haven't we? Can we go on like that?'

'On a strictly platonic basis?'

'Oh, yes, of course.'

She was silent for a moment. Then she murmured, 'Oh well. On the basis that half a loaf is better than no bread . . . Yes, all right.'

He looked at her, frowning. 'Sorry, I don't follow.'

She leaned over and kissed him lightly on the cheek. 'Never mind. Ring me next time you need an escort. 'Night!'

19

Since arriving in Lille Richard had spent a good deal of time building up his own list of contacts. Using the second set of papers which identified him as Lucien Dufrais and dressed in some old clothes Chantal had obtained for him he had frequented the bars and cafés of the university quarter, posing as an ex-student with ambitions as a writer. As a further precaution, on these expeditions he exchanged the specially built-up shoes that exaggerated his limp for a pair in which he could walk more or less normally. After long and ardent discussions of the current situation he had identified three people – a student of philosophy called Marcel, his girlfriend Jacqueline and a clerk from the Mairie by the name of Armand – whom he felt able to take into his confidence. Little by little he had become more open about his hatred of the occupying power and had hinted at a desire to find a practical way of expressing it. Finding that they shared his feelings, he finally confessed that he had 'contacts' with a resistance organisation that was in touch with London and asked whether they would be willing to join him if there was practical work to be done. He thought that they were rather sceptical of his claims and suspected him of being a bit of a fantasist, but they agreed that if ever action were needed they would be ready to help.

He had also become a regular customer at one or two bars and shops in Santes, a small town a few kilometres from the city, not far from the place he had chosen as a dropping zone. He had gained the confidence of Xavier Charlot, a blacksmith who now doubled as the local *garagiste*, and Robert Gatignon, the local vet. They, too, had pronounced themselves ready to act if the opportunity presented itself.

The day after Jack Duval had relayed the message from the BBC Richard went first to the café in the university quarter, where he found his three friends as usual, drinking pastis and arguing. He told them briefly that he was expecting a British plane to land the following night with supplies and money for the Resistance and asked them whether they were still prepared to help. He saw them exchange looks and realised that they were digesting the change in his manner and its implications.

Armand met his gaze and said, 'How do you know this?'

'I told you,' Richard replied, 'I have contacts. I can't reveal who they are.'

'Why should we trust you? You could be a German spy.'

'And you could betray me to the Gestapo as soon as you leave here,' Richard responded. 'I have to trust you.'

He watched tensely as they looked again at each other. It was a leap of faith on both sides and he was afraid that now they were faced with the dangerous reality they might regret the bravado of their earlier conversations.

It was Jacqueline who spoke first. 'We shall be there – Marcel and I.'

'And so shall I,' Armand added.

He arranged a rendezvous with them at a bar in Santes and then set off to speak to Xavier and Robert.

Xavier gave him a long look and grunted. 'I knew you weren't just a student. All right, you don't have to say anything. Where do we meet?'

Robert's reaction was equally encouraging. 'At last! It's time something happened.'

Richard spent half an hour with him, arranging details, and then returned to the flat. He had carefully kept Chantal in ignorance of his new contacts. She had resented the fact to begin with but he had eventually got her to see the sense of it. Now he persuaded her to go to the Café Bleu alone and cover for him by telling the proprietor that he had a bad cold and could not sing. Peter Cornwallis watched nervously as she prepared to leave, unsure what was going on and quite probably, Richard reckoned, not too happy at the prospect of being left alone with him.

As soon as Chantal had gone he gave him a cheery grin and said, 'Grab your gear. You're going home tonight.'

'Tonight?' the young airman gasped. 'How?'

'Special delivery. You'll see. Come on, hurry up. And for God's sake keep your mouth shut once we're out of the house!'

They made it to the rendezvous without incident, though Richard felt all the time as though his companion might just as well have had a notice hung round his neck with the legend 'escaping British airman'. Throughout the journey his senses were at full stretch, and he used every trick he had been taught at Beaulieu to make sure that they were not being followed. He saw Duval get on the same bus but was careful to give no sign of recognition. In the bar Armand was sitting with Marcel and Jacqueline, while Xavier stood at the counter. Duval strolled in after them and took a table in the corner.

Richard murmured to Cornwallis, 'I'm going to introduce you to some friends. Smile and nod and *don't speak!*'

He led him over to the table and greeted the other three as if they had just met by chance. 'And this is Pierre,' he added, slapping Cornwallis on the shoulder. 'He can't talk, poor chap, but he's OK.'

He was favourably impressed by the way the others took in the situation and reacted as if it were an everyday occurrence. He bought a round of drinks and nodded a greeting to Xavier. It was already late and people were beginning to leave in order to get home before the curfew.

'Drink up,' he admonished his companions. 'It's time to go.'

Outside, he led them round the back of the building. Parked out of sight of the road was a large closed truck. It was this vehicle that had particularly attracted Richard to Robert Gatignon, who used it to collect sick farm animals. This, together with the fact that vets were among the few categories of people who could get a pass to be out after curfew, made him an invaluable addition to the group. Seeing them approach, Robert got out of the cab and opened the rear doors. In silence they all clambered on board and seated themselves on bales of hay arranged along the sides.

When the doors were shut Richard said, 'Right. Time to put my cards on the table. You've all realised by now that I'm working for the British. Who I am doesn't matter. As far as you are all concerned, I'm Lucien Dufrais. And there is no need for you to know too much about each other, either, so first names only.' He introduced them to each other and added, 'You will have guessed, too, that Pierre here is an English pilot. One reason we are here is to get him safely back home, so he can continue the fight against the Boches. A plane is due to land at one forty-five, at a site I have selected. It will also bring money and supplies to support resistance activities. Has everyone brought a torch, as I requested?'

They all produced their torches and he went on, 'We have a couple of hours to wait. Robert, is there somewhere we can park up without attracting attention?'

'My place,' Robert replied with a shrug. 'Everyone is used to seeing the van and to me going out at night in it.'

'Right. Your place it is, then,' Richard agreed.

After a tedious hour, enlivened by a bottle of Calvados supplied by Robert, Richard looked at his watch.

'Time to move.'

Robert climbed back into the cab and they all fell silent as the vehicle reversed and bumped out of the yard and on to the road. They had not gone far when they felt the van slow down and come to a halt. Richard looked at the others and lifted a finger to his lips, but the warning was unnecessary as they all heard the German voices demanding to know where Robert was going and why he was out after curfew. In rigid silence they listened as Robert explained that a local landowner had called him out because a valuable horse had developed colic. He was on his way to collect the animal. Richard gripped the butt of his pistol and prayed that the soldiers would not want to look inside the truck. There was a delay while Robert produced his papers to be checked and then the engine restarted and the van jerked forward. In the back seven people realised they had been holding their breath and let it go in a sigh of relief.

Eventually they felt the van turn off the road and bump and sway over uneven ground, and Richard realised they were on the cart track leading to the field he had chosen. When it came to a standstill and Robert opened the doors they all climbed out in silence, stretching stiffened limbs. The landing site was an open meadow occupying the top of a low ridge and surrounded on all sides by trees. Occasionally it was used for grazing cows but at present it was empty, and Richard had made sure that it was a long way from any form of human habitation. He assembled the group and gave them careful instructions, keeping his voice low in spite of the fact that there was no one else within a mile of them.

'As soon as we hear the plane approaching I want you three, Armand, Xavier and Robert, to take up positions here, here and here.'

He walked them across the grass to indicate three points of an upside-down L with the crossbar upwind.

'I shall be here, with Armand, at the downwind end of the upright. Henri, wait with our pilot friend until I call you forward. Marcel and Jacqueline, I want you to keep watch on the track we came by. Flash your torches if you hear anyone approaching. When we hear the plane I shall flash a Morse recognition letter and he will acknowledge in the same way. As soon as you see that, Xavier, Robert and Armand, light your torches so he can see where the landing strip is. He will want to come straight in – circling just makes the chances of being spotted greater. He will land as near as possible to me and Armand, taxi to where you are, Xavier, turn and taxi back to me and turn again into the wind ready for take-off. Nobody is to come near the plane until I call. The pilot will be armed and if anyone approaches unexpectedly they are likely to be shot. As soon as the stuff has been delivered and Pierre here is on board he will take off again. The whole operation should take no more than three minutes. Everyone clear?'

They all nodded and murmured assent. Richard looked at his watch. 'OK. We still have twenty minutes to wait. Everyone get under cover of the trees and stay still.'

He and Duval settled with Cornwallis in a dry ditch at the edge of the field. There was an almost full moon and now that their eyes were night-adapted the open field looked as fully lit as a stage set. Autumn had come, and the light breeze brought a pattering shower of leaves down around them. Richard hunched his shoulders and felt glad that he had acquired a thick sweater for just such an occasion. Somewhere a little way off a fox barked.

Cornwallis shifted closer and murmured in his ear, 'I can't believe you're actually sending me home by plane!'

'It wasn't laid on specially for your benefit, so don't kid yourself,' Richard replied.

'Oh, understood! All the same, bloody good of you to cut me in on the deal. Pam will be tickled pink to get me back so quickly.'

'Who's Pam?' Duval asked.

The pilot squirmed round to look at him. 'You speak English?'

Duval caught Richard's eye across his head and grimaced. Richard shrugged. It could do little harm for Cornwallis to know who they were now. Nevertheless, Duval chose to play it safe.

'A bit,' he responded, with a very Gallic shrug.

'Pam's my fiancée,' Cornwallis said. After a whole evening of enforced silence he was obviously delighted to be able to talk. 'I've been telling Riccardo here, we only got engaged the night before I left and I don't want her to go off the boil. I mean, it doesn't do to leave a gorgeous girl like Pam at a loose end too long. You never know who might try to muscle in.'

'Quiet!' Richard said. 'I'm listening for the plane.'

Minutes passed. Richard looked at his watch: 1.49. How accurate should the timing be? Was it possible that the pilot had failed to identify the rendezvous? Then Duval whispered, 'Listen!'

Faintly and then growing stronger they could hear the throb of a plane's engine. Richard rose and from the shelter of the trees shadowy figures appeared and took up their positions. Richard looked up, straining his eyes to make out the shape of the plane. It was close now, but where exactly? Then he saw it, lower than he had expected, its wings blotting out the stars. He flicked on his torch and flashed his recognition letter and felt a lurch of relief in the pit of his stomach as he saw it repeated from the plane. He flashed his torch towards the others and saw the three lights come on. Seconds later the plane passed low over his head and touched down, bounced once and then ran on towards the second light. The noise as it revved its engines for the turn seemed so loud that Richard felt certain lights must be going on in houses for miles around, but then he reminded himself that low-flying aircraft were no novelty these days.

The plane taxied back and came to a stop a few feet away. The pilot pushed back the cockpit cover and Richard climbed up on the wing.

'Are you Artist?' the pilot asked.

'Yes.'

'Got a package for you. And there are a couple of crates in the rear cockpit.'

'Right. I'll get my people to unload them. And I've got a passenger for you.'

He took the bulky envelope the pilot handed him and waved to the others to come forward. Duval scrambled up to the rear cockpit and passed down two heavy crates to Marcel and then Richard beckoned Cornwallis. The young man swung himself up on to the wing.

'Wotcher, old boy! Peter Cornwallis, 601 Squadron.'

'Shut up and get in,' he was told crisply. 'This is not a bloody tea party!'

As soon as his passenger was aboard the pilot gave a thumbs-up sign and Richard jumped down and waved to the others to stand back. Xavier and Robert were still at their posts. The engines roared as the pilot ran them up and for a moment the plane quivered like a racehorse at the starting post, then it moved forward, gathered speed and took off. They watched as it circled, waggled its wings in salute and then headed westward for England. Richard drew a deep breath. His first operation had been a success. Then he reminded himself that they still had to stow away the supplies and get themselves home without being caught.

In the back of the truck they opened the crates. They contained half a dozen rifles that looked as though they had been left over from the first war, three handguns, of various types, a box of grenades and a packet of something that Richard instantly recognised from its strong almond smell as the explosive known as 808. Armand appraised the weapons and then looked at Richard with an ironic lift of his brows.

'And with these we are supposed to rise up against the Boches?'

'It's a beginning,' Richard said. 'There will be more. Remember, we've scarcely got enough arms to equip our own soldiers at the moment.'

'We?' queried Armand.

Richard acknowledged the slip with a tightening of his lips. 'Those of us who are pro-British and against the Nazis.'

He saw a quick look of complicity exchanged between several members of the group and knew that they had already guessed the truth about his nationality, but nothing more was said. He went on, 'We have to get this stuff somewhere it won't be found before dawn. Robert has a wine cellar that's ideal for the job, so let's get back there.'

Robert drove them back to the farmhouse by a different route, avoiding the German checkpoint. The long cellar under his house was divided into two rooms. They stowed the weapons in the second room and then stacked wine crates along the wall in front of the door. To a casual glance, there was no reason to suspect that there was anything behind them. By the time they had finished it was after 4 a.m. and they were all exhausted, partly with physical effort but mainly from tension and excitement. There was no chance of going home to bed, however. None of them could return to the city until the curfew was lifted in the morning. So they sat around the table in Robert's kitchen and he made them omelettes with eggs from his small flock of chickens. Robert, Richard had learned early on, was a widower and lived on his own – another factor that made him ideal as a member of the *réseau*. With the omelettes they drank coffee – real coffee, for packed in among the guns they had found the first packet of genuine coffee any of them had seen for months. It was a little human touch that gladdened all their hearts and increased Richard's respect for whoever was running the operation at the London end.

Afterwards Robert produced another bottle of Calvados and they settled down to pass the time till morning talking or dozing. Before long most of them were asleep.

Richard, feeling himself dropping off, got to his feet. 'I need some fresh air.'

'I'll come with you.' It was Jack Duval. They went out into the yard and sat on a low wall. Richard produced a packet of cigarettes and they both lit up. Duval said, 'How long were you babysitting that Cornwallis character?'

'Only a few days,' Richard said, 'but that was quite long enough.' He told Jack about Cornwallis's escapade while they were busy at the Café Bleu.

'Streuth!' was his response. 'These bloody Ruperts! Who do they think they are?' He was silent for a minute, then added, 'You know who he reminds me of?'

'No. Who?'

'That Captain Clandon – the one who got sent home from Wanborough for trying to bugger that Polish airman.'

'That was only a rumour,' Richard pointed out, but added with a grin, 'Yes, I can see what you mean – though I think Cornwallis means well.'

Duval chuckled. 'Do you remember that day Clandon wanted us to strip off and ford that freezing river?'

'Vividly,' Richard responded, laughing in his turn.

'Best moment of the whole course for me,' said Duval dreamily, 'standing there in the shelter of the trees, watching him wade in, and knowing there was a perfectly good bridge just round the corner. You knew I waited until he was in before I said anything?'

'Of course I knew,' Richard said, grinning. After a moment he added, 'You've changed, Jack. You wouldn't be intimidated by the likes of Clandon now.'

'You've changed, an' all,' Jack said. 'But that's Arisaig for you. You can't go through that and not change.'

'No, that's true,' Richard agreed.

'Tell you something, though. I'd never have put you down for a sentimental sort of chap.'

'Sentimental?' Richard queried. 'What makes you say that?'

'Sending that young pilot home by air so he could get back to his girlfriend.'

Richard gave a snort. 'I sent him home that way because he was a bloody liability all the time he was here. If I'd tried to send him down the line he would not only have been bound to get caught himself, he would have got whoever was with him arrested as well. I couldn't get rid of him fast enough!'

'Well, that's as maybe,' Duval commented, 'but he's convinced it was all out of the kindness of your heart. He kept telling me how grateful he was.'

'Did he?' Richard said. A slow grin spread across his face. 'Well, he may not be quite so grateful when he gets home.'

'How's that?'

'By sending him back that way I've made him privy to a whole lot of secret information that he's not supposed to have. Don't you remember what used to happen to anyone who dropped out of the course at Arisaig, because they knew too much?'

'The cooler!' Duval stared at him. 'You don't mean they'll send him to the cooler?'

'I should think it's highly probable. Six months' enforced celibacy in the Highlands will give him time to find out if the girl really loves him, don't you think?'

Duval looked at him for a long moment. Then he grinned. 'You devious bastard!'

20

Rose stood in line with the other girls along the front of the stage, trying not to breathe too hard and stretching up to look as tall as possible. There were eighteen of them and each had a number tacked to her leotard. Rose was number fourteen. She knew that only eight girls were needed for the show, and as she waited she slanted her eyes along the line, recalling the impression each of the others had made on her and trying to assess her chances. This was the fifth audition she had attended. The others had all been for major West End productions and she had known from early on that she did not stand much chance. This one was for *Mother Goose* at the Theatre Royal out at Stratford East, and she had thought that the competition might be slightly less intense, but she had to acknowledge that most of the other girls were good – very good in some cases.

Down in the shadows of the auditorium two men and a woman conferred in low tones. Then one of the men, the stage manager, came forward to the edge of the orchestra pit.

'Right, girls, sorry to keep you waiting. Will the following numbers please step forward? Numbers three, four, seven, nine, eleven, fourteen, fifteen and seventeen.'

When her number was called Rose's heart began to thud. Eight numbers! Eight girls wanted. Had she done it at last? The beating of the blood in her ears was so loud that she scarcely heard what the stage manager was saying.

'Thank you, ladies. Sorry to disappoint you. You can go home now. The other girls please wait.'

A murmur ran down the line of girls. Those who had been called forward were already heading for the wings, shrugging and sighing, hiding their disappointment. The lucky ones called out, 'Bad luck! Never mind! Better luck next time!' and some of those leaving called back, 'Well done! Congratulations!' Rose found herself alone in the centre of the stage, too stunned to move.

'Yes?' the stage manager queried sharply.

'But you said eight,' Rose said stupidly. 'You called eight numbers. There are ten left over.'

'Eight girls and two understudies. OK? Good afternoon.'

Rose stumbled into the wings, blinking back tears, her throat aching with the effort of not crying. She had forgotten what hell auditions were. There had been rejections in the early days, of course, but then she had expected them. Once she had established herself and producers got to know her she had hardly needed to audition. There was the regular booking with the Follies every summer, and when the panto season came it had been a simple matter of contacting one of the producers she had worked with before. Often the dancers had been cast without any formal auditions at all. Now that cosy network had been torn apart by the war and everyone had to fight for what work there was going.

In the dressing room she responded to the commiserations of the other girls as briefly as possible, afraid that she would disgrace herself by breaking down. They were all talking of other auditions, thumbing through the pages of *Variety*. There were still the provincial theatres, auditions in Bolton or Bradford or Exeter, but Rose suddenly felt that she could not face the prospect of traipsing round the country to meet with further rejections.

One of the girls said sympathetically, 'You new to this business? It's soul-destroying, isn't it? Cheer up, you'll get used to it.'

Rose straightened up. 'No,' she said, with careful dignity. 'I'm not new to it. I worked professionally for four years before the war. I've just had a year or so out, that's all.'

'Oh, right. Sorry!' the other girl said, and as she spoke she rolled her eyes at some of her friends. The look said 'Oh yeah? Tell that to the marines!'

Rose grabbed her bag and almost ran out of the room. Halfway down the corridor a man's voice called after her. 'Rose? Rose, hang on a minute!'

She turned, with a sudden upsurge of hope. Had the director had second thoughts? Then she recognised the small, bow-legged figure heading towards her.

'Mr Prince?'

Monty Prince, comedian and one-time proprietor of the Fairbourne Follies, waddled up to her, his frog face screwed up in a puzzled frown.

'Rose? What are you doing here? I thought you'd given up the theatre business.'

Rose shook her head. 'No – but I think it has given me up. I thought I could come back, but it's turning out to be pretty hopeless.'

Monty looked at her in silence for a moment. Then he said, 'You look like you could do with a cuppa. Come on, there's a nice little caff round the corner.'

He took her arm and she let him lead her out through the stage door into the damp chill of the November afternoon. The windows of the café were streaming with condensation but inside there was a comfortable fug of steam and tobacco smoke. Monty sat her down at a table and went to the counter, returning with a tray of tea and a plate of rock buns.

'Now,' he said, while Rose poured, 'what's all this about? I thought the surgeon told you you had to give up dancing.'

'Yes, he did,' Rose agreed. 'And it looks as though he was right.'

'Nonsense. I was out front and I saw you dance. That ankle looks strong enough to me.'

'Then why didn't I get taken on?' Rose said more sharply than she intended. 'What have those other girls got that I haven't?'

Monty put his head on one side. 'You want honest?'

'Yes, please.'

'Youth. They're just kids, the ones that got selected.'

'I'm only twenty-two. That's not old.'

Monty was silent for a moment, stirring his tea. Then he said, 'What have you been doing lately? Last time we met you were still in that convalescent home. I heard you and your family had gone to live in the country.'

'Yes, we did. Barbara Willis's parents took us in.'

'Babe's parents? What's she up to these days?'

'Oh, Babe's in the Wrens. Apparently she's loving it.'

'Well, well. Fancy a kid like that in the Wrens! But you didn't join up, did you?'

'No. Well, not exactly.'

Rose told him briefly about her time in the Women's Land Army, omitting any reference to her engagement to Matthew and playing down the horrors of her experiences at Hilltop Farm. 'Anyway, after all that I decided that if my ankle would stand up to that sort of work it must be strong enough to dance on. I've been going to classes for months – but it seems that's not enough.'

Monty frowned. 'Now, don't get me wrong. You're still a lovely little dancer. But you don't fit in a chorus line any more. It's just . . . how can I put it? Like I said, that lot are all kids. You're not. You're a woman. You're a very attractive woman but in a chorus line you'd stick out like a sore thumb. That's where the problem is.'

'You mean I look a lot older than I am,' Rose said bitterly. 'Well, that's it, then. After all, if I can't get into the chorus I'm not going to land a soloist's part, am I?'

'Now, now,' he reproved her. 'Don't go giving up so easily. And you don't look old – just different. Now, listen to me. I was out front today because I'm putting together a new show. Nothing fancy, just another touring production for ENSA.'

Rose gasped and leaned across the table to grasp his hand. 'Oh, Mr Prince! If you could find a place for me, I'd be so grateful!'

He patted her fingers kindly. 'I don't want to get your hopes up too high yet, Rose. I don't know for certain how many girls I need, or what we're going to be doing. But I haven't forgotten the work you did in that first ENSA show, before you had that accident. I'll keep you in mind, and if I can see a way to fit you in, I will. I can't say more than that at the moment.'

Rose realised that it would be foolish to press him any further, so she turned the conversation to what he had been doing over the past months and they chatted and reminisced pleasantly until the tea was finished. When they said goodbye outside the café she headed home with a bubbling sense of optimism that she tried and failed to keep under control.

21

As autumn moved towards winter Richard set about the task of establishing a series of safe houses between Lille and Brittany. The contacts he had been given by the Abbé Carpentier proved fruitful and from them he was passed on to others. In some cases he found people who had already sheltered escaping soldiers after the debacle of Dunkirk, or who had helped aircrew brought down by the Germans. In one or two places he actually discovered British airmen who were still in hiding with hosts who had no idea how to organise their escape. These men were rapidly handed over to the established *réseau* and taken south by one of its regular couriers.

One problem, which caused some argument between himself and Chantal, was what to do with the money he had received from the pilot of the Lysander. Chantal argued that since it was intended to help finance the escape line it should be handed over to Paul Cole, who ran things from the Lille end, but Richard, still unable to conquer his instinctive distrust, demurred. He would be happy to give the money to Ian Garrow in Marseilles, or to Patrick O'Leary, but not to Cole. The problem was resolved unexpectedly when O'Leary appeared at the Café Bleu in company with a small, dark man whom he introduced as Monsieur Dupré.

Back in Chantal's apartment O'Leary explained. 'Dupré is a banker, based here in Lille. He handles all the money we collect from sympathisers. He came south to talk to me because he was worried about where some of it was going. I told you that I don't trust Cole. Now I'm more than ever suspicious of him. I gave him a large sum to pass on to Dupré and then, days after I thought he had left to return here, I discovered he was living it up in Marseilles with his mistress. Dupré says the money was never handed over. I suspect Cole is using it to finance his lifestyle here, which I gather is pretty extravagant, so I've come up to check.'

'I can't believe it!' Chantal said vehemently. 'There must be some other explanation. No one has taken more risks than Paul. No one has brought more men down the line. He can't be a traitor.'

'Maybe not,' O'Leary said grudgingly. 'I admit it seems hard to credit. But at the very least he is lining his own pockets with money that should go to supporting the line, and that has got to stop.'

'On that subject,' Richard put in, 'I'm very glad you are here, because I have some funds sent by London and I should much prefer to hand them over to Monsieur Dupré directly.'

He unearthed the envelope from its hiding place under the floorboards and handed it to the banker, who counted it and was suitably impressed.

'Well, thank God London has started to take notice! It's about time,' was O'Leary's comment.

Having extended his line of safe houses as far as he could from his base in Lille, Richard decided that he needed to investigate the Brittany end of the scheme. Chantal made a few enquiries and came up with the name of a fashionable hotel in Dinard that offered entertainment in the form of cabaret. A letter to the manager elicited a suggestion that they should come down and audition for him, and as a result they were booked to perform for the whole month of November. The proprietor of the Café Bleu raised no objections, having come to the conclusion that his clientele had perhaps grown a little bored with the regular performances, but insisted that they should return in time for the Christmas trade. So at the beginning of November Richard and Chantal travelled to Dinard and found accommodation in two rented rooms in a small boarding house on the sea front.

The great advantage of their form of employment was that they worked in the evenings and so had the days free for other things. Through one of the abbé's contacts they managed to acquire a couple of ancient bicycles and the necessary *ausweisses*, the passes that allowed them to move around the restricted coastal area, and each morning they set off to explore. The coast itself was closely guarded and the beaches were out of bounds, but along the rocky and deeply indented shore of northern Brittany it was impossible for the Germans to watch every bay and cove. After some days of searching it seemed to Richard that they had found a possible location where a small boat could put in to land or take off men without being spotted. He and Chantal stood on top of a cliff and saw below them a series of deep inlets, each with a tiny sandy beach and each cut off from its neighbour by a steep headland. At the highest point along the cliffs stood a German blockhouse, but it was clearly impossible for its occupants to see down into each of the little bays from that position.

'If a sub could surface at night out there and put off a dinghy,' Richard said, 'once it was inshore the Huns wouldn't be able to see it.'

'Unless they patrol the cliff top,' Chantal pointed out.

'I've no doubt they do,' Richard agreed. 'The question is, how often.'

They retreated to the ruins of a stone cottage, where they had left their bikes out of sight, and settled down to wait. After twenty minutes or so they heard voices and saw two German soldiers strolling along the path that followed the cliff edge, chatting casually as they went. Forty minutes later they returned in the opposite direction.

When they were out of sight Richard said, 'Right, we've got a clear half-hour. I want to see if it's possible to get down to one of those coves. You wait here.'

'Oh no!' Chantal said. 'If you're going I'm coming too.'

They made their way to the path and followed it into a dip in the ground. Here, as Richard had hoped, a small stream had carved out a narrow defile, choked with rocks and overgrown with stunted bushes, but leading down to one of the tiny coves. There was even a faint path that followed the stream edge down. Slipping and sliding, and at the cost of bruised shins and hands torn by brambles, they finally achieved their object and stood on the sand a few feet from the waves. Richard craned his neck upwards.

'I was right. Once you're down here you can't be seen at all from the cliff top. If we can get people down here without alerting the Huns it should be a piece of cake.'

'Provided the navy is prepared to lend you a submarine,' Chantal added ironically.

'That's London's problem,' Richard said. 'Come on, we'd better get back.'

Going up was harder than coming down, and once they missed the path and found themselves faced with a sheer rock face, forcing them to retrace their steps. They had almost reached the top and were in the grassy dip when Richard felt himself suddenly seized from behind. Chantal flung her arms round him, pulled him to the ground and began to make violent love to him. Before he could react she had ripped open her blouse and pulled her skirt up to her waist. He was about to protest that this was neither the time nor the place when he heard the voices and a second later the two German sentries were staring down at them. Chantal started into a sitting position, feigning horrified surprise and pulling down her skirt, and Richard lay gazing up at them with what he hoped was a suitably sheepish expression. There was a moment of silence and then the two men began to laugh and one made a ribald comment to his companion.

Richard began to apologise and explain in French and broken German, but one of the men cut him short. He spoke no French but Richard knew enough German by now to get the gist of his remark. It translated roughly as: 'You've got no business here. Go and fuck your girl somewhere else, before I do it for you.'

They scrambled to their feet, Chantal still clutching her unbuttoned blouse across her chest, and backed away along the little valley. At its edge they turned and ran like rabbits back towards the ruined cottage. From there they saw the two men strolling on their way, laughing together.

Richard took Chantal in his arms. 'You were brilliant, *chérie*. You saved us both. I hadn't even heard them.'

She chuckled. 'Well, it was the first thing I thought of – and I expect it's made their day. They'll be telling the story to all their mates tonight.'

He held her closer. 'The trouble is, you've really got me going now.'

'Have I?' She moved against him and lifted her mouth to his. 'Well, you heard what the man said.'

Her blouse was still undone and he slipped his hand inside it to find the warm firmness of her breast, the nipple hard as a bullet under his caressing thumb. She kissed him and he felt her hand pulling at the buckle of his belt. The broken stone floor of the cottage was hard under their bodies and the November air was chill on his naked buttocks but he felt more excited by her than at any time since the early days when he had first returned to France. He remembered the sentries and their lewd jokes and suddenly what he was doing seemed like an act of defiance in the face of the oppressor.

When it was over they made themselves respectable and pushed their bikes back to the lane, their faces flushed with triumph.

One evening at the hotel, Chantal returned to their dressing room after her solo flushed with excitement.

'I've just made a discovery that could be very useful. You know how I always wander round among the tables when I'm singing? I couldn't believe my ears when I passed a table where two women were sitting. They were speaking in English!'

'English! That's incredible,' Richard said. 'Which two? Show me.'

Chantal led him to the door leading into the restaurant and pointed. Two women sat at a table not far from the stage area. One was fair haired and elegant, and perhaps around forty, the other younger, plump, with mousy hair and a cheerful, good-natured face. As Richard watched, a man joined them and the conversation reverted to French. He made his way to where the head waiter was hovering, his dark eyes flicking from table to table.

'François, who's the good-looking woman in the green dress over there?'

The waiter looked in the direction Richard indicated. 'Ah, that is Madame de Bernard and the gentleman with her is her husband.'

'Chantal thought she heard them speaking English. I've told her she must be mistaken.'

'*Mais non!* Madame de Bernard is half English, on her mother's side, and the younger woman with her is the English nanny employed to look after their children.'

'An English nanny! Surely that's impossible?'

'No. She was here when the war broke out, I believe, and chose to remain with the family.'

After a brief consultation, Richard agreed that Chantal

should attempt to strike up a conversation with the de Bernards. When they had finished their performance and Chantal had changed her dress, she strolled over to the table and said, in English, 'Excuse me, madame, but I couldn't help hearing you speaking in English a little while ago. I was brought up in Scotland and it made me feel very homesick. I still have many friends there and I worry about them. Do you have any news of how things are over there?'

The woman looked up. 'Scotland? No, really? My grandmother was a Scot. Please, sit down. I am Elizabeth de Bernard and this is my husband, Raoul. And this is Mary Jepson, our nanny. Now, tell me, whereabouts in Scotland did you grow up?'

Richard waited until the two women had had time to exchange news and reminiscences and then wandered over, as if looking for Chantal.

'May I introduce my partner, Ricardo Benedetti?' Chantal said.

'Please, sit down, monsieur.' Elizabeth's invitation was courteous but Richard saw that her expression had become more guarded. He could not blame her for that. The de Bernards must regard him, an Italian, as one of the enemy.

'Madame's mother is English,' Chantal informed him. 'You know how much I enjoyed my time there.'

'Indeed,' he agreed. 'And I, too, have spent time in England, before the war. I have many happy memories.'

'You were a student there, perhaps?' Raoul de Bernard suggested.

Richard remembered the advice he had been given at Beaulieu, to make his cover story as near to the truth as possible. 'No, monsieur. I was performing there, in what they call a "concert party". It is a seaside entertainment. And you, monsieur? Have you spent time in England?'

'I studied at Cambridge. I also have happy memories.'

Richard waited until Chantal and the other women were engaged in animated conversation and then leaned over and said softly to Raoul, 'I beg you to believe, monsieur, that I too hate the Nazis. That is why I am here.'

De Bernard looked at him and Richard held his gaze, with as much meaning as he could put into his look. The de Bernards left soon afterwards, but two days later a note arrived at the hotel. They were holding a little soirée on Sunday evening and would be grateful if Chantal and Ricardo would sing for their guests.

M. and Mme de Bernard lived in an exquisite seventeenth-century chateau in the village of Tregon, which was only a few miles from the bay they had selected as a landing place. There were only six others present that Sunday evening, and to begin with there was nothing about them to distinguish them from any other gathering of cultivated members of the *haute bourgeoisie*. But as the evening progressed Richard was aware that he and Chantal were being asked more and more pertinent questions and became convinced that they were being sounded out, exactly as he had sounded out so many others before revealing his purpose. At length, he asked Raoul whether they could speak privately.

When they were alone in the library Richard said, 'Monsieur, if I understand you correctly your love of England extends farther than simply a desire to speak the language.'

Raoul looked at him with narrowed eyes. 'I should not like to see Britain under the Nazi yoke, that is true.'

'And you would like to do more to help than you can do at present?'

'Help? In what way?'

'For example, there are many British airmen who find themselves stranded in enemy territory and require shelter and help in returning to the fight.'

He saw from the Frenchman's expression that he had struck a nerve.

'What do you know of this?' de Bernard demanded.

Richard knew that in every negotiation of this nature there came a moment when you had to make a leap of faith. He said, 'Let me speak plainly. I am in a position to put you in touch with an organisation run from London whose business it is to assist in the repatriation of British flyers.'

De Bernard stared at him expressionlessly for a moment. 'Why should I trust you?'

Richard said quietly, 'Perhaps it would help if I tell you that I am not Italian.'

'English?'

Richard lifted his eyebrows and said nothing. De Bernard gazed at him for a moment longer and then said, 'Come with me.'

He led him out of the chateau and across a yard to a large granary. Outside the door of this he stopped and, to Richard's incredulous amusement, whistled a few bars of 'The Lambeth Walk'. A second or two later the door was opened and Richard was ushered into a large, dimly lit space. In the centre, lit by an oil lamp, was a card table and around it sat three young men. A fourth, who had opened the door, stood between them and Richard. All four were dressed in blue overalls and might at a pinch have passed for French labourers, but three at least were fairer than any Frenchman in this part of the country.

De Bernard said, in English, 'Gentlemen, this man says he is in touch with London and can help us. I don't know if he is genuine or not. That is for you to find out. If you decide he is not to be trusted then it is up to you to dispose of him as you think fit.'

And with that he walked out and closed the door behind him.

The four men looked at Richard suspiciously. 'Well?' said

the one who had opened the door. It suddenly dawned on Richard, with overpowering irony, that whereas he had always assumed that his life depended on convincing others that he was not English, it now seemed that it might in fact depend on convincing them that he was.

'Good evening,' he said, managing a smile. 'Lieutenant Richard Stevens, South Lancashires, at your service. And you are . . .?'

The three who were seated rose slowly to their feet. 'Never mind that. What the hell are you doing here?' one asked.

'Come to get you out,' Richard told him. 'You and others like you. London wants you back, rather urgently. That is, if you are who I assume you are.'

'Oh yeah? And exactly how are you going to do that?'

'Probably the same way I got out myself after Dunkirk,' Richard said. 'Unless I can fix a quicker route, which might just be possible.'

'You were at Dunkirk?' A big, raw-boned man with sandy hair took up the questioning. 'Where did you get captured?'

'La Panne. I got shot in the legs and couldn't make it out to a boat.'

'Where was your regiment in those last days, then?' the other asked.

Richard said, 'Are you army? I'd assumed you were air force.'

'Gunner Jamieson, Royal Artillery. Wounded outside Abbeville.'

Richard caught his breath. 'You've been here, ever since?'

'Here, or hereabouts. Took a while before I was able to move. I'm asking the questions.'

The questioning went on for some time. To begin with it dwelt on British Army dispositions in France before the retreat and the names of commanders. Then the others chipped in with questions about places and people in England. Eventually the man who had opened the door, who seemed to be the senior officer, said, 'OK. I buy it.' He thrust out a hand. 'Squadron Leader Bill Bradshaw, 249 Squadron. Bloody good to see you!'

After that the questions and answers took on a different tone, though Richard refused to be drawn on his precise role or the nature of the organisation he worked for. Soon de Bernard was called back into the granary and Richard repeated as much of what he had told the others as he felt it was necessary for him to know. He promised the four Englishmen that he would make arrangements for them to be moved on as soon as possible and then returned to the house with Raoul de Bernard to find a rather concerned Chantal waiting for him.

Over the next week or two they visited the chateau several times and got to know the family. They were more than willing to play whatever part was required of them. Richard told them that, if it proved feasible to take escapers off as a regular event from the Brittany coast, their house would make an invaluable holding centre until such time as a boat could be arranged. It was agreed that Richard would contact London and ask for an experimental run, with the object of collecting the four fugitives in the granary. At that point their engagement in Dinard came to an end and he and Chantal returned to Lille.

Jack Duval came to the café on their first night back and Richard arranged to meet him in a local park the following day. Here he handed over a coded message giving the map reference of the chosen beach and asking for a pick-up to be arranged as soon as possible.

The following evening Jack was back at his usual table. 'You're not going to like this,' he muttered, his words covered by the general hubbub of conversation around them. 'London says "No ships available at the present time. Will advise".'

'Will advise? What the hell is that supposed to mean?' Richard asked.

'Wait, I suppose,' Jack said.

'Bloody incompetent crew,' Richard fulminated. 'What's the point of me running risks to find them a suitable landing site, if they can't even provide a ship?'

'Probably the RN playing hard to get,' Jack murmured. 'I imagine they're pretty stretched at the moment.'

Richard decided that he would have to return to Brittany to inform the de Bernards that their uninvited guests would be with them for some unspecified time.

'Make an excuse for me at the café,' he said to Chantal. 'Tell them I've got another cold, or something.'

'I'll tell them you've gone off with another woman again,' she said, smiling mischievously. 'They'll believe that.'

He put his arms round her. 'Just so long as you're prepared to take me back when I return repentant.'

She looked at him teasingly. 'Oh, I expect I shall. After all, I did last time.'

'And as long as you don't make it an excuse to have a fling with the next "parcel" we pass down the line.'

'You know I wouldn't do that,' she murmured, with a hint of reproach.

'Yes, I know,' he said, kissing her.

Since the misunderstanding over Cornwallis they had grown closer again. Richard had stopped feeling dissatisfied because of Chantal's reluctance to make any long-term commitments and had accepted that for the time being they must live for the day. The month in Brittany had been almost like a honeymoon, in spite of its inherent dangers, and he was more than ever aware of an intense gratitude for the pleasure and companionship that they shared.

He left Lille on 7 December and arrived at the de Bernards' chateau without incident. The four fugitives were disappointed at his news but he cheered them with a promise that if a ship were not forthcoming within the next week or two he would arrange instead for them to be passed down the line to Marseilles. The mood of everyone involved changed from disappointment to euphoria, however, as they clustered round the wireless set in the kitchen of the chateau to listen to the BBC news at six o'clock that evening. Elizabeth, who was keeping watch from an upper window in case there were any German detector vans in the area, heard the sudden outbreak of cheering and hurried in.

'The Japanese have attacked America,' her husband told her. 'Apparently they made a surprise attack on the US fleet at some place called Pearl Harbor and wiped out a lot of ships.'

'And this is good?' Elizabeth asked, puzzled.

'Yes, because now the Yanks will have to come into the war!' Raoul explained.

'God knows they've been sitting on the fence for long enough,' Richard said. 'Now, at last, we'll be able to mount a Second Front. With the sort of numbers and resources the Americans can produce we should be able to push the Nazis back over the Rhine and get rid of Hitler once and for all.'

'Does that mean we shall be free of them soon?' Elizabeth asked. 'How soon?'

Richard smiled at her. 'I don't know. I don't know how long it will take the Yanks to mobilise. It won't be soon, but at last I can actually see us winning this war!'

On the train back to Lille the next day he retained his mood of optimism. If he and Chantal could only keep their heads down for a few more months, perhaps they might survive the war after all. And then . . . For the first time he allowed himself to contemplate a possible peacetime existence, but found himself unable to visualise it in any concrete form.

The first thing he saw on leaving the station in Lille was Jack Duval, leaning on a lamp-post and reading a newspaper.

Immediately his stomach tightened with the presentiment of disaster. There was no other reason for Duval to waylay him at the station. He managed, however, to greet him in a convincingly casual manner.

'*Bonjour, Henri. Ça va?*'

'*Oui, ça va,*' the signaller replied. 'Let's walk, shall we?'

Richard followed him into a small park and waited until they were seated on a bench before saying, 'What is it? What's happened?'

'It's bad, I'm afraid,' Duval replied. 'Paul Cole was picked up by the Gestapo yesterday.'

'Cole!' Richard exclaimed. 'How do you know?'

'A character called Dowding arrived at the garage this morning,' Duval told him. 'He gave the correct password, so I had to assume he was genuine. He's a *copain* of O'Leary's – an escaper who's stayed behind to help. Apparently Garrow was arrested in Marseilles just before O'Leary got back there. Then later there was a showdown with Cole. It seems they confronted him in some doctor's flat but he escaped out of the bathroom window and came back here. O'Leary and Dowding came north to warn everyone that he's not to be trusted.'

'But now Cole has been arrested,' Richard said. 'Doesn't that mean that O'Leary was wrong about him?'

Duval shrugged. 'It doesn't really matter, does it? Either the Nazis had turned him already and arresting him was just a double bluff, or if they hadn't it's just a matter of how long he can hold out before he tells them anything. Either way, the circuit's blown.'

'Chantal?' Richard said sharply. 'Has anyone warned Chantal?'

'Dowding was going straight to the flat to warn her after he left me,' Duval said. 'I knew you were due back from Brittany today, but I didn't know which train you'd be on, so I told him

I'd hang about here to catch you. Do you have a rendezvous set up with her in case of emergencies?'

'Yes,' Richard said, 'we agreed that if we ever got separated we'd go to the Café Momus between three and four and again between seven and eight.'

Duval looked at his watch. 'It's twenty to three now. You'd better go along there. She's probably waiting for you.'

Richard's brain was racing. 'No,' he said. 'You go for me. Take her to Robert's place in Santes. I have to go somewhere else.'

'Where?' Duval demanded.

'I must warn the Abbé Carpentier. Dowding may not know about him. I'll meet you at Robert's.'

'Don't be an idiot!' Duval exclaimed. 'The Gestapo are probably looking for you.'

'They're looking for Riccardo Benedetti, an Italian with a limp,' Richard pointed out. 'Not for Lucien Dufrais. And they'll be expecting me at the flat, or at the café tonight, not in Abbeville. Now, let's get moving. Minutes could make all the difference.'

It was late afternoon when Richard reached Abbeville, and growing dark. He hurried to the abbé's house, but as he was about to turn in at the gate the front door opened and several people came out. Richard stepped back sharply into an alley running alongside the garden and watched with a pounding heart. He saw the priest appear between two men, both dressed in the long, belted raincoats that were the unmistakable uniform of the Gestapo. Following them were three others dressed in rough workmen's clothes, all handcuffed. Behind them came another Gestapo officer and a fourth man dressed much like the other prisoners, but carrying a handgun. With a feeling of sick despair Richard watched as they all piled into two waiting cars and drove away. He had come too late.

As he was about to turn away he suddenly saw a movement farther down the alley. He froze in the shadows and saw a man drop down from the top of the garden wall, pause for an instant, looking around him, and then begin to move in his direction. Someone, then, had evaded capture. There was no time to think. Richard stepped forward and said softly, 'It's all right. I'm a friend.'

He had hardly spoken before he saw the gun in the other man's hand. Instinctively he threw up his own hands and said in English, 'Don't shoot! I'm on your side!'

The man stared at him for a moment. Then he said, 'Who are you?'

'My name's not important,' Richard said, 'but I'm a friend of the abbé's. Were you waiting for papers?'

'Why should I trust you?' the other man asked.

'Because I can get you out,' Richard said urgently. 'Who sent you here? Was it Paul Cole?'

'You know Cole?'

'Yes, but I don't trust him. I think he might be behind what happened here. I came to warn Carpentier, but it seems I was too late.'

The gun was lowered fractionally and the man holding it said, 'Look, I need to know who you are. I'm not escaping. I came to warn him too.'

Suddenly Richard understood. 'Are you Dowding?'

'Yes. And you are?'

'Benedetti.'

'Good God! What are you doing here? I sent Henri Lebrun to warn you.'

'I know. He told me. That's why I came.'

Dowding moved closer to him. 'For God's sake, man! Your cover's blown. You should be thinking about getting out. Do you have a safe house to go to?'

'Yes, don't worry about me.'

'There's no chance of passing you down the line at the moment, I'm afraid. You'll have to lie low until the heat is off.'

'It's all right,' Richard told him. 'I can fend for myself. What about you?'

'I've got to warn the others. Pat gave me a list. He's doing half, I'm doing the other half. I just hope to God I'm not too late for them as well.'

'What happened in there? How did you avoid capture?' Richard asked.

'I'd just arrived. Before I could warn the abbé those four turned up, saying they were escapers needing papers. Three British airmen and one Pole. Except the Pole turned out to be a plant. His Gestapo mates were waiting outside. I was hiding in the back room. Luckily for me they didn't search.' He paused and then laid his hand briefly on Richard's arm. 'I'm sorry about the girl.'

'What girl?' Richard asked.

'Your girl. Chantal, isn't it?'

Richard felt as if all the breath had been knocked out of his body. 'What about Chantal?' he whispered.

'Oh God! You didn't know? She was picked up last night at the café where you work. I went to the flat this morning and there was no sign of her so I went to the café. They told me the Gestapo burst in in the middle of her act and took her away.'

Richard sagged against the wall. The thought of Chantal in the hands of the Nazi's brutal police force made him want to howl like an animal.

Dowding said, 'Does she know about your safe house? If she does, keep away from it. However tough she is you can't rely on her keeping quiet for long.'

Richard shook his head numbly. 'She doesn't know,' he mumbled. 'I never told her about it.'

'Then go there and stay put until you can get back to England,' Dowding said.

'I'm not going back,' Richard replied. 'Not without her. I have to get her out.'

For a moment Dowding looked as though he was going to argue with him. Then he said, 'Up to you. I've got to move. Wait here until I'm out of sight.' He pressed Richard's arm. 'Good luck!'

Then, with a quick look to right and left, he turned into the road and began to walk rapidly away.

It was late when Richard finally arrived at Robert Gatignon's farmhouse in Santes. Duval met him at the door, his face pale and tense.

'Don't tell me, I know,' Richard said brusquely. 'Chantal was picked up by the Gestapo yesterday.'

'Well, you're safe, thank God,' Duval commented. 'What about Carpentier?'

'Arrested just before I arrived,' Richard told him.

Over glasses of Calvados in Robert's kitchen he told them about his encounter with Dowding and went on, 'What matters now is getting Chantal out.'

'Look, I understand how you feel,' Duval said. 'But the Gestapo are looking for you, too. You have to think about escaping yourself.'

'I'm not leaving here without her,' Richard said. 'You can do as you please.'

'OK, it's your neck,' Duval agreed with a shrug. 'Any idea how we go about it?'

Richard had had time to think on the way to Santes. 'Armand might be able to help. He works at the Palais de Justice. Do you think he might be able to find out where Chantal is being held?'

'If he can't, he may know someone who can,' Robert agreed.

'Tomorrow I'll go and see him,' Richard said. 'It's a starting point, anyway.'

'No,' Robert said sharply. 'It's not safe for you to be wandering around Lille. Tell me where to find him and I'll go.'

Richard slept little and passed the next morning in an agony of inaction. At lunchtime Robert returned but could say only that Armand would do his best to find out what had happened to Chantal and would come that evening to meet them in the local bar. Two hours before curfew Armand slipped quietly into the little *estaminet* and joined them at their table.

'I haven't been able to locate her definitely,' he said quietly, 'but suspects are usually held at Gestapo headquarters for the first few days. Later they are normally transferred to the local prison – in this case it will be to the women's prison. If, or when, that happens we shall know about it.'

'What are the chances of getting her out of there?' Richard asked.

Armand shrugged. 'It's a prison. It's not designed to allow people to escape. On the other hand, there must be sympathisers who work there, who would help if they could. The question is, how do we find them?'

'I have a suggestion,' Robert put in. 'There must be a priest who ministers to the staff and the inmates. If we could contact him he might be able to help.'

'Good idea!' Richard said. 'Can you find out who it is, Armand?'

'It should be possible. I'll ask around.'

'Don't make it too obvious,' Richard warned. 'You need to have a reason for asking.'

'I'll say my department has received a complaint from a relative of one of the prisoners that her spiritual welfare is not being adequately provided for,' Armand said. 'That should cover it.'

Richard turned to Duval. The bar was crowded and in the general hubbub there was little chance of being overheard, but he lowered his voice to a murmur. 'We need to get a message through to London. Tell them that we may need an urgent pick-up by Lysander in the next few days.' He ran his hand through his hair, trying to force himself to think calmly. 'I think you should move. There's a chance someone may have noticed us talking together at the café and, anyway, I need you on hand to keep in touch with London. Get your set and bring it here – that is if Robert is willing . . .'

The vet shrugged. 'Why not? I'm in up to my neck already.'

'There's no reason why the trail should lead back to you,' Richard assured him. 'The Gestapo are not looking for Lucien Dufrais. They think I'm someone quite different.'

'Unless Chantal is persuaded to tell them otherwise,' Duval said heavily.

Richard felt sick. He remembered what he had been told at Beaulieu. *Everyone talks, sooner or later.* All agents were expected to do was hold out for forty-eight hours. By the end of that time it was assumed that the rest of the circuit would have gone to ground. He thought of O'Leary and Dr Rodocanachi. Garrow had been arrested. How many of the *réseau* remained at liberty?

The following days were some of the worst Richard had ever lived through. Confined to Robert's farm he could only pace the rooms and try desperately to divert his thoughts from what might be happening to Chantal. He devised a dozen hopeless plans, most of which involved giving himself up in exchange for her, but he knew that there was no way of bargaining with the Gestapo. They would simply hold both of them.

Duval returned to the farm with his precious radio set and Richard watched as he set it up in a loft above the barn and trailed the long aerial wire that was required to pick up the transmissions from London around the rafters and out through a window, where it was concealed among the ivy growing over the wall. As soon as contact had been established Jack sent off a coded message telling London what had happened and requesting that a Lysander should be put on stand-by.

On 13 December Armand reappeared in the bar.

'Chantal was moved to the women's prison this morning,' he said, 'and I have the name and address of the curé who looks after the prisoners.'

'Give it to me,' Richard said. 'I'll go and see him tomorrow.'

There were protests from the others but Richard was adamant. Any longer cooped up in the farm and he felt he would go mad.

The next morning he presented himself at the door of the priest's house, which was situated in a grey suburb dominated by the gaunt outline of the prison standing on the hilltop above it. He was admitted by the housekeeper and found himself facing a young priest who looked as if he was straight out of the seminary. He had strong, aquiline features softened by a pair of luminous brown eyes and an alert, outgoing manner that immediately gave Richard the feeling that here was a man he could trust.

He began by saying, 'I'm sorry to intrude on you, Father, but I need to make my confession.'

The priest nodded and dismissed the housekeeper. As soon as the door had closed behind her Richard lowered his voice and went on, 'Forgive me. I have not come to confess. I am not even a Catholic, but I need your help.'

The priest looked at him shrewdly for a moment and then said, 'Sit down, my son. How can I help you?'

Richard hesitated. There was no time now for the delicate probing by which he normally tried to deduce the attitude of those he was dealing with. He said, 'I understand you minister to the inmates of the prison here.'

The curé nodded. 'That is so.'

'You must be aware, then, that there are some prisoners who have committed no crime in the eyes of French justice but are simply there because they have refused to succumb to the dictates of the occupying power.'

He saw from the priest's eyes that he was already beginning to understand.

'There are some who have been sent to us by the Gestapo, yes.'

'Father . . .' Richard leaned forward and spoke with painful intensity. 'Do you condone the brutality with which some of these people are treated?'

The priest paused for a moment, then he rose and went to open the door. Having assured himself that the housekeeper was not listening he returned and seated himself close to Richard.

'Are you one of those who attempt to resist the invaders?' His face was eager.

Richard hesitated for a moment longer but there was nothing for it but to take the plunge and trust that his instinct was not wrong.

'Yes. There is a small group of us who are prepared to do anything we can against the Nazis, or to help the British.'

The priest raised his eyes to heaven. 'Praise God! I have prayed for Him to send me someone who will show me how I can do something, even a small thing, to help drive out these brutes. What do you want of me?'

'There is a young woman in the prison. She is one of us and I am afraid the Nazis will have tortured her to make her give away the names of her associates. I must get her out and take her to safety in England. Can you think of a way?'

The priest frowned. 'What is her name?'

'Her real name is Henriette Gautier, but she calls herself Chantal. She is a professional cabaret singer.'

The priest sat in thought for a moment. Then he said, 'One of my flock is a wardress in the prison. She is a good woman and I believe she hates the Nazis as much as I do. I will speak to her. She may be able to think of some way to help.' He got up. 'Come back here tomorrow at the same time. I will have an answer for you by then.'

22

The blue Lagonda roared along the country lane, the masked headlights making little impression on the darkness. At the wheel, Felix joined in the lusty singing of 'Roll Out the Barrel', bawled out by the four young pilots crammed into the vehicle with him. The cart seemed to appear from nowhere, abandoned at the side of the road, its empty shafts pointing to the sky. Felix trod on the brakes and the car skidded to a halt, but it was too late. The cart shot forward under the force of the impact, hit a tree and disintegrated into splintered planks.

Felix swore and looked round. 'Everyone OK?'

It seemed that, apart from minor bruises, everyone was. Felix got out and walked round to inspect the damage, followed by the others.

'You've pranged the cart good and proper,' one said. 'It's completely u/s.'

'Bugger the bloody cart!' Felix responded. 'Look at my car!' One of the Lagonda's headlamps was broken and there were deep scratches in the blue paint on the nearside mudguard. 'Who left the damn thing in the middle of the road, anyway?'

'It's probably old Willoughby's,' someone suggested.

Felix groaned. 'Oh no! There'll be hell to pay if it's one of his.'

His prediction proved correct. The following morning he received a summons to the CO's office. Squadron Leader

'Chips' Chatterley and he were old friends, having trained together at the beginning of the war, and they both knew that, if Felix had not suffered such terrible injuries in the crash and been out of action for so long, he would certainly have been equal in rank by now. It did not make the present situation any easier for either of them and Felix saw the embarrassment on the other man's face as soon as he entered the room. Chatterley had a job to do, however, and he was determined to behave professionally, as he made clear by keeping Felix standing to attention.

'I've had a complaint from Mr Willoughby. It seems someone ran into one of his carts last night and virtually destroyed it. From the blue paint on the wreckage, he guesses it was your Lagonda that did the damage. Was it?'

'The silly bugger had left it in the middle of the lane, without any lights or anything,' Felix said. 'He ought to be prosecuted for obstructing the highway. I came round the bend and ran straight into it.'

'How fast were you going?'

'About fifty.'

'On a narrow country lane, in the dark.'

'I was in complete control. The cart shouldn't have been there.'

'And suppose it had been an animal – or a pedestrian?'

Felix bit his lip and said nothing.

Chatterley went on, 'We already have enough trouble from the locals. We've taken over land for the airfield and Willoughby reckons the noise of the planes taking off frightens his cows and reduces the milk yield. And the villagers resent the fact that their pub is packed out with rowdy young men who drink all the beer and chat up the girls.'

'They do know there's a war on, I suppose,' Felix said bitterly.

'I take your point but we still need to try not to exacerbate local irritations,' Chatterley said. 'The Air Ministry top brass are very keen on keeping good relations.'

'Bloody penguins!' Felix muttered.

'Maybe, but you're not the one who has to carry the can when complaints are made. But that isn't the only consideration. You had four young pilots with you, as I understand it. Suppose they had been injured? A broken arm or concussion could put a man out of action for weeks. God knows, we're short enough of pilots, without you doing the Luftwaffe's job for them.'

Once again, Felix could think of no reply.

'How much had you had to drink?' Chatterley asked.

'I'd had a few beers.'

'More than a few, from what I've heard.'

'Who from?'

'Oh, not one of the boys who was with you last night. It's not the first time that it's been brought to my attention that you are drinking more than is good for you.' Chatterley looked at him in silence for a moment, then he leaned forward and clasped his hands on his desk. 'Sit down, Ned.'

Felix sat, knowing that the use of his Christian name meant a change of tone.

'Now,' Chatterley went on, 'let's try to get a few things straight. What's going on? What the hell is the matter with you?'

Felix shrugged and was silent.

'You're a good officer,' the CO persisted. 'To most of these young lads you're a hero, after what you did in the Battle of Britain. They look up to you. What sort of an example are you setting them?'

'I'm sorry,' Felix said, with a sigh.

'You battled through hell with all the plastic surgery and everything and got yourself fit again. Why let it all fall apart now?'

Felix raised his head and leaned towards Chatterley, his voice suddenly urgent. 'I'm bored, Chips! I'm bored out of my mind. You can't imagine how it feels to be stuck behind a desk, while the rest of you are swanning about up there.'

'I'd hardly call it swanning about,' his companion protested.

'You know what I mean. I'd give anything to fly again. Give me a chance, Chips! I know I can do it. If I can control a car at speed, I can fly a plane.'

'It's not the same thing. For one thing, there aren't any enemies out to shoot you down on the roads – well, give or take the odd irate farmer.'

Felix took encouragement from the momentary lightening of his commanding officer's tone. 'I can do it, Chips,' he insisted. 'I'm perfectly fit and my reactions are as sharp as they ever were. Give me a chance to prove it to you. Take me up in one of the trainers and let me take the controls. If you don't think I'm up to it you can take over and I promise I'll buckle down and never mention it again.' He saw that Chatterley was wavering. 'Please, Chips! I'm going to pieces like this. You said that yourself. Just give me a chance.'

Chatterley sat back and rubbed his hand across his face. 'If the wingco finds out he'll have my guts for garters – but all right. If that's what it takes to get you back on the straight and narrow. But not today! I want you stone-cold sober when we go up, not hung over.'

'Done!' Felix responded ecstatically. 'I'm on the wagon from now on. And I'll go and find old Willoughby and apologise and offer to pay for the cart. Thanks, Chips! You won't regret it. That's a promise.'

Soon after first light the following morning a two-seater trainer took off and climbed into a clear blue sky. Felix's heart was beating fast, but not with fear. It was all he could do to keep his hands off the controls as Chatterley circled to gain height.

Eventually the squadron leader's voice came through his headphones. 'OK, Ned. You ready to take over?'

Felix reached out and grasped the joystick. 'I've got her, Skip. You just sit back and enjoy the view.'

He tried out a few simple manoeuvres, turning and banking, climbing and diving. It was pure joy. Every move was instinctive, as if the plane were an extension of his own body. He almost began to hope that an enemy fighter might appear, until he remembered that the trainer had no armament. Too soon, he heard Chatterely's voice again.

'OK, Ned. You've proved your point. Do you want to take her down?'

Felix brought the little plane round, side-slipping to lose height, and lined it up with the runway. The wheels kissed the grass, but before the plane could lose momentum he gunned the engine and roared up into the sky again, climbing hard.

Chatterley's voice came through the headphones. 'It's OK, Ned. I'm convinced. Take us down.'

'Not quite yet,' Felix answered. Then he added, almost under his breath, 'Oh, brother! You ain't seen nothing yet!'

With a whoop of sheer exhilaration, he pushed the stick forward and put the plane into a steep dive.

It was at Suez that Merry finally got a reply to his letter. By this time they all knew that they were bound for North Africa, although they had come a long way round to avoid the danger of German attacks in the Mediterranean. Exactly where and for whom the Merrymakers were to perform, however, no one seemed to know. Merry found himself quartered in a small, stiflingly hot tent furnished with a narrow camp bed, a chair and a rickety folding table. After the general confusion of their arrival, seeing the equipment unloaded and the rest of the company appropriately billeted, it was evening before he was able to sit down and open the letter.

Dear Merry,

Great news! At least, I hope you will be able to see it in that light, knowing as you do how much it means to me. I am flying again! Not operationally, as yet, but at least I'm allowed to solo when there is a kite available. I finally managed to persuade Chips Chatterley, my CO, to take me up in one of our trainers, and it was just like riding a bike! The hand was no problem at all and I felt at once as if I was back in my natural element. I wish you flew, Merry! It's almost impossible to make anyone who hasn't flown understand how it feels – but I guess I've gone on about it often enough for you to have some idea. Anyway, after a couple of circuits it was obvious that I was fully in control, but just to make sure Chips was convinced I took him through a couple of loops and a slow roll and finished up with a spin. It was wonderful! I was yelling my head off with pure excitement. Must admit poor old Chips was looking a bit green when we got down, though. However, he had to admit that I'm quite capable of handling a plane as well as the next man and there's really no reason why I should be grounded. I'm waiting now for a medical board and hopefully soon after that I shall be passed fit and posted to a new squadron. God knows, we're short enough of pilots. There must be plenty of places where I can make myself useful.

Apart from that, life goes on much as usual. I've had a slight problem with some of the chaps in the squadron who took it into their heads that I was in need of feminine companionship, but I've solved that by inviting Harriet down a couple of times. The sight of her was enough to convince them that their efforts on my behalf were not needed. I'm sure you understand – and won't forget the promise you made last leave.

Merry re-read that paragraph twice and smiled inwardly.
Felix ended,

> *I passed on your message to F. and this is the reply,*
> *verbatim. The musical image was so apt and so beautiful*
> *that it brought a lump to my throat. I can't match it but I*
> *just want you to know that when we were together you made*
> *me utterly, utterly happy in a way no one else ever has or*
> *ever could. I miss you every day and can't wait for us to be*
> *together again.*
>
> > *Thus F., who sends fondest love.*
> > *Yours ever,*
> > *Ned*

Merry replied,

> *Dear Ned,*
> *I've just received your letter, which was waiting for me when*
> *I arrived here. It's wonderful to hear from you but letters take*
> *so long that I've no doubt events have moved on since you*
> *wrote. For a start, I expect you have had your medical board*
> *and may well be flying again by now. I'm not mean enough to*
> *say I wish you weren't – well, I'm mean enough to wish it, but*
> *that's my problem, not yours. I just hope you are being careful*
> *and not taking any unnecessary risks. Remember, you made a*
> *promise too.*

He went on to relate a few amusing incidents that had
occurred on the voyage and to explain that he and the
company were now waiting for someone to make up his mind
where they were to go next. He concluded:

> *Thank you for passing on F.'s message. If I ever have an*
> *epitaph – which I hope won't be required for some time yet –*
> *I should like it to be 'he made F. utterly happy'.*
>
> > *My love to both of you,*
> > *Merry*

He had just finished writing when a voice outside the open tent flap said, 'OK if I come in?'

Tom was standing in the opening. Merry sat back. He was tired and hot and looking forward to a shower and a cool drink in the officers' mess. The last thing he felt like at that moment was coping with the importunate attentions of the young dancer.

'What do you want, Tom?' he asked.

Tom came a step or two farther into the tent, smiling, hands in pockets. Merry, for all his dislike of military discipline, found himself wanting to tell him to take them out and stand to attention.

'Just a chat,' the boy said. 'Just a few words about you and me.'

'What about "you and me"?' Merry demanded frostily.

Tom's grin broadened. 'Oh, come on! Stop pretending. We're the same, you and me. You might as well admit it.'

Merry felt a tightening at the pit of his stomach. 'What do you mean, "the same"?'

'Well, you know what they say – takes one to know one.'

Instinctively Merry shuffled the letter to Felix back into his writing case. 'Tom, I'm tired. I don't feel like riddles. Either say what you've come to say or shove off, will you?'

Tom sauntered across to the table and looked down at him. When he spoke his tone was quieter, less confident than before. 'Look, I know it was difficult on board ship. Not much chance for any privacy. But now we're here . . . You know how I feel. I've made it pretty obvious. So, how about it? Here we are, on our own, miles from home. Why don't we give each other a few home comforts?'

Merry stared at him. Once the casual pick-up had been a necessary if undesirable part of his life. Once he would have had no hesitation in responding. But now he was at a loss as to how to deal with the situation. Against his instincts, he took refuge in his rank.

'I don't know what the hell you're talking about! And stand up straight when you're speaking to an officer. Take your hands out of your pockets. If you're not careful you'll find yourself up on a charge of insubordination.'

He saw the boy's eyes widen in pained disbelief. Then he drew himself up and stood to attention.

'Yes, sah! Sorry, sah! Permission to leave, sah!'

Merry sank back in his chair with a sense that he had betrayed his deepest principles. 'Yes, go on. Get out!'

As Tom turned on his heel and marched, with exaggerated precision, towards the tent opening, Merry was tempted for an instant to call him back, to sit him down and explain why he had been so crudely rebuffed. But it was too late and, after all, he told himself, it was probably better this way.

He learned to regret his decision over the next weeks. Tom took his revenge by adopting a mocking imitation of correct military behaviour. Whenever Merry entered a room he would leap to his feet and stand to attention. When addressed he would respond in clipped, martial tones, always ending each sentence with 'sir'. The other members of the company, used to Merry's easygoing informality, watched in bemusement, but little by little Merry could feel that Tom's behaviour was undermining his authority. Although no serving officer could have taken exception to anything he said or did, in the eyes of the company Tom was 'taking the mickey' and Merry was unable to stop him. After a while some of the others began to join in the joke.

Tom devised a particularly irritating routine, which Merry christened to himself 'the saluting trap'. He would hang around behind a building and appear suddenly as Merry approached, snapping up a smart salute and forcing Merry to salute in return. Then he would dodge round between the rabbit warren of huts and tents that comprised the camp and reappear farther on, to repeat the process. For some time Merry pretended not to notice, because to stop him and demand to know what he thought he was playing at would be simply to acknowledge that he was getting under his skin. It was when Tom succeeded in persuading Clive and the two comedians, Wally and Ray, to join him that he decided that he would have to take positive action. They would pop out from every corner of the camp, at intervals of a few seconds, pass him and reappear a hundred yards farther on, until his arm ached from returning their salutes. He did not think any of his fellow officers had noticed yet, but it was only a matter of time.

They had moved up to Alexandria by then, to entertain the troops being rested from the desert campaign, and Merry had acquired an office close to the recreation hut where they performed. One morning he sent for Tom, who marched himself into the room, saluted and stood at attention.

'At ease, Tom,' Merry said, playing the same game. 'Stand easy.'

The boy relaxed and looked at him warily. Merry said, 'Tom, this has got to stop. I know what you're doing and why you're doing it – and probably I asked for it. But it's beginning to undermine the whole atmosphere of the company. We've always behaved to each other like professionals – and I mean Professionals with a capital P, theatre people, dedicated to the job. Now I'm beginning to feel like a schoolmaster in charge of a particularly difficult class.'

Tom shifted his feet, beginning to look uncomfortable. Merry saw that his instinct, to appeal to him as a fellow artiste, had been correct. He went on, 'I think I owe you an apology. You made certain assumptions about me, which are basically correct. What you don't know, and couldn't know, is that I'm not . . . available. I'm sorry I behaved so crassly and hurt your feelings. You caught me at a bad moment and I'm afraid I reacted without thinking things through. Now, can we get back to the old relationship and forget all this toy soldier nonsense?'

He saw the colour mount in Tom's face. His large grey-green eyes were suspiciously moist and suddenly he looked very young and very vulnerable.

'I didn't mean to make things bad for you. It was funny to start with, then it sort of got out of hand. I mean, what I said that evening . . . I probably came on a bit strong. But I really like you, Merry. I always have, right from the start. And I thought you liked me.'

Merry sighed. 'I do like you, Tom, but I'm not looking for that sort of relationship. I'm afraid you just have to accept that.'

'There's someone else, isn't there?'

'Yes, if you must know, there is. No one you know, and he's miles away from here, but that's it as far as I'm concerned.'

'He'd never know,' the boy said.

'No, but I should know and that's what counts. Now, can we leave it at that?'

Tom looked down at his feet and then up again at Merry's face, obviously in the throes of an internal struggle. In the end he said, 'Yeah, I suppose so.'

'And no more playing silly buggers?'

'No, all right. Sorry.'

'That's OK. Right. Off you go, then.'

Tom fixed him with one more burning gaze, then turned and walked out of the room in a manner that would have had a drill sergeant screaming but which, to Merry, came as a great relief. He kept his word and from then on the atmosphere in the company returned to normal. He even abandoned the cheeky asides that had often brought rehearsals to a standstill. Even so, Merry was constantly aware of his eyes following his every move and in return found his own gaze drawn more and more often to the dark, tousled head and the casual grace of the dancer's body. The sensation made him extremely uneasy.

23

The day after his interview with the priest Richard returned to the house, fully aware that he might be putting his neck into a noose. The priest's vehement hatred of the Nazi occupiers could have been a deliberate pose and the appointment simply a way of luring him into a trap. As he entered the study his hand was inside his trouser pocket, his fingers gripping the butt of his pistol. If the Gestapo were waiting for him, he intended to take out as many as possible and perhaps succeed in getting away before they recovered. In the event, the only person in the room apart from the priest was a tall, severe-looking woman in a grey dress.

The priest said, 'Come in, my friend. This is Madame Constance Perrier. She is a chief wardress at the prison and she has information for you.'

Richard went to the woman and clasped her hand. 'Thank you for coming here, madame. What can you tell me?'

'The young woman you described to the father here was brought in by the Gestapo two days ago, but I am afraid she had been very badly treated by them before she arrived.'

Richard's stomach contracted. 'What have they done to her, madame?'

'I have not been in close enough contact with her to find out precisely,' Mme Perrier replied. 'All I know is that when she arrived she was scarcely able to walk.'

Richard swallowed and clenched his jaw against the impulse

to break down. 'We must get her out, madame. Please, can you see a way?'

'I have been thinking, since the father spoke to me yesterday evening. There is a possible way. Next week I shall be on the night shift. Security is a little more lax at night. I have a spare uniform at home. It would be too large for her, but I can easily alter that. I know a wardress on her wing who is sympathetic. If she is prepared to take the risk she could smuggle the uniform into your friend's cell and leave the door unlocked. Then, when the night shift goes off duty the next morning, she can simply walk out with the others.'

'I think it is a good plan,' the priest said quietly. 'What is your opinion?'

'I think it is an excellent plan!' Richard exclaimed. He caught hold of Mme Perrier's hand again. 'Madame, I shall be eternally grateful to you. I shall pray God to reward you for your kindness and your courage.'

'As He undoubtedly will,' the priest said gently. 'But now we need to think of practical matters. You will need some form of transport to get your friend out of the area, and a change of clothes for her.'

'Leave that to me,' Richard said. 'I am sure I can borrow a vehicle of some sort, and some clothes that will do. When do you expect to be ready, madame?'

'As I said, I am not on the night shift until next week. The first night will be the nineteenth. I shall need one night to make the arrangements and be sure that everything is in order. Let us say the following night, or rather early the next morning when the night shift finishes.'

'Meaning the twenty-first?' Richard said. 'And what time does the shift finish?'

'When the curfew is lifted, at six a.m.'

'I shall need to know where to wait for her – and she will need to know where to find me.'

'I know a place,' the priest said. 'At the bottom of the road leading down from the prison there is a small lane. It goes behind some houses and leads to some outbuildings that are used by some of the residents as garages. A car could be parked there without anyone thinking it unusual. But you can't drive around during curfew. It would be too risky.'

'That's true,' Richard agreed. 'So the car will have to be left there the previous evening. Would that be safe, do you think?'

'I see no reason why not,' the priest said. 'Cars are often left standing there. Bring your vehicle on the evening of the twentieth, park it in the lane – I will show you where it is before you leave – and then come and spend the night here.'

So the arrangements were finalised, and after Mme Perrier had left the priest walked with Richard up the hill towards the prison and pointed out the narrow, unpaved lane between the blank sides of two tall buildings. As he had predicted, there were two cars standing outside some dilapidated sheds, and it did not look like the sort of neighbourhood where the residents would query the appearance of another one. Richard thanked the priest and headed back to Santes.

Now that he had a plan and some positive action to prepare for he felt less distraught, though the memory of Mme Perrier's description of Chantal's condition gnawed at his mind. He had hated the Nazis before, with a kind of abstract, detached aversion, but now he loathed them with a passion that made him want to go out and shoot the first German he saw. He knew that that degree of emotional involvement was dangerous and struggled to suppress it, but without success.

The first problem to solve was transport. Robert's truck was too unusual and distinctive to serve his purpose but a farmer friend of his had an old Citroën, which had broken down and for which he was unable to obtain the necessary part. Robert persuaded him to part with it on the pretext that he needed spare parts for his own vehicle. Then Xavier and Jack Duval set to work on it and by cannibalising an old wreck lying in Xavier's yard managed to get it going. The difficulty of obtaining fuel was solved by siphoning petrol out of the tank of the truck.

Clothes presented less of a difficulty. Robert went into Lille and contacted Jacqueline, who was not too dissimilar in build to Chantal. He returned with a woollen skirt, a jersey, thick woollen stockings and an old coat. Dressed like that Chantal could be mistaken for any housewife on her way to market.

One of Richard's first actions was to encode a message to London asking for a pick-up by Lysander for the night of 21 December. The code message to be broadcast by the BBC to confirm that this would take place was 'Tell Aunt Marie that the sow has had two piglets'. The number of piglets could be varied to give the time of the aircraft's arrival.

The following day Jack came to find Richard and said, 'There's been another message from London. Would you believe they have now decided they can find a sub to take off those men in Brittany?' He showed Richard the decoded message. It informed them that a submarine would be off the coast on the night of 24 December and would put a boat ashore at the place Richard had specified at 11.30.

'Eleven thirty on Christmas Eve?' Richard exclaimed. 'Who do they think they are – Santa Claus?'

'Perhaps they reckon that the German guards might be a bit less on the qui vive at that time,' Jack suggested.

'They could be right, at that,' Richard agreed. 'But now we have a problem. Someone has to let the de Bernards know and make sure they get the men down to the beach in time. You'll have to go, Jack. I can't, and I don't want to involve Robert or any of the others for security reasons.'

Duval was reluctant to leave at that juncture but Richard insisted that it was the only solution. 'In fact,' he said, 'I think you should go with them. I'm going back to England with

Chantal and the Cole *réseau* is finished. I know he never knew about you, so you should be safe from that point of view, but I can't see that you can do much good out here on your own.'

After some persuasion Duval agreed that Richard was right and they parted with a mutual promise to 'see you in London'.

In the late afternoon of 20 December Richard took the little car and drove to the prison, where he parked as agreed in the lane at the bottom of the hill. The priest greeted him kindly and over supper they discussed other ways in which he might help in the fight against the Nazis. Richard told him that he would not be in a position to put him in touch with an escape line for the time being, but promised that either he would contact him when he returned to France, or someone else would come in his place. Neither of them felt like sleeping that night, so they sat up talking until it was time for Richard to leave. He shook the priest's hand and said, 'If I was a Catholic, Father, I'd ask you to bless me – but I'll just ask you to wish me luck instead.'

The other man smiled at him. 'God doesn't reserve His blessing exclusively for Catholics, you know.' And he raised his hand and made the sign of the cross over Richard's bent head. 'I shall pray for you both,' he added.

Richard slipped out into the darkness of the deserted street. For a few moments he stood still, straining eyes and ears for any sign of movement. Then he made his way, quiet as a cat, to where the car was parked and got into the driving seat. It was a bitterly cold morning with wisps of fog clinging around the steep sides of the hill on which the prison stood. As he sat waiting for the curfew to end and the prison gates to open he shivered, partly with cold and partly from nerves.

After what seemed a very long time he heard voices from some way off and climbed out of the car to wait at the end of the lane. A group of women was coming down the hill, all in the uniform of prison warders, talking and laughing together. For a moment he thought Chantal was not with them. Then he saw her, walking very slowly, already some way behind the others. In an agony of dread he watched her approach. It seemed to him that anyone looking down the road from the prison must realise that she was an impostor. He longed to rush out into the street and grab her and carry her to the waiting car, but he knew that that would be the worst thing he could possibly do. He shrank back into the shadows as the women passed him but none of them glanced in his direction. When he looked out again Chantal was nearer, still hobbling with painful slowness. When she was almost abreast of the end of the lane he stepped forward. She staggered the last few steps and he caught her as she collapsed into his arms and half carried her into the shelter of the tall buildings.

He heard her sob and held her tightly, whispering, 'It's all right, my darling. It's all right. You're safe now.'

After that one cry she was silent and he carried her to the car and eased her into the front seat. She was only half conscious but he managed to get the old coat on her and tied a scarf over her hair.

'Don't worry, *chérie*,' he whispered to her. 'I'll look after you. Tomorrow we'll be home – home in England. Just hang on!'

When he started the engine the noise seemed so loud that he expected windows to be thrown open in the houses backing on to the lane, but no one stirred and he nosed the car cautiously out into the road. It was still dark but by this time other people were about, hurrying to work on early shifts in the local factories. There were few cars on the road, since only those whose jobs required them could get permits to buy fuel, and Richard knew that the greatest danger was that he might be stopped and asked his business, but they arrived in Santes without incident. It was only when he stopped the car in the farmyard that he was able to look at Chantal properly for the first time.

The sight of her face filled him with cold fury. She was deathly pale, except for a purple bruise across one cheek which had partially closed one of her eyes. The other eye seemed to be sunk into its socket with pain and exhaustion. He lifted her out of the car and carried her inside the house, where Robert was waiting for them. He laid her down on an old wooden settle that stood against the wall and heard Robert say softly, '*Mon Dièu!* Look at her feet!'

Richard looked. She had kicked off the shoes she had worn to leave the prison and now he saw that she had on woollen ankle socks, which were soaked in blood. He knelt by the settle and caught her in his arms.

'The bastards! The bastards!' He could hardly get the words out. 'What have they done to you?'

She gripped his arm. 'I told them nothing, *mon cher*. Nothing!'

'I know, I know,' he whispered. 'If you had I should not be here now.'

Very carefully Robert peeled away the blood-soaked socks and Richard turned his head away to prevent himself from vomiting at the sight of her feet. All the toenails had been pulled out and the soles of her feet had been beaten to a bloody pulp.

'Oh, *ma chérie, ma chérie*,' he cried, unable to restrain his tears, 'how could they do this? You should have told them what they wanted to know.'

'No, no!' she murmured. 'I will tell those devils nothing! Better I should suffer than so many others. And I might never have seen you again, *mon amour*!'

It was the first time she had ever used that particular endearment with him. He held her close, still weeping, and covered her face with kisses.

Robert, meanwhile, had fetched warm water and the equipment he used in his practice as a vet. Very carefully he cleaned her feet and bandaged them. Then he produced a bottle and measured a dose of white powder into a glass of water.

'It's a painkiller,' he said. 'Normally I use it for horses. I just hope I have adjusted the dose correctly.'

When Robert had finished Richard coaxed Chantal into taking a little of the soup their host had made from the carcass of one of his hens and then carried her upstairs and laid her on his bed. She was drowsy from the sedative and he lay down beside her and held her in his arms until she drifted off to sleep. He even slept himself for a few hours, and when he woke it was already getting dark.

By six o'clock Chantal was awake too and the rest had smoothed away some of the lines of pain and tension from her face. Richard carried her downstairs and they huddled round the radio in the kitchen. At last the BBC broadcasts were beginning to contain some hopeful news. America was now in the war and in North Africa the British army was making some headway. The siege of Tobruk had been lifted ten days earlier and British troops were now heading for Benghazi. But it was the *messages personnels* that the three crouched with their ears to the radio set were waiting for. At last it came. 'Tell Aunt Marie that the sow has had three piglets.'

'That's it!' Richard exclaimed triumphantly. 'Three a.m. – they're coming for us at three a.m.! By morning we'll be home, my darling!'

She looked at him and managed to smile for the first time. 'It's so hard to believe, *mon cher*. I keep thinking I shall wake up and find myself back in that prison cell.'

He squeezed her hand tightly. 'You're not going back there, my sweet. I promise!'

But when Robert came in an hour later from locking up the hens he said quietly to Richard, 'I don't like the look of the weather. There's a mist coming up. Will they come if it's foggy?'

Richard glanced at Chantal, who was lying on the settle dreamily stroking one of Robert's three cats. 'No,' he answered, keeping his voice low. 'They can't land if the visibility is poor.'

'What will you do?'

'We must keep the rendezvous anyway,' Richard said. 'There might be a window. The fog could clear later on.'

'And if not?'

'I don't know.' His voice was rough with the tension of the last days and bitter with disappointment. That the weather should deprive them of this one chance of getting home seemed too cruel to contemplate. Then a thought came to him. 'Yes, I do! There's the submarine coming to Brittany. Today is the twenty-first. If the plane can't land tonight we'll drive straight to the de Bernards'. They'll give us shelter until the sub arrives on the twenty-fourth.'

'You won't have enough fuel to get that far,' Robert pointed out.

'Then I'll steal it,' Richard said. 'Or I'll steal a car. I'll get her there somehow!'

Robert shook his head doubtfully. 'Why not come back here and wait for the weather to clear?'

'For one thing because it's too risky for you. The police are bound to be looking for Chantal and someone may have seen the car. It could be traced back to the farmer who gave it to you. And anyway, I haven't got a wireless or an operator here and Henri is going back to England on the sub. I'd have no way of arranging another pick-up. No, the sub is our best bet. But perhaps we shan't need it.'

By the time they set off for the landing ground that hope was fading rapidly. They travelled in the truck with Robert driving and Richard cradling Chantal on bales of straw in the back.

Xavier was with them, to provide an extra pair of hands to set up the flashlight path to guide the plane in. Over the last few kilometres Robert had to slow to a crawl because the visibility was so poor, and when Richard climbed out the fog was so thick that he could not even be sure that they were in the right field.

'What do we do?' Robert asked.

'We wait,' he replied. 'There's still half an hour to go. Just pray for a miracle.'

The minutes passed slowly and as 3 a.m. approached Richard strained his ears for the sound of an aircraft, but he knew it was useless. No pilot would attempt a landing in these conditions. When it was clear that there was no further hope they climbed back into the vehicle and drove back to Santes, Xavier gloomily silent while Richard kept up an encouraging stream of chatter, explaining to Chantal how they would still be back in England in time for Christmas. She had said little when the plane failed to arrive, accepting the situation with a fatalism that was at odds with her normally volatile temperament.

Back at the farm Robert insisted on putting together some provisions for them, although Richard knew that he was using his own rations for the purpose. He also siphoned the last of the petrol from the truck and put it in the little Citroën. By the time the curfew was lifted everything was ready and Chantal was settled in the front passenger seat, dressed in the old woollen skirt and coat and wearing an old cap of Robert's and a pair of outsize wellington boots to accommodate the bandages on her feet. With her drawn, pale features she looked a good twenty years older, and Richard thought to himself that she was unlikely to be recognised as the beautiful and glamorous cabaret artiste the police would be looking for.

He turned to Robert and said, 'I shall never forget what you have done for us.'

'What I have done for you, I have done for France,' Robert said. 'But now you are leaving, will the struggle continue?'

'Of course it will,' Richard told him. 'I shall be back, or if it's not me someone else will come. If someone arrives and asks if you know the singer in the red shirt, trust him. He will have been sent by London to take my place. But take care, *mon ami*! You have seen how a line can be betrayed. Tell no one what you are doing unless it is absolutely essential.'

'Don't worry, I shall say nothing,' Robert assured him, 'but when the time comes I shall be waiting.'

'And so shall I,' Xavier put in.

Both of them embraced him and kissed him on both cheeks. A couple of minutes later he was driving the Citroën out of the yard, heading for Brittany.

For a while it seemed that they might reach their goal without incident. Richard kept to the side roads, which lengthened the distance but meant that they were less likely to encounter any roadblocks. This was crucial, since there had been no time to obtain false papers for Chantal or a permit for the car. Around mid-afternoon he realised that they were getting perilously low on fuel. A short time later, they passed an isolated house, outside which stood a builder's van. Richard parked the Citroën in a narrow cart track a hundred yards farther on and walked back, carrying a petrol can. He lingered for a while a short distance from the house and heard the sound of sawing from inside. Praying that the builder would not suddenly discover that he needed an extra tool from his van, Richard dropped on to his belly and crawled to the far side of the vehicle. With a pounding heart he unscrewed the cap of the petrol tank and inserted a length of rubber tube, which Robert had provided, and sucked. In a few minutes he had a can of fuel. He felt guilty and sorry for the builder, but his training had taught him that at times it was necessary to commit a small crime in the prosecution of a wider aim.

By nightfall they were a short distance from Rouen and Richard parked the car behind an isolated barn. Inside there was fresh hay for a bed and they still had enough of the food Robert had provided to keep hunger at bay. They lay in each other's arms talking softly for a while, and then Richard offered to keep watch while Chantal slept. Typically, she insisted that she would share the watch, and woke up without his prompting about three hours later.

He slept uneasily and woke to the first faint light of dawn, and the sound of a hen cackling. For a moment he could not see Chantal, but then he spotted her, on her hands and knees a few yards away, groping among the hay. A moment later she turned to him triumphantly with two eggs in her hand.

'Fine,' he said. 'How do we cook them?'

'Cook?' she exclaimed. 'Who needs to cook fresh eggs like this. *Regards, mon vieux!*' And she cracked an egg, tilted her head and tipped it down her throat.

Richard took the second egg, cracked it, tipped it into his mouth and forced himself to swallow. Then he went to the door and looked out. Long wraiths of grey mist hung over the fields and the ground was white with frost, but there was no sign of life. They splashed their faces with water from a cattle trough beside the barn and drank a little of it too. It was risky, but less so than knocking on a door and asking for a drink. As soon as the curfew was lifted, and before it was fully light, they were on their way.

By midday they were running short of fuel again and this time Richard spotted a baker's van parked outside a house. As it was *le midi* he guessed that this was the driver's home and he was inside having lunch, so he took his petrol can and rubber tube and succeeded once again in siphoning off enough to take them on their way. This time, he helped himself to a baguette as well. They ate going along, but he noticed that Chantal was only picking at tiny morsels of the bread. Since that flash of exuberance when she had found the eggs, when she had seemed almost like her old self, she had grown quiet again, huddled against him as he drove and shivering slightly.

'Eat,' he said. 'There's enough for both of us.'

'I'm not hungry,' she answered tonelessly.

Although they still stuck to the country lanes there was very little else on the roads to hold them up and they made good time. Richard knew, however, that at some point they had to cross the River Sélune, and that this was where they could encounter a roadblock. He stopped the car and carefully studied the map he had brought with him, then headed for what looked like a very minor road running towards a bridge over the river. The lane twisted and turned as it descended into the valley and the high hedges on either side prevented them from getting a clear view of what was ahead. Then they came round a final bend and saw the bridge in front of them. With a shock like a blow to the stomach Richard saw that there was a barrier across the road and that two German soldiers stood guard beside a small sentry box. There were no other turnings he could take, but a field gate offered the opportunity to turn round and he reversed quickly into it, hoping that the sentries had not noticed the approach of the little car. As he pulled out, however, he heard a shout from behind him and saw in his rear-view mirror that a third man had come out of the hut and was mounting a motorcycle.

Chantal had seen him too. '*Vite, mon cher, vite!*' she cried, and Richard heard the terror in her voice. He stood on the accelerator and the car rattled and shook, the engine howling as they headed back up the hill. Richard looked in his mirror. The German on the motorcycle was closing the gap and he knew there was no chance of outrunning him. Their only hope was to shake him off somehow. To his right a forestry road led in among trees and he swung the car into it, hoping that they might reach a bend in the track before the German arrived at the beginning. It was a vain hope. In his mirror he saw the motorbike pass the entrance, then turn and swing round into it. He swore under his breath and urged the car forward, physically pushing on the steering wheel as if that could make it go faster.

For perhaps half a kilometre they bounced and jolted over the rutted track, twisting and turning and climbing ever higher, with the German soldier getting ever closer. Then Richard saw him reach back and unsling the machine gun that he carried on his shoulder.

'Get down!' he yelled to Chantal, and as she ducked he heard the rattle of the gun and felt the car judder as the bullets struck it.

'Are you hit?' Chantal asked breathlessly.

'No. I'm OK,' he answered, and just then the engine coughed and died. Richard looked at the dials on the dashboard. '*Merde!* He must have hit the fuel tank! We're done for!'

He pressed the accelerator and the engine stuttered uncertainly into life. Ahead the road ended in a small clearing. 'Stay down!' he ordered.

He swung the car so that it was broadside on to the advancing motorcyclist, with the driver's door on the far side, and stopped. Thrusting his hand into his pocket, where he still carried the concealed .32, he waited for the German to catch up. When he was a few yards off the soldier stopped his motorbike, close enough for Richard to see the grin of triumph on his face. As he was propping the machine on its stand Richard kicked open the door and in the same movement rolled out on to the ground, momentarily hidden from sight by the car. As he came to his feet the gun was in both his hands, in the double grip he had been taught. Bent-kneed, in a semi-crouching position, he fired twice in rapid succession – the classic 'double tap' he had learned at Arisaig. The German looked surprised as the first bullet hit him somewhere in the stomach but he was already bringing the machine gun to bear. Then the second bullet took him in the chest and knocked him over backwards. He had hardly hit the ground before Richard was upon him, snatching the machine gun from his hands. Without hesitation Richard fired a short burst into the man's head. At some distant level he registered the thought that he had killed a man for the first time, but he suppressed it.

He turned away and ran back to the car. Chantal was crawling out as he reached her, white faced and wide eyed.

'*Mon Dieu!*' she whispered. 'I didn't know you could do that!'

'Never mind that now,' he said brusquely. 'We have to get out of here.'

He grabbed the few possessions they had brought with them and seized Chantal around the waist with his free arm, and together they staggered over to the motorcycle.

'We can't take this!' she objected. 'Everyone will see it is German.'

'I know that,' he said. 'We dare not ride it on the road, but at least we can use it to get out of this forest.'

He helped her on to the pillion and succeeded after one or two attempts in getting the machine started. They had a few nasty moments until he got used to controlling it over the rutted ground, but before long they were back within sight of the road. Almost at once, they saw a German jeep go by and then three other motorcyclists.

'The guards at the bridge must have raised the alarm,' Richard said. 'We're going to have to ditch this thing and go cross-country.'

Chantal got off and Richard pushed the motorbike in among some bushes, where it would not be readily visible from the road. Crouching there, they studied the map.

'We'll have to make for this bridge instead,' Richard said, pointing to a road some five kilometres from where they were. 'Come on. It's going to be dark before long.'

He got up and helped Chantal to her feet, but it was only when he saw her gasp with pain that he remembered the condition of her feet and understood the impossibility of what he had proposed.

'If I help you, can you walk a little?' he asked.

'Of course.' She nodded, her mouth closing in a line of grim determination.

He made a bundle of what was most essential and hid the rest under some dead leaves. Then he put his arm round her waist, taking as much of her weight as he could, and they set off through the trees, skirting the hill and heading up the valley. For a while they made reasonable progress, though he was aware that every step took all Chantal's will-power. The rough ground made it hard to give her as much support as he wished. Then he heard her give a little cry and for a moment she became a dead weight on his arm. Looking down at her, he saw that she had turned deathly pale.

'Sit down,' he said. 'Let's rest for a bit.' He lowered her on to the ground and sat beside her. It was almost dark now, and freezing again.

After a moment she said, 'You should leave me here. Go on yourself. You will never make it like this.'

He hesitated for a moment. 'I might be able to find some form of transport, if I can make it to a road. But then I wouldn't be able to get it back here. No, we must keep going. I'll carry you.'

'No, no!' she protested. 'I mean, you should go and leave me behind. You cannot carry me all the way to Brittany.'

'I know I can't,' he said desperately. 'Tomorrow I'll steal a car. But for tonight we have to find shelter of some sort. Come on. Get on my back.'

She continued to protest until he almost shouted at her. 'For God's sake, Chantal, I'm not going to leave you here, so will you just shut up and do as I say?'

She let him heave her on to his back then and he set off, keeping to the edge of the trees. Twice he had to stop and put her down, but at last they came out on the lane he had pinpointed on the map. By this time the muscles in his shoulders and back were screaming with agony and his legs were beginning to tremble with exhaustion, but at least on the road walking was easier and they were heading downhill.

It was an area where there were few villages, or houses of any kind, and he soon realised that the chances of finding a car they might steal were almost zero. Eventually they came to a small cottage and in a lean-to beside it Richard saw a bicycle. He put Chantal down and crept closer. For a moment he hesitated. It was obvious that the inhabitants of the cottage were poor peasants and the bike was probably their only means of getting to work or to the nearest village. But once again he reasoned that, though they might be inconvenienced by the theft of it, their lives would not be endangered. Moving very cautiously and thankful that there seemed to be no dog to alert the owners, he pushed the bike out on to the road.

It was a woman's bike, so there was no crossbar that Chantal might have sat on and no rack attached to the rear wheel, so he lifted her on to the seat and mounted in front of her, standing on the pedals. In this way they could move faster, but before long Richard's legs, already tired from carrying her, would sustain his weight no longer. He got off and pushed the bike instead, his arm round her to steady her. She sat silent, her head hanging, refusing to respond to his efforts to cheer her.

At length they came in sight of the bridge, and to Richard's dismay he saw that this one, too, was guarded. They could see the dim glow of a light inside the sentry box and the flare of a match as one of the sentries lit a cigarette. He leaned the bike against a wall and helped Chantal off.

'Now what do we do?' she asked.

'I'm afraid there's only one thing for it,' he replied. 'We're going to have to swim.'

She looked down towards the river and he knew that, like him, she was imagining the bite of the icy water, but after a moment she shrugged and replied fatalistically, '*Tant pis!* Then we swim.'

'But not tonight,' he said, thinking aloud. 'If we go now we shall have to spend the rest of the night in wet clothes, and that could be the end of us. We'll find somewhere to shelter and go across just before first light.' He searched the countryside ahead of them, on either side of the bridge. The sky had cleared a little and there was a half-moon, obscured by hazy clouds. 'Isn't that a building down there?' he asked.

She followed his pointing arm and screwed up her eyes. 'Yes, I think so.'

He got her back on to the bike and pushed her on down the lane. The building turned out to be a substantial farmhouse, but as they neared it they were greeted by the hysterical barking of a dog, which rushed to the end of its chain in an effort to reach them. Worried that the noise might alert the guards on the bridge a couple of hundred yards away, they hurried on. A little farther down, and closer still to the river, a cart track led off to the left, following the course of the stream.

'I think I can see something down there,' he breathed. 'Wait here a minute.'

He helped her to sit on the verge and picked his way silently along the track towards the outline of another building. It was a barn, much like the one in which they had spent the previous night. With a sigh of relief, Richard propped the bike against the wall and went back to fetch Chantal. It took the last of his strength to pull down a bale of hay and slit the twine that held it so that he could spread it out to make a bed. Then he helped Chantal on to it, covered her with more hay and lay down beside her.

She whispered, 'I'm not hungry but my throat is parched. I would do anything for a drink.'

'I could go down to the river,' Richard murmured, 'but I've nothing to carry water in.'

'No, forget it,' she answered. 'We'll get enough water later!'

'Try to sleep,' he said. 'I'll keep watch.'

They were silent for a while and he thought that she had dozed off but then she said, 'How far is it to the beach where we have to meet the submarine?'

'About thirty kilometres,' he told her.

'And when does it come?'

'Eleven thirty tomorrow night.'

She said, 'You should leave me, you know. We'll never be able to cover thirty kilometres in a day like this.'

'I know that,' he replied. 'Tomorrow, when we're over the river, I'll steal another car. Or, if I can't, we'll go to the priest in the nearest village, or knock at a farmhouse, and ask for help. Most people hate the Nazis. Even if they are too frightened to help they won't give us away.'

'And if we miss the submarine?'

'Then I know people in the area who will shelter us, until another opportunity comes up. Or we might stay here to run a new escape line. I still have my papers as Lucien Dufrais and we could get new ones for you – as my wife perhaps.'

'Your wife?' she said, with a small laugh. 'So we must be married after all, *mon vieux*.'

'Is that so terrible?'

'No.' She settled a little closer into his arms. 'Not so terrible.'

He did not mean to sleep but after the efforts of the day and several broken nights he could not prevent his eyes from closing. He woke suddenly in the dark, feeling cold. The space beside him where she had lain was empty. Suppressing the urge to call her name, he lay still, straining his ears. He thought that perhaps she had just gone outside to answer a call of nature, but when the minutes passed and she did not return he got up and found the knapsack in which he had carried their emergency supplies. There was a torch in it and he shone the beam around the dark interior of the barn. When he was convinced that she was not there he extinguished the light and went to the door. The moon was fully out now and he could make out the dark silhouettes of the trees between him and the river. He called softly. There was no reply.

Struggling to hold down the tide of panic that rose in his chest, he gazed around him. A narrow path led from the barn towards the river. He thought that perhaps she might have gone down to get a drink, after all. He stumbled along the path and came to a place where the river bank had been scooped away and the ground was pockmarked with hoof prints. Obviously it was where the cows came down to drink. For a moment he stood scanning the area, then he became aware of two dark objects at the edge of the water. Moving closer, he recognised them with a shock as the outsize boots Robert had given Chantal to wear over her bandaged feet. He picked them up, his weary brain refusing to accept the obvious implications. As he turned them over a scrap of paper fell to the ground. Strangling a cry he stuffed it in his pocket and began a frantic search along the river bank.

He found her quite quickly, in a little bay where the bank was higher and the flowing water had carved out an overhang. She was half in and half out of the water, her face in the mud. With a strength he did not know he possessed he dragged her, weighted with the soaked woollen skirt and sweater, up on to the bank, cleaned the mud from her mouth and tried to breathe air into her lungs. He knew from the start that it was useless – she was icy cold and there was no trace of a pulse – but he kept on anyway, sobbing and calling her name with no attempt at concealment. When, finally, he was forced by exhaustion to stop, he sat down on the wet grass, cradling her in his arms, and wept as he had not wept since he was a small child.

Eventually it came to him that he could not leave her lying there to be discovered by a German patrol or perhaps attacked by some scavenging animal. Somehow he managed to heave her on to his shoulder and stagger to his feet, and carried her back to the barn where they had been sheltering. Laying her on the straw, he switched on the torch, which he had not dared to use out in the open, and carefully wiped the mud from her face and smoothed her hair, the once burnished helmet now lank and dull. Then he took her in his arms again; but her body was already stiffening and the contrast with the warm and passionate creature he had so often embraced was so great that he laid her down again with a shudder. The question that gnawed at his mind was whether she had been attempting to swim the river on her own, or had deliberately surrendered herself to the icy waters. Then he remembered the scrap of paper he had found inside her boot. He pulled it out of his pocket. It had been torn from the paper that had been wrapped round the baguette and for a moment he thought it was rubbish. Then he saw that there were words scrawled on it. It said simply, *You would never have made it with me. Tell Rose I loved you, but we could never have been husband and wife.*

For a long time he sat gazing at it, numb with misery. Eventually, the instinct for survival forced him into action. Searching his pockets, he found another piece of paper, an old restaurant bill. Turning it over he wrote on the back of it: *This is a daughter of France who died at the hands of the brutal occupiers. Please see that she is buried with due honour.* Then he lifted Chantal's body and carried her back up the lane to the farmhouse. Ignoring the dog, which almost choked itself on its chain in its efforts to reach him, he laid her on the doorstep and tucked the note inside her coat. Above him a window was thrown open and a man's voice shouted at the dog to be quiet. Richard shrank back against the wall until the window was closed again and then faded on silent feet into the shadows of the lane.

He swam the river almost without conscious awareness of the bitter cold, which shocked the breath from his body. By the time he reached the far side the winter dawn was breaking and he forced himself into a shambling run uphill across the fields, forcing his way through hedges, oblivious to cuts and scratches, until he came out on to a road. It was full daylight now and almost at once he heard a car coming up behind him from the direction of the bridge. He turned and saw that it was a civilian vehicle and, without further thought, he stepped out into the road and flagged it down.

The driver was a respectably dressed, middle-aged man who asked him, with an expression of concern, 'What's wrong? Has there been an accident?'

Richard said breathlessly, 'I'm an English airman. I need your help.'

He had abandoned all ideas of concealment but it seemed to him that the identity of a downed pilot would be easier to explain than the fact that he was an English secret agent. The driver of the car scrutinised him sharply for a few seconds, then said crisply, 'Get in.'

In the car Richard went on, 'I need to get to Dinard. There are people there who will help me to get back to Britain. Can you take me there?'

The man looked sidelong at him as the car pulled away. 'You swam the river?'

'Yes, it seemed the only way across.' He became aware for the first time of how wet he was. 'I'm sorry. I'm making a mess in your car.'

'It's not important,' the other replied, 'but if you don't get some dry clothes quickly you are going to die of exposure. I will take you to my house first. It is close by. When you are warm and dry again I will drive you to Dinard.'

This kindness and the ease with which he had found help after the travails of the past days almost reduced Richard to tears again. His Good Samaritan went on to explain that he was the local doctor, returning home after attending a difficult confinement on the other side of the river. At his house Richard was given a hot bath and a suit of clothes that had belonged to the doctor's son – his only son, who had been killed fighting the Germans during their initial push into France.

The doctor's wife made them breakfast as if the arrival of a bedraggled escaping airman was an everyday occurrence, and as soon as they had eaten they returned to the car and set off in the direction of Dinard. A few miles farther on they were stopped at a roadblock. Richard still had his identity papers as Lucien Dufrais, which he carried in a waterproof pouch. He produced them and the doctor explained that he was suffering from some as yet unidentified infection and was being taken to hospital for further tests, a story that gained added colour from the fact that he was shivering with a quite genuine fever. The guards were happy to wave them through with the minimum of formality. Just before midday they arrived at the chateau belonging to Raoul and Elizabeth de Bernard.

By this time he was only semi-conscious. He was aware of the welcoming expressions on the faces of the de Bernards and Jack Duval turning to anguished distress as he recounted what had happened. He vaguely recalled saying goodbye to the doctor. Then he was helped upstairs and laid on a bed. After that, everything was blank. When he returned to full consciousness he was stumbling down the narrow path leading to the beach, supported between Jack and the gunner who had quizzed him on his first visit to the de Bernards'. Led by Raoul and followed by the other three men, they slipped and scrambled as silently as possible over the rocky terrain until they stood in the darkness by the edge of the water. Richard was aware of the jubilation, hastily stifled, when the recognition code flashed from somewhere out to sea, but could not share it. Then came the seemingly endless wait until the dark shape of a rubber dinghy materialised on the waves and grounded with a soft susurration of rubber on sand. There were handshakes with two sailors in black clothes with camouflaged faces, hasty farewells to Raoul, embraces all round, and then they were off, paddling out into open water until the dark shape of the submarine loomed above them.

Hands reached down to help them up the rope ladder to the deck, and as he grasped one of them Richard was suddenly taken back to the beach at La Panne and almost thought he heard the sailor say, 'Never mind, mate. There'll be another one along in a minute.' In his confused state he almost let go and dropped back into the water, but this time the hand grasping his held fast and he was drawn up on to the deck and then led quickly below, where an officer waited to greet them.

'Welcome aboard, old man!' he said, shaking Richard warmly by the hand. 'Oh, and since it's after midnight – Happy Christmas!'

Rose had never intended to return to Wimborne for Christmas. She had convinced herself that by then she would be working in the theatre. When that ambition failed to materialise she was tempted to say that she could not leave the shop, but an emotional appeal from her mother forced her to change her mind. She went, but in spite of the determination of everyone involved, the festivities were muted by memories of the previous year.

True, it was good to see her mother and Bet again, and the two boys, and the Willises were as welcoming and hospitable as ever. But she missed Merry and Felix and this year there was no invitation to the Big House and no young farmers' dance. Even the Christmas fare was less plentiful than the previous year. Bob Willis had managed to fatten a capon, as before, but there was no pair of pheasants from Matthew Armitage, and no bottles of good wine charmed from the local publican by Felix. Rationing was stricter than ever, and the few little luxuries that people had managed to preserve in store cupboards and cellars from before the war had all been exhausted long ago.

The Willises' daughter, Barbara, was home on leave, and so was Bet's husband, Reg. This meant that Rose had to vacate the room she had shared with her sister and move in with Barbara, in the big double bed that Merry and Felix had been so happy to share. No longer Babe of the schoolgirl face and the ingenuous manner, Barbara now assumed an attitude of hard-bitten sophistication. She was glad to be home, happy to see her mother and father again and effusively pleased that Rose was there as well, yet she could not resist boasting about the many sailors who had been queuing up to take her out. Rose felt that behind her happy chatter there was always the suggestion that she could have been having a much more exciting time if she had stayed on the base for all the festivities.

Reg was finding it difficult to adjust to the fact that he was a guest in another man's home rather than master in his own. He compensated by demanding a great deal of Bet's time and attention and by asserting his authority over the two boys, who, he declared, had been allowed to run riot in this household of women. Billy and Sam responded by becoming sullen and cheeky and did not help matters with constant cries of 'Mum lets us!' or, worse still, 'Uncle Felix would have let us!' or 'Uncle Merry said . . .'. Bet, torn between her sons and her husband, veered from attempts to placate all three to angry remonstrations.

All this made for an uncomfortable atmosphere, but what disturbed Rose most was the constant fear of accidentally encountering Matthew. Every time someone came to the door she was afraid that it might be him, and whenever they went for a walk she was constantly looking ahead or over her shoulder in case he should suddenly come round a corner. Every lane and field brought back memories. She even re-cognised individual cows. After all, a year ago she had known them all by name. She tried not to think that, if Richard had not suddenly reappeared that last New Year's Eve, she would now be a married woman, perhaps even a mother, and that all this land, this quiet, fruitful countryside, could have been hers – not to possess, but to live in and share. Sometimes she asked herself whether, if Richard had died in France as she had thought, she could have been happy with Matthew, and she knew that the answer was probably yes. But Richard had not died. Richard was alive somewhere, so far as she knew,

although he had not answered her letter. And as for Matthew –
it was too late now. There could be no going back.

The one hopeful thought, which she hugged to herself when
sleep refused to come, was Monty's suggestion that there
might be a place for her in his new company. She did not
mention the possibility to her mother or Bet. It had been hard
enough confessing that she had failed so many auditions. She
was aware that they were tiptoeing around the subject, not
wanting to hurt her feelings, and she did not want to raise
hopes that might once again be dashed. Instead, she told them
that she was thinking of taking her teacher's certificate.

'I might even have my own dancing school one day, like
Sonia and Irena,' she said, trying to sound optimistic.

'Well, that sounds like a really good idea,' her mother said.
'After all, teaching a few classes in the evenings or at weekends
is something you could keep up after you're married.'

'Married?' Rose said, startled. 'Who to?'

'Well, how should I know?' her mother asked. 'But someone
will come along, you just wait and see.'

Rose was glad when Christmas was over and she could use
the excuse of having to reopen the shop to get back to London.
She was in the shop on New Year's Eve when a telegraph boy
came in.

'Telegram for you.'

Her heart bumped. In these wartime days telegrams almost
always meant bad news, but who might it be about? If anything had happened to Felix or Merry no one would telegraph
her. Could it be Reg? Perhaps something had happened to Bet
or her mother . . . She ripped the envelope open and read,
TELEPHONE ME AS SOON AS POSSIBLE STOP I MAY HAVE SOME-
THING FOR YOU STOP MONTY PS HAPPY NEW YEAR.

On New Year's Eve in Alexandria, Merry and his band were
asked to play for a dance in the officers' mess. It was an

uproariously noisy evening, in spite of the fact that most of the men present had recently returned from the battlefield. After a month of fierce fighting Operation Crusader had finally succeeded in relieving the siege of Tobruk and, although casualties had been heavy on both sides, there was a sense of victory in the air. The atmosphere in the room was stifling and Merry and the others sweated their way through the popular standards of the day – 'Don't Sit under the Apple Tree', 'Tangerine', 'You Are My Sunshine', 'Run Rabbit Run' and, of course, the big hit of the season, incongruous though it was in the circumstances, 'I'm Dreaming of a White Christmas'. They were all glad when the speeches and the toasts were over and 'Auld Lang Syne' had been sung and they were able to play the last waltz.

Merry had drunk very little during the course of the evening, so he felt justified in appropriating the remains of a bottle of brandy that had been left on one of the tables. With the strains of 'Who's Taking You Home Tonight' still running through his head he went out into the sudden chill of the desert night and walked back to his tent in a mood of dreamy nostalgia.

When he entered the tent, however, his relaxed frame of mind was abruptly dissipated. Tom Dyson was lying on his bed, clad only in his underpants. As Merry came in he raised himself on his elbow and greeted him with a smile.

'Hello, Merry. Happy New Year.'

Merry walked over to his table and put the brandy bottle down. 'Push off, Tom, there's a good chap. It's late.'

Tom sat up. 'Oh, come on, Merry! It's New Year's Eve and we're the only ones without a date. We might as well cheer each other up.'

'I don't need cheering up,' Merry said.

'Well, I do,' Tom replied, with a sudden change of tone. 'Can't you see that?'

Merry sighed deeply. 'Look, I'm sorry, Tom. I've told you, there's nothing doing.'

Tom leaned forward and gazed up at him appealingly. 'But you like me, don't you? I mean, I can't be that repulsive.'

'You're not repulsive,' Merry said patiently. 'You're a nice lad and you're very attractive, but I'm still not interested.'

Tom got up and came to within a few feet of him. 'It's him, isn't it?' he said, nodding towards the table, and Merry saw for the first time that the photograph of Felix, which he kept tucked into the back of his writing case, had been taken out and was lying there.

'Bloody hell, Tom!' he exploded. 'You've been going through my things! That's unforgivable.'

'What happened to his face?' Tom asked, unabashed.

'He got shot down during the Battle of Britain and badly burned – not that it's any of your business.'

'Oh, I get it,' Tom said. 'He's a bloody hero so you've got to be faithful because otherwise it would look as if you were dumping him because he's disfigured.'

'It isn't like that at all,' Merry replied. 'As it happens, our relationship didn't start until after he was shot down. Now, get out, Tom, please. I'm tired and I want to get some sleep.'

Tom hesitated, searching his face. His brash confidence had evaporated and he looked what he was, a lonely boy desperate for comfort and reassurance.

'OK,' he said finally, 'but give me a kiss before I go. Just one, to wish me Happy New Year – please?'

He had moved closer and Merry could feel the warmth emanating from the naked young flesh a few inches from his own. The boy's lips were trembling and Merry saw that the long eyelashes were dewed with tears. With an inward sigh of defeat he bent his head to the kiss. Tom's lips were dry, slightly roughened by the desert sun, but his tongue was moist and agile and very experienced – and Merry had been celibate for four months.

It was all over very quickly and as soon as he had recovered himself Merry sat up on the edge of the narrow camp bed.

'I didn't want this to happen,' he said.

'I know,' Tom answered.

'Go now, please,' Merry continued, in a low voice.

There was a momentary pause, and then he heard Tom get up and pull on his clothes. The boy went to the entrance of the tent and then stopped and looked back, his expression a mixture of distress and injured pride.

'My mistake!' he said. 'You're not such a great lay after all!'

When he had gone Merry got up and went to the table and poured himself a slug of brandy. He looked down at the photograph of Felix, which gazed back with that enigmatic, far-away smile, and raised his glass ironically.

'Happy New Year, Felix.'

But his voice was rough with regret and self-loathing.

Felix spent the Christmas period on duty at his RAF station on the south coast. As usual, leave over the holiday period was restricted to men with families, especially those with young children. After having been on the sick list for so long he was perfectly willing to stay and hold the fort and there were plenty of parties going on in and around the base. Harriet came down for some of them and they had a good time. He had forgotten temporarily how much he enjoyed her company.

Which was not to say that he did not miss Merry. He was frequently reminded of the musical metaphor that Merry had used in his letter. The thought of him, and the sensation of loss that his absence produced, was like a piece of constant background music. It had become so familiar that most of the time he was hardly aware of it, but then a sound or a smell would spark a memory and he would be pierced with almost unbearable longing. He dealt with those moments by heading for the bar in the mess and losing himself in the chatter and jokes with which his pilot colleagues defended themselves against the reality of their situation.

There was another reason why he was content to stay on the base. He had passed his medical board and was waiting for the order that would post him to another station and put him back on the active list. On New Year's Eve an orderly came to tell him that the CO wanted to see him in his office. The squadron leader greeted him with a broad grin.

'Got something for you, Ned.'

He held out a sheet of paper. Felix read it. It was the order posting him to 126 Squadron as flight commander of A Flight, with effect from the following day.

'Bloody marvellous!' he exclaimed. 'Thanks, Skipper!'

The CO regarded his obvious delight with ironic amusement.

'Glad you're pleased. Happy New Year!'

Richard stood on the balcony and looked out over the darkened city. Somewhere to the east he could see a faint glow, the remains of a fire started by an incendiary bomb the night before, and farther away to the south searchlights patterned the sky, seeking out a suspected invader. Behind him, in the flat, he could hear voices and laughter from the party he had temporarily escaped.

For the past week, since he was picked up from the beach in Brittany, he had behaved like an automaton. Victor, his conducting officer, had met him when the submarine docked at Portsmouth and whisked him up to London by car. He had been taken to Maurice Buckmaster's flat, where he had been given the use of the luxurious, black marble bathroom and offered the sort of meal he had only dreamed about for the past five months but which he had been unable to eat. He was still shivering with shock and fever and he had been transferred within hours to a private nursing home. The following day he had woken to find Priscilla sitting by his bed.

Two days of rest had cured the fever and he had been discharged, to return to the flat he had stayed in while waiting to leave for France. It was no surprise to find that Priscilla was already installed there. While he underwent a long and intensive debriefing from Buckmaster and Victor she pampered him with little delicacies, procured from God knew where, and apparently inexhaustible patience and tenderness. He was too exhausted to be interested in sex, but they shared a bed and she held him in her arms until he dropped off and then soothed and comforted him when he woke, crying out, from the nightmares that came every time he slept. She asked no questions about what had happened, knowing he would have had enough of that with Buckmaster, but instead tried to distract his mind with music and casual chatter about what was going on in the London theatre scene. To his mind, racked almost beyond endurance by the strain of leading a double life and the tragedies of the last days, she came to represent everything he valued and missed – gentleness, normality, the world of music and art he would have chosen for himself if the war had not intervened.

In his debriefing he forced himself to be unemotional, retailing the facts of Cole's apparent betrayal and the disintegration of the escape line, giving details of the new contacts he had set up, setting out the bare outline of Chantal's fate and his own escape. He knew that if he once allowed himself to begin to express his sense of loss, his anger, his feeling of guilt, those feelings would overpower him and he would be swept away into an uncontrollable maelstrom of emotion from which he feared he might never surface.

Buckmaster congratulated him, gave him three weeks' leave and offered him a rail pass to go home to Didsbury, which he declined. He knew that at present he simply could not cope with the well-intentioned questions of his family. Instead he opted to stay in London with Priscilla. It was she who had persuaded him to come to the New Year's Eve party being given at the flat of a composer whose music was newly fashionable. It had seemed a good idea at the time, but after an hour of listening to people discussing concerts he had not attended, books he had not read and plays he had not seen – all of which seemed unbearably trivial and futile – he could stand it no longer and had escaped on to the balcony.

He looked down into the street, but with no gleam of light from windows or street lamps it was impossible to tell how many storeys up he was. The dark abyss below him reminded him of the river where he had found Chantal. Once again he felt the icy shock of the water and the dead weight of her body in its soaking garments, the chill of the lifeless flesh. Behind him there was a sudden outburst of shouts and laughter and then voices joining in 'Auld Lang Syne'. He wanted to rip the curtains back and scream at the men and women inside, to ask them how they could sing and laugh and wish each other Happy New Year when gallant, lonely souls were risking their lives and losing them, when one of the bravest and most vividly alive now lay in icy death. He turned again to the balcony rail and strained his eyes into the darkness below. It would be so easy to let go, to give himself up to the dark waters and be carried away . . .

Behind him the curtain was briefly lifted, letting a shaft of light play across the windows of the houses opposite, and then Priscilla's voice said, 'Darling, here you are! I've been looking everywhere for you.'

She came to him and put her arms round his neck, scanning his face in the moonlight. 'I'm sorry, my sweet. I shouldn't have persuaded you to come. You're not ready for all this, are you?'

Her intuitive understanding came as such a relief that he caught her in his arms and clung to her, as a drowning man might cling to a rock in the middle of the torrent. She held him tightly and murmured, 'It's all right, my love. It's all going to be all right. You'll see.'

Through his tears came the sudden recognition that in his arms he held warmth and security and the promise of continuing life. He kissed her passionately and whispered, 'Oh, my darling, marry me! Please, please, darling Priscilla, say yes! Will you?'

She drew her head back enough to look up into his eyes. Her own were huge, still pools that reflected the stars.

'Darling Richard, of course I will. You know I will!' She kissed him again. 'Happy New Year, my love!'

Rose entered the restaurant at the Cumberland Hotel with her heart thumping. On the phone Monty had been enigmatic, merely requesting that she meet him here at 12.30. The little man was already at the table and he rose to greet her with a kiss on the cheek. She longed to blurt out the question that had been boiling up within her ever since receiving his telegram, but she restrained herself until they had ordered the meal.

Then Monty leaned across and put his hand over hers. 'Now, Rose. I don't want you to get too excited, because what I've got in mind probably isn't quite what you're expecting.' Rose's spirits sank but she said nothing and he went on, 'I've got my four dancers, which is as many as I can use for a show like this. They're nice kids and very talented, but they are just that – kids. The youngest is seventeen and the oldest hasn't reached twenty yet. Now, you remember what it was like in the old days with the Follies. Some of the girls there were very young and it was the first time they had been away from home. They needed someone to keep an eye on them, make sure they didn't go off the rails.'

'Madame,' Rose said, with a reminiscent smile. Monty's wife, who gloried in the stage name of Dolores da Ponte although everyone knew she had been born plain Dolly Bridges, was a character not easily forgotten. A gorgon with a heart of gold. 'She kept us all in order.'

'Exactly,' Monty agreed. 'But that wasn't all she did. She arranged all the dance numbers, for one thing. Now, I haven't forgotten that when you were with me last, in that show we took to France before you hurt your ankle, you choreographed the dances we did then.'

'I didn't do it all on my own,' Rose said. 'The other girls helped.'

'Maybe, but you were the one with the real knack for it.' He paused while a waiter set bowls of soup in front of them. 'OK. This is the deal. As you know, Madame has given up touring for the time being. She's got her hands full looking after the refugee kids from Poland that we've taken in. So I need someone to do what she used to do – choreograph the dances and be mother to the younger girls. And that's where you come in.'

'You don't want me to dance, myself?'

'Not for the time being. Later, when the show gets bedded in . . . maybe. Who knows? What matters is that you're a sensible, mature young woman and you know what you are doing on the stage. You're someone the other girls can look up to. How about it?'

Rose blinked back tears. She remembered how she and the others had laughed at Dolores, with her pretensions and her assertion that she had once danced for Diaghilev. They had been irritated by her insistence that they get home to bed immediately after the show each evening, refusing all invitations from the 'stage-door johnnies' who queued up to take them out. They had been amused by the fact that she forbade them to sunbathe, because she wanted them to look like young ladies, not cabin boys. And they had evaded her strictures at every opportunity. Was she now to put herself in the same position?

Then she straightened her shoulders. What Monty had said was true. Young girls away from home for the first time did need someone older and wiser to turn to. And it was a compliment that he thought she was capable of choreographing a whole show – even a small one. More importantly, she would be working again – and working in the only milieu where she felt happy. It had to be better than the shoe shop, better than being a dance teacher. It was a new beginning, for a new year.

She smiled at her companion. 'Thank you, Monty. I'd like that very much. When do I start?'

HISTORICAL NOTE

As usual, the main characters in this book are fictional, but some of the peripheral ones really existed. Colonel Basil Brown and Captain George Black were the moving spirits behind the army's entertainments unit, Stars in Battledress. Archibald McIndoe was the society plastic surgeon who turned his skills to rebuilding the faces of young airmen terribly burned when their planes were shot down in flames. Paul Cole, whose real name was Harold, was a sergeant who was left behind after the Dunkirk evacuation. Masquerading as a captain, he was responsible for escorting a number of escaping servicemen over the demarcation line into unoccupied France and on to the south coast. It is generally accepted, however, that at some point he became a German double agent and was responsible for betraying the rest of the *réseau*, as escape lines were called. 'Pat O'Leary' was the *nom de guerre* of Albert-Marie Guérisse, a Belgian doctor who offered his services to the British after the fall of his own country. He took charge of the *réseau*, which became known as 'the O'Leary line'. He was arrested by the Germans and sent to Dachau, where he was tortured but survived until the camp was liberated. He received the George Cross and the DSO for his services and died in 1989. Ian Garrow was a captain in the Seaforth Highlanders who chose to stay in France to assist the escape line. He was arrested but later escaped and survived. Dr and Mrs Rodocanachi were Greeks who had taken French nationality. They sheltered many escaping servicemen in their flat in Marseilles, at great risk to themselves. Dr Rodocanachi was arrested and died in Buchenwald in February 1944. The Abbé Carpentier was another member of the *réseau*. He kept a printing press in his back room and provided brilliantly forged documents for escapees. He was arrested in December 1941 and was executed at Dortmund in 1943, along with Bruce Dowding.

Those wishing to learn more may like to consult the following:

Stars in Battledress, Bill Pertwee, Charnwood Library, 1993

The Greasepaint War, John Craven Hughes, New English Library, 1976

Showbiz Goes to War, Eric Taylor, Robert Hale, 1992

Safe Houses Are Dangerous, Helen Long, Kimber, 1985

Escape and Evasion, Ian Dear, Cassell, 2000

Saturday at MI9, Airey Neave, Hodder and Stoughton, 1969

Six Faces of Courage, M.R.D. Foot, Eyre Methuen, 1978

McIndoe's Army, Peter Williams, Pelham, 1979

The Last Enemy, Richard Hillary, Macmillan, 1959

All Muck and No Medals, Joan Mant, Isis, 1995

Landgirl, Anne Hall, Ex Libris, 1993